ROTTER APOCALYPSE

ROTTER APOCALYPSE

by Scott M. Baker

Also by Scott M. Baker

Novels
Operation Majestic
Nurse Alissa vs. the Zombies
Nurse Alissa vs. the Zombies: Escape
Nurse Alissa vs. the Zombies III: Firestorm
Nurse Alissa vs. the Zombies IV: Hunters
Nurse Alissa vs. the Zombies V: Desperate Mission
Nurse Alissa vs. the Zombies VI: Rescue
Nurse Alissa vs. the Zombies VII: On the Road
Nurse Alissa vs. the Zombies VIII: New Beginnings
The Chronicles of Paul: A Nurse Alissa Spin-Off
The Chronicles of Paul II: Errand of Mercy
The Ghosts of Eden Hollow
The Ghosts of Salem Village
The Ghosts of the Maria Doria
Frozen World
Shattered World I: Paris
Shattered World II: Russia
Shattered World III: China
Shattered World IV: Japan
Shattered World V: Hell
The Vampire Hunters
Vampyrnomicon
Dominion
Yeitso
Rotter World
Rotter Nation
Rotter Apocalypse

Novellas
Nazi Ghouls From Space
Twilight of the Living Dead
This Is Why We Can't Have Nice Things During the Zombie Apocalypse
Dead Water

Anthologies
Cruise of the Living Dead and other Stories
Incident on Ironstone Lane and Other Horror Stories
Crossroads in the Dark V: Beyond the Borders
Rejected for Content
Roots of a Beating Heart
The Zombie Road Fan Fiction Collection
The Collector
Vlada: Tales of the Damned
Through the Aftermath: A Post-Apocalyptic Anthology

A Schattenseite Book
ISBN-13: 978-0-9963121-2-7

Rotter Apocalypse
by Scott M. Baker.
Copyright © 2015. All Rights Reserved.
Print Edition

To Curtis

This one is for you. I wish you were still here to
finish the journey.

BOOK ONE

CHAPTER ONE

MIKE ROBSON LAY beside Natalie on the beach. Her arm was nestled against his, their fingers intertwined in a tender embrace. He basked in the warmth generated by the sun as it dried the sea water that still moistened their bodies. A few yards away, the surf washed against the sand in a steady, lulling rhythm. The briny smell of low tide filled his nostrils. He savored every moment, every sensation. At least until sleep drifted away, making him painfully aware that he was dreaming.

Robson opened his eyes, hoping to find solace in his surroundings. Instead, reality rampaged through his fantasy. He was reclined in the passenger seat of the black Hummer H3 they had confiscated from Price, the leader of the rape gang attacked last night. It sat on the road opposite the construction company garage his team had been using as a makeshift camp. The seatbelt wrapped around his right hand. The air inside the enclosed vehicle had grown hot and stagnant, and sweat soaked his skin and clothes. Even rolled up, the windows could not keep out the stench of decay from the pile of corpses one hundred feet in front of him. Tom Caslow stood between the Hummer and the funeral mound, digging a mass grave along the shoulder. The fleeting glimmers of Robson's happiness drained away, leaving behind the soul-crushing routine that had become his daily existence.

As his dream faded into a hazy memory, the events of the past twenty-four hours came back into focus. His team had raided the storage facility outside Barnston that Price's gang used as their camp. The main reason for the attack was to rescue Windows, although he did want revenge on them for destroying their camp at Fort McClary and murdering everyone inside. Even though Robson's team had defeated the gang and revenged the slaughter at their camp, the raid had been less successful than he had hoped. They had failed to save Windows. Some of the other hostages had reported seeing her and a young girl escape during the melee. Despite sending out search parties, Robson's team never found her.

However, they had rescued thirty-eight survivors, most of them dehydrated and emaciated from weeks of being confined to the human defense perimeter set up around the storage facility. Five were young women who had been forced into being camp followers and had been repeatedly brutalized. Their psychological wounds would take much longer to heal. To compound the situation, Robson had lost three of his own people, casualties he could not afford given their small number.

Worst of all, he still had no idea what had happened to Natalie and the Angels.

Opening the door to the Hummer, Robson stepped out and stretched. He had come out to the Hummer to get away from the hustle going on inside the garage while the survivors settled in. When he had dozed off for a quick nap, it had been close to dawn, and the sky had a light blue tint. Now the sky was marginally brighter. Although he could not have been asleep long, he felt surprisingly well rested for such a short power nap.

Caslow glanced up at Robson and raised his hand to wave. Robson walked away. Out of the corner of his eye, he saw Caslow slump over and resume digging. Moving around the front of the Hummer, Robson strolled across the street and entered the construction company's parking lot. Roberta Giovanni and Charles DeWitt stood by the main door talking with Neal Simmons.

Roberta was middle-aged and, at one time, probably quite attractive. However, one year of an apocalypse and several days on the road had sapped the beauty and vitality out of her. She stood between the two men, the worn and dirty clothes hanging loosely on her gaunt frame. Her brown eyes seemed sunken and listless. She tied her brunette hair into an oily and frayed ponytail that hung down her back. DeWitt fared slightly better. He had worked out at camp and kept himself toned, if underweight. Yet his face betrayed the wear and tear of everything that had transpired. Dark circles had formed under his eyes, and a days-long growth of beard covered his face and neck. DeWitt and Roberta were the only ones to survive both the massacre at the camp and the raid on the storage facility. They were lucky to be alive.

Frakes and Allard had also gone into battle with them. They had been killed during a gunfight. And, of course, there was Jennifer, who had been murdered in cold blood by the gang's leader. Jennifer's death hit him hardest of all for personal reasons. Robson bore the guilt of getting all three of them killed. He knew they lacked tactical training and should not have participated in last night's raid. Robson never would have exposed any of them to such danger had he not been desperate for manpower.

Simmons and Isaac Wayans were newfound friends and a godsend. Former Boston cops who barely escaped the collapse of the city, the two had moved north and set up a good life for themselves in the rectory of the town of Gilmanton. When Robson's group happened upon them, they had been gracious enough to not only let Robson use the town as a staging area for the action against the storage facility, but assisted in the raid, an act of kindness that left Wayans with a minor bullet wound in the chest and Simmons with thirty-eight starving mouths to feed.

Simmons glanced in Robson's direction and grinned. "It's about time you woke up."

"What are you talking about? I've barely been asleep half an hour."

Roberta shook her head. "You've been asleep all day."

That explained why he felt so rested. "Why didn't you wake me?"

"You needed to rest," said Simmons. "Besides, we're taking care of everything here."

"At least what we have control over," added DeWitt.

Robson knew what DeWitt referred to. "How many did we lose?"

"Seven," answered Roberta. "All of them were those rescued from the defense perimeter. Most died right after eating."

"What did you feed them?"

"Reconstituted scrambled eggs and bacon, plus water," replied Simmons. "They're all so badly malnourished, I doubt half of them will make it through the next few days."

Robson turned to where Caslow dug the mass grave. "I assume he didn't want to help with the survivors?"

"*We* didn't want him to help," Roberta spat.

Simmons glanced over at Caslow with contempt. "Earlier this afternoon, he asked if he could help. I told him to dig graves so we can give the dead a proper burial. He prepared three graves for your people, plus a mass grave for those from the camp who don't make it."

"He agreed to that?"

"I didn't give him much choice."

Robson did not blame Simmons and the others for despising Caslow. Even he could not stand him. Middle-aged and of average height and looks, his entire demeanor reeked of cowardice, from the constantly hunched shoulders, the inability to make eye contact, and his avoidance of confrontation. Caslow had allowed his wife and little girl to be kidnapped by the rape gang, hiding in a store while they were abducted and doing nothing to protect them. The only reason Robson had allowed Caslow to go on last night's raid was to give him a chance to redeem himself. However, his wife already had committed suicide and his daughter had disappeared, presumably being the little girl the survivors reported seeing leaving the compound with Windows. After the raid, he found Caslow cowering in one of the abandoned storage units.

By now the sun had dropped below the tree line, leaving a reddish-orange glow along the western horizon. The office door to the garage opened, and Dravko and Tibor stepped out into the parking lot. Robson felt sorry for them because of the fate that had befallen their coven, which seemed ironic considering one month ago he could have easily been convinced to feed them to the rotters. The Revenant Virus the vampires released against mankind to stop humans from hunting the undead nearly made their own kind extinct. The small group of vampires that had been allowed into their camp had been granted asylum out of necessity, the humans needing the strength and agility of the undead to bolster their ranks. An uneasy alliance existed between the two species that lasted for eight months until the trip to Site R when the vampires proved their loyalty. None of Robson's team would have survived the ordeal at the underground military facility, or last night's raid on the storage facility, had it not been for the vampires. The past few weeks had solidified the friendship between the two species, although at a loss of three members of the coven, a casualty rate of sixty percent. Pockets of humans still existed across the country. As far as Robson knew, Dravko and Tibor were the last of their kind.

Robson suppressed a sigh. His team now consisted of the last two vampires on Earth, a pair of untrained guards, a useless coward, and thirty-one survivors, most of whom were knocking on death's door.

As the vampires approached, Dravko nodded. Tibor remained his usual stoic self.

"How did the survivors make out?" asked Dravko.

"Not good," answered Roberta. "We lost seven and will

probably lose several more before long."

Tibor cast a disdainful look at Dravko that sent a shiver down Robson's spine.

Dravko seemed genuinely sympathetic. "Let me know if there's anything we can do to help."

"I will."

"Do you want us to take the Hummer and go looking for Windows?" asked Dravko.

Robson shook his head. "I doubt you'll find her. She's long gone by now."

"We don't mind."

"I can't risk losing any more people right now. Windows is on her own."

Roberta nudged Robson in the shoulder and motioned toward the raised door of the garage. "We have company."

One of the survivors stood by the opening and peered around the jamb. Robson recognized her as one of the camp followers from inside the compound, although he did not know her name. She ducked out of view when she saw him.

"It's okay," Robson called to her. "You're safe now."

The woman came out from behind the wall and cautiously walked across the parking lot. She reminded him of a frightened deer approaching a campsite. Her time in the rape camp had sucked all dignity out of her. Unkempt, dirty brunette hair hung past her shoulders and her face and body were gaunt from lack of food. She had the sunken eyes and vacant stare of someone who had witnessed or experienced an event too horrific for the mind to bear. He had seen that stare too frequently in those who had survived the first few weeks of the rotter outbreak, but never before from someone who had suffered at the hands of fellow humans. She stopped ten feet away and lowered her head.

"What can I do for you?" asked Robson.

"I'm sorry to bother you, sir."

"What's your name?"

The woman raised her head. "My name?"

"Yes."

"Linda Prowell, sir." She averted her gaze again.

In all his years with the sheriff's department he had never seen a woman beaten down this badly. He had no regrets about taking out Price's gang.

"Linda, my name's Mike. Please stop calling me sir. You're not at that compound anymore. I promise, no one here is going to hurt you."

Linda made eye contact with each of the men, gauging whether she had anything to fear from them. When her gaze fell upon Roberta, Roberta smiled, assuring her everything would be all right.

"Linda, do you trust me?" asked Robson.

"I… I want to."

"That's a start. Now, what can I do for you?"

"I wanted to talk to you about the physical condition of those you rescued from the Line."

"They're in bad shape. And while I know your intentions are good, bacon and eggs aren't going to help them recover. We lost seven people, and we're going to lose a lot more unless you can get them a proper diet."

"I take it you're a nurse?"

"I was a…." Linda paused, and then proceeded with more confidence. "I *am* a doctor. A pediatrician, to be exact. I dealt with a lot of eating disorder cases in my practice, so I know what I'm talking about."

"I'm not questioning you," said Robson in his most reassuring tone. "What do we need to do?"

"To start with, they need a high calorie and high protein diet. Things like peanut butter, cheese, and beef jerky. Even though they're dehydrated, don't give them too much water. If they take in too much liquid too quickly it could seize up their stomachs. The best thing would be powdered milk or protein shakes. If you have any, multi-vitamins will help them get back on their feet. Also, because they've been out on the Line for so long, their clothes are soiled with urine and feces and are infested with bugs. I know all this sounds unreasonable under the circumstances, but we need to get these people properly fed, cleaned up, and into new clothes as soon as possible if they're to have any chance of surviving."

"Setting up showers shouldn't be too difficult," said Roberta. "DeWitt and I could have them running in a few hours."

"That's all well and good," Robson said, running his hand through his hair. "But where are we going to find the food they need, as well as a fresh change of clothes for everyone?"

Simmons cleared his throat to get everyone's attention. "I actually know where we can get everything on Linda's list."

Robson fixed his gaze on Linda. "See? That was easy."

Simmons smirked. "Who said anything about it being easy?"

CHAPTER TWO

"**D**AMN," WINDOWS MUTTERED under her breath.

The RAV-4 bucked as the engine stuttered, jarring Cindy from her nap. She sat up in the passenger seat, her eyes wide with fear.

"What's wrong?"

"Nothing bad." Windows reached over and wrapped her hand around Cindy's, giving it a reassuring squeeze. "We're about to run out of gas, that's all."

"Oh." The girl visibly relaxed. The RAV-4 bucked again, a little harder this time. Cindy giggled. "It's like being on a ride at Canobie Lake Park."

Windows grinned. After what the world had gone through this past year, she doubted anyone would ever be excited again about amusement park rides, if society even reopened them. She admired how Cindy could retain her childhood innocence after everything that had happened, especially after spending so many months in that camp.

Windows closed her eyes tight and swallowed back the bile as the memories of that place rushed into her memory. She knew she would relive those events for the rest of her life. Windows' time in that Hell had only lasted a few days, beginning with her kidnapping after the gang had destroyed her original home at Fort McClary, and lasting until the raid last night when she and Cindy used the commotion to sneak out, find the RAV-4 prepared for a quick escape, and headed northeast. However, in those days she had experienced more sexual abuse and psychological torment than she ever thought imaginable. Thankfully, Cindy had been spared from being molested, but not because of any moral standards on the part of their captors. Cindy had been kept out of harm's way because her mother Debra and Windows had allowed themselves to suffer degradation and humiliation in order to keep her safe. The emotional strain had been too much for Debra and she committed suicide, leaving Windows to care for Cindy. To do that, Windows had killed a man, broken out of a secure facility, and went on the run. Not bad for a woman who should be graduating from college right about now.

The RAV-4's engine sputtered and died. Windows maneuvered it toward the side of the road and braked. The sun had set only a few moments earlier, leaving enough light for her to scan the surrounding area. Woods stood off to the right, and a large field to the left. The road ahead ran straight for a mile before becoming lost in the shadows. She saw what mattered most–there were no rotters nearby.

"Where are we?" Cindy asked.

"I have no idea."

Windows opened the map and spread it out, knowing it was futile. They had traveled all last night, first heading north for several hours before traveling northeast along the foothills of the White Mountains. The last city she remembered passing through had been Berlin, and she had spent over an hour trying to navigate the outskirts of town to avoid the living dead. A few miles north of Berlin they had come across an old gas station/service center, pulled into one of the empty bays, closed the doors, and slept for most of the day.

After setting out again, the two had stayed off the main roads, which allowed them to avoid the living dead. It also meant they often had to retrace their steps due to fallen trees, washed out roads, or abandoned roadblocks. Having spent so much time on the back roads, none of which were listed on the map left inside the SUV, Windows had no idea what their current location was or even in which direction they had been heading when they ran out of gas.

Getting out of the RAV-4, Windows went around to the back deck, opened the hatch, and sorted through the four backpacks. Cindy joined her, watching quietly while Windows transferred all the food, water, and ammunition into two backpacks, making sure the lighter stuff went into the smaller one. When finished, she slung the heavier of the two backpacks across her right shoulder and one of the AK-47s over her left. She held out the second pack to Cindy.

"Do you think you can carry this?

Cindy looked apprehensive as she took the bag. Her face lit up when she realized how light it was. "No problem."

Windows helped the girl slide it over her shoulders and picked up another AK-47 with her right hand. She placed her left behind Cindy's head and ruffled her hair. "Okay, let's move out."

"Where are we going?"

"I have no idea." Windows walked down the road in the direction they had been heading. "We'll know it when we get there."

CHAPTER THREE

"Jesus," Robson muttered under his breath.

"I told you it wouldn't be easy," Simmons replied.

From their vantage point on top of the hill, Robson used his night vision goggles to scan the Super Walmart a quarter of a mile away. The building looked pristine. Along the front, the doors remained closed, and the glass was intact. No debris lay spread across the parking lot, so the store had not been ransacked. The only things in the parking lot were a dozen vehicles left by their owners in scattered spaces. And, of course, a few hundred rotters that milled around the building.

Robson passed the goggles to DeWitt on his right. He said to Simmons, "We've seen worse."

"Are you serious?"

"Yes," said Robson.

"*You* have," DeWitt chimed in as he looked through the goggles. "This is a whole new Hell for us."

Sadly, what DeWitt said was true. Robson had seen worse, much worse. During those times he had an entire raiding party behind him, including the Angels, four vampires, and his own team of six. Because of the trip to Site R, the assault on the rape camp, and sending the Angels west with the vaccine for the Revenant Virus, those numbers had dwindled down to Dravko, Tibor, DeWitt, and Roberta. Bringing along Linda had been a necessary evil. Although not psychologically ready to face a rotter horde, she was the only person in the group with medical experience, and they needed her to gather supplies inside the pharmacy. Robson had left Caslow back at Gilmanton, ostensibly to take care of Wayans. In reality, he did not want him around. Which left him with a total of seven people, half of them untrained, to break into a Walmart, steal enough food and supplies to accommodate more than thirty people, and sneak out, all while avoiding the horde of the living dead.

He must be fucking insane.

"You and Wayans have never actually been inside?" asked Robson.

"No need to. We already had everything we needed. We considered this our emergency reserve. And what better way to protect it?"

"Lucky for us no one overrode your security system."

DeWitt huffed. "Do you really think we'll have any luck getting past all those rotters?"

"No," said Robson. "We don't have to get past them."

"What do you mean?"

"Watch and learn." Robson turned back to Simmons. "I'm going to need you to create a diversion. Take the Hummer and drive through the west end of the parking lot. Once you get their attention, lead them away from the building. Take Dravko and Tibor with—"

"No," Dravko interrupted. "We're going inside with you."

"You're not vaccinated against the Revenant Virus. If one of them bites you, you have no protection."

"Our extinction is inevitable no matter how hard you try to protect us. Besides, we're tired of being relegated to the sideline. Tibor and I are part of this team. If you go into that building, we're going with you."

The determination in Dravko's eyes told Robson it would be futile to argue.

"Do you mind being on your own?" Robson asked Simmons.

"Not as long as I don't have to mix it up with the living

dead. Don't you need me to hang around in case you need help?"

Robson shook his head. "If we get into more trouble than we can handle, there's nothing you'll be able to do. Lead the rotters away from us for as long as possible, and then head back to Gilmanton."

"Roger that."

Robson faced the rest of his team "Okay. Let's do this."

SIMMONS LED THE three-vehicle convoy along the county road leading to Super Walmart. Ahead of him he could see the southern entrance to the parking lot and, two hundred feet beyond that, the northern entrance. He continued to the furthest one and entered. Robson swung the Ryder truck in behind Simmons, stopped before entering the lot, and shut down the engine and headlights. Dravko pulled his Humvee alongside the Ryder and did the same. Both vehicles sat silent, leaving the black Hummer H3 as the only noise in the parking lot.

As anticipated, it attracted considerable attention.

Every rotter in the vicinity shifted their gaze onto Simmons. He took a deep breath to steady his nerves. Instinct told him to gun it for the other entrance and get out of there. Instead, he coasted through the parking lot, careful to avoid concentrations of the living dead. The deeper in he drove, the harder it became as rotters swarmed him. Simmons ignored those closest to him and blared the horn to attract the ones on the perimeter. One by one, each of the living dead lumbered toward him. Some staggered around the sides of the building or emerged from around back. A small group clustered around the front doors, their attention directed inside the building, was the last to focus on him. Within a minute, several hundred rotters converged around his Hummer.

Simmons' heart raced and his body tensed. He warned himself to stay calm. If he panicked and allowed the rotters to overwhelm his vehicle, he would never make it out alive. Concentrating on the parking lot rather than the oncoming horde, Simmons calculated the path of least resistance and maneuvered through them, making his way toward the southern entrance. Several times he had to swerve around rotters, and occasionally ran some down. Others clawed against the side of the Hummer, grasping at him until he could barely see out the side windows because of the decayed flesh and gore stains. Flies and wasps covered the windshield, blocking his view. The sound of bones and fingernails scraping against the glass, accompanied by the incessant moaning, threatened to paralyze him with fear. He felt himself clenching his bladder and sphincter, and his thinking becoming frenzied. Just as Simmons felt his nerves about to give way, he broke through the outer perimeter of living dead and into an empty portion of the parking lot, heading toward the exit.

When Simmons glanced in his side mirrors, he could see the mass converging on him. He slowed his speed enough for them to keep up with but not catch him. The seconds dragged by like minutes as he passed through the exit and turned left onto the main road, leading the rotters out of the area. Eventually, Super Walmart and Robson's other two vehicles disappeared from view. With only the mass of living dead following close behind, Simmons felt like he was some sort of demonic Pied Piper.

IT TOOK AN hour for Simmons to clear the rotters out of the parking lot. Robson waited an extra ten minutes to make sure the horde was far enough away before starting the Ryder. He headed around back, with Dravko close behind him. When they pulled behind the building, Robson saw half a dozen rotters milling around the back lot, stragglers that had not followed the main herd. Nothing they could not handle. When they cruised along the rear façade, the few living dead shambled toward them.

The rear entrance was located in the center of the building, fifteen feet from the loading dock. A military-style Humvee in camouflage paint was parked diagonally between the two. Its doors had been left open. A body lay on the pavement near the vehicle with an M-16A2 automatic rifle resting nearby. As the headlights illuminated it, Robson noticed the body had been picked clean of flesh and muscles except for some residual chunks of tissue attached to the shoulders and skull. Its head fell to the side and its jaws snapped at the air.

"Looks like someone had the same idea you did," said Linda from the passenger seat.

"We'll have better luck." Robson maneuvered around the military Humvee and backed the Ryder into the loading dock. When he felt the truck's rear thump against the rubber bumpers, he shifted into park and shut down the engine. "Let's go."

Dravko had parked close to the entrance. While Tibor checked the door, DeWitt and Roberta fanned out, neutralizing the few rotters with head shots.

Robson joined the vampires by the door. "Can we get in?"

"It's locked," responded Tibor. "I can break it, though."

"Go ahead."

Tibor pulled on the handle, the muscles along his neck and shoulders straining. The steel around the jamb groaned under the pressure until the deadbolt snapped. He opened the door and smirked. "After you."

Slipping on his night vision goggles, Robson raised his Atchisson AA-12 assault shotgun, an automatic version of a shotgun that held twenty rounds in a drum magazine, and stepped into the storage room. He scanned the area from right to left and saw no signs of danger. Pushing the goggles onto his forehead, he motioned for the others to follow. One by one they entered and switched on their flashlights, each checking the area for themselves. Tibor entered last, closing the door behind him, sliding a broom through the handle, and resting it against the jamb.

Robson stepped over to the double doors leading onto the main floor and motioned to the others. "Douse the lights."

When the storage room went dark, Robson slid the goggles back over his eyes and pushed open one of the swinging double doors leading onto the main floor. He half expected to be greeted by a wall of the living dead. Instead, everything seemed normal. No signs of movement. Not even any indication the store had been looted. From this vantage point, it appeared as though the place had been closed prior to the outbreak and never visited again.

Robson stepped back into the storage room and pushed the goggles up onto his forehead. "You can turn the flashlights back on."

As their glare lit up the storage room, he continued. "I don't think this place has been touched, so this should be easy. That doesn't mean you can be careless. We've seen easy turn to shit too many times before. Linda and Tibor will head for the pharmacy and gather medical supplies. DeWitt and Roberta will be responsible for clothing. Dravko and I will get the food. Any questions?" When no one responded, Robson said, "Move out."

The three groups exited the storage room and spread out through the store.

DEWITT AND ROBERTA made their way to the center of the store to the clothing department. They stood between the men's and women's sections.

"Now what?" DeWitt asked.

Roberta searched around until she found a wheeled clothing rack upon which hung dresses and children's garments. She gathered them in her arms, lifted off the hangers, and tossed the pile onto the floor. She pushed the rack over to DeWitt.

"Grab sweatpants, jeans, and t-shirts for men and women. Make sure you take only small sizes. Load this up and meet me back here in a few minutes."

"Where are you going?"

"To get everything else we need." Without waiting for a response, Roberta headed for the footwear department. She found a shopping cart at the end of one of the aisles stacked with shoe boxes. The staff must have been in the process of restocking when they abandoned the store. That made it easier for her. She emptied the shopping cart and proceeded up and down each aisle, filling it with running shoes of various sizes. When she felt she had collected a wide enough variety to accommodate all the survivors, she headed over to the underwear section and grabbed boxers, panties, bras, and socks. By the time Roberta had made her rounds and returned to the clothing section, DeWitt had finished gathering his items.

"Are you ready?" she asked.

"I think so. I can't fit anything else on this thing."

"Then let's get out of here." Roberta spun the shopping cart around and led the way toward the storage room.

ROBSON AND DRAVKO approached the food section. The vampire raised a hand and placed it on his friend's chest.

"Do you smell that?"

Robson inhaled. He did. It was the stench of decayed flesh.

Robson raised his AA-12, shut off his flashlight, and lowered his night vision goggles over his eyes. Dravko morphed into his vampiric form, his human features changing into a furrowed brow and fanged mouth. His fingers elongated, the nails becoming two-inch talons. Together, the two walked into the food section, anticipating the inevitable rotter attack.

Moving down the cereal aisle toward the bakery, Dravko took the lead. He sniffed the air and pointed toward the back. Robson nodded in acknowledgment. At the end of the aisle, Dravko peered around the corner and waved on his friend. Robson fell in behind the vampire and they made their way toward the rear of the store. He scanned behind the bakery counter and down each aisle they passed, searching for rotters. His fingers tensed around the trigger. When Dravko reached the rear wall, he laughed.

Robson moved up beside him. "What's so funny?"

"There are our rotters." Dravko pointed to the refrigeration units along the rear wall. With the electricity out, the units had failed, allowing hundreds of pounds of meat to spoil. Numerous cellophane wrappers had broken open, and the exposed meat swarmed with maggots and flies.

"Thank God for small favors." Robson lifted up his goggles and shone his flashlight along the rear wall until it fell upon the dairy section. "Come with me."

"Everything there is spoiled."

"I'm not looking for food." Robson walked down to a cart in the center of the aisle stacked with milk crates, half of them empty. He removed the full ones and dumped the gallon cartons onto the floor. "We can use these to carry the food."

Dravko helped empty the crates. "You get the peanut butter and powdered milk. I'll take care of the cheese and jerky."

"Gotcha." Robson placed half the empty crates back on the cart and wheeled it toward the grocery section. He emptied the shelves of peanut butter before switching aisles and doing the same with the powdered milk. When he pushed the cart back toward the dairy section, he found Dravko crouched, examining something on the floor. The concern on the vampire's face bothered him.

"What's wrong?" Robson asked.

"Look at this."

Robson knelt beside Dravko and flashed his light onto a

dried pool of blood staining the tiles. The blood had been smeared around. Hand and footprints were mixed in among the streaks.

"Fuck," mumbled Robson.

"We definitely are."

LINDA FOUND THE health and beauty section and headed straight for the vitamin aisle. She ran the flashlight along the shelves, relieved to find the bottles still there. Waving for Tibor to follow, she wandered to the pharmacy. As expected, the gates had been pulled down over the service windows and secured. The door leading to the office had been bolted shut.

She stepped back and motioned to the handle. "Can you open it?"

"No problem."

Tibor stepped around Linda. Leaning to one side, he slammed his shoulder into the deadbolt. The frame shook but did not give. Tibor rammed it again, this time harder. The metal door swung open and crashed against the wall. Moving to one side, he made a melodramatic gesture with his hand for Linda to proceed first. She entered and shone the flashlight around. Jackpot. No one had touched the stocks since the outbreak. Everything she would need to assist the others in recovering was right here.

Off to her left sat a two-wheeled dolly stacked with four gray plastic crates used to transport pharmaceuticals. She picked up the two top crates, emptied the contents onto the floor, and handed them to Tibor. "Take these. Fill one with multi-vitamins and the other with protein mixes."

Tibor took the crates and left. Linda emptied the next two containers and proceeded to fill them with antibiotics and other drugs.

ROBERTA AND DEWITT approached the double doors leading to the storage room when they heard a noise that sounded like something being dragged across the floor. They spun around, panning their flashlights into the store, but saw nothing.

"What was that?" DeWitt whispered.

"I don't know, and I don't feel like hanging around to find out." Roberta grabbed her cart and pushed it into the storage room. "Let's load this stuff on the truck so we can get out of here when the others get back."

TIBOR FINISHED LOADING one crate with multi-vitamins. When he knelt down to close the lid, he heard something running, followed by a snarl. Four swarmers in soiled National Guard cammies were rushing toward him. The nearest, only ten feet away, had no left arm, Tendons and strips of decayed flesh hung from the empty socket. A second swarmer followed, with a third fifty feet to the rear, hobbling along on legs with chunks of flesh and muscle chewed out of them. The last of the living dead broke away from the pack and headed down a separate aisle toward the pharmacy.

Lowering his right shoulder, Tibor dove to the side, colliding with the closest swarmer's legs and knocking it to the floor. Coming out of his roll, he jumped up in front of the second swarmer. It lunged at him. Tibor dug his left hand into the swarmer's chest to hold it in place and wrapped the right behind its head, cupping its chin. The swarmer flailed its head, trying to find flesh to bury its teeth in. Tibor yanked his right arm to the side, twisting the swarmer's head around. The vertebrae crunched as the bones shattered. The swarmer dropped to the floor, motionless except for its mouth that still bit at its missed meal.

A hand clasped Tibor's shoulder. The one-armed swarmer had gotten back to its feet and resumed its attack. Tibor tried to yank himself free, but the swarmer clutched his jacket and would not let go. The two fell forward, crashed against the shelves, and sprawled to the floor amidst a cascade of plastic vitamin bottles. Tibor tried to stand but could not find a good foothold. He moved forward and twisted from side to side to keep the swarmer off balance. If it bit his exposed neck or shoulders, he was as good as dead. He crawled to a section of the aisle free of plastic bottles and stood, dragging the one-armed swarmer with him. It leaned closer, Tibor felt its teeth near his neck. He spun to his right to throw the swarmer off balance.

Tibor stared directly into the lifeless eyes of the leg-ravaged swarmer that had closed the distance between them.

LINDA HEARD THE commotion outside the pharmacy and looked through the customer window, unable to see anything because of the closed grating.

"Tibor, are you okay?"

Something growled. Linda knew right away what had made the noise. She sprinted to the door. A swarmer in National Guard cammies with the skin stripped off its chest, its abdomen exposed and empty, rushed toward her from inside the store. She reached the door first, closed it shut, and reached up to secure the bolt. The swarmer slammed into the other side. The door burst open, smashing Linda in the face and knocking her back against a shelf of prescription drugs. The swarmer pushed its way into the pharmacy and lunged, pinning her against the shelf.

Though stunned, she had the presence of mind to stop it. Her fingers clutched its ribcage, slipping through the rotting muscles and gore. She swallowed back the vomit rising in her throat and locked her elbows, keeping the swarmer at arms' length. It tore at her arms, snarling and gnashing.

Linda felt her muscles giving way under the onslaught.

ROBSON AND DRAVKO had pushed their cart halfway back to the storage room when they heard the commotion around the pharmacy near the center of the store. Both men stopped. Robson shut off his flashlight and switched to the night vision goggles. He could not see the entire store, However, in those sections within his line of sight, rotters climbed to their feet. He counted over a dozen, each spread out across the main floor. They twisted their heads, trying to determine where the noise came from. A loud bang from the pharmacy caught their attention, and the rotters lumbered off in that direction.

"Take this back to the truck," ordered Robson, pushing the cart toward Dravko. "I'll check on Tibor and Linda."

"No." Dravko grabbed his arm. "Tibor is from my coven. Let me go."

"Yell if you need help."

Robson pushed the cart toward the storage room. Dravko headed for the pharmacy.

ROBERTA AND DEWITT pushed open the double doors leading into the storage room when they heard all hell break lose in the pharmacy. DeWitt raised the flashlight. Roberta placed her hand on the light and lowered the beam to the floor.

"Don't do that," she whispered. "If there are rotters in here, the light will attract them."

"What about the others?"

"They'll be heading this way soon."

DeWitt stared at her in disbelief and contempt.

Realizing how cowardly her remarks sounded, she explained. "Robson expects everyone to meet back here. If we go off searching for them, we're liable to get separated."

DeWitt scrunched his lips. "Makes sense."

Roberta shoved the cart inside, and then took the wheeled clothes rack from DeWitt. "Wait here by the door. If anyone calls for help, we'll go after them."

"What are you going to do?" DeWitt asked.

"I'm going to load this stuff onto the truck."

Roberta pushed the cart and rack over to the loading dock door. She panned the flashlight from one end of the storage room to the other. Once certain lurked in the shadows, she crouched down, grabbed the handle, and lifted. The sickeningly sweet stench of rotting flesh wafted through the opening, accompanied by a dozen decaying hands. One clasped her ankle and pulled, knocking her over backward. Her flashlight fell to the floor and rolled so the beam shone outside. Roberta saw a dozen rotters on either side of the Ryder, crowded in front of the loading deck. Another twenty or thirty moved toward them from a clump of tress on the opposite side of the parking lot.

A second and third pair of dead hands grabbed Roberta's ankle and tried to pull her off the platform.

THE RAVAGED-LEG SWARMER reached out for Tibor. Raising his right leg, Tibor kicked it in the chest. The swarmer fell back several feet, giving the vampire the few seconds he needed. Tibor brought down his leg, bent the knee, and crouched to his right while simultaneously digging both hands into the one-armed swarmer's right shoulder. The move pulled it off Tibor's back and he threw it over his shoulder. When it crashed to the floor, Tibor took the talons of the middle and forefingers of his right hand and plunged them through the one-armed swarmer's eyes. It spasmed once and went limp. Tibor jumped back to his feet to confront the ravaged-leg swarmer, which had closed to within five feet of him.

Dravko stood in the center of the aisle. "Are you okay?"

"Nothing I can't handle," Tibor grinned. He motioned with his head to the pharmacy. "Help the human."

Dravko rushed off. The ravaged-leg swarmer spun around toward him. Tibor took advantage of the opportunity. Launching himself at the swarmer, he grabbed its head in both hands and pushed. The two tumbled over. Tibor straightened his elbows and leaned forward so that, when they hit the floor, all his weight was distributed to his hands. The swarmer's head erupted beneath his palms, splattering brains and skull across the floor and shelves.

Standing up, Tibor flicked away the gore. He heard a muffled snarl. Glancing behind him, he saw the first swarmer whose head he had twisted around spread out amongst the spilled vitamin bottles. Tibor walked over and stared down at it. Its eyes still focused on him, its teeth snapping and grinding. He sneered.

"You'll never beat me, motherfucker."

Tibor stomped his foot on the swarmer's head, crushing it beneath his boot.

ALTHOUGH LINDA TRIED pushing away the swarmer, she knew she could not hold it back any longer. Weeks in the rape camp had left her with no strength. Giving in to the inevitable, she closed her eyes and prayed that the end would be quick. She let her arms collapse.

The swarmer fell against her. Linda cried out in anticipation of being bitten. Instead, something lifted it off her chest. She opened her eyes to see Dravko behind the swarmer, his hands clasping its neck and head, dragging it away. He smashed its head against the wall several times until the skull shattered, spurting brains and gore in a fan-shaped pattern. Dravko flung the carcass to one side. Linda stared at the corpse, still in a semi-state of shock.

"Are you alright?" asked Dravko.

Linda stared at him. She had not heard the question.

"I asked if you're alright."

She responded with barely a nod.

"Good." Dravko offered his hand. "We have to get out of

here."

"No." Linda's head suddenly cleared. She went back into the pharmacy, stopped in front of the plastic crate, and resumed filling it with prescription medicines, grabbing bottles off the shelf and making quick decisions about their usefulness.

"Are you crazy?" Dravko stepped into the pharmacy. "Rotters are closing in on us."

"A lot of good people are going to die if we don't bring this stuff back, so let me work." Linda glanced over at Dravko "I'm almost done. Give me a few minutes."

Dravko shook his head and stood by the door.

ROBSON AVOIDED THE few rotters throughout the store because their attention was focused on the commotion up front. He breathed a sigh of relief at his good fortune until he neared the storage room and heard Roberta screaming in terror. Leaving the cart in the center of the aisle, Robson swung the AA-12 off his shoulder and raced the few yards for the swinging double doors.

He burst through to find Roberta lying by the open door of the loading dock. More than a dozen rotters swarmed around the edge, clutching at her legs. DeWitt crouched behind her, his hands under her arms, trying to pull her away. Too many dead hands grasped her. Roberta yelled and kicked frantically. Every time she broke one rotter's grip, another took its place. Her pants were torn and blood covered her legs. Robson rushed up beside Roberta, aimed the AA-12 at the rotters closest to her, and pulled the trigger. A rapid-fire barrage of shotgun shells tore into the horde. A cloud of gore formed as heads exploded, torsos burst open, and limbs were severed. Roberta kicked and screamed even louder. This time, with so many of the rotters cut down, DeWitt pulled her away. He dragged her across the floor, still thrashing and screaming. When Robson knelt beside her to offer comfort, she lashed out at him, nearly kicking him in the jaw. Robson grabbed Roberta by the collar, yanked her to her feet, and slapped her across the face. She calmed down instantly.

Robson placed a hand on her shoulder. "Sorry."

"Don't be." Roberta avoided his eyes. "I didn't mean to panic like that."

"It's understandable." He stepped back and examined her legs. "Were you bit?"

Roberta followed his gaze, her eyes widening as she noticed the blood for the first time. "I... I don't know."

"We'll check later." Robson headed back to the loading dock.

"What if I've been bit? I'll turn."

"No, you won't. You've been vaccinated. Remember? DeWitt, there's a cart outside the doors loaded with food. Bring it in here."

"Roger that."

Robson stepped over to the loading dock. The Ryder sat in the center backed up against the edge. To the left of the truck, another horde of rotters had moved into the gap where he had gunned down the previous lot. A second group swarmed around the gap to the right. As Robson approached the back of the truck, the living dead leaned in for him. Their arms were not long enough to reach, yet he felt uncomfortable with dozens of pairs of dead hands clutching at him only inches away. Pulling the latch up and to the left, he unfastened the Ryder's rear door and slid it open. He moved back into the storage room and grabbed the clothes rack. Tapping Roberta on the arm, Robson pointed to the shopping cart. "Bring that with you."

Getting behind the cart, Roberta pushed it toward the truck, stopping several feet from the edge of the loading dock. Robson loaded the clothes rack into the back of the Ryder and shoved it toward the front. He took the cart from Roberta and did the same. DeWitt entered the storage room pushing the cart with the crates of food.

"Bad news," warned DeWitt. He rushed past Robson and headed for the Ryder. "We have five rotters heading this way."

"Shit." Robson removed the empty magazine from his A-12, replaced it with a full one, and took up a firing position in front of the swinging double doors.

LINDA CLOSED THE lid on the second plastic crate and piled both onto the two-wheel hand truck. "I'm ready."

"Is that everything?" asked Dravko.

"It's all we can carry." She pushed the hand truck toward the door. "Now let's get Tibor's boxes and get out of here."

Dravko led the way. When they reached Tibor, he had his two crates filled and placed them on top of the others.

Linda saw the dead swarmers. "What happened?" she asked.

Tibor smirked. "These little shits are no match for us."

"Gloat later," Dravko reprimanded his friend. He said to Linda, "There are no more than eight rotters between us and the exit. You'll have to use the flashlight to see where you're going, which is going to attract them. Stay close to us and we'll get you out of here safely. Okay?"

"I trust you," said Linda.

"Then let's go. Tibor, you lead."

Tibor set off for the storage room. Linda tilted the hand truck and followed. Dravko brought up the rear. She kept the flashlight beam lowered to the floor to make certain she did not trip over anything. That allowed her to see the rotters moving in the shadows around her.

A female in a blue Walmart apron stained dark with blood stumbled out from behind a clothing display. Tibor morphed into his vampiric form and rushed forward. He swiped at it with his right hand, his talons catching it on the cheek and tearing off its lower jaw, then shoved it aside. The rotter moved toward Linda as she rushed past. Without a lower jaw it posed little threat.

Linda heard a snarl approaching from behind, followed by a muffled grunt and the sound of a body dropping to the floor. She barely noticed, her attention drawn instead to the two rotters coming at them from the front. The closest wore a tattered sundress that hung in rags around its waist, its chest and shoulders stripped of all flesh and most muscles. The one behind it hobbled along on a right leg with a compound fracture of the femur. Tibor hunched over and raced forward, smashing his left shoulder into the abdomen of the sundress rotter, and sending it careening backwards into the one with the fractured leg. Both of the living dead tumbled to the floor and slid into a DVD display. Tibor waved them on.

A minute later they burst into the storage room where Robson stood with his automatic shotgun aimed at them.

ROBSON TIGHTENED HIS finger on the trigger at the sound of approaching feet. He lowered the weapon the moment he saw Dravko and the others.

"We were about to come looking for you."

"We're okay," said Dravko. "We have half a dozen rotters on our tail."

"Tell me about it." Robson motioned behind him to the horde around the Ryder. He pointed to Linda. "Get those in back."

Linda maneuvered the hand truck onto the Ryder.

"Get on board," Robson ordered. "We're getting out of here."

"Only one problem," said Dravko. "How are we going to get into the front?"

Robson swore under his breath, partly because of his own stupidity. He had not realized there was no access to the front cab from the truck bed. The Ryder's roof sat flush with the top of the loading dock door, leaving only a few inches to crawl through. The only way to get to the driver's seat was to jump off the dock and make his way to the front. With close to twenty rotters on that side of the Ryder, he would never make it. They were screwed.

Robson stepped back and examined the storage room. Ten feet to the left sat the exterior door leading into the parking lot. He had an idea. A really bad idea, yet at this point they were out of options.

"It's only twenty feet between that door and the truck. If you keep them distracted, I should be able to make it."

DeWitt shook his head. "You won't get ten feet."

"Do you have any better ideas?"

DeWitt averted his gaze.

"I do," said Dravko. "I can crawl up the side of the truck onto the roof and make my way to the cab."

Before Robson could respond, the swinging double doors leading to the main floor burst open and a rotter dressed in a flannel shirt and jeans hobbled into the storage room. Robson raised his AA-12 and fired two rounds that tore off its head. Before the body hit the floor he began shouting, "Everybody on the truck! Now!"

The others ran into the back. Robson and Dravko stepped to the left side of the loading dock. The living dead crowded around the rear of the Ryder, moaning and clutching at them.

Robson took a deep breath. "Are you ready?"

"No, but let's do it."

Two more rotters pushed through the double doors into the storage area. Robson lowered his AA-12 at the loading dock and pulled the trigger, swinging the shotgun from left to right and blowing apart the nearest rotters. The shattered bodies dropped to the ground. Before the other living dead could move into their place, Dravko morphed into his vampiric form and jumped onto the side of the Ryder. With his taloned fingers, he scaled the side of the truck onto the roof before the next tier of rotters could get to him, and then ran down toward the cab.

In one fluid motion, Robson spun around, dropped the empty magazine from his AA-12, and loaded a full one. Five rotters from inside the store came across the storage room, the closest only a few feet away. Robson raised the shotgun and pulled the trigger, sending two rounds into the closest rotter's head, churning it into a cloud of red dust. Taking careful aim, he dispatched the other four with head shots. Three more pushed their way into the storage room and headed for him.

Once on the cab's roof, Dravko leaned over. The door was closed and the window rolled up. Seven rotters gathered around, reaching up for him. Dravko jumped down onto the Ryder's hood and kicked at the windshield until it cracked and the frame bent inward. Grabbing it by the exposed corners, he ripped it out, tossed it aide, and crawled in behind the steering wheel. When he turned on the ignition, the rotters outside the cab became frantic, clawing and scraping at the door. Dravko rolled down the window halfway and yelled to Robson.

"Are you ready?"

"Yes. Swing by the Hummer so I can pick it up."

Dravko shifted into gear, and Robson stepped into the bed of the Ryder, firing several rounds at the three rotters in the storage room. When the truck pulled away, he held on to the strap so he did not fall out. The horde of rotters gave chase.

Robson leaned back and yelled, "Roberta, Dewitt. Get up here and cover me."

Dravko swung the Ryder around and pulled the back end by the driver's door of their Humvee. The rotters were twenty feet away. Robson jumped down from the truck, raced over to the Humvee, and climbed inside. He had the vehicle started before any of the living dead could reach him. Flashing the headlights to let Dravko know he was ready, he fell in behind the Ryder. The two vehicles accelerated across the parking lot and away from Super Walmart. He glanced into his rearview mirror to see the rotters still chasing them.

Reaching the far end of the lot, the convoy turned right at the exit and followed the side roads that would take them back to Gilmanton.

CHAPTER FOUR

N ATALIE BAZARGAN STOOD in front of the window to her holding cell. She had been staring out of it for over an hour, her attention focused on Alcatraz Island in the middle of San Francisco Bay. The abandoned prison complex, which used to symbolize despair for the inmates incarcerated there, now represented the best chance for humanity's survival. Alcatraz was where the government-in-exile had established itself and been marshaling forces. If mankind hoped to take the world back from the living dead, it would begin here. If they succeeded, it would be in no minor part due to Natalie and her Angels having transported the vaccine for the Revenant Virus across the country.

For the first time in almost a year, the world saw a glimmer of hope that it could finally stop this rotter apocalypse and take back the planet. Even if it was the dullest of glimmers, it was more than the world had a few days ago.

Natalie, more than anyone, needed that thread of hope to hang on to.

Now that she had time to reflect on the past few weeks, she realized how much her life had changed. A month ago, she and the others in her group of survivors had been living a comfortable life along the coast of Maine, or as comfortable as one could in a post-apocalyptic world. They had established a nice community for themselves at Fort McClary, an early-eighteenth century fort outside of Kittery that once had been a tourist attraction. They had food, comfortable living conditions, and, most of all, security. Natalie had gathered fourteen other women from the camp and formed a zombie hunting team, respectfully referred to as the Angels of Death. She had even fallen in love with Mike Robson, the leader of the camp's raiding party. Their lives had settled into a semblance of normalcy until Dr. Compton, the creator of the Revenant Virus that had caused the outbreak, arrived at camp. He claimed to have a vaccine that could give the survivors the ability to fight back. It was kept in storage at Site R, an underground military facility more than five hundred miles away. The camp elders decided the benefits of acquiring the vaccine outweighed the risks and ordered Robson's raiding party and Natalie's Angels to accompany Compton to retrieve it.

That mission ended in disaster.

Having lived in the shelter of their own camp for so long, no one had been prepared for the journey down to Site R. The group had grown used to dealing with minor numbers of rotters, and now had to confront entire cities infested by them. They lost several good people on the way, although nowhere near as many as when they arrived at the underground facility. The vaccine for the Revenant Virus was effective only on humans because it had been cultured with human DNA. If given to the vampires, it would change them into the living dead. Compton wanted to use the vaccine to infect the vampires and murder them. When Robson refused, Compton released a horde of close to four hundred rotters into the compound and tried to escape. They had been able to stop Compton and fight back the living dead, at the cost of almost every member of Robson's raiding party and one of the Angels.

Their situation had deteriorated even further after arriving back at camp. A rape gang they encountered on the trip south had followed their tracks back to Fort McClary. The gang destroyed the camp and murdered everyone except for one four-man group out on patrol and Windows, who had taken back to their compound. Robson made the decision to split the group. He and the rest of the camp survivors would attempt to rescue Windows. Meanwhile, Natalie and her Angels acquired a yacht and headed down the East Coast and then west via the Mississippi River to the government-in-exile in Omaha.

Natalie felt a cold shudder race down her spine at the thought of that voyage. The Angels' morale had been shattered by the battle with hundreds of rotters at Site R and, psychologically, they were in no condition to make such a dangerous trip. They eventually made their way to Omaha, only to find the government-in-exile overrun by rotters, and then traveled by plane with the last military unit leaving the city to the new government in San Francisco. Everyone on that flight would have died fighting thousands of the living dead on the Golden Gate Bridge if the government had not sent out a rescue party to save them and bring them back to the Beachhead, the old San Francisco Port of Embarkation located inside Fort Mason that served as the gateway to the new government-in-exile on Alcatraz Island. Natalie had succeeded in bringing the vaccine for the Revenant Virus to the government, although at a cost of five of her Angels dead and two missing. Those who survived were lucky to be alive.

It had been a long time since Natalie felt safe and secure in her surroundings. She had only been away from camp for a few weeks, yet those had been some of the most difficult and dangerous weeks she had experienced since the initial outbreak. Since the group's departure from Site R, every waking moment had been spent on the edge, anticipating the next danger. Christ knew they had encountered more than their fair share of mishaps until she trusted no situation. Even while being escorted into the Beachhead, she had expected the worst, especially after their group had been separated and detained for forty-eight hours in a holding cell. Thankfully, their captors were gracious hosts, offering a hot meal and a good night's sleep, both of which Natalie took full advantage of. She slept for seventeen hours, a deep REM sleep that allowed her to wake refreshed.

The group spent most of their first full day in detention being debriefed. The government personnel were especially interested in Ari, who had been bitten on the hand during the battle on the Golden Gate Bridge and showed no signs of infection. Natalie had been questioned by Brian Thomas, the chief of staff for Secretary Fogel, on the vaccine and what she knew about it, as well as her knowledge of rotters. Although Natalie had no medical expertise to answer questions about the former, she had been more than happy to describe her experiences with the living dead. Other than the debriefings, the past two days had passed without excitement.

Now, on the morning of the third day, their detention was almost over. Natalie studied herself in the window's reflection, taking in the change. Physically, the changes were insignificant. Her brunette hair still flowed down her shoulders, although the ends were frayed and desperately needed a trim. The brown eyes staring back at her were fatigued. Of course, she could have said that about every part of her body. Her face and five-foot-six frame were gaunt from the strenuous nature of the past few weeks and the lack of food. No, the change was in her attitude and how she bore herself. The desperateness, the hopelessness, and the fear had been replaced by confidence. Not confidence in herself, because that had never wavered.

Confidence that humanity had a future.

She only wished she knew whether or not Robson was still alive.

Natalie heard a commotion by the door leading from the main building to the detention area. The rest of the Angels who shared the space with her stood up from their cots and joined her. Each seemed more optimistic than a few days ago. Stephanie, the oldest member of her group, pushed her shoulders back and pulled down on the hem of her jacket. Josephine, a petite young woman of Asian descent, smiled at

Natalie. She had a slight bounce in her step, a sign she was anxious to begin her new life. Amy, who usually wrapped her long blonde hair in a ponytail, let it flow naturally down her back, something she had not done since arriving at camp. Ari pushed her librarian-style glasses up her nose and ran her fingers through her shoulder-length dark hair to straighten it. She then reached out, clasped her hand against Natalie's, and gave it a reassuring squeeze.

A few seconds later, Captain Rogers, the Army officer who had led the rescue operation on the Golden Gate Bridge, centered himself in front of their cell.

Captain Duane "Butcher" Everett, the pilot who had flown them out of Omaha, and Private Carver Duncan, the only soldier with them on the bridge to survive the battle, stood off to the side. Everett favored his right leg, his left thigh wrapped in bandages from where he suffered an injury during his crash landing on the emergency airstrip north of the bridge. A corporal came up with a set of keys and unlocked the door.

"Good news, ladies." Rogers clapped his hands together and rubbed the palms. "Your forty-right hours are up. You're free to go."

"Go where?" Ari asked as she exited the cell.

"Alcatraz. We've arranged accommodations for you. Once you get there, we'll give you your passes to the mess hall."

"Three hots and a cot," said Stephanie.

"More like two hots and a cot," Rogers chuckled. "But you get the drift. You'll also get hot showers and a change of clothes."

Ari performed a vertical fist pump and hugged Stephanie. Natalie stepped out in the hall and said, "Thank you."

"You're part of the team now, and we take care of each other." Rogers headed for the exit and motioned for the women to follow. "Once you get settled in you can either choose a job posting or we can assign one to you. We've got plenty of openings in the armed forces. There's no need to make any decisions yet. First, let's get you cleaned up." The captain glanced over at Natalie. "I'll have to show you your quarters later."

"Why's that?"

"Right after you take your shower, Secretary Fogel wants to see you."

CHAPTER FIVE

B RUCE DENNING STOOD on the front porch of his house, a
cup of warm coffee in one hand and an apple in the other,
alternating between the two as he looked out over his farm.

A bright morning sun balanced perfectly with the cool air.
Birds chirped in the surrounding woods and a pair a squirrels
chased each other around the trunk of an oak tree. On the far
end of his pasture, a family of deer ventured out into the open
to graze. Denning took a sip of coffee, savoring the flavor for a
few seconds and relishing another perfect, quiet morning.

He was probably the only person who enjoyed the rotter
apocalypse.

"Enjoy" sounded too harsh. A better phrasing would be
"least affected." When the outbreak spread, civilization
collapsed because the infrastructure supporting it fell apart.
One by one, utilities and services ground to a halt. Most of
those who had survived the dead hordes could not cope with
living in a world that had regressed by more than a century.
Those who had been weaker or unready were either absorbed
into larger, more prepared groups, or culled out by those who
were tougher. The strong survived, or the incredibly lucky.
More often than not, they were people you did not want as
neighbors. None of this had any impact on him, however,
because Denning refused to rely on anything most people
associated with their day-to-day lives. Since the death of his
wife ten years ago, he had gone off the grid and become self-
sufficient.

The thought of Anna always brought a brief flicker of happiness to his heart. Sadly, that flame soon fanned itself into a raging conflagration of anger. Not at Anna. He loved her more than anything in the world. She had been his wife of twenty-seven years. More than that, she had been his best friend, his lover, and his soul mate. No, he directed the anger at the cancer that ravaged its way through her body. At the insurance company that refused to pay for a procedure which could save her life because, despite its success rate in clinical trials, they deemed it "experimental." At the hospital that denied the treatments to save Anna's life without getting their payment up front. At the real estate agency that agreed to help him sell half his farm so he could raise the money for Anna's surgery then tricked him into selling it at fifty percent of its value after making a corrupt deal with a land developer. Not a day went by when he did not imagine every one of those assholes as one of the living dead. If he ever came across one, he would let them suffer for eternity like they had made him suffer rather than put them out of their misery.

A smile crossed his lips as he imagined Anna chastising him for having such a negative attitude and for not being very Christian. She had always been his better half and lovingly called him "her misanthrope."

Her pet name for him happened to be closer to reality than even she realized. Denning had associated within society because of Anna. Their friends were her friends. After Anna's passing, contact with them became less frequent until it stopped altogether. He never owned a cell phone and only maintained the landline in case of emergency. Anna had used the Internet and cable television and, with her no longer around, he had gotten rid of both, limiting what little TV he viewed to the local channels he could tune in with the antenna in his backyard. He learned how to do things for himself so he could avoid relying on contractors or repairmen and spending money he did not have. A well and a septic system provided his plumbing. A few years back he installed solar panels to remove himself from dependency on the utility companies.

Over time, his attitude became full-blown self-reliance. Whatever Denning could not produce for himself, he stock-piled. Many of his neighbors thought he had gone nuts, while some of the more gracious referred to him as a survivalist. He would agree with the latter, although not with the negative connotation that it implied. If the death of Anna had taught him anything, it was life could be unpredictable and unfair. As far as Denning was concerned, if disaster struck, he did not want to rely on anyone.

Denning took a bite of apple and chewed. He wondered what the locals thought of him now… if any of them were still alive.

Finishing his apple, Denning flung the core toward the pine tree near his house so nature would recycle it. Drinking the last of the coffee as he stepped inside, he placed the empty mug in the sink and prepared to make his morning rounds of the perimeter. He strapped on his utility belt with the hunting knife and machete, grabbed his 450 Bushmaster rifle with scope, and headed out the back door.

His farm covered twenty acres. Denning had surrounded the property with a five-foot-tall, reinforced wooden fence interlaced with barbed wire and topped with rusty nails. At the time, he had considered the measure overkill since his property sat a mile from the closest public road. Over the past year, he had thanked God for his paranoia. That fence kept out trespassers and the living dead, although he rarely encountered either. In the beginning, four or five groups of people came across his farm and wanted to stay, and every time he refused, not wanting to bring strangers into his house. His caution had been justified when the first four groups became belligerent. The third had been the worst, threatening to take his farm away since they outnumbered him seven-to-one. Denning used the Bushmaster to narrow the odds to three-to-one before the survivors broke and ran. The only group he had felt guilty about turning away was the last, a family with three kids, all under ten. That had been ten months ago. He had not seen another human since. He occasionally came across a rotter sauntering outside the fence or entangled in the barbed wire and would dispatch it with the machete. The last of those had been four or five months ago. The only reason he continued to walk the perimeter every morning was out of force of habit and the need to exercise.

The main property consisted of five acres of yard surrounding the sides and back of his home, a two-thousand-square-foot ranch style house. In front of that sat ten acres he farmed to raise the grains and vegetables he lived on, as well as the chicken coop and pig enclosure. Denning crossed behind the house to the eastern border of his property and proceeded south. As usual, he saw nothing out of the ordinary.

Making his way along the south and west perimeters, he eventually backtracked to the front of the property where he had enclosed five acres of land into a pasture for Walther, his prized bull from when he had unsuccessfully tried his hand at raising cattle. The business failed because Walther was an ornery son of a bitch who did not get along with other cows and hated everyone except for Denning, which explained why he and Walther got along so well. Most mornings his friend waited by the corner of the fence to greet him as he made his rounds. Not today, though. At first, Denning thought Walther might be ill until he saw the animal at the far end of the pasture, its attention focused on the road leading to the farm.

Two figures approached from half a mile away. Crouching by the wooden fence surrounding the pasture, he raised his Bushmaster and centered the scope on them. They were a young woman with short blonde hair and a little girl about ten years old. Each carried a backpack. The woman sported two AK-47s, one strapped over her right shoulder and the second clutched in her hands. Denning watched carefully for several minutes to make certain these two were not being used as bait to lure him out. Using the scope, he scanned the surrounding area for any signs of an armed group but saw no indication they were with anyone else. Well, he might as well confront the intruders and get this over with.

Standing, Denning held the rifle in front of him so it appeared non-threatening but so he could raise it to fire in an instant, and then moved forward to greet the newcomers.

Upon seeing him, the woman stopped and grabbed the girl's shoulder, signaling for her to do the same. She stepped in front of the girl, her body shielding the youngster, and waited for Denning. She held her weapon the same way, sending the signal she posed no danger yet should not be trifled with. Denning sized them up. Both wore filthy clothes that had seen better days. They had not washed in God knew how long and smelled from twenty feet away. The woman's demeanor stood out most. The slumped shoulders and drawn face indicated she had gone through Hell, an impression reinforced by the partially healed gouge taken out of her left cheek. Despite her physical appearance, a spark of defiance in her gestures and eyes warned she still had some fight left in her. Her spirit had been beaten, not broken. The situation out there must have been far worse than he imagined.

As Denning approached, the blonde spoke. "I'm Windows. This is Cindy. We're not looking for trouble. We just need a place to stay for a while."

Smart girl, he thought. *Take the initiative and try to get the upper hand.*

"This is the only place around for miles," he replied. "You must've been walking for some time."

"All night. Our car ran out of gas yesterday."

"Where'd you come from?"

"We left the car south of here, maybe fifteen or twenty miles away."

"No," said Denning. "Where'd you drive from?"

"Southern New Hampshire."

Denning laughed, which caught the woman off guard. "You're a long way from home, miss."

"How so?"

"You're in Canada now. We're about twenty kilometers south of Quebec."

The woman glanced down at the little girl, who wrapped an arm around her waist and hugged. The woman loosened her grip on the weapon and her finger moved off the trigger.

After a few seconds, she asked, "Is it okay if we stay here a little while, at least until we can rest and clean up?"

Denning considered it. He had refused to take in anyone since the outbreak, mostly to avoid the hassle of having to deal with people or be concerned over whether they would attempt to take over. Yet he still felt bad about turning away that family, so this might assuage his guilt. Besides, at sixty-three he was no longer as young as he used to be, and it would be nice to have someone to help around the farm.

"I'll let you stay as long as you're willing to do some things around here."

The woman sighed. Her shoulders slumped again, and her body lost that fighting edge she had displayed a moment ago. Moving away from the little girl, she stepped up to Denning and spoke in a soft voice.

"I'll do anything you ask me to, but don't touch Cindy."

The comment took Denning aback for a moment, and then everything fell into place. He could not even begin to imagine what this poor woman had gone through. He stepped back a few feet to put some distance between them.

"I'm talking about helping with chores around the farm. That's all."

"Thank God." She lowered her head. A tear ran down her cheek. "I'm sorry. I didn't mean to imply—"

"Yes, you did. That's okay. You'll be safe here."

Her facial expression softened.

"I'm Bruce Denning." He held out his hand. "You said your name is Windows?"

Windows raised her head and sniffed. "Yes, it is."

"That's an unusual name."

"It's my nickname. I got it because I'm really good with computers."

He bent down on one knee in front of the little girl. "You must be Cindy."

Cindy glanced over at Windows for guidance, who nodded. The girl extended her hand. "Yes, sir. It's a pleasure to meet you."

"The pleasure is mine." Denning gave her hand a friendly pump. "Have you ever fed chickens or slopped pigs?"

Cindy shook her head.

"Would you like to?"

The girl's face beamed.

"I'll introduce you to them later." Getting to his feet, Denning motioned to the farmhouse. "First, let's get you ladies inside. You both could use a warm meal and a hot shower."

Windows sniffed back a tear. "Thank you."

"Don't thank me yet. You haven't tasted my cooking." Denning headed back to the farmhouse and waved for Windows and Cindy to follow. The two fell in behind him, hugging each other tight.

Denning could almost hear the teasing Anna would give him if she were alive at the moment.

CHAPTER SIX

ONCE THE RAIDING party got back to Gilmanton, Linda took over and organized the team to care for the survivors, leaving Robson with nothing to do and no orders to give. Which suited him fine. Though he never admitted it to the others, he had grown weary of being in charge. Leading his people had proven difficult enough. Now he had thirty others, most of whose names he did not even know, to be responsible for. If someone else wanted to step up and take over for a while, Robson would not complain.

Linda oversaw the unloading of the Ryder and organized the effort like an assembly line. Simmons prepared each of the survivors a breakfast of peanut butter on stale crackers, cheese, and beef jerky. Wayans, who was still experiencing pain from his wounds but had grown restless lying around doing nothing, mixed powdered protein drinks. As each survivor finished eating, he or she would be seen by Linda, who provided a cursory physical, treated any illnesses with the prescription medicines commandeered from Super Walmart, and started them on a regimen of vitamins.

They then headed outside to where Roberta and DeWitt had set up a makeshift shower stall fed from a thousand-gallon water container located behind the garage. They stripped out of their old clothes, threw them into an empty fifty-five-gallon drum, and received a buzz cut and a shave of the pubic region, with DeWitt assisting the men and Roberta the women. Everyone got a long shower with medicated shampoo to kill lice. After cleaning up, DeWitt or Roberta led each person to a windowless back room inside the warehouse where Dravko and Tibor distributed clothes.

After that, the survivors were free to do what they wanted. Several went back inside the garage, found a place to lie down, and slept. A few went off into a private corner to cry. Most, ventured outside and collected into groups, chatting amongst themselves.

After wandering through the garage for an hour and realizing the others had everything under control, Robson went outside. He saw Caslow expanding the size of the mass grave. Robson crossed the street and stepped up beside him.

"How many more did we lose last night?"

Caslow did not even look up. "Four."

Damn. "It looks big for four people."

"I assume we're going to lose more, so I figured I'd dig them all while I'm at it."

"Good idea," Robson said. "When you're done here, Roberta and DeWitt have collected everyone's old clothes in a drum out back. They're infested with lice and bugs. Burn them before they spread into the camp."

"Sure."

As Robson walked away, Caslow said, "Other than to bark orders, no one has spoken to me since the raid the other night."

"So?"

"What's up with that?"

Robson faced Caslow. "Do you really want to know?"

"Yes."

"You're a coward and you're unreliable."

"That's not fair."

"It's the truth," Robson said, trying to hold his anger in check. "You allowed your wife and daughter to be taken by that rape gang and did nothing to help them."

"I told you, I was outnumbered."

"Quit making excuses. You should have tried. Instead, you

chickened out and let the gang have them. Because of you, your wife committed suicide and God only knows what happened to your daughter."

"Don't I get credit for going with you to save them?"

Robson moved forward to confront Caslow, who stepped back and almost toppled into the open grave. With his left hand, Robson grabbed Caslow by the shirt to prevent him from falling in.

"I teamed you with Jennifer so you could provide backup for each other. Jennifer was shot and killed while you cowered in one of the storage units. She might be alive if you had been there for her."

Robson realized his right hand had balled into a fist. He yanked Caslow forward and away from the grave. When he released his shirt, Caslow fell forward onto his hands and knees. The little shit remained in that position, refusing to face Robson.

"I deserve better than this," he whimpered.

"No, you don't. *Jennifer* deserved better. *Your wife and daughter* deserved better. As for you..." Robson inhaled deeply to calm his anger. "...be thankful you're here. I almost left you at the storage facility."

"Why didn't you?"

"Because when I let you join our group, I took responsibility for you. I wasn't going to leave you in the middle of nowhere, no matter how useless you are."

Robson started to leave, stopping when he heard Caslow mumble a question under his breath. "What was that?"

"I asked what'll happen to me when you move on." Caslow lifted his head. He tried to show defiance, although Robson detected the underlying fear in his eyes. "Are you going to leave me on the side of the road like an abandoned dog?"

Robson stared at Caslow a moment, not attempting to conceal the disgust on his face. After a few seconds, he headed back to the garage, though not because he refused to answer.

Robson had not yet considered what he wanted to do about Caslow.

★　★　★

DRAVKO WATCHED IN fascination as Tibor handed out clothes to the survivors. In their hundreds of years together, he had never seen his fellow vampire so outgoing. Dravko had wanted to reinforce to Robson that he and Tibor were still part of the group. However, because the sun had risen, the only job they could handle was distributing clothes in the windowless back room of the garage. Dravko had been concerned that, after all these people had gone through, none of them would want to be enclosed in a room with two vampires. Thanks to Tibor, those fears were unfounded. Tibor chatted with the humans, asking them their names and how they were getting along. Everyone entered the room feeling apprehensive, and all of them left with higher spirits. Some even grinned and laughed. One young blonde came around the table and hugged Tibor, thanking him for being concerned. When the last human had left, Tibor packed up the remaining clothes.

Dravko stepped up beside him and patted his shoulder. "You did a good job."

"Thanks," replied Tibor while putting a stack of sweatpants back into the plastic crate.

"When did you become so friendly with humans?"

"When I got the idea to recruit them."

"Recruit?" Dravko took a step back. "You're talking about turning them?"

"I'm talking about making them want to join the coven."

"You can't be serious," protested Dravko.

"I am." Tibor glanced around the room to make certain no one could hear him. "Robson and the others are vaccinated against the zombie virus, and are taking chances they normally wouldn't, like last night's raid. We're the last two vampires in the world. At this rate, our species will be extinct in a few weeks."

"You can't turn these people against their will."

Tibor's lips sneered in disgust. "There was a time when vampires were superior to humans. We were stronger, faster, and immortal. We never used to worry about who we sired and whether or not we did it against their will. Our only limitation was in keeping our numbers low so as not to alarm the humans. What happened to you? Do you feel a sense of guilt because we released the Revenant Virus and nearly destroyed the humans? Do you feel like you have to treat them with deference to atone for our sins? Maybe we deserve to be extinct."

Dravko could not respond, his mind trying to come to grips with Tibor's tirade.

Tibor went back to packing the extra clothes. "I've obeyed your request to leave Robson and the others alone. The survivors from the camp are different. They're not part of our original group. Robson hasn't even talked to most of them or learned any of their names."

"And you have?"

"Yes." Tibor's gaze bore into Dravko, emphasizing his point. "Thanks to me, they don't see us as monsters like most other humans do. I'm not going to turn anyone against their will. However, I'm winning over their trust. If they ask to become a vampire, I won't hesitate to rebuild the coven."

"What makes you think they'll want to become one of us?"

"They're sick and weak, and they know their chances of survival are slim." Tibor's tone became energized as he tried to convince Dravko. "They've been raped, beaten down, and dehumanized. They're tired of being taken advantage of. I can see it in their eyes. I can sense it on their souls as easily as I can sense the blood flowing through their veins. They don't want to be part of a collective with someone else in the lead. They want to take charge of their own lives, and some of them see becoming a vampire as the way to do that."

Although Tibor made a rational argument, Dravko knew Robson would never allow it. "We can't do this."

"Why not?" pleaded Tibor. "We've worked with the humans for a year to survive. Sultanic and Tatyana gave their lives to save them. The humans are rebuilding their numbers. Don't we also have a right to exist?"

Dravko could not answer. This was a decision he had hoped to avoid. Of course, vampires had a right to exist. As the only remaining vampires, he and Tibor had a solemn obligation to rebuild the coven. Doing so would place him at odds with Robson. While the two were friends and covered each other's backs, Dravko doubted Robson would sit by and let him turn the survivors. If Robson tried to stop them, he and Tibor did not stand much of a chance.

"I don't see how we can do this," said Dravko.

"Leave it to me."

"What about Robson?"

Tibor sighed in exasperation. "In deference to you, and to all Robson's done for us, I'll be as considerate of him as possible. But when the time comes, we'll rebuild the coven, with or without his approval."

CHAPTER SEVEN

T HE HOT SHOWER and change of clothes had been the best
thing to happen to Natalie in the past four weeks, except
for those intimate moments spent with Mike. Judging by the
reaction of her Angels, she assumed they felt the same. She
heard several of her girls giggling in the shower. When a female
staffer took them to the storeroom for a change of clothes, most
of the Angels acted like teenagers on a shopping spree, holding
the garments against each other and asking the others how they
looked. The selection was limited and functional, mostly earth-
toned ACUs, or Army combat uniforms, sand-colored t-shirts,
and black or tan boots. No dresses, skirts, or heels. Natalie
found it strange not to see her girls in what their traditional
uniforms. Not that it mattered. For the first time in a year, her
girls had the opportunity to wear something other than their
well-worn leather pants, white shirts, and leather jackets.
Coming to Alcatraz symbolized a break with everything they
had gone through previously, although Natalie seemed to be
the only one who noticed. They looked like women and not the
Angels, and she had not seen them this vibrant since before Site
R. When the girls left to be escorted to their new quarters, she
was the only one to take with her anything from her past life,
asking the staffer if she could have her leather jacket.

Rogers and an enlisted woman in a blue-toned ACU waited for them outside the storeroom. Rogers stepped forward
when he saw the Angels. "How do you feel?"

"Like a new woman," said Natalie. "Thank you."

"No need to thank me, ma'am. We're building a new society here, and we can't do that if we all smell like the revenants." Rogers motioned toward the woman beside him. "This is Corporal Bechtel. She's going to show you ladies to your quarters."

Bechtel stepped forward. "You arrived at a good time. A large contingent moved out of the cellblock two nights ago, so we have quarters available. I arranged to have you in adjacent cells so we don't have to separate you. It's two people to a cell, but it beats the tent farm out on the parade ground."

"You'll hear no complaints from us," said Natalie.

"If you ladies will follow me, please."

Rogers motioned to Natalie. "Secretary Fogel is waiting to see you."

"Lead the way."

Rogers escorted Natalie outside the cellblock, leading her around the northeast façade to the main entrance of the administrative offices at the far end of the building. Upon entering, they took the first right, passed through two offices, and found themselves in the warden's secretary's room. Brian Thomas, the chief of staff for Secretary Fogel, sat behind a dented and scuffed metal desk in front of a set of windows that overlooked San Francisco Bay, with Oakland in the distance. He wore the same outfit he had on when he debriefed her— black slacks and shoes, a white dress shirt, and a tie. Natalie assessed him to be in his mid-fifties because of the gray streaking his dark hair along the temples, which accentuated his lean face and brown eyes. She found him to be professional, pleasant, and polite. Upon seeing her enter, he stood and came around the desk.

"Miss Bazargan, it's good to see you again." He extended his hand.

"Likewise." She gave it a firm pump.

"I see you've had a chance to freshen up. I hope everything is to your satisfaction."

"It's much better than anything we've had in a long time."

"We do our best."

Captain Rogers cleared his throat. "I hope we're not late."

"Not at all, Captain." Thomas motioned toward a card table set up in the corner with a coffee pot on top. "Help yourself to a cup while you wait."

"Thanks."

"Come with me, please," Thomas said to Natalie. "Secretary Fogel is anxious to meet you."

They crossed Thomas' office to the interior wall. The chief of staff knocked on the door, waited for a response, and opened it. "Excuse me, Mr. Secretary. Miss Bazargan is here to see you."

"Excellent," said the voice from inside the office. "Send her in."

Thomas stepped aside and ushered Natalie into the warden's office. The room appeared as Spartan as the outer office, with the same plain white walls and dirty floor tiles that had been in place when the prison was shut down back in 1963. Two large support beams ran down the center of the room. To the left opposite the single window and door leading outside sat the Secretary's desk, an old, scratched up piece of furniture with drips of dried paint scattered along the surface and sides. The only other pieces were three easy chairs, one behind the desk and two in front for visitors, each of a different design with frayed, mismatched fabric. The office appeared as if it had been furnished from an old basement.

When Fogel stood to greet her, Natalie barely recognized him. Prior to the outbreak, she had seen him on the news quite often due to his being a vocal advocate for improving the country's declining educational standards. She remembered him as being robust. Now he was thin, although his loose-fitting black suit made him seem gaunter than he actually was. His blond hair had gone gray, and he squinted to see through his glasses. Coming around the side of the desk, Fogel steadied himself on its surface before approaching. Other than the signs of age and exhaustion brought on by living through the outbreak, he seemed in good health and greeted her with a firm handshake.

"It's a pleasure to meet you, Miss Bazargan."

"Please, call me Natalie, Mr. President."

Fogel snickered. "I'll make a deal with you. I won't call you Miss Bazargan if you don't call me Mr. President."

Natalie became confused. "I don't understand. I thought you *were* the President."

"That depends on who you talk to," replied Thomas.

"What do you mean?"

Fogel gestured toward one of the easy chairs in front of his desk for Natalie to sit, and he took the other. Thomas propped himself on the edge of the desk. "With the collapse of the government-in-exile in Omaha and the chaos throughout the nation, the presidency is up for grabs."

"I'd heard that from the troops at Offutt. I thought it was only a rumor."

"I wish." Fogel shook his head. "Sadly, most politicians are looking out for themselves. The highest-ranking surviving official still alive that we know about who is in line to succeed to the presidency is Secretary of Defense Wilson. He was returning from a summit in Europe when the president banned all air travel. He made it as far as Montreal. Some say he's ineligible to be president because he resides in a foreign country. It's all moot, though. No one has had contact with him in five months. Assuming Secretary Wilson is dead, I'm the next highest-ranking official known to be alive, even though I'm sixteenth in the line of succession."

"The problem is, some of the governors have declared the United States dead and buried and are trying to set up their own fiefdoms," Thomas said. "Shortly after the outbreak and the fall of Washington, D.C., Governor Peters of Texas declared himself the only legitimate government left in the country. Ham operators report Peters is still in the game, although he's lost most of Texas and is falling back to Mexico with a handful of people."

"Sort of an Alamo with revenants," Fogel chuckled.

"Then this past spring, Governor Dean of Wyoming declared himself the most capable official to handle the outbreak. The winter was cold with an unusual amount of snow, and it stopped the revenants. Dean used that opportunity to regroup and organize his defenses. By the time the thaw hit, he had cleaned out most of the state and had set up fortified enclaves throughout the region. He hasn't declared himself president, but he's trying to usurp power."

"At least Governor Sanders isn't vying for power," Fogel chimed in.

"Who?" Natalie asked.

"Governor Sanders of Alaska," said Fogel. He stood and crossed over to the window, gazing out over San Francisco Bay. "She used the winter to her advantage, just like Dean, and shared her information with the Canadians. By the time spring rolled around, the revenants had been pushed out of the north. Sanders and the Canadians have formed a defensive line from the southern tip of Alaska, running east south of Edmonton to the southern tip of Hudson Bay, and then turning southeast to north of Quebec. For six months, they've been taking in survivors and using them to reinforce the defense line. Me, Governor Dean, and the president have been doing the same thing. Well, the president was until the government-in-exile became infected. We've been organizing, planning, and preparing for months. Showing up when you did with the vaccine is a sign from God that we'll be successful."

"Wait a minute," Natalie interrupted. "I'm confused. What are you talking about?"

Fogel stepped away from the window. "Forgive me. I forgot you're not privy to this. In three days, we launch an operation that will take North America back from the living dead."

Natalie could hardly believe what she had heard. "Three days?"

"We've been coordinating this offensive for months." Fogel sat down at his desk. "The Canadians and Alaska will begin the campaign by pushing down from the north, clearing each square mile of revenants before moving on to the next. At the same time, we here in San Francisco, Governor Dean in Wyoming, and other smaller pockets of resistance will initiate their own offensives with the goal of meeting up with the Canadians. Major cities will be bypassed and contained."

"Are you abandoning them?" Natalie asked.

"Not at all. We've formed special units and developed tactics to clear out large cities, though the methods are going to be destructive."

"Not as the destructive as those used by the Russians," Thomas chimed in. "They nuked every major city to stop the outbreak. Moscow. Saint Petersburg. Volgograd. That only slowed the spread of the outbreak. The blasts destroyed millions of revenants inside the cities, not those in the suburbs."

"The fallout killed thousands of survivors who might otherwise have escaped to Siberia," Fogel continued. "We're determined not to make the same mistake, which is why we have a boots-on-the-ground approach to dealing with them. We were counting on the vaccine to keep our losses low, and had given up hope of ever getting it when we lost contact with Dr. Compton after he left Site R. Then you showed up."

Natalie swelled with pride for her Angels. "Thank you, Mr. Pres... Secretary."

"You'll be pleased to know we've already used the vaccines you provided to inoculate some of the troops here in San Francisco. We've flown copies of the CDs to Wyoming and to Alaska so the vaccine can be produced there and distributed to the troops. It may take a few weeks to produce enough to protect everyone. This will give us the advantage we need to take back our country. It's a shame Dr. Compton couldn't be here to see this."

Natalie forced herself to keep silent, well aware that Compton wanted to use the vaccine to infect and murder the vampires within their group and, when Robson refused to go along, released four hundred rotters into the underground facility to distract everyone while he escaped. Although it pissed Natalie off, under the circumstances she opted to maintain the fallacy of Compton's patriotism for the Secretary's benefit.

"On to other things." Fogel slapped his knees. "We have news about your missing comrades."

Natalie forgot all about Compton. "That's good."

"Not necessarily," said Thomas. "They were taken hostage by the Deaders."

"Deaders?"

"It's one of the local gangs that carved out turf for themselves following the outbreak. They've been trying to push us out but don't have enough firepower. Instead, they've taken to kidnapping our people and ransoming them back to us for supplies."

"You have enough firepower. Why don't you take them out?"

"We tried," Thomas sighed. "The bastards use hollow point ammunition filled with revenant blood. On our first raid against them, we lost ten dead and fifteen wounded who later had to be euthanized."

"Jesus."

"Tell us about it," said Fogel. "We're going to finally put an end to this. We have a drop scheduled for later this afternoon where we'll trade supplies for your three people who were taken hostage. Only this time, we'll be using troops we've inoculated, and will have a surprise for them."

Natalie thought for a moment. "Do you need any more guns?"

"What do you mean?" asked Thomas.

"Two of my girls are among the missing," said Natalie.

"And we're already inoculated. I'd like to have a chance to offer some payback."

A grin pierced Fogel's lips. "I think that can be arranged."

CHAPTER EIGHT

ROBSON GLANCED AROUND the table at the others in the rectory's dining room: Simmons and Wayans, Dravko and Tibor, DeWitt and Roberta, and Caslow. There were fewer than the last time they had all gathered for dinner, which had been two nights ago when the group had attacked Price's camp. Since the raid, they had spent most of their time caring for the survivors, making the supply run to Super Walmart, and burying the dead. Now that the situation had stabilized, their routine had returned to normal. The lull had also given Robson a chance to consider their plans for the future, which did not present any truly viable options. He had appreciated the distraction of the last few days because it provided an excuse not to deal with this. Robson would honor his promise to Simmons not to remain in Gilmanton and be a burden while at the same time meet his obligations to his own people and those they had saved. Every scenario he developed had more flaws than benefits. He decided on their future course of action late that afternoon and assumed he had made the correct choice because he knew everyone would be against it.

As the others chatted amongst themselves, Dravko leaned over toward Robson and whispered, "Is everything all right?"

"Yeah. Why?"

"You've barely said a word during dinner."

"Sorry," Robson responded halfheartedly. "I have a lot on my mind."

"I understand. If there's—"

A knock at the doorway to the dining room caught their attention. Linda stood in the entrance. "Sorry to interrupt."

"You're not interrupting," said Simmons. "We're almost finished. Is everything okay at the warehouse?"

"Everything's fine." Linda stepped into the dining room. "He asked me to come by."

Everyone focused their attention on Robson. He motioned for Linda to enter. As she took a seat near Simmons and Wayans, Robson said, "I asked Linda here so we can discuss our plans."

"Good idea," said Roberta. "We need to coordinate what we want to do next."

"There's nothing to coordinate," Robson said firmly, hoping to preempt any debate. "We're going to link up with the government-in-exile in Omaha."

DeWitt snorted. "You mean hook back up with Natalie in Omaha."

"I'm not going to lie and say it wouldn't be nice to get back together with Natalie. We'd all want to see our loved ones again." Robson made eye contact with everyone at the table. "That's not the reason I'm doing this. We know there's a large group of survivors in Omaha. Our best option is to make our way to them where Linda's people have the best chance of being taken care of properly and where the rest of us can be of use."

"Why?" asked Roberta in a soft tone. "Mike, your responsibility now is to those of us sitting here at this table, and to those people in the warehouse who are looking to you for guidance."

"I agree," said Robson, "and the most responsible thing I can do is get them someplace where they can be properly taken care of."

"That's not Omaha," said Simmons.

"They're right," Dravko stated. "You, me, and Tibor are the only three experienced enough to even attempt a cross country trip like this. And we'll be taking with us three dozen people who can barely travel, let alone fight rotters. Even if we headed north to where there are fewer living dead, I doubt we'd make it to Canada without getting overrun."

"What are you suggesting?" asked Robson. "That we give up?"

"That we survive," Roberta stated. "Linda, how long will it be before your people are back on their feet?"

"It'll be weeks before they reach full strength. If you're talking about being well enough to travel, they'll be able to do that in a few days," Linda added hesitantly.

"Thanks." Roberta focused her attention on Robson. "We're going to have a hard enough time surviving the next month, let alone trying to reach Omaha. We have plenty of food and medicine from last night's raid, so we have enough to keep going for a month, more if we ration food once people feel better. Our best bet is to head north, find a location where we can settle down, and rebuild what we had at Fort McClary."

Robson contemplated this for a minute before asking DeWitt, "I assume you agree?"

DeWitt nodded.

Robson gestured to Dravko. "And you?"

"It's the best choice under the circumstances."

"Tibor?"

The vampire grunted. "I'm with Dravko."

"What do you think?" Robson asked Caslow.

"Me?" he asked, surprised.

"For better or worse, you're part of the team now."

Caslow was uncertain how to respond. "I agree with Roberta. It's better to hunker down and ride this out."

"I knew he would," Tibor whispered loud enough for the others to hear.

"I know I don't have a say in this," said Simmons. "It's your best option."

"Yeah," added Wayans. "It's the only friggin' way you're

going to survive."

"What about you?" Robson asked Linda.

She lowered her head. "I don't have a say in this."

"Yes, you do. Do you think your people can handle traveling and setting up a new camp?"

Linda raised her head to meet Robson's gaze. "Honestly, no. One encounter with rotters and most of them will be killed. And they don't have enough strength to build a compound. But what choice do we have?"

"Then it's settled. In two days, we'll head out and find ourselves a new location to set up camp."

CHAPTER NINE

S NAKE RUBBED HIS calloused hand across Doreen's cheek. She tried not to focus on his face. She didn't know what repulsed her more, the greasy dark hair, the three-day growth of stubble, or the tattoo of a rattler than ran from one cheek, over his forehead, and down the other. When he leaned forward, Doreen almost gagged. Between his diseased gums and the front teeth rotted away by habitual crack use, his breath smelled as bad as a rotter. Like Sandy and Sergeant Batchelder to her right, she rested on her knees, her ass sitting on her ankles and her wrists handcuffed behind her back, which allowed Snake to tower over her.

"You're the prettiest hostage we've ever had in here." Snake slid his grimy fingers through her long red hair.

"You say that to all of them," said Snake's partner, One Eye, from the doorway. He stood in the opening, his AR-15 slung over his shoulder, his patched-over left eye facing them as he kept watch down the hall.

"This time I mean it."

One Eye chuckled. "You say that to them, too."

"Come on, baby," said Snake. "How about giving me some before the transfer?"

"Fuck you."

"That's what I had in mind." Snake clutched her hair and yanked, raising Doreen onto her knees, her face inches from his crotch.

One Eye moved away from the door and unslung his AR-

15. Coming up behind Snake, he slammed the stock between his shoulder blades. "Cut that fuckin' shit out."

"Screw you. I'm just having some fun."

"You know the rules." One Eye shoved his face into Snake's, shifting his head slightly to one side so his good eye locked onto Snake's. "None of the hostages are to be harmed in any way. That was the deal with the Rock. We send back damaged goods, and they stop paying ransom. You want to fuck up this arrangement on the Boss, go ahead. Let him break your legs and throw you out of the compound so those things can get you. I ain't gonna be deader food so you can get your rocks off. Clear?"

Snake averted his gaze. "Yeah."

"Good." One Eye stepped back. "Now, guard the door. I'm going to the loading dock to see what the holdup is."

As Snake walked away, Doreen sat on her ankles. She glanced over at Sandy and Sarge to see how they were doing. Sarge made eye contact and nodded his approval. Sandy winked. The three of them had held up well considering they had been hostages for two days.

It began during the escape from the rotters on the Golden Gate Bridge. They had been ahead of the others when the living dead swarmed the group. Sarge ordered them to keep moving forward, telling them that was what Pandelosi would be ordering the others to do. They made it to the banks of San Francisco without incident only to be ambushed by five members of the Deader gang. Their captors disarmed them and brought them to an apartment complex a mile south of the bridge off of Baker Beach. The complex had been fortified with a makeshift wall of Jersey barriers and chain link fences, with an old school bus parked across the entranceway serving as a gate. They had been escorted to a windowless room in the basement and had remained there until an hour ago. No one had bothered them during the duration of their captivity, at least until now, which had suited Doreen fine. The only contact came from those who had brought them their breakfast and dinner, and then Snake and One Eye who had arrived an hour ago to prep them for the transfer. With luck, they would be out of here in a few minutes.

NATALIE CROUCHED IN the back of the tractor trailer by the sliding door, holding the M-16A2 in her hands and placing the stock on the floor to steady herself. Ari, Amy, Stephanie, and Josephine gathered around her, in addition to one hundred soldiers from Alcatraz who had been inoculated with the vaccine.

The voice of Jim, the truck driver, crackled over their headphones. "We pulled onto Lincoln Boulevard. We should be at the Deader's compound in a few minutes."

Beside Natalie, Captain Endo, the platoon leader, spoke into his microphone. "Copy that."

The soldiers readied their weapons. Each of the Angels had a look of determination on their face, although Natalie could detect traces of fear in their eyes. She understood their trepidation because she felt it, too. They were used to battling rotters. This would be the first time they would go into combat against humans. Thankfully for the Angels, the plan to attack the compound was simple. These prisoner exchanges had gone on for so long security had become lax. In the beginning, the Deaders had examined every truck before allowing it inside the compound. Since Fogel had not wanted to do anything to endanger the hostages' safety, he never used the transfers to launch a rescue mission. Over time, the procedure had become so commonplace that the gang stopped checking the trailers. Endo planned to use that trust to his advantage. Once inside the compound, the unit would secure the area, take down the Deaders, and rescue their missing people.

The truck slowed, turned left, and rolled to a stop. They all listened to the conversation over their headphones.

"Hey, man. It's good to see you again."

"Thanks," said Jim. "How's your deader situation been?"

"The motherfuckers have been all riled up after the commotion on the bridge. What happened out there?"

"Some survivors coming in from Oakland got into a gunfight with them and shot up a propane truck. Blew out the center span in the process."

"Fuck."

"Tell me about it. The deaders in our section are still stirred up," said Jim.

"I hear you. Let's get this over with so we can get you on your way." The voice changed in pitch. "Open up the gat—"

"Wait," ordered another voice with a Puerto Rican accent. "The Boss wants us to inspect the truck before bringing it onto the compound. He's jittery after what happened on the bridge. Is it unlocked?"

"I think so," Jim replied, a hesitancy in his voice.

"Hang on while I check it out," said the man with the Puerto Rican accent. "You guys come with me."

Natalie looked to Endo for guidance. He and the soldiers along the rear row had already raised their weapons into firing position and trained them on the sliding door. She heard footsteps walking down the length of the trailer, followed by the sound of the locking device being unhitched and swung to the side. A second later, the door slid up. The three faces that stared at them registered a brief moment of shock before a fusillade of gunfire tore through their heads and upper torsos. The bodies had not even hit the pavement before Endo and his men poured out of the truck and spread out, laying down suppressing fire. Natalie raced forward and jumped off as all Hell broke loose.

Automatic weapons raked the front end of the truck and the flanks where Endo's men tried to deploy. The soldiers dropped to the ground, some taken down by return fire, most going prone to present a smaller target. Bullets punched through the thin metal container, thudding into the first few rows of troops packed against the front wall and transforming the inside into a charnel house as chunks of bodies and spent rounds ricocheted off the walls. A stream of weapons fire slammed into the rear corner of the truck beside Natalie's head, showering her with wood splinters. She ducked under the trailer.

From the two-story apartment complex off to the left, more than a dozen gang members fired from the windows or the flat roof. While a few engaged Endo's troops, most concentrated on the left corner at the rear of the truck, shooting those trying to get off. The same thing happened on the right. After the first eleven soldiers fell, the rest clustered around the end of the trailer. The troops still inside the truck, exposed and unable to get out, screamed frantically for the others to move.

A heavy staccato drumming cut through the din of battle. A line of bullets walked their way along the left flank, kicking up geysers of dirt or, when one struck a human, vomiting up a cloud of blood from the wound. One round slammed into Endo's face, blowing out the rear portion of his head. The heavy gunfire paused for only a moment before resuming, this time directed at the left side of the trailer. The bullets punched their way through the metal as if it was tissue paper and ripped apart the troops still trapped inside. They pulled the bodies of their dead friends on top of them as protection against the slaughter. Natalie searched for the next in command. Anyone on flank who tried to take charge died before he could give more than one or two orders. Those sheltering inside and behind the trailer seemed more concerned about surviving the next few seconds.

From the back of the truck, Josephine cried out and tumbled onto the driveway, holding her left shoulder. A tear ran across her uniform and blood seeped through the material.

"How bad were you hit?" Natalie asked.

"I don't know. I don't think it's fatal."

Natalie knelt down behind Josephine and checked the wound. An abrasion five inches long ran from the tip of her shoulder blade toward the spine. The bullet had not punctured the skin, but instead tore a gash across the surface half an inch deep, exposing the muscle beneath. Though it would hurt like a son of a bitch, Josephine would live—provided they could get out from behind the truck.

"Jesus motherfucking Christ!" screamed the private standing behind her.

"They've got a fucking .50 caliber," called out another soldier from inside the trailer.

"Where the fuck did they get a .50?" yelled a third.

"Cut the shit," ordered Natalie. She saw a corporal crouched three feet away who did not seem on the verge of panic. He had the name BROWN stitched onto his uniform nameplate. "Do you have any rocket launchers?"

"We have SMAWs," said Brown. "They're shoulder-launched assault weapons."

"Get them up here now."

"Yes, ma'am."

Ari moved up to Natalie. "What are you planning on doing?"

"I'm going to get us out of this slaughterhouse," Natalie stated resolutely. "Are you with me?"

The face that stared back bordered on panic, yet the eyes showed trust. "Of course."

"Wait here."

Still crouching, Natalie made her way to the right side of the truck. Machinegun fire came from the balcony window of a second-floor apartment. Another seven or eight gang members shot at them from various locations inside the building and on the roof. Two of Endo's men had advanced as far as the perimeter wall, a makeshift structure composed of three Jersey barriers stacked on top of each other, where they were pinned down.

Brown knelt beside her. "We're ready."

"How many SMAWs do you have?"

"Six."

"Put three on each side. The machinegun is in the second window from the left on the top floor. I need half a dozen of your men to provide cover fire. Do you have smoke grenades?"

"Yes, ma'am. But…." Brown motioned toward the dead troops on either side of the truck.

"We'll we have to do without it."

"No offense, ma'am. I should lead this attack."

Natalie shook her head. "Once we take out that machinegun, you're leading the charge on the front gate."

"Hoo-ah," said Brown. He barked orders to the rest of the troops and then focused back on Natalie. "On your order, ma'am."

Natalie waited until the fire from the machinegun paused. She prayed they were reloading and not waiting for a target of opportunity.

"Now!"

Natalie dashed out from behind the truck and ran to the right, her M-16A2 trained on the apartment building. Automatic weapons fire came at her. Nothing from the .50 caliber. When the others joined her, enemy gunfire tapered off as the defenders sought cover. The two-man teams carrying the SMAWs deployed. One of the weapons operators dropped to his right knee, raised the multipurpose assault weapon to his shoulder, aimed at the roof where a gang member reloaded, and fired. Natalie heard a swoosh and followed the trail of white smoke as it struck the building beneath the gang member. The rocket punched its way through the wall and exploded inside the apartment, blasting a hole through the roof. Body parts and blood mixed with black smoke and tile. Rockets from the other two SMAW-equipped soldiers struck the corner of the building, one entering through the balcony doors where the machinegun nest stood, the other slamming into the wall beside the bedroom window to its left. The simultaneous explosions gutted the apartment, and two fireballs burst through the window casings. The machinegun was ejected from the apartment and fell to the ground. Three explosions on the other side of the trailer told her the gang members there had met a similar fate. The teams' ammo bearers had already reloaded the SMAWs with more high explosive rockets.

"Move it! Move it!" ordered Brown, standing behind the trailer and waving everyone out.

Those who had survived the initial onslaught jumped off the back of the truck and swarmed the wall and front gate, shooting at anything that moved. A lanky soldier with a red beard crawled up into the cab, pulled out Jim's body, and took his place. Shifting into gear, he headed up the entry road. Gunfire erupted from the school bus blocking the entrance, slamming into the front of the truck. A rocket from one of the SMAWs punched its way into the bus and exploded. The truck shoved the burning vehicle away from the wall and into the parking lot. Taking advantage of the breach, the soldiers rushed the gate.

The rest of the Angels hovered around Josephine. Natalie rushed over to them. "We have to find Doreen and Sandy."

The women hesitated, responding when Josephine said, "Go on. I'll be safe here."

With that, the Angels raced up alongside the truck toward the front gate. By now, the fighting had shifted inside to the compound.

THE SOUND OF battle shattered the silence in the basement. Doreen, Sandy, and Sarge looked between each other, trying to figure out what was going on.

"Is that gunfire?" asked Sandy.

Sarge nodded.

"Does this mean we're under attack by rotters?" Doreen asked.

"Shut up in there!" Snake yelled from the corridor. He stood with his gaze focused on the door leading to the basement.

A second later, more gunfire joined the fray. Sarge glanced over at the women, a glimmer of hope in his eyes. "There's a lot of weapons fire, and some of it sounds like it's outside the compound."

"Hey!" Snake centered himself in the door. "I thought I told you to shut the fuck up!"

Sarge whispered. "I think our people are coming to get us."

Snake stepped up and placed the barrel of his AR-15 against Sarge's forehead. "Then maybe I oughta shoot you rig—"

Three explosions rocked the building above them. Dust drifted from the ceiling. Snake forgot about Sarge and ran out of the room. "Come on, man. Where are you?"

BY THE TIME the Angels passed through the gate, the battle had pushed deep inside the compound. Two-thirds of Brown's remaining men had secured the parking lot north of the entrance and were clearing the three buildings in that area of combatants. The rest had set up a defense line across the drive leading to the five buildings in the southern sector of the complex and had engaged the enemy. Bodies littered the area opposite the gate, most belonging to the Deaders. Near the makeshift perimeter wall, a gang member dragged himself through the grass toward the first building on the right, leaving a trail of blood. Natalie waved for the others to follow.

"What's your hurry?" Natalie asked as she squatted beside the gang member. She rolled him onto his back. He had a gaping wound in his abdomen the size of a baseball and dragging it across the ground had not done it any good. "Where do you keep your hostages?"

"Fuck you, lady."

Natalie shoved her hand into the open wound and twisted. The gang member convulsed around her fist and attempted to sit up, screaming in agony. She removed her hand after a few seconds. He fell back onto the ground, gasping for air.

"I'll ask you again. Where do you keep the hostages?"

"You can... kill me... if you want... bitch. I'm not... telling."

"No. I won't kill you." Natalie shoved her fist inside the wound again, this time deeper. Her fingers wrapped around something that felt like intestines. She grabbed and yanked. The gang member's body went rigid and his eyes rolled up into his head. His cry cut off in his throat.

"I'll keep this up until you tell me what I want to know."

To emphasize her point, Natalie twirled the intestine.

The gang member raised a hand and shook it in supplication. Natalie released the intestine and removed her hand. The gang member went limp.

"Well?"

He pointed to the building ahead of them. His voice croaked out a whisper. "In there.... basement.... third door.... on right."

"How many guards?"

He could not muster the energy to speak. Instead, he raised two fingers, although they barely moved.

Natalie stood up and focused on the apartment building in front of them. "Let's go get our people."

THE FIGHTING OUTSIDE intensified. As it drew closer, Snake became more agitated, changing position every few seconds and keeping his weapon trained on the door leading into the basement. Doreen eyed him carefully, trying to determine if he would panic and run, or kill them out of spite.

She never considered that Batchelder would attack.

Sarge jumped to his feet and raced for the door, bending to tackle Snake. Without hesitating, Doreen jumped to her feet and followed, knowing Sarge would need all the help he could get. She lost her balance and righted herself. The noise drew Snake's attention. He turned in time to see them charging him. Snake spun his AR-15 around. Being so close to the doorway, the barrel hit the jamb. He backed up and readjusted his aim as Sarge body checked him. The weapon discharged. Sarge grunted and collapsed, blood pouring from a wound in his left leg. Snake fell to the floor, dropping the AR-15.

He started to get back up when Doreen slammed into him, driving her right knee into his chest. The two slid down the wall. Doreen straddled him, with one knee on his chest and the other on his stomach. Walking on her knees, she moved up toward his neck. Snake regained his second wind. He grabbed her by the belt with his left hand, holding her in place, and punched her in the face. The first blow glanced off her cheek because of the angle. Doreen shifted her torso so her back faced him. Snake grabbed a handful of her red hair and yanked, pulling her off balance.

Sandy rushed into the corridor and dropped to her knees, the right one landing on Snake's crotch. Doreen heard one of his testicles pop, like a walnut being cracked. Snake's body went rigid. He cried out, tears streaming down his face, and released Doreen's hair. She took advantage of the opportunity and shifted on his chest. Her left knee slid down his sternum and against his neck, choking off his sobs of pain. Balancing herself on her right knee, she raised her left and slammed it down again on Snake's neck. A loud cracking of bones filled the corridor and Snake went limp. Only then did Doreen fall against the wall and begin crying.

A commotion sounded further down the corridor. Doreen did not have any fight left in her. She rolled over to face the door leading into the basement and accept her death. Relief washed over her when she spotted Natalie and the rest of the Angels approaching, their weapons raised and aimed. Natalie headed straight for her and Sandy while the others checked each of the rooms along the corridor. Natalie dropped to her knees when she reached her girls, placed her weapon on the floor, and hugged them. Ari stood to the side, keeping her eyes on the opposite end of the corridor.

"I'm fine," said Sarge with a heavy tone of sarcasm. "Thanks for asking."

"I'm sorry." Doreen raised her arms behind her back to show Natalie the handcuffs. "Get us out of these things."

Natalie patted down Snake, found the key in his shirt pocket, and used it to free Doreen and Sandy. Doreen took the keys and stepped over to Sarge. He shifted so she could reach the handcuffs. When his hands were free, he massaged his wounded leg.

"It feels funny. Almost like a burning sensation."

"What do you expect? You've been shot."

"I was shot once before in Iraq. I know what it feels like," Sarge grunted. "This is different."

"Don't worry about it," said Doreen. "You'll be okay."

Natalie patted her on the shoulder. When Doreen looked up, Natalie shook her head.

Shit, thought Doreen. *Will anything ever be all right again?*

CHAPTER TEN

D ENNING WOKE UP at his usual hour, although not under the usual circumstances. Rather than listening to the chirping birds and the wind blowing through the trees outside his bedroom window, he heard the clanking of dishes and laughing coming from the kitchen. Even more pleasing was the aroma of coffee, eggs, and bacon wafting through the house. Anna was the last person to have made him breakfast. A momentary tinge of sadness over her memory tainted his contentment. Windows and Cindy were preparing a special treat for him, and he intended to enjoy it.

Sitting up and swinging his feet onto the floor, Denning paused for a few moments to catch his breath. He got up, dressed, and went downstairs. Windows and Cindy sat at the table eating breakfast and chatting. Both had showered and changed, borrowing some of Anna's old clothes. The jeans and white cotton button-down shirt Windows wore hung loosely on her, mostly because of being underweight. Cindy's dress engulfed her like a tent. Windows had patched it as best she could by using a belt to hold the material tight against the girl's waist and lifting the hem two feet with safety pins.

At first, Denning felt irritated that they had borrowed his wife's clothes without asking permission. He pushed those feelings aside. They looked so much better than the two lost souls who had wandered onto his property yesterday, both physically and mentally. The shedding of the grime and dirt had been a psychological break with their past. Besides, if Anna had been here, she would have offered her clothes to these two as well as helped mend them to fit better.

When Windows saw him standing in the door, she said, "Good morning."

Cindy stared down at the tabletop. "Good morning, Mr. Denning."

Denning realized he must have been frowning because Window's demeanor went from pleasant to apologetic. "I'm sorry we borrowed your wife's clothes without asking. Our stuff has to be washed and mended before we can wear it again."

"The only thing they're good for is burning." Denning entered the kitchen and sat beside Cindy. "Anna's sewing kit is the guest bedroom closet. You can use it to take in your clothes. Especially hers. The girl looks like she's wearing a potato sack."

"I do not," Cindy retorted in a playful tone.

"That should be my nickname for you. Potato."

Cindy's mouth contorted into that half smile/half frown only children can pull off.

"You're not mad?" asked Windows.

"I will be if you didn't make me breakfast."

"I got you covered." Windows jumped up and went over to the stove. Pulling down the oven door, she reached in and removed a plate containing scrambled eggs and three strips of bacon, which she placed in front of Denning. "I've been keeping it warm for you."

"Thanks."

Windows stepped up to the counter, removed the pot from the coffee maker, and poured some into a mug that she brought to Denning. "It took me a few minutes to figure out how to make breakfast. I didn't realize you still had electricity. How did you manage that?"

"Solar panels on the roof. They can't run anything heavy duty like air conditioners, but they provide enough power to keep the appliances and lights going." Denning scooped a forkful of eggs into his mouth. "These are excellent. What did you do to them?"

"I mixed in some onions, ground up bacon, and pepper. You like them?"

"I may let you do all the cooking," he joked.

"That won't last long. The only meal I ever learned how to make in college was scrambled eggs."

"I'll teach you."

"Are you serious?"

Denning nodded, unable to speak with a mouthful of scrambled eggs.

"Thanks. Do you still want me and Cindy to make the rounds with you this morning?"

Denning swallowed. "If you're going to stay here for a while, you'll need to know the layout of the farm. Plus, I'll show you the chores I want you to help me with."

"That's fine." Windows gathered the dirty dishes. "I'll start cleaning. Let us know when you're ready."

THEY WALKED TO the five-foot-tall, reinforced wooden fence that surrounded the property. Denning wore his utility belt with the hunting knife and machete and carried his rifle over his shoulder. The girls followed. Windows paid careful attention as he showed her the various plots of land where he raised food and what was required to cultivate each crop. Cindy traipsed along behind them, running a blade of grass along the barbed wire, clearly bored with the tour. When they approached the coop and she heard the chickens clucking, she became excited, rushing past the adults to see them. When Denning and Windows reached the coop, they found Cindy kneeling in front of the chicken wire, her fingers through the openings and thirty hens and one rooster flocking around her on the other side.

Cindy's head shot up, a huge grin on her face. "I've never

seen chickens before. They're so friendly."

"They're hungry. They think you have food." Denning stepped over to a metal trash can half filled with chicken feed and removed the lid. Taking a plastic bowl from the top of the pile, he scooped up feed until it was full and handed the bowl to Cindy. "Would you like to feed them?"

"Really?"

"Sure." Denning replaced the lid on the trash can. "Take some in your hand and sprinkle it around. If any fly up at you, brush them away. Ready?"

Cindy nodded. Denning opened the coop door and Cindy rushed inside. The clucking became frantic as the chickens swarmed her, pecking at her legs and each other. The frenzy died down when Cindy grabbed a handful of feed and sprinkled it across the ground.

Windows moved up alongside of Denning and spoke softly. "Thank you. It's been a while since she's been able to act like a little girl."

"She seems like she could use some good times."

"She does."

"The same could be said of you."

Windows closed her eyes as if that could blind her from the memories.

"Was it that bad?" he asked.

"Not at first. I was lucky and hooked up with a good group of people who took me in and gave me shelter. We had a nice camp set up along the coast of Maine. I led a pretty sheltered life until a few weeks ago."

"What happened?"

"A rape gang found us. They destroyed the camp and killed everybody. They took me back to their compound. I was forced to do things...." Windows choked up.

"I can imagine."

"No, you can't." The young woman said it without anger or accusation. "Cindy and her mother had been there for months. After I arrived, Cindy's mom committed suicide and left me a note begging me to look after her daughter. The things I had to do to protect that little girl were disgusting."

"None of that was your fault."

"Not when it came to being assaulted. Three nights ago, our compound was attacked. I used that opportunity to get Cindy out. In order to escape, I… I wounded a man and left him to die."

"You had no other choice."

"I know." Windows faced him. "What bothers me is that I enjoyed hurting him and leaving him to bleed out."

Denning stared at her, saddened by what he saw. Windows could be no more than twenty-five, yet she had that toughened appearance about her as if she had already experienced a long life of suffering and hardship. In reality, she had, except all those horrible experiences had been crammed into a few weeks. Outwardly, her appearance and demeanor warned others not to fuck with her or Cindy. The eyes betrayed the truth. He detected a sadness in them her rough exterior could not hide. Windows had not fully coped with the pain and what she had become. She seemed to be begging for absolution.

"You had a right to enjoy it," said Denning.

"That's not me."

"That's what they *made* you into." Denning faced Windows and placed a comforting hand on her shoulder. "You didn't do those things to save yourself. You did them to save Cindy, and she's not even your responsibility."

"Yes, she is."

"Now she is, only because her mother took the easy way out and pawned off that responsibility onto you. You didn't have to accept it. You didn't have to take her with you when you escaped. You didn't have to take the risk of bringing her to this farm not knowing how I would treat you. You've been through a lot, and it's made you tough."

Windows lowered her head. "It made me a monster."

"You're not a monster. You're an incredibly strong woman."

When Windows raised her head, she fought back the tears. Denning did not know what to say.

Cindy provided a welcome distraction when she exited the chicken coop, giddy with excitement. "That was so cool."

"I'm glad you liked it. Come on." Denning placed a hand on Cindy's shoulder and led her away. "Let's complete our rounds."

The three of them walked along the southern and western perimeter fence, no one saying a word. After a few minutes, they approached the pasture where Walther grazed. As usual, the bull waited by the corner to greet Denning. When they got to within a few feet, Cindy broke away and ran up to Walther. The bull snorted.

"Cindy!" yelled Denning. "Don't go near him!"

The warning came too late. Cindy jumped up onto the fence, reached over the top, and stuck her hand into the pen. Walther lifted his head. Denning thought he would bite or ram Cindy. Instead, he allowed her to pet him. As her hand glided across his scalp, Walther closed his eyes and pushed against her palm, making sure she continued.

Denning shook his head. "Well, I'll be damned."

"What's wrong?" asked Windows.

"Walther is an ornery son a bitch. He hates everyone except me."

Cindy glanced over her shoulder. "He's just like you. All he needs is someone to be nice to him."

"Cindy!" Windows' jaw dropped. She turned to Denning. "I'm so sorry. She never—"

Denning was laughing too hard to hear her. "Don't worry. They say animals and kids are good at judging character."

"Still."

"She's right. My wife would have agreed with her." Some of his good mood drained away at the memory of Anna.

"I hope you don't mind my asking. The set up you have here...." Windows hesitated. "Are you a survivalist?"

Denning chuckled. "I prefer the term prepper. Survivalist sounds like someone who is heavily armed and anticipating the end of the world. This is the only weapon I own. That and a .38 revolver I keep in my nightstand."

"You were prepared for this," Windows pointed out.

"Not for this." Denning looked beyond the perimeter fence to the dead world beyond. "I always knew society would collapse someday. I assumed it would be a financial collapse or a pandemic. Maybe even a natural disaster. If anyone had ever told me the dead would come back to life and start eating the living, I would have laughed at them. Who's insane now?"

"The world." Windows grew sullen.

Denning nodded. "It's a good thing I planned ahead, otherwise I would never have survived this long. I didn't intend for this to be permanent, though."

"Are you saying you're running out of food?"

"No. I've stockpiled canned goods and coffee, but they have a limited shelf life. Other than that, I'm fine. I have plenty of farmland to plant on, and I never eat all the eggs, so I'll have a continuous supply of chickens. I also have rain barrels located across the farm, so I'll always have a supply of fresh water. What I don't have is time."

"What do you mean?"

Denning tried to hide the vulnerability in his voice. "I'm seventy-two years old, have high blood pressure and a bad heart, and ran out of my medication two months ago. Living like this is not doing my health any good. Eventually, I'm going to die. It could be tomorrow. it could be in ten years. I have no idea."

"And you don't want to die alone."

"I've been alone for the past ten years, so dying alone doesn't bother me. What I am scared of is having a stroke or coming down with something that incapacitates me. That's one of the reasons I allowed you and Cindy to stay, to be certain that if anything happens to me, someone will be here to make sure I cross over. Will you promise to do that?"

Before Windows could answer, Cindy stopped petting Walther and raced up to the two adults. "I love Walther. Can I visit him again tomorrow?"

"Of course you can, honey." Windows wrapped her arms around Cindy and hugged her close. "You can visit him every day. We're going to stay here for a while."

"How long?"

"As long as it takes to make sure we take care of things for Mr. Denning."

"Really?" Cindy grinned at Denning. "Thank you."

"And thank you," said Denning, more to Windows than to Cindy.

CHAPTER ELEVEN

NATALIE SAT IN the waiting room outside the warden's office still wearing the ACU she had gone into battle with. The battle had not lasted long after they rescued Doreen, Sandy, and Batchelder. Most of the Deaders had been killed during the breaching of the main gate and the securing of the northern compound. The southern sector contained living quarters and housed mostly camp followers. Resistance had crumbled quickly. Two school buses were called in to pick up the survivors as well as a pair of U-Hauls to cart away the bodies and any supplies that could be salvaged. The final casualty figures were sixty-three gang members killed and fourteen captured, as well as fifty-five camp followers rescued. Their losses totaled forty-four dead and twenty-nine wounded, all but one of whom would not become a rotter thanks to the vaccine the Angels had brought to Alcatraz. Having been kidnapped before he could be inoculated, Batchelder was the only one who would die from his wounds.

Thomas stuck his head out of the warden's office and motioned for Natalie to join them. When she entered, Secretary Fogel stood in front of his desk. He greeted her with a warm handshake.

"Natalie, it's good to see you again."

"Same here, Mr. Secretary."

He motioned to one of the two easy chairs in front of his desk. "Please, have a seat."

Natalie took one of the chairs. Fogel sat in the one opposite her. As usual, Thomas perched himself on the end of the desk.

"Corporal Brown briefed me on the raid on the Deader compound. It's a shame about Captain Endo and the others. We've all lost good people since setting up the government here at Alcatraz, most of them due to the Deaders. We don't have to worry about them anymore, thanks to you." Fogel leaned back in his chair. "Now we can concentrate on the important matter. Taking the battle to the revenants and making America right again."

Natalie shifted her gaze between Fogel and Thomas.

"The revenant outbreak caught the government by total surprise," Fogel explained. "Too many politicians on both sides of the aisle saw the outbreak as a way to gain political advantage. Some members of my own party criticized the president for not taking decisive action, even though initially no one knew how to deal with the situation. A few wanted to go through the charade of an impeachment hearing. Those around the president blamed the previous administration. The Christian Right called it God's judgment for accepting homosexuality. One Muslim cleric declared it Allah's will against Islam for not ridding the world on infidels. While political and religious leaders dicked around, the American people had to fend for themselves. Everyone thought the world had come to an end."

"Hasn't it?" Natalie asked.

Fogel shook his head. He squinted through his glasses to see her better. "Our planet is like a living organism and, sadly, we're the parasites feeding off it. If we abandon a town or leave behind an environmental disaster, in time nature reclaims the land. When the population grows too large and becomes a drain on resources, the planet purges itself through pandemics, such as the Black Death or the Spanish Influenza. In that sense, Earth is like us. If we become overstressed, we get sick. Once the virus has run its course, we get better."

"The Revenant Virus wasn't natural, though," said Natalie.

"It was bioengineered in a lab and released into the population on purpose."

"We know that," said Thomas. "The concept is still the same."

"Exactly," continued Fogel. "However it came about, we see this outbreak not as the end of the world but a resetting of it."

"I don't understand."

Fogel sat forward. He spoke in a quiet, reassuring voice. "The world was going to Hell in an overcrowded hand basket. Overpopulation strained our resources. Our government had a twenty-trillion-dollar debt and no way of paying it off. The disparity between the richest and the poorest people was worse than ever, and the middle class had all but disappeared. People no longer trusted the government, the police, or the courts. The social fabric of society was falling apart. And the institutions we'd normally turn to for guidance didn't care. The church was either covering up its own scandals or trying to influence politics. Our elected officials were too busy taking care of their careers to do the right things. You know, when I entered government thirty-odd years ago, both parties didn't get along, but they agreed to disagree, and every American called this country the land of the free. Prior to the outbreak, politics had become a blood sport where you got what you wanted by lying and defaming your opponents, and no one thought we were free anymore.

"The Revenant Outbreak was a reset button. There are no banks, police, courts, or governments. No one cares about reality TV, social media, gun control, illegal immigration, or the thousands of other petty things that dominated our lives. There are no more liberals or conservatives, rich or poor, Christians or atheists. There are only people who have survived and are trying to get their lives back in order. I want to rebuild society, but not the one we had prior to the outbreak. I want to abolish all the laws on the books, except the Constitution, and start from scratch. When Congress is re-established, there'll be a whole new set of politicians who are not beholden to the system, and they can decide which laws are good enough to keep. This is our chance for a new beginning."

Natalie found herself intrigued by the proposition. "Do you really believe you can change things for the better?"

"Maybe not permanently, human nature being what it is," said Thomas. "We can at least try. Hopefully, we can get two or three good years out of it."

"Five, if we're lucky." Fogel chuckled. "I'm a realist. I know it won't last. Whenever there's an election for president, someone will try and get votes by blaming this on the other party. The rich and powerful will do whatever they can to get back what they've lost. I doubt it'll be long before the world is in turmoil again."

Fogel reached out and took Natalie's hand. His voice possessed a sincerity and optimism she had not heard in ages. "We have to try. We owe it not only to ourselves, but to the hundreds of millions who died in this war. History is going to view this moment with a critical eye. If we fight our way back from the brink of extinction only to embrace everything bad about society that put us in this predicament in the first place, this will be our darkest moment. If we try to salvage something better from the wreckage of our past, even if we fail, future generations will have a beacon to guide them. They're going to have a difficult enough time as it is. We owe it to future generations to give them a good foundation to build on."

Natalie felt inspired, something she had not felt in a long time. It had nothing to do with presentation, because Fogel gave his speech without any of the finesse or oratory flair she would have expected from a politician. Instead, he spoke with a heartfelt honesty. For the first time since the outbreak occurred, and especially since the destruction of their camp, Natalie felt like she had a chance to rebuild her life. She placed her hand on top of the Secretary's and clasped it. "Count me in."

"I was hoping you'd say that." Fogel released his grip on Natalie's hands and sat back in the easy chair. "Corporal Brown had some exceptional things to say about you. Discipline had fallen apart after Captain Endo was killed, and the outcome might have been different if you hadn't taken charge."

Natalie felt embarrassed. "All I did was shake them out of their initial shock. Endo's troops did the rest."

"True. Yet you saw they had faltered and kicked them back in line. That's the type of leadership we need. Only a handful of my people are professionally-trained soldiers, including a number of vets or people with police training. Most are civilians who signed on because they want to take this fight back to the revenants. They want to clear them out of our cities and towns, take back their homes, and start over. You and your Angels would be a major asset to the cause."

"I'm definitely on board," said Natalie.

"What about the other Angels?" Fogel asked.

"Let me talk to them. I don't see why they'd say no."

CHAPTER TWELVE

"**N**O FUCKING WAY!**"** Amy practically shouted.

Natalie looked to each of the other Angels seated around the table in the empty dining hall. Doreen, Sandy, and Stephanie were with Amy on the opposite side. Josephine sat to Natalie's left, her arm in a sling, and Ari to her right.

"Why not?" Natalie asked.

"Haven't we done enough?" Amy answered in a calmer voice.

An awkward silence followed. When Natalie had gathered her girls together to present Secretary Fogel's offer, she had anticipated they would accept. She never expected such a vehement reaction. She wanted to respond, to shout back, to defend her position, or try to reason with the Angels. Truth be known, however, after what they had gone through the past month, Natalie could not blame them. She slumped her shoulders and sighed.

Amy cared for her friend too much to allow her to lose face. Reaching out, she clasped Natalie's hand. "You know as well as any of us that we've done more these past few weeks to end this apocalypse than most of the people here. We were not ready to deal with any of it. It took a toll on us, and not only in the friends we lost. I'm not afraid—"

"I never said you were," Natalie cut in.

Amy squeezed her hand reassuringly. "We all know what's going to happen next is far worse than anything we've gone through up until now. I can't take any more. Maybe if I'd spent the last eight months sitting safely on Alcatraz training for this, I'd be more willing to participate. After what we've been through.... well, it's time to let someone else take up the fight."

"Do you all feel this way?" Natalie asked.

Everyone except Ari and Doreen nodded or replied yes.

Natalie tried to hide her disappointment. "What are you going to do?"

"Most of us have already been recruited," Stephanie answered.

"Are you serious?"

"Manpower is short, especially with the majority of people gearing up for war," said Stephanie. "Based on my experience fighting rotters, they asked if I would train new recruits."

"I'm getting medical training," said Sandy. "Then they're going to place me with one of the mobile surgical units that will follow the front."

"I've been assigned to the mayor's office," said Josephine. "I'll be helping restore order in the city once it's cleared of rotters and reestablish the government here."

"And you?" Natalie asked Amy.

"Logistics. I'll be driving a truck for the duration."

"Doreen?"

"They asked me to become one of Secretary Fogel's bodyguards. They liked the way I handled myself at the Deader compound." Doreen chuckled. "I declined."

"Why?" Natalie asked.

"None of us would have made it this far without you. I like those odds."

"What about you?" Natalie asked Ari.

"I go where you go."

"I guess that's it." Natalie could not hide the resignation in her voice.

"Please don't take this the wrong way," pleaded Amy. "We love you and respect you. We've followed you to Hell and back more times than we care to imagine. But we can't make that trip again."

"I understand," Natalie said. She meant it.

"Thank you." Amy stood and came around the table to hug Natalie. "Good luck. And God bless."

Josephine was next, hugging Natalie with her one good arm. "We'll see each other again."

"Take care of yourself," Stephanie said, embracing Natalie.

And Sandy. "I'm going to miss having you around to always save me."

As the Angels left the dining hall, Natalie felt the depression fill her soul. She had known the Angels for a year. She had lived with them, fought with them, and, in many cases, watched them die. Now she had an unsettling certainty that, except for Ari and Doreen, she would never see any of these women again.

CHAPTER THIRTEEN

ROBSON STOOD IN front of the survivors, who now numbered twenty-five. Last night, Linda had relayed to them his plans for setting out in two days to find a new place to settle down. This morning after breakfast, she came to him and passed along a request to meet with everyone. He assumed it was to answer questions about the resettlement. Upon entering the warehouse, though, he detected an air of hostility.

Linda walked up and stood beside Robson, forcing herself to meet his gaze. "We want to thank you for coming to talk to us. Last night, I informed every one of your plans for moving on, and some of us had questions we—"

"Are you going to make us go with you?" asked a tall, thin man who stood at the front of the group.

"I'm sorry?"

"Are you going to make us go with you when you leave here?"

"You can't stay here," explained Robson. "I promised Simmons we would—"

"I know that. I'm asking if you're going to make us go with *you.*"

"Please," Linda snapped at the tall man. "We had a long talk last night about our future. We understand we can't stay here, and none of us want to take advantage of Simmons' hospitality. However, not everyone wants to find a new place to stay."

"Where would you go?"

The tall man started to speak when a young brunette cut him off, trying to be more polite. "On the way in here the other night, we saw an abandoned community at the end of the road. We want to live there."

"You realize that community was trashed by the same gang that held you prisoner. None of the houses are livable."

"It doesn't matter," said the brunette. "We'll make the necessary repairs. It's better than how we've lived since being captured."

"Or being on the road," added the tall man.

"You have to understand," continued the brunette. "We know it's less than ideal conditions, and it'll take a while to get things back in order. We don't care. We're too tired, physically and mentally, to do what you're proposing. We want to start rebuilding our lives now, and that's the closest place to do it. All we're asking is that you give us our share of the food and medicine you got from Super Walmart, and then leave us be."

"I don't know," Robson hesitated. "The odds of you surviving won't be good. I have a responsibility to take care of you."

"What's my name?" asked the tall man.

"Excuse me?"

"What's my name?" he asked again. When Robson did not answer, he pointed to the brunette. "What about her, then? Other than Linda, do you know any of our names?"

Robson had no response. He saw where this was heading.

"I didn't think so," spat the tall man. He paused and took a deep breath. When he spoke again, his tone had switched to one of understanding. "We know it was never your intention to save us, and that you wanted to rescue your friend Wendy."

"Windows," corrected the brunette.

"You didn't have to help us," the tall man continued. "And we're all grateful you didn't leave us to fend for ourselves. You've given us a place to stay and risked your lives to get us supplies. We appreciate that. But we're not your responsibility. You know that, too."

"That's not true," Robson replied weakly.

"It is. There's nothing wrong with that. And you're right. Maybe we won't survive if we try to set ourselves up in that community. Maybe we'll die of starvation, or be overrun by deaders, or attacked by another gang. We know that. You have your own agenda, your own goals. Don't ask us to be a part of it. Let us live our own lives."

"How many of you want to stay here?" Robson asked.

Fourteen of the survivors raised their hands.

"Excuse me," said a blonde woman near the back of the group. She pointed to the three women seated around her. Robson recognized them as the camp followers he had rescued from inside the compound. "We have our own favor to ask."

"Go ahead."

"We don't want to go with you either. We also don't want to stay with the larger group." She spoke to the tall man. "After what we went through, we don't feel comfortable with large groups of people. No offense."

"None taken," Robson said. "What do you want?"

"We want to set out on our own. Give us one of the smaller vehicles and some supplies, and we'll take care of ourselves."

"And the rest of you?" Robson asked.

The last six survivors looked amongst themselves. Finally, a short black man said, "We'd feel safer with you."

"Who do you want to go with?" Robson asked Linda.

"I'd rather take my chances with you, if that's okay."

Robson said nothing. Everyone stared at him, waiting for a decision. Finally, the blonde woman asked, "So, will you allow us to go our separate ways?"

Robson knew they were right, although he did not want to admit it. While saving these people had been the decent thing to do, expecting them to follow him as their leader was egocentric. He would have a hard enough time keeping his own people alive, let alone a group that preferred not to be there.

"Yes, I'll let you go your own way if you like."

A murmur of excitement washed through the survivors, and they talked excitedly amongst themselves. Not wanting to spoil their good mood, Robson stepped back and exited the warehouse, motioning for Linda to follow.

Once outside, she said, "Thank you."

"No problem. I'll talk to Roberta and DeWitt, and tomorrow you and the other survivors can coordinate the logistics with them."

Linda smiled, the first time he had ever seen one from her. "I know a lot of them won't make it through the next month, but you gave them something they haven't had in a long time."

"What's that?"

"Hope."

CHAPTER FOURTEEN

AFTER BREAKFAST, WHEN Denning went off to make his rounds of the perimeter, Windows and Cindy cleaned up the kitchen and set off to feed the chickens and take care of the crops. It had taken them all morning and most of the afternoon, partly because Windows was unfamiliar with the procedures, and partly because Cindy had so much fun Windows did not want to take her away from the chickens. Cindy spent over an hour playing and laughing, two things Windows had not seen her do before. She watched Cindy the entire time, experiencing lightness in her heart, something *she* had not felt in weeks. For the first time since being kidnapped by Price, Windows felt confident and hopeful about the future.

Not until late morning did it dawn on Windows that she had not seen Denning all day. At first, she was not worried. concerned. By mid-afternoon, she became concerned. As midafternoon rolled around, her concern became fear. The thought occurred something bad might have happened. Once finished tending to the crops, she took Cindy and searched the compound, starting at the east side of the perimeter fence near the ranch house and heading north.

It took only a few minutes to come across Denning. He was in the ten acres reserved for Walther working on the engine of a combine, the bull standing a few feet away, keeping an eye on his master. Cindy raced ahead and jumped up onto the fence, calling to Walther. The bull strolled over and extended his head, begging to be petted. Windows headed for the fence opposite the combine.

Denning placed his tools back in the box. "Hello."

"Hi," said Windows. "Where've you been?"

"Right here. It hasn't been that long."

"You've been missing all day."

Denning turned toward the sun. He raised his right hand vertically to the horizon, placed the left on top of it, then the right on the left, and the left on the right again. "Man, you're right."

"What are you doing?" Windows asked.

"Telling the time."

"How?"

Denning raised his right hand again. "You hold your palm up with the bottom on the horizon. Each finger represents approximately fifteen minutes, and one hand equals an hour."

"You're fascinating."

"I'll take that as a compliment."

"It was meant as one. You didn't muddle through the end of the world like the rest of us. You survived it. You kept on going as if nothing had happened. That's impressive."

Denning laughed. "My wife would have called me paranoid."

"Your wife would be proud of you."

Cindy walked over. "Do you farm anymore?"

"Just the patch of crops for myself."

"Then why do you have that thing?" She pointed to the combine.

"That's a Massey-Ferguson 850 combine." Denning pointed to the front end of the machine. "See the device that looks like teeth?"

"Yeah?"

"That's the maize header. When I used to farm, I'd drive this through the fields. The header would scoop up the stalks and feed them into the conveyor. Cylinders inside the combine would grind up the stalks, leaving the grain in a bin and spitting the empty stalks out the back. It made my life a lot easier."

"If you don't farm anymore, why do you need to fix it?"

"Let me put it this way." Denning leaned over the fence so he could be closer to Cindy. "Before the dead came back to life, you used to play with toys so you wouldn't get bored, right?"

Cindy nodded.

"Well, that's my toy. I keep it running so I don't get bored."

"No offense, Mr. Denning," Cindy said, "but I'd rather have a doll."

"I wish I could help you there."

"Does it work?" asked Windows.

"Let's find out."

Denning closed the cowling to the engine compartment and climbed into the cab. Sliding into the seat, he switched the ignition into the ON position, pressed the start button, and the engine roared to life. Walther jumped to one side and snorted. Upon realizing it was only the combine, he gave the machine a disdainful glance and strode off.

Denning shut down the engine and leaned out of the cab. "Success."

The two girls clapped.

Denning climbed down from the cab. He lifted the toolbox and passed it across the fence to Windows, who held it for him while he climbed over, pausing for a few seconds on the other side to catch his breath.

"Now what?" Windows asked.

"I think it's time we head back to the house so I can make you gals supper. We've got a lot to do in the days ahead." Denning passed by Cindy and leaned over. "Come on, I'll race you back."

Cindy giggled and darted off, with Denning chasing after her, although he soon fell far behind. No matter. It was great to see her acting like a little girl again.

Windows tagged along, lugging the toolbox, and hoping this would last a while.

CHAPTER FIFTEEN

N ATALIE, ARI, AND Doreen sat at their table in the dining hall comparing notes.

"Where were you assigned?" Ari asked.

"An armored unit." Natalie took a sip of coffee.

Doreen paused as she raised the fork to her mouth. "You mean tanks?"

Natalie nodded.

"What do you know about tanks?"

"I don't have to. I talked with the unit commander this morning. Since this isn't traditional combat, and since they're short on qualified tank crews, they're doubling up on functions. The tank commander will also be the driver, and the gunner will be the loader. I'm the observer."

"What does that mean?" Ari asked.

Doreen chuckled. "It means she's the one who gets out and pushes in case they get stuck."

Ari flashed Doreen a stare that could have killed. Doreen did not see it.

"I'm their eyes," explained Natalie. "The other two will be stuck inside the tank with a limited view. I'm the one who gets to pop the hatch and see what's going on around us."

Ari scooped up a forkful of beans. "Isn't that dangerous?"

"It shouldn't be. Rotters can't climb. Besides, the commander says once the operation begins, we'll be moving all the time."

"Are you nervous?" Doreen asked.

"None of the tank crews I've met seem nervous, so I figure there's no reason I should be." Natalie broke her biscuit in half. "What about you two?"

"We've been assigned to a mop up battalion," said Ari. "There are a couple of dozen cruise ships and naval vessels sitting off the Pacific Coast with almost a hundred thousand troops on them, plus ten thousand civilians who are going to start rebuilding the city once it's secure. When the main operation begins, we're going to land on a twenty-mile front from the Presidio down to Morris Beach then push east until we reach the Bay, mopping up any rotters you miss. The civvies will come ashore later and start rebuilding."

"And they're keeping us together," Doreen told her. "We're going ashore near the San Francisco Zoo. They'll be flying us out to our ship later tonight."

"I just realized," said Ari, "that means we may not see each other for a while."

Natalie saw the concern in Ari's eyes. "Don't worry. This doesn't seem anywhere near as dangerous as what we've already gone through. I'm sure we'll all be back here before—"

"Ladies and gentlemen," bellowed a voice from the other end of the dining hall. A tall, burly, African-American colonel in Army ACUs stood in the center of the door. "I hate to break up this merry gathering, but it's time to deploy. Gather your gear and be on the Parade Ground in ten minutes. Choppers are coming in to fly you to your respective units. God help anyone who comes to me and says they missed their flight. I want to see asses and elbows, people."

A bevy of excitement broke out as those assigned off the Rock jumped up from their tables to bus their trays and head back to their quarters to get their gear. Doreen stood and nudged Ari, "Come on. We don't want to be late."

"I thought we'd have more time," Ari responded.

"I'll take those for you." Natalie stood and crossed around the table.

"Don't you have to hurry?" Doreen asked.

"No. I'm taking the ferry over to the Beachhead later to-night." Natalie hugged Doreen. "You be careful. Don't do anything foolish."

"Have I ever?" Doreen hugged back. "Good luck."

Natalie moved over to Ari. "That goes for you, too. I don't know what I'd do without you."

Ari wrapped her arms around Natalie and embraced her, holding her for several seconds. "I love you. Take care of yourself."

Doreen took Ari by the arm and led her across the dining hall. Ari kept her gaze on Natalie until they disappeared into the corridor.

Once her friends had left, Natalie piled all the garbage onto one tray and stacked the two empty ones underneath. She waited until the commotion had died down before taking the trays up to the counter. As she headed back to her quarters, she felt a sense of optimism. When Dr. Compton had first arrived at their camp talking about the vaccine and using it to fight back, she had considered him delusional. Now she knew better. Too many people around here were too optimistic about the prospects of success. She could feel it as well.

Tomorrow morning, humans would engage the living dead for the ultimate control of Earth.

CHAPTER SIXTEEN

TWO HOURS AFTER sundown, everyone still remaining in Gilmanton gathered in front of the warehouse to say their final goodbyes.

Earlier that morning, Robson, DeWitt, Roberta, and Caswell had helped move the fourteen survivors to the community along Suncock Valley Road. They had stayed for five hours, patrolling the neighborhood to make sure there were no rotters or squatters and helping the others settle in. Roberta had found a house at the end of a cul de sac that had been vacant during the raid, so the gang had not bothered to smash its windows or break down its doors. Once his team had unloaded the supplies, Robson tried to offer some advice to the tall man, whose name was Jim, on how to survive. Jim listened politely, although it had been obvious to Robson he was not interested, so Robson gathered his team and headed back to Gilmanton.

Once back at the warehouse, the group packed the remaining vehicles for their upcoming trips. The camp followers asked if they could take Price's black Hummer H3. Robson had agreed, seeing it as the perfect irony that their former captor's vehicle would now be their means to salvation. Robson had made sure each woman had their own weapon, plenty of ammunition, and extra rations. Of the two groups who were going their separate ways, Robson knew these four had the best chance of survival and the roughest time. After making their farewells, and after an emotional and tearful goodbye with

Linda, the four women climbed into the black Hummer and set out north.

Robson had decided to take only four vehicles to decrease the amount of gasoline they would need to scrounge while on the road: his military-style Humvee, the Humvee Tibor had converted to accommodate the vampires during daylight, the RAV-4, and the Forester commandeered from the storage facility. Each vehicle contained an equal share of food, medicine, ammunition, and canned gasoline in case they became separated. Robson would drive the lead Humvee. Linda, Cory, a smarmy teenager with dark hair down to his neck that he refused to trim, and Magda, a young woman from Germany on vacation in the States who became trapped when all flights were grounded, rode with him. Roberta would follow in the RAV-4 along with Gary, a middle-aged man who had lost his glasses during the apocalypse and had trouble seeing, and Ed, a Marine whose unit had been overrun by rotters outside of Albany and who had been on his own until captured by Price's gang. DeWitt would drive the Forester and would take the last two camp survivors, a middle-aged Japanese woman named Yukiko whose nose remained disfigured following a beating at the camp, and an African-American male who refused to give his name. Robson had begun to refer to him as Clint. Dravko, Tibor, and Caslow would bring up the rear.

Right after sundown, once all the gear was packed away and the survivors were on board, Robson called his people together for one last briefing.

"Remember, our primary goal is to find a location we can easily secure. We want to avoid all population centers. I plan to stop every couple of hours so we can give everyone a chance to stretch their legs." To Dravko and Tibor, he added, "We'll find a place where we can safely hole up during the day."

"Thanks," answered Dravko.

"You all know the direction we're heading. Each vehicle

has a radio, so if for some reason we get separated we'll try to regroup. If we don't, then you're on your own, and I wish you the best of luck. Any questions?'

None.

"Good. Load up. I'll be back in a minute."

While the others climbed into their respective vehicles, Robson crossed the warehouse parking lot to where Simmons and Wayans stood.

"I guess this is it," said Simmons.

"I guess so."

"Where are you heading?" Wayans asked.

"Northwest. We're going to follow the back roads as much as we can to avoid heavy population centers. Until the survivors are on their feet physically, we're vulnerable on the road. The first place I find that makes a halfway decent encampment, I'm setting up shop."

"Makes sense," said Simmons.

"Who knows? If we're really lucky, we'll find our friend Windows."

"That'd be friggin' nice."

An awkward silence followed. Finally, Robson said, "Guys, thanks for everything. I never would have been able to pull this off without your help."

"I wish we could have done more," said Simmons, who offered his hand.

"You did more than enough." Robson shook the hand, then pulled Simmons in close and wrapped his left arm around his back.

Robson broke the hug and offered his hand to Wayans. "Sorry you took a bullet for us."

"I've gotten hurt a lot worse for less noble causes." Wayans shook his hand and offered a fist bump. "You friggin' take care of yourself."

"You can count on it." Robson bumped fists with Wayans. "Good luck."

Walking back to his Humvee, Robson slid into the driver's seat. "Are we ready?"

"No," said Linda. "But we don't have a choice."

Starting the vehicle, Robson pulled away from the warehouse and headed for the parking lot exit, waving to Simmons and Wayans. Once out onto North Road, he veered left and accelerated, passing the rectory. The other vehicles in the convoy fell in behind him at one-hundred-foot intervals. He kept his gaze on Gilmanton until it was no longer visible. This moment reminded him of the last time he had departed Fort McClary for the run down to Site R.

Everyone remembered how badly that turned out.

BOOK TWO

BOOK TWO

CHAPTER SEVENTEEN

THE PROVISIONAL JOINT Chiefs of Staff at Alcatraz had devised a simple method of conducting Operation Lazarus, the clearing of revenants out of San Francisco. They had established four RCZs, or Revenant Collection Zones, where the living dead would be herded for PDS, or Permanent Death Status. Each RCZ had to be large enough to contain vast numbers of revenants, be on open ground, and be of minimal importance to the city's infrastructure to minimize collateral damage. The four RCZs chosen were Golden Gate Park, TPC Harding Park, the runways of San Francisco International Airport, and Candlestick Park Stadium. Ten days prior to the initiation of Lazarus, helicopters placed battery-operated loudspeakers on rooftops in a three-hundred-and-sixty-degree radius around and at a half-mile distance from each RCZ. These speakers played music that lured the revenants away from the residential areas and toward the zones. Five days prior to Lazarus, helicopters moved these speakers inside the RCZs.

Today, the four armored units assigned to the collection zones, twelve tanks in total, would herd stray revenants back to their respective zones for PDS.

Natalie sat in the commander's cupola of an M1 Abrams tank designated RCZ4/3, the third tank assigned to Revenant Collection Zone 4, or Candlestick Park Stadium. Their tank idled on the southbound lanes of Route 101, a thousand feet from the interchange with Interstate 280 and across from the remnants of a burned-out Jack in the Box. She had anticipated that hordes of the living dead would be swarming the highway. Instead, only a dozen or so were visible, most on the side streets paralleling Route 101 and blocked from getting to the tank by concrete barriers separating the highway from the surrounding neighborhoods. One rotter lay two hundred feet ahead, its legs crushed into pulp, its arms stretching for the vehicle. Another, a female in a gray business pants suit stained brown with dried blood, stood in front of the tank, scratching at the glacis plate, its dead eyes fixed on Natalie.

Something from inside the tank grabbed her leg. Natalie cried out, then realized with embarrassment it was Lieutenant Hendricks, the tank commander. He motioned for her to put on her Combat Vehicle Crewman (CVC) helmet. When she did, Hendricks asked over the integrated communication system, "Jumpy?"

"A little," she admitted.

"It's only natural," Hendricks said reassuringly.

"Listen to the lieutenant," Corporal Preston said from the driver's seat. "First time I did this, it literally scared the shit out of me. Thank God the smell from the dead was so bad no one noticed."

"Lovely image." Hendricks shook his head. "I'll toss my cookies later."

"You know it's the truth, man. You were there."

Hendricks waved for Natalie to come inside the tank. She crawled down from the cupola and closed the hatch. The lieutenant spoke to them both.

"All right, listen up. Units One and Two are in position. They're going to patrol the neighborhoods around Candlestick Park to lure the revenants to the stadium. We're going down the 101 to pick up stragglers. Think of us as a heavily fortified Pied Piper for the living dead."

"I have a question," said Preston. "How come we don't have a gunner?"

"Because we don't have a working gun," Hendricks explained. "All the tanks in the unit have been cannibalized of everything except the drive gear to repair those going into combat."

"Great," Preston huffed. "We're in a fucking expendable."

"Get used to it," said the lieutenant. "Miss Bazargan, we—"

"Call me Natalie."

"Natalie, wear your M50 at all times."

"What's an M50?"

Hendricks made a visible effort not to roll his eyes. "It's your gas mask."

"Why do we need a gas mask?" Natalie asked. "The virus hasn't gone airborne, has it?"

"It blocks the stench," Preston answered. "It's the worst thing I've ever smelled, and I worked in a slaughterhouse one summer."

"Can the chatter," Hendricks ordered. "We'll be moving out soon, so get ready."

The three crew members got into position and waited. Natalie peered through her optical periscope. The business suit rotter still clawed at the front of the tank.

ARI AND DOREEN sat in the back of the fifth and last CH-47 Chinook helicopter in line along with thirty-eight other soldiers. They still traveled over water, with the coastline a few hundred feet ahead of them. After a few minutes, the Chinook slowed, swung its tail around one-hundred-and-eighty degrees, and lowered the rear ramp. They hovered over Ocean Beach at an altitude of two hundred feet and were descending. She could see the San Francisco Zoo in front of them and, to the right and off in the distance, TCP Harding Park.

When the ramp touched the sand, a stout second lieutenant biting down on an unlit cigar centered himself in the center of the ramp. "Haul ass, ladies and gentlemen. What are you waiting for? This ain't no fucking beach party."

Everyone inside the helicopter stood and double timed down the ramp and onto the beach. Master Sergeant Napier, their platoon sergeant, stood fifty feet away, directing everyone to the fifteen-foot-tall escarpment separating the beach from the main road. The troops deployed before them had already taken up position and waited. The Chinook raised its ramp and flew away.

Ari and Doreen knelt by the cement stairs leading up from the beach while Napier made his way down the line, pausing every twenty feet to issue orders.

"Don't fire unless Lieutenant Nowack or I give the order. We don't want to lure the revenants away from the zone. And keep your heads down until the PDS is over."

After Napier moved on, Ari leaned closer to Doreen. "What's the PDS?"

Doreen shrugged. "I guess we'll find out."

HENDRICKS CHECKED HIS watch. "It's time."

Preston revved the M1, and its Honeywell turbine engine roared to life. The noise excited the business suit rotter. It clawed frantically at the glacis plate. The Abrams lurched forward, knocking the rotter backwards. Natalie watched through one of the vision blocks as it disappeared under the tank. Preston approached the rotter with the crushed legs, steered right, and ran over the body. The rotter exploded beneath the treads like a package of ketchup. Straightening the tank, he headed for the highway interchange.

"Why aren't there any vehicles on this section of highway?" Natalie asked into the CVC's microphone.

Preston answered. "Some fucktard in a semi-trailer came off the 280 overpass too fast and dropped his tanker onto the

101. Damn thing exploded and closed the highway in both directions. It's clear on this side of the interchange, but the other side is packed tighter than a fat guy's colon."

"Quit giving a Goddamn tour and pay attention," snapped Hendricks. "The road ahead is blocked."

"Roger that." Preston accelerated the M1 and aimed for the center lane of the congested highway. "Let's give the fat guy an enema."

Natalie peered through her periscope. Beyond the charred debris from the exploded tanker, abandoned vehicles clogged all three lanes of traffic on both sides of the highway as well as the breakdown lanes. Natalie braced herself for a collision. Instead, the M1 barely slowed as its treads dug into a taxi and an SUV sitting in the center and passing lanes. The Abrams' front end lifted momentarily, then its sixty tons of steel and armor brought the tank crashing down on the two vehicles, crushing them under its weight. A shower of shattered glass cascaded across the road. The Abrams rolled along the taxi and SUV until its treads caught the hoods of the next two cars in line. The crunching of metal was audible even over the roar of the turbine engine.

"Natalie," said Hendricks.

She keyed her microphone. "Yes?"

"I need you to keep watch for an open wooded area off to our left. That's our exit."

"Roger that."

They rolled across the third set of vehicles in line, jostling Natalie, causing her to bang her helmet against the interior hull. "How far ahead is it?"

"About a mile, so sit back and enjoy the ride."

ARI HAD BEEN waiting over fifteen minutes for something to happen when she heard a commotion off to her left. Napier came down the line again. "The extraction of our people from the RCZ has been completed. The Air Force is coming in now to perform the PDS. We'll be moving out shortly."

When he moved on, Doreen asked Ari, "Any idea what he said?"

Ari shook her head.

Their squad leader, Corporal Mesle, moved closer to the two women. "It means the tank crews have lured as many revenants as possible into the collection zone, and the B1s are on their way to napalm them."

"Aren't we too close?" Doreen asked.

Mesle shook his head. "We'll be fine unless the Air Force drops short. Then we'll have bigger problems to deal with."

"That's not comforting," said Ari.

"Don't worry about it," said Mesle. "Even the Air Force can't screw this one—"

"Here they come," a voice called out farther down the beach.

The three B-1 bombers approached the zone. Their wings swept forward and their bomb bay doors opened. Descending to an altitude of one thousand feet, the bombers passed over the beach in a V formation and continued southeast. Once over TPC Harding Park, each aircraft released a string of seven-hundred-and-fifty-pound Mark 77 incendiary bombs that tumbled toward the park. As each bomb struck the ground, the one-hundred-and-ten-gallon mixture of kerosene-based fuel combined with benzene ignited, dousing the area and the surrounding Lake Merced in a napalm-like fuel gel mixture. From their vantage point on the beach, the troops saw the fireballs billow above the tree line and devolve into the familiar thick black smoke. What they did not see was that the oxidizing agent added to the compound kept the gel burning, and white phosphorous allowed it stick to the living dead. Fire consumed the dry, leathery flesh like kindling and ate its way through muscles until the revenants lost all functions in their limbs and collapsed. The intense heat vaporized tissue and melted fat. Protected by the skulls, it took longer for the brains to fry, forcing the revenants to lay motionless in one massive heap for several minutes until permanently dead.

Before the smoke had dissipated, the stench of kerosene mixed with charred, decayed flesh wafted along the beach. It was the most ungodly odor Ari had ever smelled. She swallowed the bile in her throat. Most of the others along the beach, including Doreen, puked into the sand.

"When are we gonna get off this beach?" protested a private several feet down from Ari.

"Relax," said Mesle. "They haven't even firebombed Golden Gate Park yet."

"Shit," Ari mumbled.

Mesle tapped her on the shoulder. "How are you ladies doing?"

"We're better off than they are." Ari motioned with her head toward the park. "I almost feel sorry for them."

Mesle chuckled. "You should see what they have planned for the revenants on the other side of the city."

THE ABRAMS HAD traveled over half a mile and crushed scores of vehicles beneath its treads when it came upon three tractor trailers side by side stretching across Route 101.

"The road is blocked," said Preston.

"Go over it," replied Hendricks.

Preston accelerated and the M1 surged ahead. "Hang on!"

Natalie grabbed the chicken handle on the interior hull and braced herself as the two trucks to the right loomed larger in her periscope. One was painted dark brown, probably belonging to UPS. The other bore the twin concentric circles of the Target logo. A jolt shook the Abrams when it collided with the cabs. Its speed decreased as the treads ground into the engine compartments, pulling the tank over the hoods and windshields. For several seconds, the tank hovered at a forty-degree angle before toppling forward, the twin treads crushing the fronts of the trailers. The sidewalls exploded outward, sending packages and boxes spewing across the highway. A slight pause ensued before the treads regained traction. The M1 lurched forward, flattening the trailers beneath it, the twisted metal sidewalls scraping against the undercarriage. The tank crossed over onto a pair of sedans and continued down the highway.

Natalie looked through the periscope again and gasped.

"What is it?" asked Hendricks.

"The highway is filled with rotters."

"With what?"

"The living dead. Revenants. Whatever you call them." Natalie switched her gaze to one of the forward vision blocks. Rotters wound their way amongst the abandoned vehicles, hundreds of them, all shambling toward the oncoming tank.

"I see them." Preston accelerated. "They're no match for us."

Natalie saw the familiar snarling faces, gore-encrusted teeth, and milky white eyes she had witnessed so many times before, and the outstretched decayed hands grasping for her as they disappeared beneath the glacis plate. This time she felt secure. Rather than facing them down the barrel of a gun, she did so from the safety of an armored tank.

When Natalie pivoted her periscope to the rear, her stomach threatened to heave. She had been battling the living dead for a year and had never witnessed such a slaughter. Every rotter in the path of the treads had been maimed. Some had limbs or heads crushed into the road. Others had been ground into the vehicles, body parts mixing with the twisted metal. Those few not trampled followed the tank.

When Natalie spun the periscope around front, she saw their designated turn off point—the Bay View Children's Play

Area.

"There's our turnoff," said Natalie.

"Roger that," said Preston. "Hang on. This is going to be bumpy."

Preston veered the M1 left and exited the northbound lanes of traffic. The tank slammed over the guardrail, clawed its way down to the empty access road paralleling the highway, tore through a chain link fence, and proceeded across the sandy lot at the base of the hill. After three hundred feet, Preston stopped the tank and let it idle.

"What's wrong?" Natalie asked.

"Nothing," the corporal replied. "I'm letting those things on the highway catch up to us. Let me know when most of them get here."

Natalie rotated the periscope one hundred and eighty degrees. A handful of rotters from inside the sandy lot had reached the rear of the M1 and clawed at the armor, leaving streaks of gore on the surface. Her eyes were not on them. Natalie focused her attention on the hundreds of rotters that flowed off the highway, through the ripped-out section of fence, and staggered toward the Abrams.

ANOTHER SERIES OF fireballs erupted to the north. Ari found herself ducking from instinct, even though the explosions were a mile away.

"That would be the PDS of Golden Gate Park," Mesle announced.

A whistle blast sounded farther down the beach. Napier walked along the line. "Move out and keep it tight. Remember, we're here to clean out revenants, not see who can reach the Bay first."

Mesle headed up the stairs leading off the beach, with Ari and Doreen following. The entire line of troops surged forward from the beach and advanced inland, maintaining a tight line. As they crossed the highway, the troops checked each vehicle. A Coop ahead of Ari held a single rotter, a young woman still wearing her seatbelt. The skin on the left side of her face, shoulder, and arm had been chewed away. It stared at the approaching food and snarled through half a mouth. For a moment, Ari hesitated.

Mesle pushed past her, raised his M-16A2, and put a single round into its head.

"We're here to clean these things out," he snapped. "Get your head in the game or get out of line."

"Sorry," she said. "It won't happen again."

Upon reaching the other side of the highway, the line flowed like a wave. Ari's section passed through a copse of trees and entered the parking lot of the San Francisco Zoo. Several dozen vehicles sat at skewed angles around the main gate, in most cases the doors left open. Those troops that reached the exterior wall bordering the parking lot stopped. The rest flowed around the side walls and continued into the city, the occasional sound of weapons fire punctuating the day. Napier blew his whistle again and summoned his platoon to the main gate. They totaled forty-one men and women.

Napier stepped up to Mesle. "You know what to do."

Mesle nodded. "I'll take my squad."

"Are you sure that's enough?"

"If I need back up, I'll call for it. If this goes south and we get overwhelmed, why lose more than that?"

The master sergeant frowned but agreed with the reasoning and walked off.

Mesle gathered up the eight members of his squad. "I don't want anybody playing the hero in here. We go in, do our job, and get out as quickly as possible. If we run into any revenants, dispatch them without discharging your weapon. If there are too many, we fall back and abandon the mission."

"What mission?" Ari asked. "I thought we were bypassing

buildings and enclosed areas."

"We are. In this case, we need to gather intelligence. Let's move out."

The main entrance to the zoo had been barricaded from the inside. Two of the soldiers hoisted Ari to the roof of the Education Center on the left. She climbed to the peak and looked inside the compound. Some of the interior barrier had been taken down, and dried blood smeared the cement. She saw no signs of activity and backed down to the edge of the roof.

"Everything is clear," she reported.

"Any chance of removing the barricade?" Mesle asked.

She shook her head. "It's wooden planks and sections of chain link fence held in place by cinderblocks, wooden beams, and metal poles. But there are a pair of ladders on the roof."

"Then we go over. Lower one of the ladders to us," Mesle ordered.

Five minutes later, the squad stood inside the zoo surrounding Mesle while he studied the mounted visitor guide. He snapped his fingers to get their attention, motioned to the right, and moved out.

In the distance was the distinctive moan of rotters, probably no more than ten. Ari raised her M-16A2 into the high ready position. The squad came to an open enclosure on the right set up to resemble the African Savanna. They climbed onto a pile of boulders overlooking the interior. Seven rotters milled about. Two animal carcasses lay on the dried grass. One appeared to be a zebra based on the striped coloring of its leathery skin, with most of its midsection eaten away. The other animal was a giraffe, the neck of which had been picked clean of flesh and muscle. Those portions not devoured had decomposed and been baked by the glaring sun. Upon seeing the squad, the rotters issued a deep groan of hunger and stumbled toward the retaining wall.

Several of the troops raised their weapons to fire. Mesle

waved them down. "They can't get to us. It'll draw others."

"What do we do about them?" asked a young man with red hair.

"Leave them for the clean-up squad."

Climbing down from the rocks and returning to the main path, the squad continued until it reached a large open area near the center of the zoo. Three rotters blocked their path. Two wore casual street clothes. The third appeared as though something had mauled it. Half its face had been ripped away, one of its arms torn off, and chunks of flesh and muscle gouged out of its chest. The three rotters headed toward them.

Ari stepped toward the mauled rotter. It reached out its one good arm toward her. She raised the butt of her M-16A2 and slammed it into the rotter's face, then swung her right leg behind it, knocking out its legs. The rotter fell to the ground. Ari pounded at its head with the butt of her weapon until it shattered. Doreen and the red-headed soldier did the same to the other two living dead.

Moving on, the squad came across a scene of carnage outside of Cat Kingdom. Dried blood covered the area for a hundred square feet. The remains of a snow leopard, lion, and tiger, as well as eleven rotters lay scattered across the walkway. The snow leopard had its abdomen torn open and its insides emptied of all internal organs. A twenty-foot-long streak of blood trailed behind the tiger's carcass, indicating that even in its death throes it had fought to get away. The lion had multiple bite wounds across its body and one eye gouged out. Each of the big cats had been brought down and eaten, although not before mauling their attackers, because interspersed among the melee were decayed human limbs and heads. The eyes on one of the heads followed the group as it approached. Its mouth moved in anticipation of a meal.

"What happened here?" Doreen asked.

Mesle stared at the killing zone. "Somehow the big cats got out and fought the revenants. From the looks of it, they gave as well as they got."

"How horrible," Ari said.

"At least they went out fighting, not like those other animals."

The red-headed soldier moved toward the rotter head and raised his M-16A2. Mesle stopped him. "Don't waste the energy. We still—"

A moaning from further down the walkway and to the right caught their attention. Ten rotters approached from the front and another seven on the flank, enough for the squad to handle. They raised their weapons to fire. Again, Mesle intervened.

"We're almost done here. Fall back."

The squad double-timed to the African Savanna section when Mesle ordered them to stop. "Wait here. Fire a shot when those things get to within fifty feet." To Ari and Doreen, he said, "You're with me."

Before they could respond, he ran up the stairs to the elevated walkway that ran through the Primate Discovery Center, with the two women behind him. He raced down the length of the walkway, pausing every few seconds to stare into the multistory primate building off to the right. Because of the overgrown rainforest inside and the dust-covered windows, they could not see in. Mesle swore under his breath and backtracked along the front of the building. A single round of automatic weapon fire cut through the stillness. The women continued back toward the rest of the squad. Mesle turned left and circled around the end of the primate building.

"What are you doing?" Ari called out.

"I have to check something."

"The rotters are here."

"Go on. I'll be there in a minute."

Ari told Doreen to go on without her and followed Mesle. The corporal raced to the reviewing area at the far end of the walkway overlooking the outdoor chimpanzee compound.

Over a dozen chimp carcasses lay across the compound. Though a few showed signs of having been eaten, most lay near the base of trees and had died from starvation.

Mesle studied the enclosure for a moment and then whispered, "Thank God."

"For what?"

Before he could answer, a barrage of automatic weapons fire erupted from the walkway.

"Let's haul ass." Mesle darted away from the reviewing area, making sure Ari was with him.

They raced down the stairs to the walkway where the squad stood in line abreast, aiming at the approaching dead. Eight rotters lay in a crumpled heap ten feet in front of them, with another twenty or so drawing near. A second volley of fire cut that number in half.

"Let's move," ordered Mesle.

The squad fell in behind Mesle and they made their way to the front entrance. Napier had found a pair of ladders and placed them on either side of the Education Center, allowing Mesle's squad easy access to and from the roof. The squad climbed out of the zoo, with Mesle being the last to leave. He and the red-headed soldier pulled up the ladder from inside the compound and laid it on the roof, then climbed down the second one to join the others. Napier greeted him at the bottom.

"Did you get the information we needed?"

Mesle nodded. "It's good news. We're safe."

"Excellent. I'll tell the lieutenant and he can forward it to Secretary Fogel." Napier shook Mesle's hand. "You all did an excellent job. Now muster the rest of your forces and go support Abercrombie. He ran into a pack of revenants on Sloat Boulevard and could use some back up."

"You heard the master sergeant," yelled Mesle. "Fall in behind me and let's double time it. We have a city to liberate."

★ ★ ★

AN INCREASING NUMBER of rotters gathered around the Abrams, nearly seventy-five in the past fifteen minutes, with several hundred still staggering in from the highway. Natalie wondered how many would have to swarm them before the Abrams would not be able to move.

A voice coming through the headphones of her CVC interrupted her thoughts.

"RCZ4/3, what's your location?"

Hendricks keyed his microphone. "We're off Route 101 less than a quarter mile from the collection zone. We're waiting for the revenants to catch up."

"Forget about that. Units One and Two have already been extracted. The MC-130 is airborne and ready to deploy. Proceed with the rest of your mission. The Chinook is standing by to extract your team."

"Roger that." Hendricks rekeyed his microphone so only the crew could hear. "You heard that. We're heading in."

The Abrams lurched forward, pushing away the rotters gathered on its flanks and crushing those that had moved around to the front. The tank skirted the base of the hill before turning right, cutting down an access road between two sets of apartment buildings. Preston swung left onto Harney Way and gunned the engine. Candlestick Park towered over the roofs of the surrounding apartment complex. The M1 raced out of the side street, across Hunters Point Expressway, and into the stadium parking lot.

"Oh, my fucking God," Natalie mumbled into the microphone.

The southern parking area was one mass of rotters extending from the stadium to the far ends of the lot and stretching from the expressway around the front of the building. Tens of thousands of the living dead, perhaps one hundred thousand or more, with their attention centering on the Abrams as it approached.

"Hang on," warned Preston. "This is going to get interesting."

The Abrams crashed into the rotters, its weight and speed slicing through the ocean of living dead. Natalie could hear the moans of hunger and the crunching of bones over the roar of the tank's engine. Even worse, the destruction of so many rotters sent airborne the flies and wasps feeding off their bodies. So many attached themselves to her periscope and vision blocks she was unable to see.

The Abrams slowed. Preston keyed his microphone.

"I can't see a damn thing because of these insects. Natalie, you need to direct me."

"Mine are blocked, too."

"Then go topside and direct me from there."

Natalie reached up, unlatched the hatch, and pushed it open. The stench of thousands of the living dead wafted into the turret, gagging her despite the gas mask. She pulled it off and vomited across the top hull of the turret, which only made things worse. Without the mask, the smell was overpowering. It stung her eyes and infiltrated her sinuses, making it difficult to breathe. Flies and wasps hovered around her face, threatening to get into her mouth and nostrils. Every time she flicked her head or brushed them away, others replaced them.

"Talk to me," said Preston.

Natalie used one hand to wipe her mouth and the other to push the microphone close to her lips, cupping it so no insects could get inside. "Where are we heading?"

"There's a truck entrance on the north end of the stadium."

"Continue straight. I'll tell you when to turn."

"Roger that."

Natalie shifted around to avoid the swarm of flies and wasps the tank passed through and wished she had not. The treads kicked up a splash back of blood that sprayed the rear end of the Abrams and left a wake of gore in the mass of living dead. The nauseating stench of decay mixed with the overpowering odor of ammonia from hundreds of ruptured stomachs and intestines. Natalie retched again, spilling what remained in her stomach down the open hatch.

"Jesus," complained Hendricks as the puke splattered off his helmet. "What the fuck is going on up there?"

Natalie ignored him. When she spit out the last of the vomitus, several flies entered her mouth, forcing her to swallow them. She grimaced, trying to prevent herself from vomiting again.

"I need a location update," Preston yelled into his microphone.

"Hang on," Natalie hacked. Glancing forward, she said, "Turn left thirty degrees."

The Abrams swung left and continued plowing its way through the parking lot. A few seconds later, they passed by the front entrance to the stadium. More rotters occupied the eastern and northern sectors of the parking lot, surging toward the noise.

"Where are we now?" asked Preston.

"We passed the front entrance."

"How big is this fucking stadium?" he asked.

Natalie kept turning her head to the back to avoid the swarming insects. When she looked forward for the third time, they had reached the far corner.

"Turn left again, forty degrees."

Preston complied. Natalie scanned the side of the building for the vehicle entrance. After a few seconds she spotted it. The doors had been pushed in by one of the previous tanks.

"I see it. Turn ninety degrees to the left on my mark." Natalie waited until the Abrams had pulled parallel to the entrance. "Now."

The M1 lurched hard left and headed for the stadium. After a few seconds, Preston said, "Everyone hang on."

The Abrams stopped. Preston locked the turret in place and rotated the chassis three hundred and sixty degrees, repeating this maneuver several times. The spinning chassis plowed through the horde of rotters, scattering them in every direction, and propelled off the insects. On the third revolution, the chassis stopped and the M1 moved forward.

"What was that about?" asked Hendricks.

"I needed to clean the bugs off my periscope so I can see where we're going."

"Good idea. Natalie, get back in the tank."

She did not need to be told twice. Climbing down into the turret, she closed the hatch. Dozens of insects followed, although they were nowhere near as aggravating as the swarm topside. She peered through the periscope as the Abrams entered the stadium. She found it difficult to see because of the darkened interior, although she did notice that the walls were splattered with blood and dripped with crushed internal organs, evidence the other two tanks had passed this way. A few seconds later, the Abrams exited through the other end into the stadium.

Natalie thought this was what Hell must be like.

Rotters jammed the stadium bowl. Every inch of the playing field contained living dead, as well as most of the seating area, until the structure itself seemed like a single pulsing organism. The only portions not occupied by rotters were the two spots where the other Abrams had been abandoned. A cloud of flies and wasps hovered over the horde.

Preston maneuvered to the center of the stadium and shut down the M1.

Hendricks yelled into his microphone to be heard above the din. "This is RCZ4/3. We're ready for extraction."

"Roger that. We're inbound to you now. Please be waiting by the curb for your ride."

"Hurry up, I don't want to be here any longer than I have to." Hendricks pulled off his helmet and gas mask and called up to Natalie. "Crack the hatch and head topside. The chopper will be here in a minute."

Natalie removed her helmet, pushed open the hatch, and climbed out onto the turret. Only then did she appreciate the full horror. A sea of decayed, outstretched arms greeted her. Several tried to crawl up onto the M1, unable to get a grip on the gore-covered surface. Even those in the seating area reached out, many tumbling over the guardrail and crashing into the mass of living dead on the levels below. The stench was more intense within the confined space of the stadium. The moaning of tens of thousands of rotters and the buzzing of hundreds of thousands of insects drowned out all other noise. Natalie moved toward the rear of the turret, trying to ignore the mass of living dead.

Her foot slipped on a piece of intestine and Natalie fell backwards, sliding along the turret's slick surface toward the rotters. Those closest to her became frantic in anticipation of a meal, tearing and clawing at each other to get to her. Natalie closed her eyes and prayed.

A hand grabbed her arm before she slid off. Natalie opened her eyes to see Hendricks crouched on the turret, one hand holding her wrist, the other clutching the machinegun mount. For a moment Natalie thought she would be all right until hands clutched at her legs. One wrapped itself around her ankle and yanked, threatening to pull her out of the lieutenant's grip. She kicked desperately. The rotter let go of her ankle and others took its place. She glanced down and stared into dozens of hungry mouths only a few feet away.

"Give me your hand!" yelled Preston, who crouched beside Hendricks, leaning out and extending his arm. "Hurry or we're going to lose you!"

That snapped Natalie out of her confusion. She swung her free hand up and clasped onto the corporal's. Both men pulled her onto the turret and steadied her.

"Are you okay?" Hendricks asked.

"Yes, but I feel like an idiot for falling."

"Don't. It takes a while to get used to crawling around armor." Hendricks patted her on the shoulder. "Secure the antenna before the Chinook shows up, otherwise it will cut us to shreds."

Natalie had finished tying it down when a heavy burst of wind slammed into her face. A Chinook entered the stadium, the pilot positioning it over the Abrams. The back ramp lowered, and the helicopter descended until its ramp hovered one foot above the front end of the turret Preston jumped on first, holding the hydraulic joist with one hand and helping Natalie on board with the other. Hendricks boarded last. The other two tank crews sat on a bank of seats. One of the crew members spoke into his headset. The Chinook lifted off and headed out of the stadium. Once at a safe distance over San Francisco Bay, the helicopter hovered.

An MC-130 flew northwest at an altitude of six thousand feet. While still over the Bay, the rear landing deck lowered. When the aircraft passed over the stadium's eastern parking area, a gray cylindrical object thirty feet long and three feet in diameter rolled down the ramp and off the plane. A parachute on the blunt end of the device opened, allowing it to float toward its target. A second, similar object rolled off the ramp three seconds later and also deployed a parachute, this one over the stadium. The MC-130 banked left, increasing speed and altitude to evacuate the blast zone.

The devices exploded twenty feet above ground and created donut-shaped clouds of liquid-gel that spread out across the eastern parking lot and stadium, each covering an area of one thousand square feet. Five seconds later, a second explosion occurred inside each cloud, generating a spark of fire that detonated the liquid-gel mixtures with the equivalent of forty-four tons of TNT. Outside the stadium, the flames incinerated everything within the cloud's radius. A massive overpressure twenty times normal atmospheric pressure raced through the parking lot and expanded into the northern and southern sectors, crushing everything in its path. In an instant, tens of thousands of rotters not burned in the fireball were shattered, limbs and heads torn from bodies, torsos ruptured, and skulls caved in. The blast wave slammed into the eastern façade of the stadium, shearing off the klieg lights, leveling the entrance, and collapsing the concrete ramps.

The device that detonated inside did similar damage, the fireball incinerating almost two hundred thousand of the living dead on the field and in the bleachers and blasting through the exterior corridors. The elevated seating directed the overpressure back on itself, generating a shockwave that gutted the interior of the stadium and blew chunks of debris into the parking lot. As the smoke dissipated, nothing could be seen moving in the area of the blast.

All Natalie could say was, "Holy fucking shit."

"Tell me about it." Hendricks grabbed her shoulder and squeezed, intending it as a comradely gesture. "I told you we were taking this war back to the revenants. Payback is going to be a bitch."

The Chinook headed back to the Beachhead, the remnants of the stadium receding in the distance.

Damn, we might just win this.

CHAPTER EIGHTEEN

THE PUSH DOWN Sloat Boulevard had fallen into a routine after the first few hundred feet. Ari admired the efficiency of the operation. The troops walked line abreast and stretched from one sidewalk to the other, with a foot between each person. If they came across any living dead, the closest soldier would take it down with a single shot to the head. At every intersection they paused to check out the cross streets and allow any stray revenants to close with the line, then dispatched it and moved on to the next intersection. Every fifteen minutes, platoon leaders would check with their counterparts on the parallel streets to the north and south, either stopping so the other lines could catch up or moving ahead with their own people. By this method, a stable front steadily made its way across San Francisco from the Pacific Coast toward the Bay.

A second line of troops followed one thousand feet behind the first. Their job was to mop up stray revenants that wandered out of buildings or alleys and to ensure the main line did not get surrounded. A third, much smaller group brought up the rear, leaving a pair of guards along Sloat Boulevard every five hundred feet to police the area and report any large numbers of the living dead they found, most likely those stuck in buildings that emerged after the main line had passed.

Those on the line encountered only a score of revenants in their push across the city, most having been previously lured to the RCZs and eliminated during the morning's PDS operations. Most of those they came upon were trapped inside abandoned vehicles or immobile. A few buildings, like the Lucky Supermarket and West Portal Lutheran School, contained a considerable number of living dead trapped inside. Penal squads would come by later and clean them out before the city was declared safe for habitation.

The line eventually reached the intersection of Portola Drive and Junipero Serra Boulevard. Napier's platoon continued through the intersection to where Sloat Boulevard narrowed and became St. Francis Boulevard. The going was uphill through a residential neighborhood. Rotter activity increased in this sector, although nothing to be alarmed over.

When St. Francis Boulevard ended by a large stone water fountain, Napier ordered, "Take fifteen, people. Stay alert in case there are revenants in the area."

"Beautiful view from up here, isn't it?" Doreen remarked.

Ari turned around. For the first time, she realized they were on one of the many hills overlooking San Francisco. Looking back the way they had come, she saw the coastline a few miles in the distance, the azure water reflecting the late morning sun. Off to the northeast, the various residential neighborhoods ascended the hill's terrace up to the peak of Mt. Davidson Park. The homes were large and elegant, many with red terra cotta roofs. The horrors of the outbreak had not reached this neighborhood, None of the houses had been ransacked or destroyed, and no corpses lay strewn across the street. The only indications of an apocalypse were front lawns where grass and weeds had grown untended for a year and the four pillars of black smoke rising in the distance from the RCZs.

"It makes me want to move here when this is finally over," said Doreen.

"Fuck that. There are too many bad memories associated with this city. Besides, if I make it through this, I'm moving to the mountains where I'll be safe if this shit ever goes down again."

"Won't you be lonely by yourself?"

Ari wanted to avoid answering that question. She got the chance when Mesle strolled by. Ari excused herself and stepped over to him.

Mesle paused in front of her. "What's up?"

"I'm curious why going to the zoo was so important?"

"We've heard rumors the Revenant Virus had species jumped and needed to check the zoo to verify that."

"Species jumped?" Doreen came over and joined the conversation.

"Yes." Mesle nodded. "The Revenant Virus was originally designed as a medical application to regenerate scar tissue. It had the unintended effect of killing off the host's living tissue and reanimating it. Since the virus had been bioengineered for humans, it only infected humans. Over the past few months, we've been receiving reports from across the country, none of which could be substantiated, that the virus had adapted and could infect animal hosts."

Ari exhaled audibly. "Jesus."

"Exactly," answered Mesle.

Doreen scrunched her eyebrows. "I don't understand."

"If the virus species jumped," explained Mesle, "we'd be dealing with revenant animals. Can you imagine the clusterfuck if a pack of infected rats or a flock of infected birds got loose in an unaffected area? The rumors almost convinced Secretary Fogel not to proceed with the plan to take back the country and limit the reclamation to San Francisco. Luckily, none of the animals we found in the zoo that were bitten had come back to life, so we can rule out those reports as rumors."

"Thank God," said Ari.

"You rest up," said Mesle. "We're going to have a long afternoon ahead of us."

"Why do you say that?" Ari asked. "This has been easy."

Mesle pointed to the area east of the water fountain. "So far, every street in our sector has been laid out in a grid pattern, so most of the revenants were lured to the RCZ. Once we get on the other side of this fountain, the neighborhoods become a winding labyrinth of roads stretching for over a mile until we reach the flat ground on the opposite side. According to our intelligence, there are large concentrations of revenants in there."

Mesle walked away. Ari looked over to the fountain and the area beyond it. All she could mumble was, "Shit."

CHAPTER NINETEEN

ROBSON SAT IN a lawn chair on the roof, partially hidden by the sign that read Waits River General Store. He rested his AA-12 on his lap, his right hand on the trigger guard, and drank from a warm bottle of Coke. From this position, he had an excellent field of fire on the parking lot beneath him and could see DeWitt across the road. DeWitt had set himself up in a copse of trees, far enough back to guard both ends of the road and yet not be easily seen by the casual observer. Everyone else rested, either sleeping in their vehicles parked behind the building or camped out in the store itself. Roberta and Caslow would change out with them at noon, and Linda and Clint would take over four hours later.

Though the guards were a necessary precaution, Robson felt nothing would happen. This area appeared devoid of both humans and rotters.

After leaving Gilmanton last night, the convoy had traveled north until it reached the town of Tilton, which had access ramps to Interstate 93. Both northbound and southbound lanes were jammed with abandoned vehicles and their now living dead occupants. The State Police had blocked the ramps leading to and from the highway, so no vehicles blocked the roads in town. The convoy doglegged onto Route 132, which paralleled the Interstate for several miles before passing beneath it, and followed the back roads to Newfound Lake, their first objective. Robson had hoped to find a cabin or campsite where the group could settle in.

Those hopes were dashed when they drove through the community along the lakefront. They found several hundred rotters in the area, people who had the same idea. They came across a few residences off the beaten path that could have been converted into a new camp. However, their proximity to the rotter-infested community made them too dangerous to attempt, so Robson moved on.

Leaving the Newfound Lake area, they continued into Vermont and traveled north to Bradford where Robson hoped to pick up either Route 3 or Interstate 91. Both highways were filled with abandoned vehicles and rotters, just like I93. The convoy drove until they came upon the deserted town of Waits River and found the general store. Since the sun would be rising soon, Robson had decided to set up camp. The store had been broken into but not ransacked, with those who had looted it taking only the basic necessities. Robson's team had found some medical supplies and a few canned goods, plus some luxuries like three twelve-packs of toilet paper, several boxes of stale cookies, and a case of Coke. After the least healthy breakfast anyone had eaten in ages, everyone had settled in for the day, with Robson and DeWitt agreeing to take first shift.

Robson heard the ladder to the roof squeak. Putting down his Coke, he wrapped his finger around the trigger of his AA-12. A few seconds later, Linda's head appeared over the edge of the roof.

"Am I bothering you?" she asked.

"Not at all. Come on up."

Linda climbed up the rest of the way and joined him. She leaned her arms on the top of the sign and stared out over the surrounding area.

"You can't sleep?" Robson asked.

"I don't know if it's because I'm nervous or excited about the prospect of starting over."

"Why are you nervous? Are you afraid we'll run into more rotters than we can handle?"

Linda shook her head. "I'm afraid we'll never find a place to settle down."

"We will. Trust me."

"I do trust you. It's…."

"What?"

Linda leaned against the sign. "You were fortunate that you had a fortified compound to live in for most of the apocalypse. You've only been homeless and on the road for a few weeks. Most of us have lived that way since the outbreak. For some of those you rescued, being in Price's camp wasn't the first time we had been assaulted, it was just the worst experience."

"I didn't know."

"I'd been gang raped by two separate groups before being captured by Price. I was an Emergency Room nurse in Concord when the outbreak erupted. Seven patients brought into the ER with bite wounds turned in the space of a few minutes. They attacked other patients and staff and infected them. A National Guard unit assigned to protect the hospital shot those who had become zombies and then began shooting the wounded. The police on duty tried to stop them, and a gun fight broke out. While they were killing each other, those who had been bit died, came back to life, and attacked the rest of us.

"Gary and Phil had dropped off another patient with bite wounds when the fighting erupted. They were ambulance drivers. I'd known them for over a year. They were always dropping people at my ER. When they offered to take me with them, I figured I'd be safe. Somehow, we made it out of the city. When we stopped to rest, that was the first time they forced me to have sex with them. That happened almost every night for three weeks until one day, while we were stopped at a gas station, the living dead came out of the woods. I was inside scrounging for food and water. Those assholes left me. None of the living dead saw me, so I snuck out the back door and headed out on my own."

Robson stared at Linda, dumbfounded. He did not know

what bothered him more, the fact this woman had endured so much, or the fact she could relate the details as if she were talking about a trip to the mall. He felt guilty about pitying himself over his own misfortunes.

"What about the second time?"

Linda shrugged. "That was my own fault. A week later, I ran into these five guys who seemed decent enough. I thought I couldn't be assaulted twice, so I made contact and asked if they had any food to spare. They gave me something to eat and drink, and then took turns with me that night and the next morning before leaving me alone in the woods. After that, I avoided all contact with people until one of Price's teams found me asleep in a Seven Eleven."

"So that's why you were so leery of us."

"Do you blame me?" Linda said without recrimination. "I still am."

"Why did you come with us?"

"You offer the best chance of survival. The other girls who were with me won't last two weeks before they're either dead or camp followers again. Those who stayed at that looted bed-and-breakfast community won't make it through the winter. If anyone's going to survive, it'll be your group. That's why I'm here." Linda stared out again over Waits River. "I only hope we don't all die on the road while searching for the perfect spot."

Robson thought the perfect spot would be back at Fort McClary with Natalie. That dream had been crushed forever.

"We don't need to find the perfect spot," he said. "Only the right one."

"Why can't this be the right one?"

"There's no defensible position. If another gang or a sizeable number of rotters find us, we're screwed. I know we're vulnerable on the road, and I want to find a place where we can settle down as much as you do. Trust me."

"No offense, trust is an extremely hard thing for me to offer nowadays."

"Fair enough. Go below and get some rest. You and Clint can take over in a few hours."

"Clint?" Linda furrowed her brow. "You mean the African-American?"

Robson nodded.

"He told you his name?"

"No."

"Then how do you know his name is Clint?"

"I'm calling him that because of Clint Eastwood."

Linda stared at him as though he had rotters sprouting from his head.

"In *High Plains Drifter* Clint Eastwood played the man without a name."

Linda's confusion became amusement and, for the first time since Robson had rescued her, she laughed. "That's awful."

"I was never known for my stand-up humor."

"I'll go get some sleep." Linda headed back to the ladder and paused. "Thanks."

"For what?"

"For listening. And for being a decent guy."

"I'll do everything I can not to let you and the others down."

"I want to believe that." Linda descended the ladder, leaving Robson alone.

Robson went back to watching the road. He had meant what he said to Linda about not letting them down. He hoped he had it within him to still do what was right for the group.

CHAPTER TWENTY

T HE LAST HALF hour had gone better than expected. After setting out again, Napier's platoon had moved through a stand of trees before emerging into the neighborhood known as Westwood Highlands. Here the streets curved, following the slope of Mt. Davidson. Because of the meandering layout, the platoon moved forward in a straight line, pushing their way through residential yards and common areas, and only breaking as the soldiers flowed around the thousands of homes dotting the area. They moved slower than they had earlier in the day due to the terrain.

The platoon ran into fewer revenants here than along Sloat Boulevard, mostly those trapped inside homes, which they bypassed. A few wandered the streets or had been corralled in backyards, and those were put down with little effort. However, the squad saw abundant signs of earlier revenant activity— numerous abandoned vehicles parked at odd angles with the doors left open, suitcases and travel bags abandoned on lawns and streets, houses with broken doors or shattered windows, patches of dried blood, and dozens of bodies eaten so thoroughly the corpses did not reanimate.

After walking for forty-five minutes, the platoon came upon a section of the neighborhood at the base of Mt. Davidson where the streets ran west to east. Ari and Doreen lucked out. They stood across from Cresta Vista Drive and got to follow the street rather than traipse through backyards. Two hundred feet down Cresta Vista Drive, Ari heard the all too familiar moaning of a rotter but saw nothing nearby.

Doreen tapped her on the arm and pointed to a white VW Beetle parked sideways across the street with the passenger side facing them.

"It's in there. I can see something moving."

The driver's side was open with a single rotter strapped inside. As she moved around the car, it became frantic, pushing against the seatbelt to get at her and snapping its jaws. It wore black high heels and a gore-encrusted skirt. Its blouse had been ripped off, and all the skin devoured from its left arm, chest, and head. The face that stared at them was part decayed flesh and part skull. When it opened its mouth, Ari could see through the jaw into its throat.

"I've got this," said Doreen.

"I'm fine." Ari moved toward the car, removing the bayonet from her belt. The rotter reached out for her with its right arm, the left dangling by its side, useless from being stripped of flesh and muscle. Ari grabbed the rotter's arm and pulled it toward her while plunging the bayonet into the left side of its skull. She felt the blade hesitate when it touched bone before breaking through. The rotter convulsed. Ari twisted her wrist, twirling the blade around inside the rotter's head and scrambling its brain. It went limp and slumped against the steering column. Ari withdrew the bayonet, wiped the blade on the headrest, slid it back into its scabbard, and rejoined the others.

Mesle had moved on ahead to another rotter laying in the middle of the street. This one had been stripped of most of its flesh and muscles except for the head. What little tissue remained had been dried and tanned until it appeared like leather. It stared at them with eyes bleached white and blinded by constant exposure to the sun. It heard the approaching humans and snarled, its head tilting to one side. Mesle stepped up and crushed its skull with a single blow from the butt of his M-16A2, putting the rotter out of its misery.

Doreen sighed. "It only gets worse."

"What gets worse?" Ari asked.

"Everything. We used to think fighting rotters around the Kittery Trading Post was important until we fought those four hundred at Site R. Those were nothing compared to what we encountered on the trip out here. Now we're doing this."

"This is a lot easier than fighting hundreds of rotters at once."

"It's more personal, which is demoralizing," Doreen said to her friend. "When I'm fighting hundreds at once, I don't see them as individuals. They're a lifeless horde. Killing them one at a time, I can't help wondering who they were, how did this happen, who did they leave behind?"

"Try to think of this as the dark before the dawn."

"I want to, but it always seems to get darker. If only—"

Mesle moved up behind the women and interrupted Doreen, his voice firm yet quiet. "This isn't *The View*, ladies. Can the chatter and concentrate on what you're doing."

"Sorry."

The platoon continued on for another third of a mile and approached the end of Cresta Vista Drive where it connected with a cross street. Ari heard it first, a low moaning in the background. It grew louder as they approached the cross street. She moved over to Mesle.

"Do you hear that?"

"Hear what?"

"That background noise that sounds like humming of a beehive."

Mesle listened for a moment, His eyes widened. "Revenants?"

Ari nodded. "It sounds like a lot of them."

When they emerged onto the cross street, Mesle paused his people and waited for the other squad leaders. When he spotted them, he motioned to hold their position and rushed over to explain. Mesle chatted with one squad leader a block to their south when another squad emerged from the line of houses off to the north, crossed the street, and kept on going, ignoring the stopped line of troops. Half a dozen soldiers marched along an open grassy area between the row of houses in front of them and those located at the corner. Ari went to warn them. She had only gone a few yards when gunfire erupted behind the houses. The soldiers retreated through the open area, firing behind them.

One of them screamed, "Revenants! Hundreds of them!"

A moment later, rotters poured out of the grassy area. Rather than fall back and form a line against the living dead, the retreating troops pushed past their comrades and headed west. Those left behind had no idea how to respond. Some took up a defensive position and fired into the revenants. Most joined the others and ran. The rotters followed, threatening to spread into areas already cleared.

Ari walked a few steps up the street and stopped. She switched her M-16A2 to fully automatic and fired into the horde. Only a few rounds resulted in head shots, the rest slamming into dead torsos or overshooting their mark. She never intended to stop them, though. She hoped to distract them, and it worked. The horde ignored the fleeing humans and went after Ari. The rest of the squad fell in beside her and began firing. For each rotter that went down, three more took its place. Every few seconds, the line had to fall back or risk being overrun. Other squads joined them. The tide of living dead slowed, although Ari knew it would not be enough. At some point they would have to retreat and give up ground.

Mesle walked up and shouted. "Try to hold on for another minute. We've got air support on the way."

It better hurry, Ari thought, firing a round into the face of a rotter in a soiled 49ers t-shirt and shorts. The bolt of her M-16A2 stuck open. Stepping out of line, she discarded the empty magazine and switched it out with a full one from her ammo pack. The rotters had closed to within thirty feet.

The thumping of a helicopter's rotor blades cut through the

sounds of battle. Mesle ordered, "Fall back."

An AE-64 Apache approached from the south, stopping a few yards behind the line and hovering one hundred feet above the street. Once the soldiers had safely pulled back out of its line of fire, the pilot descended until its rotor blades practically touched the surrounding roofs and dropped the nose a few degrees. An electronic whir came from the 30mm chain gun mounted in the Apache's nose. A moment later, all Hell broke loose.

A stream of bullets firing at the rate of sixty hundred and twenty-five rounds per minute decimated the living dead, churning those in the front into a cloud of blood and body chunks. A rain of spent shell casings clattered to the street. The pilot swept the chain gun from side to side, walking the stream of gunfire along the horde until the street had been cleared. Raising his elevation, the pilot moved the Apache to the open grassy area and swung right. The chain gun came to life again, cutting down more revenants. Keeping the Apache's nose trained on the area behind the townhouses, the pilot rotated his helicopter in a one-hundred-and-eighty-degree arc and fired a series of Hydra-70 general purpose rockets from its stub wing mounts. Over a dozen explosions ripped through the area, sending balls of fire and clouds of smoke billowing above the rooftops. The pilot remained over target another minute, firing a few quick bursts from the chain gun before ascending to an altitude of one hundred feet and flying off to the west.

"The pilot said everything is clear," Mesle called out after the noise from the Apache's rotors had died out. "Let's form up and move out."

"Are you sure?" Ari asked.

"The pilot says there's nothing left but squirmers."

Ari did not want to ask what squirmers were. She found out soon enough as the line reformed on the eastern side of the carnage area. The chain gun had chewed up most of the revenants until they were hardly recognizable as once being human. A few of the rotters had lost legs and thrashed about in the pile of inhumanity. Others had shattered arms or torsos, preventing them from standing. Some had their bodies ripped apart from under them, leaving only heads that remained alive. Doreen raised her M-16A2 to shoot a disabled rotter in a UPS uniform that reaching out to her with the one remaining arm on its legless torso. Mesle stepped forward and pushed the barrel down.

"Don't waste the ammo. Only shoot those that are mobile. The penal battalions will take care of these."

Placing a hand on her friend's shoulder, Ari squeezed gently and ushered her forward. The two women avoided looking at the remains of the living dead, although they could not avoid their presence. By ripping them apart, the Apache had ruptured their intestinal tracts so that the pent-up methane and feces mixed with the sickeningly sweet stench of decayed flesh. Several of the troops fell out of line to vomit. Ari's eyes watered and bile burned the back of her throat. She fought back the urge to retch. Once they made it off the street, she would be fine.

She kept telling herself that until she crossed the open grassy area, now covered in body parts, and moved to the open space behind the homes. Several hundred rotters had congregated in this area. The Apache had generated even greater devastation, its rockets blasting body parts across the open field. Intestines and limbs hung off trees, dangled from roofs, or lay strewn across back decks where the explosions had tossed them. Coagulated blood splattered the rear walls of the outlying houses. Back here, the stench was even more intense than out front. Flies and wasps had descended to feast on the fresh remains, creating a nightmare for the platoon as they passed.

"Go around them," Mesle offered. "If you see any that are mobile, shoot them. We'll meet up on the other side."

The squad moved south, giving the area a wide berth. Doreen moved up beside Ari.

"Remember what I said earlier about settling down here after this is over?"

"Yeah?"

"No fucking way."

CHAPTER TWENTY-ONE

"**T**HAT WAS A great meal," said Windows.

"It was, Mr. Denning," said Cindy. "Thank you."

"You're welcome." Denning tossed his napkin on the table. "I'm glad you enjoyed it."

"Where did you get pork chops?" asked Windows.

"I used to own a pig. He died of old age shortly after the outbreak, so I butchered him. Most of the meat went into jerky, which is long since gone. Some of it went into pork chops which I froze for special occasions. This seemed as special as any."

Windows appreciated the act of kindness.

Cindy asked, "What was his name?"

"Whose name?"

"The pig."

Denning grinned. "My wife named him. His name was Porky."

Cindy giggled. "Porky Pig?"

"I know. It's stupid."

Cindy lifted up her fork with a piece of pork on it. "Th-th-that's all, folks."

Cindy and Denning both laughed.

"At least we missed the rain today," Windows remarked after the two settled down.

"The crops could have used it, though." Denning frowned. "It's been a while."

"With all that thunder we heard from the north this afternoon, I'm surprised we didn't get a downpour."

"The funny thing was, there were no storm clouds in the sky." Denning shrugged. He stood up and began to collect the dishes.

Windows stopped him. "I'll take of those."

"No need for that."

"Yes, there is. It's the way my mother raised me. Whoever cooks, the other cleans."

"Well, your mother raised you right. At least let me help bring them to the sink."

While the adults gathered the dirty dishes and placed them in the sink, Cindy asked, "Can I go outside and play?"

"I don't know," said Windows. "It's already dark."

"I'll be okay."

"She should be safe as long as she stays near the house," said Denning.

Cindy clapped her hands and headed for the door. Denning called out after her, "Don't go off to see the chickens or Walther. Understand?"

"Yes." Cindy pushed through the kitchen door out into the backyard.

A few minutes passed before Windows said, "Thank you."

"For what?"

"For taking us in."

"It's the least I could do."

"No..." Windows picked up a dinner plate and rinsed it. "You didn't have to give us a place to stay. You didn't have to trust us. You didn't have to...to...."

"Treat you decently?"

Windows averted her gaze.

Denning reached out and placed a reassuring hand on her shoulder. "It's my pleasure. Besides, there was no way I could turn you two away. I would have to have been—"

"Windows!" Cindy yelled from outside. "Mr. Denning!"

Windows dropped the plate she held, shattering it into a

dozen pieces, and raced for the door. Denning followed, grabbing his Bushmaster on the way out. Windows ran up to Cindy and hugged her. "Are you okay?"

"I'm fine."

"Then why did you call us?"

Cindy pointed north. "The sky's glowing."

Windows and Denning looked in that direction. A yellowish-orange tinge spread across the horizon.

"Is that the sunset?" Windows asked hesitantly.

"No." Denning pointed to the west. "Sunset is in that direction."

"It's pretty," said Cindy. "I like the way it reflects off the clouds."

"Those aren't clouds, Cindy." Denning shook his head. "That's smoke."

"Smoke?"

"Something's on fire. And judging from the direction and distance, I'm guessing it's Montreal."

Windows felt a cold chill race down her spine. "Are we safe?"

"It should burn itself out long before it gets here."

Windows noticed that Denning did not sound as certain about his answer as he usually did on other matters. That chill down her spine made its way into her gut.

Denning forced a smile. Some of his certainty returned. "I think it's safe to say that what we heard this afternoon wasn't thunder." Wrapping an arm around Cindy's shoulder, he escorted the young girl back to the house. "Come on. You can help me clean the dishes."

The two went back inside. Windows stayed in the backyard a few moments longer, her gaze fixed on the conflagration in the far distance.

CHAPTER TWENTY-TWO

"**W**E SHOULD LEAVE tonight." They were the first words Tibor had spoken that evening.

It caught Dravko by surprise. "What are you talking about?"

From the top of the general store where he and Dravko kept guard, Tibor stared with contempt down on the rest of their party as they ate dinner. "Robson is the only one who knows what he's doing. DeWitt and Roberta are somewhat useful. The rest... they're going to get us all killed. If we run into rotters, these humans won't know how to defend themselves. Robson will die trying to save them and will expect us to go to the slaughter with him. He's putting everyone in danger for them."

"It's Robson's way," Dravko argued, although not convincingly. "He can't abandon anyone. He lost half his people fighting for us at Site R."

"These people are not our responsibility. We owe it to ourselves to save what's left of our own race."

What bothered Dravko most was that he agreed with Tibor. After defending Robson for the past few weeks, he could no longer condone this course of action. It seemed as if Robson compensated for failing to rescue Windows by helping everyone else. Dravko had agreed with the raid on Price's camp and the freeing of the hostages because they were going after one of their own. There was no rationalization Dravko could use to convince himself to go along with this folly any further. Robson's decisions were no longer made based on the needs of the group, but to satisfy the inner demons eating away at him. He had always thought of Robson as one of the few humans he liked and could rely on. Dravko could no longer allow sentimentality to cloud his judgment. He needed to do what was best for him and Tibor.

"What are you suggesting?"

Tibor shifted his position to face his Master. "That while we're on the road we go our separate way."

"You're no longer considering turning any of the survivors?"

Tibor shook his head. "That would put us in conflict with Robson. I don't want that. We owe him that much."

"What about Caslow? He rides with us."

"We'll take him to feed off of." Tibor chuckled. "The others have a better chance without that little *mudak*."

Dravko hesitated. Out of the corner of his eye, he saw the dissatisfaction on Tibor's face. He finally said, "Okay. We'll do it."

"Are you serious?"

"Yes, with one caveat. We wait until the right moment. Either we run into rotters and use that to cover our escape, or we find a place that's good for us and break away."

"Deal."

Dravko had not seen his friend this happy since before the outbreak. Not that he blamed him. Dravko himself felt a satisfaction he had not felt in months. He had followed his mistress' orders to join with the humans to survive and to keep the other vampires in line, even though it meant having to banish one of their own, Vladimir, from camp. With the camp destroyed, his mistress murdered, and most of their human allies dead, it was time to set out and rebuild the coven.

And hopefully to spread vampirism around the world again.

★ ★ ★

ROBSON FINISHED THE stale granola bar and washed it down with a mouthful of water, forcing himself to swallow. He spread out his roadmap on the asphalt. The others gathered in a circle, some standing, some crouching. Only Clint did not join them, instead leaning against the RAV-4 fender.

"Here's the plan for tonight. We're here." Robson pointed to the location on the map for Waits River, then dragged his finger northwest toward the Vermont-Canadian border. "This is where we're heading."

"Why there?" Linda asked.

"According to the map, there are a lot of ski resorts and bed and breakfasts in this region. I'm hoping we can find an isolated one to set up camp. With luck, we'll find one with a fireplace and wood stoves so we can keep warm. Once we get settled in, we'll make some supply runs, stockpile our resources, and sit tight for the winter. When spring arrives, we can start planting crops and building up our camp."

"It's a sound plan," said Ed, the former Marine. "I'm sure a lot of others had the same idea. What if we run into other camps?"

"We'll avoid anyone we run into and make sure we establish our own camp in an isolated area."

"What if they're friendly?" asked Corey, the teenager. "You're assuming that anyone we run into will be assholes like Price. There's a chance they may not be. Suppose they're like you, or that dude Simmons? I mean, if we find a camp that's already set up, wouldn't it be easier to join forces with them rather than start from nothing?"

"The kid makes a good point," DeWitt said. "You remember how long it took us to set up, and how difficult that first winter was. And we had a lot more people than we do now."

"It's not as simple as that," Robson said. "Joining another

group means we'll have to put ourselves under their control."

"What? Is the boss man afraid to give up some of his precious power?" chided Corey.

Gary chimed in. "We didn't give up Price to be under your rule."

"You didn't give up Price," snapped Roberta. "We saved you from him."

"So that gives you control over us?" Gary asked, squinting without his glasses.

"Leave them alone," snapped Yukiko. "I can understand him not wanting to trust others. I trusted Price when I first met him."

"What are the chances of that happening twice?" asked Magda, the German exchange student.

The group began to all talk at once until a deep, quiet voice said, "Cut the shit, people."

Everyone stopped talking and looked over at the RAV-4. Clint pushed himself off the SUV and strode over, stopping behind Caslow.

"None of us have to be here," Clint said slowly. "You could have gone off on your own, like the camp followers. Or you could have thrown your lot in with the others who stayed behind. You put your trust in this man, and now you're all second guessing every decision he makes. I got news for you. He's in charge, so you all do as he tells you or go your separate ways. For what it's worth, this man drove a thousand miles through zombie country to find the vaccine for this virus, took down Price and the other assholes holding us prisoner, and is now offering us a second chance. He's earned my trust, and that means he deserves my respect. Does anyone disagree?"

No one did.

Robson met the man's gaze. "Thanks."

"James."

"Excuse me?" Robson asked.

"My real name is James."

"Thanks, James."

James nodded once and walked back over to the SUV.

"That's it, then." Robson picked up the map and stood. "We'll leave in fifteen minutes."

The others sauntered off. Robson called over to Caslow. "Go on the roof and tell Dravko we'll be leaving soon, so we're ending the watch."

"Sure thing."

After Caslow ran off, Robson contemplated what had happened. Corey may be a pain in the ass, yet in this case he was correct. Their best chance of survival would be to find a like-minded group and team up with them, assuming anyone would be willing to take them in. Joining another group would also mean relinquishing power, which meant giving up control over their destinies. What good would it be to save these people from Price only to turn them over to someone like him? He was not sure if he could do that yet.

Folding the map, Robson placed it inside his jacket pocket and went to check on his vehicle.

CHAPTER TWENTY-THREE

ROBSON'S CONVOY SET out an hour after sundown. He took the lead, followed by Roberta in the RAV-4 and DeWitt in the Subaru. The vampires brought up the rear in their modified Humvee. They traveled until they reached Route 302 and headed west toward Barre and Montpelier. The plan was to race through Barre, pick up Route 14 in the center of town, and head north into resort country. As they entered the suburbs, Robson breathed a sigh of relief. The streets were wide open, with no signs of abandoned vehicles or rotters. This should be easy. He keyed the microphone button on his radio.

"We're almost at Route 14, so be prepared to turn."

"How far?" Roberta asked.

"Less than a mile on the right." Robson raised the map to glance at it. "There should be a park in the middle of the intersection with a statue on one end. That's where we—"

Linda yelled out, "Mike!"

He looked up in time to see the street blocked by a mass of vehicles parked in both lanes and on the sidewalks. He slammed on the brakes. The other vehicles in the convoy did the same.

"Is anything wrong?" Dravko asked from the rear Humvee.

"The road's blocked. Hang on a minute." Still holding the radio in his hand, Robson checked the map. The building off to his right bore a sign indicating it was the Vermont Historical Society, which meant the three-story brick building to his left must be the Health Department. "There's a street about a hundred feet behind us on the right that cuts through the neighborhood and will bring us out onto Route 14. Let's back up and go that way."

Dravko and DeWitt shifted into reverse and backed down the street a hundred feet to wait for the others.

WHEN THE ROAD behind was clear, Roberta shifted her RAV-4 into reverse. Initiating a three-point turn to the left, she accelerated too quickly. The RAV-4 bounced over the curb with a heavy jolt and rammed into a tree. The yellow tire pressure light on the console lit up.

"Shit."

Ed leaned forward from the back seat. "Don't tell me we've got a flat."

"Let me check." Opening the driver's door, Roberta slid out and examined the tire on the left side. "These seem okay. Gary, how's the other side?"

Gary opened the door and leaned out to check the back tire, then stood up and peered over the door to check on the front. "I don't see a flat."

"Good."

A single beep of a car horn caught her attention. Robson had pulled his Humvee alongside the sidewalk and had rolled down the window. "Are you okay?"

"I backed over the curb too hard. No problems, though. I'll be—"

Linda screamed at the same instant Roberta heard the moaning. A horde of rotters broke through the hedges surrounding the Health Department parking lot and swarmed the RAV-4. Roberta jumped back into the vehicle and slammed shut the door. Dead hands scratched at the rear window and scraped along the side of the SUV. She shifted into drive. Then she realized Gary still stood on the door landing.

"Get back in the car."

"Fuck that." Gary jumped out of the RAV-4 and ran across the lawn. He made it only a few feet before a rotter in blood-stained scrubs grabbed him by the neck and knocked him to the ground. Panic stricken and desperate, Gary struggled to his feet and tried to break free. He might have made it if two other rotters did not fall on him. One clutched his arm and bit into the wrist, the other clasped his head and took a chunk out of his neck. Gary collapsed to his knees and wailed as three more of the living dead fell on him, each pushing their way through to feed.

Roberta noticed none of this. Her concentration focused on the passenger door Gary had left open and the approaching rotters. Ed attempted to close it, but the front seats were in his way. Roberta climbed across the center console and reached for the handle. When she did, her foot came off the brake. The RAV-4 rolled forward until the front end collided with Robson's Humvee. Roberta used the brief reprieve to scramble across the passenger seat, grab the handle, and slam the door. A rotter in a Vermont State Trooper uniform had grabbed the jamb, and its fingers prevented her from shutting it tight. She held on as two more sets of dead hands pried their fingers between the door and the jamb and attempted to yank it open. Strewn out across the front seats, she had little leverage to hold them back.

"Ed, help me,"

ROBSON LEANED OUT the open window to assess the situation. The RAV-4 had drifted to its left when it rolled so that the front bumper had struck his left rear wheel, and the angle of its fender prevented Robson from opening his door. He could not get out and help Roberta and could not risk moving the Humvee without tearing up its tire.

A moaning caught his attention. Robson glanced to his

right to see a rotter in a nurse's uniform only a foot away lunging at him. Out of instinct, he raised his right arm to block it, and felt its mouth on the top of his hand. He shut his eyes and braced himself for the bite. It only scraped its teeth across the top of his hand. When Robson opened his eyes, he saw that the rotter had no lower jaw, only a gaping maw that dripped coagulated blood onto the white uniform. Robson drew back his hand, balled it into a fist, and punched the nurse rotter between the eyes. It staggered back, pushing away three others closing in. Robson rolled up the window.

Thankfully, Linda had sense enough to get on the radio and had already called for back-up.

"HELP US!" LINDA'S panicked voice blared over the radio. "We can't move and, rotters are swarming us."

DeWitt grabbed his weapon. Since none of the rotters were paying any attention to him or the vampires, he had a chance to take the pressure off the others. He opened the door to the Subaru and climbed out. Yukiko clutched his right arm and held him in place.

"Don't leave us."

"I'll only be a minute. You'll be safe."

Yukiko maintained her grip.

James reached between the seats, placing one his hands on Yukiko's wrist. "You have to let him go. I'll stay here and protect you."

"No!" she cried.

The more James tried to break her grip, the tighter she held on. DeWitt glanced ahead of him. Rotters surrounded Roberta's RAV-4 on three sides and had closed in around the front of Robson's Humvee. They were losing precious time.

"SCREW THIS." DRAVKO backed up their Humvee another

twenty feet.

"Are we leaving now?" asked Tibor.

"No." Dravko shifted into drive and accelerated. "We're saving their sorry asses."

Dravko steered the Humvee around DeWitt's Subaru and accelerated. When he reached the other two vehicles, he turned hard left. The right fender of his Humvee scraped the rear end of Robson's vehicle, doing only minor damage. It then swiped along the RAV-4, ripping away the rotters gathered along its right side, either crushing them between the two vehicles or flinging them out of the way. Dravko veered left again, continuing up the embankment to the Health Department parking lot and stopping. He repeatedly revved his engine to draw attention to himself. It worked. Half the rotters forgot about Roberta and moved toward the new sound.

"WHAT THE FUCK?" Ed asked.

Roberta saw Dravko's Humvee bearing down on her. She lowered her head and prepared for impact. Instead, he raced past, tearing away the rotters. She felt the pulling on the door stop. It opened for a moment as severed fingers and hands lost their grip and dropped to the ground. Roberta slammed the door tight and slid back into the driver's seat.

"Hang on."

Shifting into reverse, she depressed the gas pedal and spun the steering wheel hard to the left. The RAV-4 backed up the embankment, this time avoiding the tree behind her.

THE INSTANT ROBERTA moved her RAV-4 away from the Humvee, Robson accelerated and backed out of the area. He continued down to the next street, used it to initiate a three-point turn, and headed back along Route 302 in the direction they had come from. Roberta gunned it off the embankment and followed. DeWitt made a tight U-turn and fell into third place. Pulling off the embankment, Dravko headed for the side street, planning to use this opportunity to make their escape. At the last moment, he steered straight and followed the others.

Tibor stared at him. "Now would be a great time to make our break."

"What 'break'?" Caslow asked from the back seat.

"Shut up, human," Timor barked. "You're not changing your mind, are you?"

"No." Dravko glanced over at his friend. "Something tells me to stay with them a little while longer."

Tibor snorted. "Fear?"

Dravko ignored the taunt. "Instinct."

CHAPTER TWENTY-FOUR

Windows woke up from a restless sleep and glanced around the darkened bedroom. Cindy lay beside her, clutching a pillow tight against her face, and with the lion's share of the covers wrapped around her. The girl seemed at ease, lost in her dreams and breathing deep in what amounted to a child's version of a snore.

Something did not set right with Windows. It was not a sense of danger but of unease, as if bad karma had settled over the farm. Gently sliding out of bed so she did not disturb Cindy, Windows crossed over to the window. The yellowish-orange colors still painted the northern horizon, appearing more eerie in the full darkness of night. Denning stood in the front yard, a steaming mug of coffee in his hand, his gaze intent on the distant glow. Throwing on her sneakers and a bathrobe, Windows went downstairs, fixed herself a cup, and stepped outside to join Denning. She sipped from her mug, trying to appear as casual as possible.

Denning saw right through her. "You couldn't sleep either?"

"No."

"Worried about that?" Denning pointed to the horizon.

"I guess."

"I don't blame you. I've been watching it for close to two hours trying to determine where it is and what direction it's heading."

"Any luck?"

"I still think it's either Montreal or something in the suburbs."

"How long will it take to reach us?" Windows asked, not really wanting to know the answer.

"I doubt it will." Denning pointed to the trees their left. "The wind has been blowing from west to east, which will drive the flames perpendicular to us."

"That's good." Windows saw the concern in his eyes. "Isn't it?"

"It's good because we don't have to worry about it spreading to the farm."

"But...?"

"That fire is going to disturb whatever made its home around Montreal."

"Rotters?"

Denning shook his head. "Those things are as dumb as cow shit. They'll swarm into the flames thinking that's where the food is, which is good for us. I'm talking about the living."

"You mean packs of wild animals."

"I mean humans."

The implication dawned on Windows. She glanced up at the bedroom window, realizing that they might soon be in danger. "How long will it be before they show up here?"

"Don't go jumping the gun," Denning said, trying to sound reassuring. "We don't know if there are any other survivors in the area and, if there are, whether they'll even find us. To be on the safe side, carry your weapon and a sidearm with you at all times. I have some two-way radios in the house. I'll give you one so you can keep in touch. Don't let Cindy out of your sight until we know better what's going on."

"You can count on that." Windows felt her heart racing fast and her breathing grow rapid and shallow. After all she and Cindy had gone through, after all they had endured to find this sanctuary, only to face the possibility of it being violated by others like Price... she could not bring herself to think about it.

Rationally, she knew Denning was right. The odds were in their favor. Assuming groups of survivors were displaced by the fire, the chances of them coming across the farm and of being hostile were thin. However, the time she spent in the camp had taught her to consider the worst possible realities. How would the two of them defend themselves if a group of thugs like Price showed up at the farm and wanted to take it over?

An explosion to the rear startled Windows, until she realized it was only thunder. Gray clouds moved in from the south. A bolt of chain lightning lit up the sky as it arced to earth.

"Good," said Denning. "Maybe if it moves far enough north it'll put out the fire. Come on. Let's get inside before it starts raining."

"What'll we do if someone shows up at the front gate?" Windows asked.

Denning thought for a moment, then placed a hand on Windows' shoulder and led her back to the house. "We'll cross that bridge when we come to it."

CHAPTER TWENTY-FIVE

THE CONVOY HAD parked along the banks of the Thurman W. Dix Reservoir. This place presented a pleasant contrast to rotter-infested Barre. A peaceful quiet engulfed the reservoir, broken only by the chirping of crickets and the croaking of frogs. Robson sat inside his Humvee and used a flashlight to read the map he had spread out on the steering wheel. The others milled about, either chatting amongst themselves or wandering off to calm their nerves after the encounter a few hours earlier.

After escaping from the horde, Robson had given up on the idea of traveling through town because it was too risky. Instead, he backtracked a few miles and headed north until he reached the reservoir where he stopped to take a break and get his bearings. He studied the map, realizing the detour would not hurt them. They could still reach the resort area where he hoped to find a location to set up camp. They would have to do it from a different direction. In hindsight, he should have chosen this route when first planning the trip rather than risk going through a city, no matter how tiny it appeared on the map. That screw up had already cost one person his life, and almost got four others killed. Robson knew he had better get his head back in the game quickly.

"Are you okay?" Linda asked.

He had not heard her approach, so when she spoke it startled him.

"Sorry," she said, lowering her head.

"Don't apologize. I'm a little jumpy after what happened back there. How is everyone else doing?"

"Your people are fine." Linda leaned back against the open door. "Mine are still pretty shaken up, especially over Gary."

"I'm sorry about that..." Robson let his sentence fall off, not wanting to say what was on his mind.

"No one blames you. He panicked and ran, and almost got Roberta and Ed killed in the process. We've all experienced death before, although this is the first time any of us have run into a situation like that."

"You get used to it after a while."

"How many times have you gone through something like that?"

"More than I care to remember." Robson could not remember how many encounters he had survived with rotters, always being superstitious that if he kept count his luck would run out that much quicker.

"I guess we have a lot to look forward to," Linda said, trying to make it sound like a joke, but her voice sounded heavy with resignation.

"I wouldn't worry. We're heading north to where the population is thinner. We'll arrive tomorrow night. In two nights, three at most, we should have set up a new camp. After that, we won't have to worry about the dead."

"I hope you're right."

"Trust me."

"Okay." Linda glanced over at him and smiled. The smile morphed into terror. She moved away a few feet. "You've been bitten."

It took a moment for Robson to realize what Linda referred to. The top of his right hand had scratch marks from where the rotter with no lower jaw had tried to bite him. Two of the marks were bright red and oozing blood.

"He didn't bite me. See?" Robson held up his hand so Linda could see better.

She backed further away. "It doesn't matter. It broke the skin, so you're infected. You're going to turn."

"No, I'm not." Robson lowered his voice and tried to sound soothing. "Linda, I've been vaccinated with a strain of the Revenant Virus that makes me immune to infection. Remember?"

"I forgot." Linda halted. "I guess I'm jittery."

"Don't worry about it." Robson placed the folded map between the dashboard and windshield of his Humvee, and then stepped out. "Let's check on the others."

Dravko and DeWitt came forward to meet them.

"So," said DeWitt, "how far off of our planned route are we?"

"Not far at all. I was telling Linda that—"

Dravko held up his hand to cut off Robson. "Listen."

The area was silent.

"I don't hear anything," said Robson.

"Exactly. What happened to the crickets and frogs?"

Robson expected to find rotters converging on them. He listened for rustling in the woods and bushes to their right, or splashing from the reservoir to their left, some sound to indicate where the danger came from. Linda moved behind Robson for protection. DeWitt raised his weapon, scanning the area for a target.

"It can't be," Dravko muttered, his tone possessing an uncertainty unusual for the vampire.

"Can't be what?" Robson asked.

Dravko looked over at Tibor, who also sensed it. Tibor seemed excited rather than confused.

Robson was about to demand Dravko tell him what he sensed when something bolted out of the woods. At first, he thought it might be a swarmer, except it moved too quickly and did not snarl or moan.

The shadow raced by DeWitt. DeWitt convulsed once and his eyes widened. A gash formed across the man's neck that opened up, spilling blood down the front of his shirt. DeWitt dropped his weapon and fell to his knees, swaying in that position for a moment before collapsing face first onto the asphalt. Other shadows rushed out of the woods and took up positions behind the rest of his group. Before Robson could react, he heard Linda gasp. A pallid hand clasped her neck, the tips of its talon-like fingernails resting on her throat.

"Dear Satan," muttered Dravko. "It can't be."

"It is," Tibor said, a growing excitement in his voice.

A tall figure crossed the road and walked up to Dravko. He stood over six feet in height. His clothes fit poorly, hanging loose on his lean frame. What he lacked in physical appearance was more than compensated for by a poise displaying arrogant self-confidence. Several strands of blond hair fell across his long, angular face. The figure pushed the hair back behind his ears, revealing piercing blue eyes that mirrored a penchant for violence and cruelty. Robson immediately recognized him, and a chill raced down his spine.

The figure strode up to Dravko and stared at him with a cold, hateful glare. "I never thought I'd run into you again."

"Vladimir. Is it really you?"

"Yes. I survived, no thanks to you." Vladimir studied the others. "I see Elena still bids you to be the servant for the humans."

Dravko became defensive at the slight against his mistress. "Elena is dead. I'm master of the coven now."

Vladimir leaned in close to Dravko. "I'm master here."

When Dravko tried to protest, Vladimir cut him off with a menacing glare. He moved closer to Robson, a note of recognition in his dead eyes, and stepped up to him. "I don't know any of the others. I remember you."

Robson never saw Vladimir's hand swing at him. He experienced a brief moment of searing pain, and then everything went black.

CHAPTER TWENTY-SIX

CONSCIOUSNESS RETURNED SLOWLY to Robson. He opened his eyes. He could make out nothing of his surroundings. Everything was a blur, partially because of the dark, partially because he lay face down in dirt, and partially because of the throbbing in his left temple. When he attempted to lift himself up, the pain spiked, blacking out his vision. Robson moaned and dropped back down onto the dirt.

In the background, Linda said, "He's awake."

Roberta's voice cut through the dark. "Mike, are you okay?"

"I'm alive," Robson answered. He rolled onto his back. The pain throbbed again in his temple. This time he expected it. When he opened his eyes, he squinted against the sunlight filtering in through the gaps between the wood. A few moments passed before his vision adjusted. They were inside a barn. "Where are we?"

"An abandoned farmhouse less than a mile from the reservoir," said Roberta.

"I remember being attacked and Vladimir knocking me out. What happened next?"

"The vampires escorted us here and chained us up." She held up the chain for emphasis. The link ran five feet, with one end entwined around the wooden support beam of a horse stall and the other wrapped tightly around her ankle, both ends secured in place with padlocks.

"That's trusting of them." Robson rose to his feet. "Did

they really think we wouldn't try—"

The moment he stood on his right foot, a searing sensation burned its way from his ankle up through the leg muscles. Unable to support himself, he toppled onto the dirt and clasped his ankle in agony.

"After they chained us, they sliced through our Achilles tendons with their talons." Roberta sighed. "Even if we try to escape, we won't get far."

"They've got us trapped in here like cattle," said Linda.

"Blood cattle," added James.

Robson bent over and checked his ankle. Sure enough, someone had torn a gash two inches deep across his Achilles tendon. "How many did we lose last night?"

"Only DeWitt," Roberta answered.

"What about Dravko and Tibor?"

"Those motherfuckers joined the other bloodsuckers," Corey, chained up at the far end of the stalls, spat.

"Even Dravko?"

"Yes," Roberta said gently. "I'm sorry."

That disappointed Robson. Of all the vampires, he had trusted Dravko the most, and always thought the two of them could work out their differences. He could beat himself up later for being naïve. Right now, he had to figure out a way to save his people.

"How many vampires were there?"

"Nine," answered Roberta. "Not counting Dravko and Tibor."

"Nine that we saw," Ed chimed in from somewhere behind him.

"What about our weapons?"

Roberta shook her head. "The vampires made us leave everything by the reservoir. We have no idea where our vehicles and equipment are."

"What do we do now?" asked Caslow, his voice barely concealing his desperation.

Robson leaned back against the support beam he had been chained to. "We wait."

"Wait for *what?*" Roberta asked incredulously.

Yukiko lowered her head and cried. "I don't wait to die."

"Me neither," said Magda. "We need to do something."

"Do what?" James cut in. "We're outnumbered, we have no weapons, and we're in no shape to take on vampires."

"So, this is it?" asked Ed. "Game over?"

"If Vladimir wanted us dead, he would have killed us out there by the reservoir," Robson stated, hoping he sounded more confident than he felt. "The fact that he didn't means he wants us for something."

"Yeah," Caslow snorted. "He wants to feed off of us."

"It doesn't matter," said Robson. "As long as we're alive, we have a chance of figuring a way out of this."

CHAPTER TWENTY-SEVEN

THE COVEN HAD made its nest in the blacked out living room of the farmhouse, opting to reside in the same area for security and safety in numbers. Mattresses and sofas from the other rooms had been dragged in and pressed into corners or against walls. The only illumination came from a set of candles atop a coffee table in the center of the room. A love seat and three easy chairs surrounded the coffee table. They had secured the room well, painting the glass black in the three windows along the north wall, nailing boards across the frames, and draping heavy curtains over the interiors to block any sunlight. The sliding double doors, as well as the single swinging door to the kitchen, had also been closed, with heavy curtains stretching across their length and deadbolts inserted into the jambs. The coven was impervious to sunlight, and neither rotters nor humans were breaking in without waking them.

Most of the coven had wandered off to their respective corners and fallen asleep once the thrill of meeting new vampires had worn off. Four still remained awake: Dravko and Tibor, who each sat in an easy chair, plus Vladimir and a female vampire with long auburn hair who he had introduced as Gabrielle, who cuddled together on the love seat. Tibor and Vladimir chatted animatedly, mostly discussing the good times before the Vampire Council had initiated the outbreak that slaughtered billions of humans and nearly wiped out their own species. Gabrielle sat beside her Master and remained silent, rubbing his chest or running a hand along his thigh, playing the role assigned to her. Dravko kept to himself, not wanting to discuss certain uncomfortable subjects.

"So how did you survive being banished from the camp?" Tibor asked, bringing up one of the subjects Dravko had wanted to avoid.

"I almost didn't." Vladimir's tone lost none of its pleasantness. "I'll admit, I hovered around the camp for several days, plotting a way to sneak back in and murder Paul and Elena—especially Elena—for throwing me out like they did."

"Why didn't you?"

"Because I knew that would turn the humans against you. The rest of you would either have been killed or banished and, with nowhere to hide, you wouldn't have lasted long. I thought it was better to let the coven survive than to get revenge."

Tibor laughed. "How noble of you."

"It was always my best quality." Vladimir chuckled. He glanced over at Gabrielle. "Isn't that right?"

"Lord of the manor," she replied. Dravko noted she said it with more fear than affection.

"At first, I headed south, hoping to meet up with any survivors from the raiding party we had sent to shut down the nuclear reactor at Seabrook, but had no luck. I did find Gabrielle held up in an old diner in Hampton. She had been one of seven people who had set themselves up there shortly after the outbreak. Four had died in supply runs, one succumbed to pneumonia, and the last had committed suicide a month earlier. Gabrielle had been alone for weeks when I ran across her, and she begged me to make her one of us."

When Gabrielle lowered her eyes and bowed her head, Dravko assumed Vladimir was not relaying events precisely as they had happened.

"We headed north. I figured we'd be safer where there were fewer rotters. Any humans we came across were given a choice. Join the coven or be bled dry. You'd be surprised how many chose death over immortality."

"I wouldn't," said Tibor. "I lived among humans long enough to realize not everyone is strong enough to be immortal."

"Exactly." Vladimir shoved Gabrielle aside and leaned toward to Tibor. "That's why I gave the humans a choice, and why I only accepted into the coven those who asked to be immortal. Our bloodline has been diluted by bringing in those who were weak in mind and body. We've polluted our species to the point that our leaders thought releasing the Revenant Virus would be beneficial."

"Those assholes nearly killed us all," Tibor agreed.

"Which is why, when I decided to rebuild the coven, I swore I wouldn't make the same mistake. I wanted to ensure the purity of our species going into the future. Only those who asked to be immortal, and who I thought were worthy of it, were allowed to join." Vladimir pointed to the fireplace where a tall vampire in a leather greatcoat and blond crew cut, and who was in his mid-thirties, curled up by the hearth. "That's Miles. He was part of a biker gang holed up in a bar outside of Concord that had been overrun by rotters. I found him ten miles away after his bike spun out and tossed him in a ditch, breaking his leg and shattering several ribs. He begged me to turn him so he could get some payback on the rotters. Good thing I did. He's the toughest son of a bitch in the coven."

Vladimir motioned to the far end of the room where three other vampires slept, one propped up in the corner and the other two at his feet. They each were in their early twenties and wore street clothes. "Those three are Jonathon, Stamos, and Sean. I came across them in a Stop & Shop in Hanover. There were eighteen people hiding inside, and they had a fairly good set-up until I came along. The coven ate well that night. Me, Gabrielle, and Miles overpowered the guards and drained them, and then rounded up the others. We spent over a week feeding. Several of the survivors begged to join us."

"They were the ones who begged?" Tibor asked.

Vladimir shook his head. "No. The ones who begged were terrified for their lives. I would never have let them in. Those three were the last to die. I taunted them, telling them that if they wanted to be immortal all they had to do was ask. Jonathon said he would love to be immortal but would rather die than beg for it. The other two agreed. I liked their spunk, so I turned them. They've been loyal."

"What about her?" Tibor motioned toward a female spread out by the sliding doors.

"That's Mia. I found her collapsed by the side of a road, almost dead from hunger and dehydration. She wasn't even worth feeding from. She begged me not to let her die and promised eternal loyalty if I saved her. I did."

Vladimir looked to the opposite corner where a young brunette with bobbed hair wearing a knee-length skirt cuddled against a blond teenager in a flannel shirt and denim jacket. "He's Lewis, the only one sired against his will. When we attacked him in Barre, Lewis overpowered and staked one my vampires. There was no way I was going to kill someone who fought that tough, so while Miles and Stamos held him down, I turned him. His girlfriend Tamara begged me to do the same to her so they could be together, so I obliged."

"Wait a minute," Dravko interrupted. "You said Lewis killed one of your vampires?"

"Uh-huh."

"How big was your coven?"

"At one time it numbered fifteen," answered Vladimir. "Lewis killed one. Another was taken down by some humans we had captured who escaped. That's why I hobble them now. Three more died when the coven was swarmed by rotters in the White Mountains. And the last committed suicide."

"You're shitting me," said Tibor.

"She was a punk seventeen-year-old. I don't even remember her name. When the coven found her, she threatened us with an axe. I gave her a choice: die quickly or join us. She chose the latter. Two weeks later, she left the group in the middle of the day and walked out into the sunlight."

"First time I ever heard of that happening," said Tibor.

"It makes sense, though. Every time a master sired one of us, they would mentor us in how to be a vampire and would teach us what we needed to know. Now we turn a vampire and hope he or she survives the next few weeks. It's why I moved here." Vladimir sat back and gestured to the farmhouse around him. "The coven was losing vampires as fast as we could create them. I figured there were fewer rotters, so our chances of survival would be greater. A lot of humans thought the same way, so we've not gone hungry. I wish I could say the same for you. You two look terrible."

"Tell me something I don't know." Tibor gave Dravko a disapproving stare.

Vladimir settled into the love seat and drew Gabrielle close to him. Dravko noticed how comfortable Vladimir handled not only being in charge, but in being able to manipulate the situation. "What happened to the coven after I was expelled?"

Tibor spent the next hour relating what had transpired since that first incident between humans and vampires at the camp that resulted in Vladimir being banished, with the emphasis on the last month. Tibor detailed the journey down to Site R and how Sultanic had been bitten while trying to save Whitehouse from rotters. How Dr. Compton had wanted to exterminate the vampires inside Site R and released four hundred rotters on Robson's team when he refused to go along. How Tatyana's human boyfriend infected her with the virus, forcing Tibor to kill her. How they had gotten back from Site R only to find the camp destroyed by Price's gang and Elena and the others murdered. And the attack on the gang's compound. Vladimir said nothing, allowing Tibor to tell the story. Only when he was done did the Master speak.

"I mourn for Sultanic and Tatyana. It's a shame they died

because of humans."

"What about Elena?" Dravko asked.

"She got what she deserved." When Dravko tried to protest, Vladimir held up a hand to cut him off. "I don't mean to be disrespectful. She was the mistress of our coven, and I obeyed her. The fact remains, she never should have joined forces with the humans. I've proven we can survive on our own. When you lie with dogs you can't complain if you get fleas."

Tibor nodded his assent. Dravko remained silent.

"So let me get this straight," Vladimir said to Tibor. "When Compton developed the vaccine, it was only effective on humans?"

"Yes."

"Because he had used human blood to create the vaccine," added Dravko. "Our vampire blood is different, so the strain of Revenant Virus used in the vaccine would have infected us."

"Did he offer to create a vampire-effective vaccine?" The tone of Vladimir's voice indicated he already knew the answer.

Dravko lowered his head. "No."

"Fuck," Tibor chimed in. "The asshole wanted to use it on us and then, once we were infected, put us down."

"This is what I'm talking about." Vladimir slammed his palm down on the love seat's arm for emphasis. "The humans created a vaccine to help them survive the rotter apocalypse and engineered the vaccine so it's lethal to vampires. The humans are going to use this to enact genocide on us and blame it on the outbreak. We never should have trusted them."

"That's not true," Dravko protested. "Robson's people have been good to us."

"Wasn't it O'Bannon who sided with Compton and used the vaccine to infect Tatyana?" Vladimir asked with a melodramatic flair.

"Robson stopped him."

"No!" shouted Tibor. "*I* stopped him. Robson was too busy

trying to retrieve the vaccine."

Dravko shook his head. "Robson has treated us well."

"Has he?" Vladimir pushed Gabrielle aside again and leaned closer to Dravko. He spoke like a professor leading a student to realize something he knew already. "Has he ever allowed you to go after a meal like the hunters you are, or have you only been allowed to feed off animals or humans at their discretion?"

"We hunted members of the rape gang."

Vladimir raised an eyebrow. "With his permission or by instinct?"

Dravko said nothing.

"I thought so. Tell me, after leaving Site R, did Robson feed you regularly?"

"It was difficult. The blood supply at camp had been destroyed. And once he had decided on going after the gang—"

"Once Robson decided to go after the gang," Vladimir surmised, "saving his precious human was his top priority rather than making sure all the members of his team were fed. Tibor, didn't he make a run to a Walmart to get supplies for his people?"

"Yes," Tibor hissed the word like a snake.

"Did he offer to feed you? Did anyone volunteer to give you blood?"

"No."

Vladimir turned back to Dravko. "Robson may have treated you well, but he saw you as nothing more than pets, as attack dogs to be used when needed. Don't get me wrong. Most humans like their pets and treat them well. But they don't treat them the same as other humans."

"That's not fair," Dravko said halfheartedly, no longer sure if he believed it himself.

"It *is* fair because it's true. If you and Tibor were truly part of his group, he would have put your needs before those of humans he had never met. He didn't. Humans come first to him. He has shown that repeatedly."

Tibor's eyes were pleading for his friend to accept the truth. "I've been telling this to you for weeks. You know I'm right."

"No one is blaming you for any of this," said Vladimir. "Once Elena was dead, you did what was best for the coven under the circumstances. Now things have changed. It's not the two of you anymore. I've started a new coven. I'm growing the vampire population again. And this time we won't take second place."

"What do you mean?" asked Tibor.

"Releasing the Revenant Virus was a stupid move because it nearly wiped us out. It also nearly wiped out the humans. Both species are going to try and rebuild, except this time they don't have the numerical advantage they've had over us for the past two millennia. We finally have an opportunity to increase our numbers so vampires rival humans as the dominant species."

"If you don't count the rotters," said Dravko.

"They won't be around forever. At some point the humans will regroup, fight back, and take care of them for us. Once they do, they'll be in for a surprise."

"What about them?" Tibor used his head to gesture toward the barn. Dravko picked up on the fact that he didn't use Robson's name.

"They'll be given the same choice the others have. They can join us, or they can feed us."

"Do you think they will?" asked Tibor.

"From what you've told me, most of them will be happy to put an end to their suffering, one way or another."

"What about Robson?" Dravko asked. "Does he get to make the choice?"

Vladimir shook his head. "I have something special planned for him."

CHAPTER TWENTY-EIGHT

A RI STOOD IN the open hatch of the M1127 Stryker Reconnaissance Vehicle while the convoy made its way down Route 101. Doreen and half the squad sat comfortably inside, with Mesle and the others in one of the accompanying vehicles. Every time the Stryker swerved to avoid an abandoned vehicle, she reached out to steady herself on the mount of the M2 .50 caliber machinegun. It reminded her of standing in an open sunroof, only your typical car was not followed by three more Strykers and ten two-and-a-half-ton trucks loaded with troops.

The Battle of San Francisco had played out much easier than anyone had anticipated thanks to the use of the RCZs. Despite isolated incidents like Westwood Highlands, the ten-mile-long line of troops had reached the Bay by dusk, clearing the streets of rotters. This morning, they were redeployed across the peninsula in a line running southeast from Pacifica on the West Coast to north of Burlingame on the east. Intelligence indicated that most of the locals not trapped inside San Francisco had escaped south during the outbreak, leaving much of the peninsula abandoned, which meant fewer humans had remained behind to become the living dead. Since the eastern corridor would be pushing through cities, the government-in-exile had provided them with ten Abrams tanks, sixteen Strykers, fifteen M3 Bradley Fighting Vehicles, three mobile M270 Multiple Launch Rocket Systems, and fifty troop transports.

The initial push had run into minimal activity, with various units encountering nothing more significant than stray rotters. By the time the line had reached the southern outskirts of San Mateo, the Revenant Body Count had numbered less than two thousand, so command decided to take advantage of the lack of resistance. The mechanized units were divided into four groups, three recon units of four Strykers and ten transports each to travel south along the three major highways running down the peninsula, and the fourth group, which remained behind as a reserve. The ground troops would continue their block-by-block advance on foot. Mesle's squad had been assigned to Tango Alpha, the recon unit moving down Route 101, the easternmost of the three highways. They had been on the road for close to an hour and had run into no more than a hundred rotters.

Ari felt someone pull on her pants leg. Doreen stood beneath her and lowered the microphone of her CVC to her mouth. "How far do you think we've traveled?"

"We've covered thirty miles, give or take. We passed Moffett Airfield in Sunnyvale a few minutes ago. San Jose is about five miles ahead of us."

"Can the chatter," said Lieutenant Barnes, the commander for the Tango Alpha recce unit in the Stryker ahead of them. "Keep this line open for official communications."

Doreen waved and stepped back to her seat.

Ari scanned the area for rotter activity. The column passed through a residential neighborhood, with an AMC movie theater off to their left. She thought the number of rotters was increasing, although not by enough to pose any threat. A voice over the CVC headphones interrupted her thoughts. She recognized it as the commander of the Stryker scouting ahead of the column.

"Tango Leader, Tango Alpha Two."

"Tango Alpha Two, Tango Leader," responded Colonel Allen from his Bradley Battle Command Vehicle (BCV) back with the main column.

"Tango Leader, we have reached Objective Blue. We got slowed down by abandoned vehicles. Hostile activity is minimal."

"Tango Alpha Two, Tango Lead—"

"Jesus Christ!" The expletive came from Reynolds, the driver in the Stryker behind hers. "We have heavy hostile activity on our right."

Ari shifted her position in the hatch to get a better view. The column approached the northern end of Mineta San Jose International Airport, which sat a few hundred feet from the highway. Tens of thousands of rotters stretched the length of the runway. Those closest to the column clutched at the surrounding chain link fence, pulling at it to get to them. The commotion spread like a wave, and soon every one of the living dead inside the perimeter swarmed the fence. Rotters also approached from the neighborhood to their left and from farther down the highway. A quick estimation put their number in the thousands, all converging on the Strykers. They would be overrun within minutes.

"Tango Leader, Tango Alpha One," Barnes said into the CVC. "We have heavy contact with hostiles at our nine, twelve, and three o'clock positions."

"Tango Leader copies. Tango Alpha One, set up a defensive line to cover the withdrawal of your exposed troops."

"Tango Alpha One copies."

The Strykers ground to a halt in a line abreast across Route 101 with ten feet between each vehicle. The transports pulled into three-point turns and headed west. By now, the rotters had approached to within fifty feet of the recce unit. Ari wished she was on one of those retreating trucks.

"All Alphas, Tango Alpha One. Line up your shots and make them count. Fire on my command."

Rotating the machinegun to face forward, Ari lowered the weapon and aimed at the approaching horde, which had closed to within thirty feet. She lined up her site on a rotter with no arms draped in the remnants of a flight attendant's uniform.

Twenty feet.

"Fire!" Barnes ordered.

Four .50 caliber machineguns fired simultaneously in short, well-aimed bursts. Ari and the others had become so familiar with close-in contact with the living dead that no one paid attention to the stench or the swarms of insects hovering around them, concentrating instead on making each shot count. Each time the gunners pulled the trigger, they tore the rotters apart. Limbs were dismembered, torsos shredded, heads shattered. A pool of blood and body parts formed around the Strykers. However, the numbers were stacked against them. For each rotter taken down, dozens more filled the gap. The concentrated fire only slowed their advance.

Reynolds' voice came over the CVC again. "Tango Alpha One, Tango Alpha Three. Things are about to go FUBAR on our right."

Inside the airport, the mass of living dead pushed against the perimeter fence, their weight bending the supports at a forty-five-degree angle. The entire structure would soon give way, releasing a massive horde to join the melee.

"Tango Leader, Tango Alpha One. We have a situation developing inside the airport."

"Tango Alpha One, I'm already on it. We should have incoming rockets from Tango Charlie Five in a few minutes."

"Tango Alpha One copies."

Rotters had begun to outflank both ends of the line of Strykers. "Lieutenant, we're about to be swarmed."

"Copy that," said Barnes. "All Alphas, Tango Alpha One. Fall back three hundred feet. Stop at a ninety-degree angle to the right so the 7.62s can engage."

As instructed, the four Strykers pulled back and swerved so their right flanks faced the horde, allowing a soldier to open one of the hatches and arm the rear-mounted 7.62mm machinegun. A kill zone had formed, and the living dead surged forward into a storm of concentrated fire. The barrage took its toll on the rotters, churning them in a mist of blood and gore. A barrier of corpses formed in front of the horde, tripping many of those surging ahead and creating an obstacle for those behind. The advance slowed. The weight of the rotters to the rear pushed forward, and the barrier of human detritus could only hold them back for so long. It reminded Ari of the videos she had seen of the massive tsunamis that struck the Japanese coast years ago where retaining walls held back the water only so long before the tidal waves flooded over the tops and swept away coastal towns. It would be the same here, except this time it would be a tidal wave of living dead.

A whoosh off to her right caught Ari's attention. A dozen contrails from twelve rockets from Tango Charlie's M270 Multiple Launch Rocket System streamed from the northwest, each spaced three seconds apart and converging on the northern end of the airfield. When each rocket was at an altitude of twenty feet, it released its payload of six hundred and forty-four M77 submunitions, each about the size of a hand grenade, over a six-hundred-foot diameter area. The submunitions detonated on impact with the ground, fragmenting the grenade's steel casing and sending the shards ripping through everything within a twelve-foot radius. For half a minute, thousands of explosions burst from the perimeter fence down the runway toward the terminal.

When the smoke cleared, Ari saw a killing field. Every rotter, except those on the far edges of the horde, had been ravaged by the barrage, their bodies eviscerated and their legs torn out from under them. Where the wounds inflicted by the submunitions would have been fatal to the living, they succeeded only in immobilizing the rotters. The piles of bodies still pulsed as one organism, with torsos thrashing around and arms clutching at the air. Their moans of hunger could be heard even from this distance.

Barnes' voice came over the CVC. "Tango Leader, Tango Alpha One. We are running low on ammo. Where is my supply train?"

"Tango Alpha One, it's about three klicks behind you and on the way."

"Tango Leader, copy that."

The roar of battle diminished as the gunners' weapons ran low on ammunition and they slowed their rate of fire. The decrease in gunfire allowed the rotters to regain the momentum. An increasing number made it past the line of corpses and shambled toward the Strykers.

"I'm out," one of the gunners announced.

"Same here," said another a few seconds later.

One by one, the machineguns on each Stryker went silent. Fifty rotters had closed to within ninety feet of the recon vehicles, with another few hundred following. As the noise of battle faded, the only sound came from the idling of the four Stryker engines and the moaning of the living dead. They had slaughtered most of the horde, yet a few hundred still remained.

"We're screwed now," Reynolds said over the CVC.

"Tango Alpha One, maybe we can help," said a new voice over the radio.

"Who's 'we'?" Barnes asked.

"Tango Delta One."

From the north, five Bradleys bore down on the Strykers.

"Tango Delta One, we are glad to see you. Tango Alpha has expended its ammo."

"Then we arrived in the nick of time. You can't get much more American than that." The five Bradleys pulled up in a line abreast across Route 101 and stopped two hundred feet from the Strykers. "Tango Alpha, fall back behind our position."

Barnes did not need to pass on the message; the Strykers had already started to withdraw. Once the recon vehicles were out of the way, the five Bradleys opened fire, raking the horde with their 25mm 242 Bushmaster chainguns and chewing apart the line of living dead, decimating what remained of the horde. A cloud of blood and body parts formed, making it impossible for the Bradleys' gunners to clearly identify targets. They continued to fire, knowing they would hit something hidden behind the grotesque mist. Even over the heavy staccato of the chaingun motors, Ari could hear the thumping of 25mm shells impacting against bodies. By the time the chainguns went silent, only a few dozen rotters still stood. These staggered into the pile of gore, tripped, fell, and were not able to get back up. Ari almost felt bad for them.

"Tango Leader, Tango Delta One. Hostile activity neutralized."

"Tango Delta One, copy that. Set up a Forward Area Rearm Point at your location. Your supply train should be there any moment. The rest of Tango Alpha will join you within the hour."

"Tango Leader, Tango Delta One copies. All Alphas and Deltas, deploy and set up a watch in case any stray hostiles wander into the perimeter."

As the main hatches on the Strykers and Bradleys opened and the troops poured out, Ari looked around at the devastation. She had experienced some scary moments since the outbreak began, although nothing as intense as today. This was only the second day of the war. She wondered what other horrors were in store for her.

CHAPTER TWENTY-NINE

"**C**AN I PET Walther?" Cindy asked.

Windows continued purifying the bull's drinking water, hesitating in her response. Given what was going on up north, she wanted to keep Cindy close at all times. On the other hand, she did not want to hurt the girl's feelings or, even worse, alarm her.

For God's sake, Windows chastised herself. There is being cautious and there is being paranoid.

The situation had not changed dramatically in the last twenty-four hours. Sure, they could still see black smoke rising from whatever was burning. They had not had to fight off hordes of rotters or marauders yet, so Cindy would be safe. And Walther was milling around by the fence three hundred feet away.

"Go ahead," Windows said. "Just keep in my sight at all times."

Cindy dramatically sighed and spun around. She trudged away, huffing, "Yes, mother."

Mother? Windows could not hold back the tear that streamed down her cheek.

She went back to purifying the rainwater from last night's storm, adding a few drops of bleach into the barrel and stirring it before transferring the water into sealed containers to prevent the sunlight from turning it into a Petri dish of diseases. She had used the hand pump to transfer half the rainwater into the sealed tank when she heard a soft voice call out, "Help us."

Windows stopped what she was doing and looked for Cindy. The girl stood in front of the fence by Walther, standing on the middle slats and reaching over, with the bull lifting his head to be petted and swishing his tail. The call had not come from her.

"Please! Help us!"

Windows grabbed her AK-47 and stepped back from the fence to get a better view down the access road leading to the farm. A woman stumbled along the road, holding the hands of two children, a boy and a girl, approximately seven and ten, respectively, pulling them along behind her. Nine rotters pursued them, the closest less than a hundred feet distant. Windows raced along the perimeter fence to the pasture and removed the two-way radio from her pocket.

"Denning, are you there?"

A few seconds of silence elapsed.

"Denning, can you hear me?"

"Yes. What's the urgency?"

"We have a woman and two kids heading for the farm followed by a pack of rotters. They're coming down the access road."

"Shit. I'll be there in a few minutes."

Windows reached Cindy, whose gaze shifted between her and the approaching threat. Fear welled up in her eyes. "Are we going to help them?"

"I am. You're going back to the house."

"I want to help."

"Do as I tell you."

Windows waited until she saw Cindy heading away then focused back on the threat. The woman and kids were still several hundred feet from the compound, and the rotters were closing in. Windows ran to the perimeter fence. The little boy tripped and crashed onto the road, yanking the woman to a halt. The closest rotter, a male in a blue and red flannel shirt with half its neck torn open, moaned and quickened its pace.

The woman tried to drag the boy to his feet, but he would not move. Releasing the girl's hand, the woman told her to run. The girl refused, so the woman shoved her toward the farm.

"Run!"

The girl broke into a sprint and headed for Windows, wailing at the top of her lungs. The woman leaned over to protect the boy from the living dead.

Stopping at the fence, Windows unslung the automatic weapon from her right shoulder. She was not a good shot, but she had no choice. The rotter was twenty feet from the woman and boy, and she would never get to them in time. Resting her left elbow on the support post, she focused down the sight on its head and jerked the trigger. The bullet missed its target and thudded into the chest of a rotter in a fireman's uniform forty feet to the rear. Readjusting her aim, she slowly squeezed the trigger. This time the bullet hit the flannel-shirted rotter in the sternum, knocking it off balance. Windows aimed again, held her breath, and pulled the trigger. The rotter's head exploded. It teetered for a moment and fell forward, its carcass landing on the woman's back and sliding to the road. The woman screamed in terror and held the boy tighter.

Windows raced down to the gate and opened it. She ushered the little girl inside the compound and pointed to the farmhouse. "Head for that house. You'll be safe there."

"What about my mother and brother?"

"I'll get them."

Windows didn't bother to see if the girl obeyed. She rushed toward the woman and boy. "Come this way. Hurry!"

The woman did not respond, remaining hunched over the boy.

Windows reached her at the same time as a naked male rotter. She raised her automatic weapon into its face and fired, ducking as the exploding skull splattered her back and shoulders in chunks of brain and bone. Facing the rest of the horde, she lined up a shot on a rotter in a blue down jacket which had been torn open so that blood-encrusted feathers covered the front. Windows fired. The bullet thudded into its upper left chest, jerking its shoulder back. She aimed, fired carefully, and took the rotter down with a shot right between the eyes. Switching to the next nearest rotter, the abdomen and chest of which had been torn open leaving a gaping cavity, she brought it down with a headshot. The remainder of the horde was a good thirty feet away.

Windows reached down and grabbed the woman by the arm. The woman screamed and clutched the boy.

"I'm here to get you and your son to safety." When the woman still would not respond, Windows yanked her arm. "Come on. We have to get out of here."

The woman stared up at Windows, gradually registering the figure above her was human. Her gaze drifted to the left and she screamed again. A rotter in soiled fireman's gear approached, its arms outstretched and its mouth opening to feed. Windows surged forward, slammed the stock of the automatic weapon into its chest, and pushed it over backwards onto the ground. Lowering the barrel, she fired off three rounds into its head, vaporizing it. The bolt had locked in the open position. Windows did not have a spare magazine with her. The last four rotters moved in.

Windows crouched down and stared the woman in the face. "If you don't haul ass now, we're all dead, including your son."

The woman blinked once, and then understood. Grabbing the boy by the shoulders, she lifted him into a standing position and the two raced for the house. A female rotter in tattered red silk pajamas had closed to within ten feet, its single arm reaching for her. Windows raised her automatic weapon and waited, preparing to slam the stock into its face when it got close enough, concentrating on the forehead where she intended to strike. Suddenly, the forehead blew apart and the rotter dropped to the ground.

"I got this," Denning said from behind her.

Denning stood at the perimeter fence, his rifle against his shoulder. Ducking to be out of the line of fire, Windows dashed toward the fence, keeping herself between the woman and the rest of the horde. Denning continued shooting. By the time Windows she reached the fence, none of the living dead remained standing. When Denning met her at the gate, he was inhaling long, deep breaths.

"Are you okay?" she asked.

"Yeah," he panted. "I'm winded... from running... from the other end... of the compound." Denning held his chest and inhaled. After a few seconds, he pointed to her clothes. "You're covered in blood. Did one of them bite you?"

"No. It's backwash from shooting one of them too close." Windows patted Denning on the shoulder.

She stepped over to check on the woman and boy. Cindy stood on the other side of the perimeter fence talking to the little girl, who had calmed down considerably now that the crisis had passed. The two girls chatted like old friends.

"I thought I told you to go back to the house," Windows said sternly.

"I was heading there, and then I saw Rebecca running for the fence. I went back to help her."

The little girl waved at Windows. "I'm Rebecca."

Despite her motherly instincts telling her to be mad at Cindy, Windows admired her for showing such courage. "I'll let it slide this time."

Cindy tried not to grin.

"Are you a right?" Windows asked the woman. "Were you or your son bitten?"

She shook her head. "Th-thank you for saving us."

"No problem," said Windows.

"First things first," said Denning. "Let's get these people back to the farmhouse, clean them up, and feed them. Then we can chat."

CHAPTER THIRTY

DENNING SAT AT the end of the kitchen table while the woman and her two children devoured their meals. Between the three of them, they had eaten a dozen scrambled eggs and drank a gallon of water. No one had spoken much since the incident on the access road, the newcomers being too shaken to talk, and him and Windows agreeing to give them a chance to calm down. Cindy sat across from the little girl, studying her intently. Windows leaned against the sink. The only information Denning had gotten out of the woman was that her name was Miriam and her kids were Rebecca, age eleven, and Philip, age seven.

Fortunately, the kids' clothes were in good shape other than being slightly worn and dirty, nothing a good washing would not fix. The same could not be said of Miriam's outfit. By protecting Philip, her blouse and slacks had been splattered with blood, making them impossible to clean. Like with Windows, Denning lent Miriam a pair of jeans and a sweater from his wife's closet. The clothes fit her better than they had Windows. In fact, Miriam and her kids appeared to be in decent physical shape.

When their guests had finished eating, Windows collected the dishes and placed them in the sink. As she took Miriam's plate, the woman placed her right hand on top of Windows' wrist and squeezed. Her eyes shifted between Windows and Denning.

"Thank you both so much for taking us in."

Windows patted her hand and continued clearing the table. "No need to thank us."

"We're glad we could be of help," Denning said warmly.

"You have no idea how grateful I am. We wouldn't have lasted much longer. We'd been on the run for a full day."

"Cindy and I can relate. We were on the road for days before we came across this farm."

Miriam shook her head. "No, I mean *literally* we were on the run since yesterday morning. Those things were right behind us the whole time. We tried outrunning them and, when we stopped to rest, they'd catch up. Finally, we kept on walking, always trying to be a little faster. We haven't slept, we haven't rested, and we haven't even stopped to pee for over a day. We pissed our pants on the run if we had to go. I'd been dragging the kids along with me for the past few miles. If we hadn't come across...."

Miriam broke down in tears.

Windows stepped back over to the table. She placed her hands on the Miriam's shoulders and squeezed sympathetically. Miriam reached up and clasped the hands.

"Can you tell us what happened?" asked Denning.

Miriam nodded. She snorted back tears and ran the back of her hand across her nose and eyes. "We lived in the LaSalle neighborhood of Montreal north of the Saint Laurent River in a townhouse complex. When the outbreak occurred, most of the others fled the city. We stayed holed up in our townhouse because we had several months of food and water, and my husband Paul thought we could wait it out."

"Was he a survivalist?" Denning asked.

"No, just cautious. During that last Ebola scare he began storing food, canned goods, and medicine in the basement in case the virus reached Montreal and officials placed the city under lockdown. He wanted to be able to ride out a three-month crisis, so he bought a solar-powered generator and learned how to purify rainwater. When the outbreak reached

Montreal, he figured we'd be safer staying put. And he was right. Hundreds of thousands died trying to get out. While the city fell apart around us, we remained safe. We were even lucky enough that when the living dead took over, there were none in our neighborhood. We weren't doing too bad, at least compared to what we heard was going on elsewhere."

"What did you hear?"

"Paul had a ham radio. He kept in touch with others who had survived. They all compared notes. About a month ago, rumors started surfacing that the Canadian and American governments were getting ready to wage war on the rotters. Apparently, a vaccine was being prepared that would make people immune from a bite. We didn't put much stock in them until a few days ago when the Canadian army began pushing its way into northern Montreal. Paul and I were happy. We thought we'd be rescued. That didn't happen. As far as I can tell, one of the military units used flamethrowers against the living dead and set fire to one of the neighborhoods. Without a fire department to contain it, the flames spread through the city. We barely made it out and to the Mercer Bridge. That was yesterday morning, and we've been on the run ever since."

"I would have thought the rotters would be attracted to the flames," said Windows.

"Most were. Thousands of those things walked right into the fire. The problem was, any that saw survivors trying to escape went after them. At one point, we had fifteen people with us. A few broke off and went on their own, hoping the swarm would follow the larger group. Rotters took down the rest."

"What happened to your husband?" Denning asked.

Miriam lowered her head. "Early last night we stopped to rest. We were concentrating on the ones following us and didn't see the group approaching from out of a side street. They would have gotten all of us if Paul hadn't dived into them, sacrificing himself so we could escape. After that, fear and instinct kept me going, and the need to keep Rebecca and Philip alive. I got off the main road and came this way hoping to find a stream or something where I could lose those things. It's a miracle I found you."

"You did," said Windows, patting Miriam on the shoulders. "And you're safe now."

Miriam fought back her tears. "All I ask is that you let us stay here a few days to rest up, and then we'll be on our way."

Denning shook his head. "You and the kids are welcome to stay until the military gets this far south."

Miriam's face showed signs of hope. "Are you sure?"

"The only rule is that everyone pulls their weight, so you and the kids will have to help out with the chores."

"What type of... chores?" A note of apprehension seeped into Miriam's voice.

"They're not that bad," Windows reassured her.

"I'll teach you how to feed the chickens and Walther," Cindy said to Rebecca.

"Who's Walther?" the little girl asked.

"He's Mr. Denning's bull."

"Isn't that dangerous?" Miriam asked.

"Not at all," answered Cindy. She looked at Rebecca. "Walther loves it when you scratch behind his ears."

"Enough of that, girls," said Denning. "Right now, Rebecca needs her sleep."

Miriam sighed. "That sounds so good."

"You take my room tonight," said Windows. "I'll sleep on the sofa."

"I can't do that. We'll—"

"I insist. Tomorrow we'll work out better sleeping arrangements. Cindy, will you show our guests to their room?"

Cindy sprang from her chair. "I'd love to. Come on, Rebecca."

Windows waited until the others had reached the second floor before saying to Denning, "That was good of you, letting them stay."

"Well, I couldn't turn them away, could I?"

Windows stepped up to him, leaned forward, and gave him a quick kiss on the cheek.

"I am concerned about one thing," he said.

"What?"

"Miriam said t other survivors had fled Montreal, and revenants followed them."

"You're thinking there may be more heading this way?"

"Exactly."

"What do you want to do?"

Denning moved to the kitchen door to make sure no one else could hear, and then faced Windows. "We should take turns staying up at night to make sure no one or nothing shows up here without us knowing about it. You take the first shift until midnight, and I'll take over until dawn. Keep your radio with you at all times, even when you're sleeping."

"Sounds reasonable."

"Hopefully I'm being paranoid." Denning headed for upstairs. "I'm going to go take a nap. I'll spot you at midnight."

CHAPTER THIRTY-ONE

NATALIE FIDGETED WITH the M50 general purpose gas mask, adjusting it so the fit would be more comfortable, and sending the half dozen flies resting on the faceplate into flight. By doing so, she inadvertently moved her headphones, pushing off the one covering her right ear, and something flew into the canal. Natalie shook her head to dislodge it and dropped the headphone back before another insect took its place.

"Is everything okay?" Sergeant North, the leader of their twelve-man squad, asked over the headphone.

"Yes," she responded. She gestured toward the gas mask. "I'm not used to wearing one of these things."

"You never will be. It's better than the alternative."

"That's for damn sure."

Natalie had thought the most disgusting thing she would endure during the rotter apocalypse would be the drive through San Francisco in the Abrams, crushing tens of thousands of the living dead and wallowing in their stench and gore. This was far worse, because at least then she was inside a steel fortress that isolated her from the majority of the sights and smells. When she had signed up as part of the security detail for the clean-up crew policing San Francisco International Airport, she assumed she would walk the perimeter and provide fire support for any stray rotters that had survived the firebombing. She had no idea what special hell she had volunteered for.

The liquid-gel air-fueled explosive dropped yesterday afternoon had incinerated the estimated eighty-three thousand revenants in and around the airport and its runways. Except for a few hundred of the living dead inside the terminal been protected by the blast, all the others had their skin and muscles either seared off or burned to the point the bodies could not move, leaving behind piles of charred skeletons. The runways around the airport had been turned into a killing field littered with bodies that stank like barbecued decayed meat. The security detail stood on the outer fringes. The gas masks and headphones had been provided to the crews not to prevent infection, but for their comfort.

Natalie ignored the scorched sea of living dead stretching around her and concentrated on the construction equipment that went about the mundane task of clearing the runway. The clean-up crew had been following the same routine since half a dozen Chinooks had airlifted in four front loaders and two dump trucks after dawn. The front loaders scraped up bones and ash and placed them into the bed of one of the dump trucks. When full, the truck would drive to the southeast end of one of the runways and unload the remains onto a barge moored on shore. Here, a second crew distributed the debris until the barge was full, covered the mound with a tarpaulin, and towed it to a tugboat anchored four hundred feet offshore. An empty barge would take its place and the process would continue. Once the airport was cleared, the barges would be towed to the commercial docks where they would be loaded into a derelict supertanker that would be taken out fifty miles and sunk. Natalie knew similar operations were proceeding in the other RCZs. Working this way over the past eight hours, the clean-up crews had managed to clear a thousand-foot section of the twin runways they had been working on.

The seventh barge had pulled away from shore when Natalie heard a helicopter approaching from the north, a Sikorsky UH-60 making its way across the bay and heading for the cleared section. It swung around and came in from the southeast, setting down between the shore and the construction equipment. The backwash from the propellers blew a cloud of ash down the runway. By the time the engine had shut down and the blades slowed to a stop, the crews had gathered around the UH-60.

A tall Asian man in a well-starched ACU stepped out of the rear compartment. He wore the eagles of a colonel and had the name NAKAJIMA embroidered in the nameplate on his chest. He did not wear a gas mask. If the stench bothered him, he never showed it.

"Who's in charge of this detail?"

"That would be me," the man to Natalie's right mumbled through his gas mask.

"What's the revenant situation like here? Can you spare your security team?"

"For the rest of the day?"

"Permanently."

"I guess so," the clean-up supervisor hesitated. "There are a few hundred revenants held up inside the terminal, but we've seen nothing out here in hours. What's up?"

"We've run into heavier than expected revenant activity near San Jose. Secretary Fogel wants to send in reinforcements."

"Are we in danger of being swarmed?" someone asked off to the right.

"The Apaches and the napalm are keeping them at bay. However, there are so many the going has been slower than anticipated and the troops on the line are getting tired. We're looking for relief who can spot those on the front and get the advance moving again. The secretary is pulling troops from those sectors in San Francisco where revenant activity is light and shifting them south."

"I can spare my security team," said the clean-up supervisor.

"Thanks." Nakajima nodded. "Don't take any chances. If you see revenants, abandon your equipment, take a barge over to the tug, and call for backup."

"Yes, sir."

"Your relief chopper should be here in about an hour." Nakajima climbed back into the UH-60. "What are you waiting for? We're heading for the fighting. Come on."

Natalie and the others climbed on board. Five minutes later, the Sikorsky was airborne and heading south for San Jose.

CHAPTER THIRTY-TWO

ROBSON TRIED TO sleep and save his energy for what he knew would be a difficult night, which was easier said than done. He had meant it earlier when he had told the others Vladimir wanted them alive or he would have killed them at the reservoir. What he failed to mention was he had no idea what Vladimir intended for them, although he knew it could not be good. Nor did Robson mean it when he told the others that so long as they lived, they had a chance of getting out of this situation. He knew his group could never overpower eleven vampires and escape, especially in their condition. The only ace in the hole he could count on was Dravko.

Shortly after nightfall, activity inside the barn woke Robson from his slumber. He heard the others chatting amongst themselves, as well as the sound of footsteps approaching from outside. Pushing up into a sitting position, Robson leaned against the roof support he had been chained to and brushed himself off, wanting to display as much confidence as he could under the circumstances.

The footsteps stopped by the barn doors. Chains rattled and the doors swung open. Vladimir led the coven inside. Except for the master, each vampire held a kerosene lamp. They spread out and formed a circle among their captives, the light from the lamps illuminating the interior. Vladimir grabbed an old wooden chair that sat inside the barn and carried it over to Robson, placing it so the rear faced him. Vladimir straddled it and rested his arms on top of the back rest.

"Do you remember me, human?"

"You're Vladimir. You used to be part of Elena's coven."

"Until you banished me."

"Banishing you was Elena's decision. I only enforced it."

"Fair enough." Vladimir nodded. "Still, you both threw me out to certain death."

Robson motioned toward the rest of the coven. "You haven't done too badly for yourself."

"Because I was exiled while I still retained my vampire instincts, while I still lusted for the hunt and remembered my superiority over humans. I built this coven so it's strong. Elena turned hers into a pack of tamed dogs for you and Paul. Look what she did to them." Vladimir motioned with his head toward Dravko. "He's nothing more than a puppy that follows you everywhere. Tibor is the only one who still has *strigoi* blood running through his veins, and you keep him on a tight leash."

Robson leaned to one side to see the two vampires from his group. Tibor glared at him with the same disapproving sneer he had come to know all too well. Dravko lowered his head and refused to make eye contact. He seemed emotionally beaten down. Robson ruled out being able to rely on Dravko as his ace in the hole. He directed his attention back to Vladimir.

"If you want to take revenge on me for banishing you, go ahead. None of these people were involved, so let them go."

"First, anything I do to you is not revenge, it's justice." Vladimir stood and spun around so the others could see him. "As for the rest of you, I cannot let you go. However, you do have a choice. You can join the coven as one of my progenies or we can feed off you."

"It's not going to work," Robson said. "None of us—"

Linda hobbled to her feet and stood on her one good ankle. "I want to join your coven."

Vladimir stepped over to Linda. "Why do you want to be one of us?"

She met the vampire's gaze, her eyes burning with anger and passion. "Ever since this outbreak began, I've been raped, beaten, and taken advantage of. I've had enough. I've seen how strong and confident Tibor is, and how he's not afraid to take on half a dozen walkers at once. I'm tired of being scared and vulnerable. Make me one of you."

Vladimir clasped her hands. "You realize that if I sire you, you are beholden to me as the leader of this coven and must give me your loyalty."

"I've been forced to obey someone else for the past year. This is the first time I get to do it of my own free will."

"You can't be serious," said Robson.

Linda glared at him. "Don't you dare try and stop me. This is not personal. You've been good to me, but I'm tired of being at everyone else's mercy. It's time people fear and respect *me*."

Vladimir flashed Robson a snide look, knowing full well he had won.

"I'm ready," said Linda.

"So be it. This will hurt only for a moment, and then you'll drift off into death. When you wake up tomorrow night, you'll be one of us." Vladimir positioned himself in front of Linda and placed his hands on her upper arms. "Close your eyes."

When she did, Vladimir morphed into his vampiric form, leaned forward, and plunged his fangs into her neck. Linda's body tensed and she yelped when he pierced her skin. After a few seconds, she relaxed as Vladimir drank from her artery, draining away her life blood. Linda's face showed an erotic pleasure. Her expression changed to one of inner peace, and soon became vacant as the last vestiges of life slipped away. She slumped forward into Vladimir's arms. He wrapped his right hand around her waist and held her up. Removing his mouth from her neck, Vladimir bit his left wrist. Blood flowed from the wound. He placed the wrist over Linda's mouth.

"Drink."

Linda slurped with hardly any effort.

"You have to take as much of my blood as you can. That's the only way you'll become one of us."

Linda pressed her mouth down on his wrist and sucked. Blood pooled around her lips and ran down her chin. She drank for several seconds before slumping forward, dead. Vladimir lowered her to the floor and gently placed her head onto the dirt, then stood and pointed to Tibor.

"Take her back to the house and put her in the upstairs bedroom with the blacked-out windows. No one will disturb her during the transformation."

"My pleasure." Tibor placed his kerosene lamp on the dirt and came forward, scooped up Linda's body in his arms, and exited.

When Tibor had left, Vladimir walked around the barn, making eye contact with each of the humans. "You see how easy it is? A few brief moments of pain, and you drift off into immortality. When you wake up, you'll have nothing to fear, from either the living dead or other humans. Think about it. I'll be back tomorrow night to see if anyone else wants to join us."

Vladimir walked out, followed by the rest of his coven. None of them bothered to look at the humans, not even Dravko. Once outside, they closed and chained the doors, leaving their captives alone in the barn with nothing but Tibor's kerosene lamp.

The lamp cast only a meager amount of light through the barn, leaving most of the interior in shadows, which was okay with Robson. He bowed his head and stared at the dirt, grateful no one glanced in his direction or bothered him. Vladimir had made a fool out of him. Robson had hoped that by presenting a united front they might be able to bargain their way out. Those hopes were dashed when Linda joined the coven. He felt certain some of the others would, too. Everyone who did would weaken the resolve of the others. His leadership over those whom his people had rescued from Price's camp had been tenuous to begin with, now it had become untenable.

After fighting off thousands of rotters over the past year, he found it ironic that he would lose to an overconfident vampire who had once been part of the group.

Resting his head back against the support beam, Robson closed his eyes and forced himself to sleep. Anything would be better than waiting for the next humiliation.

CHAPTER THIRTY-THREE

A RI SAT ON the open rear hatch of the Stryker with a bottle of water and a sand-colored MRE. MEAL, READY TO EAT was printed across the front. The military personnel in her unit always laughed at that, joking that none of those words were an accurate description. Ari disagreed, although she never admitted it. She thought the MREs were good, especially after what she had been eating the past month. This one contained spaghetti and meatballs, one of her favorites, even if she ate it for breakfast. Ripping open the top, she emptied out the contents, picked up the Flameless Ration Heater, slipped the entrée packet inside, added water, and closed the top. She leaned it at an angle against the hatchway and checked her watch. It would take twelve minutes for the chemical reaction inside the heater to warm her spaghetti. In the meantime, she opened the packs with crackers and peanut butter and snacked on those, gazing out on the row of Jersey barriers blocking the street two hundred feet in front of the line of recon vehicles.

On the other side of the barrier, a few score of rotters clawed at the cement, frantically trying to get to the humans.

When the rest of Tango Alpha had reached the Forward Area Rearm Point across from Mineta San Jose International Airport yesterday afternoon, they had established a defensive perimeter on Route 101. In a bit of good fortune, one of the squads had discovered a number of Jersey barriers stored on one of the side streets for use by the local police to control the flow of traffic escaping from San Francisco and never put into play. These were used to barricade the highway and some of the adjacent roads. Barnes had ordered his men to make noise to attract the living dead, flushing out any from the surrounding neighborhoods so the troops could keep an eye on them. Not that many made it to the barricade. Apaches had spent the afternoon sweeping back and forth across San Jose. If they found any large concentrations of rotters, the pilots called in a rocket strike from the M270s or handled it themselves. The position of groups was radioed to the local ground commanders who gathered together all available information to piece together an intelligence assessment for the next stage of the operation.

Doreen stepped over to the Stryker, an MRE clutched in her hand. "Mind if I join you?"

"Sure, if you don't mind the view."

Doreen sat on the ground beside Ari. "A month ago, that might have freaked me out. Since Site R...."

"I know. After what we've gone through, having those things leer at us while we eat is nothing."

Doreen leaned over toward Ari's MRE. "Smells good. Wanna trade?"

"What do you have?"

"Vegetarian chili with beans."

Ari shook her head.

"Damn." Doreen ripped open her packet. "Can't blame me for trying."

"Any idea what time we're kicking off?"

"According to Mesle, we're not moving out until tomorrow. Headquarters doesn't want a repeat of yesterday. They'll spend most of today conducting air recon of San Jose and the surrounding cities so we'll know what to expect. In the meantime, San Francisco is sending down reinforcements and supplies."

"No arguments here. I could use a day of R&R." A chorus of moans emanated from the Jersey barriers. "Well, a day of rest at least."

Doreen dropped the packet of vegetarian chili into the heater and added water. "Do you think the world will ever go back to normal?"

"Normal as we knew it, no," Ari replied. "I do think we'll see a time when there are no rotters."

"Really?"

"Yeah."

"What do you think things will be like then?" Doreen zipped the heater and laid it at an angle against the rear wheel. "I'm assuming the world will be a better place. We've all had to pull together to fight the rotters. Don't you think we'll be more unified once this is all over?"

Ari grew sullen. "I doubt it."

"Why?"

Ari opened the heater pack, removed the MRE, and ripped open the seal. "We're still in the middle of the apocalypse and there are those who are out only for themselves. Compton. O'Bannon. That gang in New Hampshire. The Deaders. Human nature will never change. Those things out there are more reliable than us."

Doreen turned toward the rotters behind the barricades. "Them?"

"They won't betray you, or rape you, or take advantage of you. All they want to do is eat you. We know where we stand with them. I can't say that for everyone else we've encountered."

Doreen appeared as if she had the enthusiasm sucked out of her, which she had. Ari regretted speaking her mind. Too late now. She reached into the MRE with the plastic fork, dug out a chunk of spaghetti, and stuck it into her mouth. She chewed and swallowed, forcing herself to do so. Her appetite had suddenly vanished. Holding out the MRE to Doreen, she waved it in front of her friend.

"Do you want this?"

Doreen shook her head. "It's yours."

"I'm not hungry."

"If you're sure." Doreen grabbed the packet and began eating.

Ari marveled at how the simplest things now brought such pleasure in the new dead world.

The two women ate breakfast and chatted. Neither was aware of Mesle's approach until they heard him say, "I have someone here who wants to join the squad. Is there any room?"

"Sure. We always have room for fresh meat to feed—" Ari glanced up to greet the new recruit. Her heart soared when she saw Natalie standing there. "Oh my God!"

Natalie grinned. "I'm glad you think I'm still fresh. I was feeling old."

Ari jumped up and wrapped her arms around Natalie, holding her as tight as possible and not letting go.

When the hug became awkward, Natalie reached up and patted Ari on the back. "It's good to see you, too."

Ari hugged tighter for an extra second, then broke the embrace and stepped back. "Sorry. I... we weren't sure if we'd ever see you again."

"Well, I'm back."

"Thank God." Ari nodded in the direction of San Jose. "You ain't seen nothing yet."

"Don't be so sure," said Mesle. "Your friend has seen some shit that makes what we went through seem tame. Christ knows we can use someone like her."

"You're really joining our squad?" Ari asked.

Natalie nodded.

"She requested to join us, and Headquarters granted it." Mesle patted Natalie on the shoulder. "Get her settled in and brief her up. And get some rest. Word is we're taking San Jose tomorrow."

CHAPTER THIRTY-FOUR

THE ALARM WOKE Windows at 5:30 AM. She crawled out of bed and opened the window to check the perimeter. It was still dark, so she was unable to see anything. Listening for a few moments, she heard nothing other than crickets and an owl hooting in the distant woods. Closing the pane, Windows got dressed, checked on Cindy and the others, and went downstairs. None of the lights were on. She stepped into the kitchen and flicked on the switch.

A knocking on the living room window caught her attention. Denning sat on the front porch, gazing in at her. He swung his horizontal hand back and forth across his neck. Windows understood. She flicked off the light, crossed the living room, and opened the front door.

"What's going—?"

Denning raised two fingers to his lips, then used them to motion Windows to the wooden chair beside him. When she sat down, he leaned closer and whispered.

"There's several rotters along the perimeter fence down by Walther's pen."

"How many?"

"Five or six as of two hours ago. I thought I heard moaning about two in the morning, so I made a sweep of the perimeter. That's when I found three of them. I went back at four and there were a few more."

"Do they know we're here?"

Denning shook his head, although Windows could barely

see it in the dark.

"Any idea where they came from?"

"I'm assuming Montreal, like Miriam and the kids."

"That means there'll be more," Windows said, louder than she meant to.

Denning placed his fingers against his lips again. "We'll have to prepare for that."

"How?"

"I didn't want to be out there alone with them in case there were more. I figured we can go take care of them at dawn."

WINDOWS HAD WOKEN Cindy and the others right before sunrise and warned them about what she and Denning intended to do. After ordering them to stay together in one of the upstairs bedrooms facing the southern side of the house, she joined Denning in the kitchen. He sat at the table sipping a cup of coffee. A machete and a hunting knife had been laid out on the counter.

"Are you ready?" he asked.

"Not really."

"At least you're honest." Denning put down his mug, pushed out of the chair, and stepped over to the counter. He picked up both edged weapons and extended them to Windows. "Which do you prefer?"

She took the hunting knife and slid the sheath between her right hip and jeans. Denning ran his belt through the top loop of the scabbard and tied the bottom string around his leg. He picked up the mug, took several large gulps of coffee, and grabbed his weapon.

"Let's get this over with."

Exiting the back door, the two stepped to the west end of the house and peered around the corner. The sun had not yet crested the tree line. However, they had enough light to see to the end of Walther's pen. Five rotters were bunched around the outer fence, their attention focused on the bull as he paced the pasture, oblivious to the living dead nearby. When he trudged to one end, the rotters followed. When he came back, so did they. It was almost comical to watch.

"When Walther walks away from us, we'll go after those things," Denning whispered. "They're distracted, so hopefully we can sneak up on them and take down a few before the others know we're there."

"Why not shoot them?"

"If there are more on the road, the noise will attract them."

Windows frowned. "Makes sense."

They waited until Walther had reached the southern end of the pasture and turned north. The rotters shambled after him. Denning and Windows darted across the open space between the house and the perimeter fence. They crouched, ran to the gate, and passed through to the other side. After resting a moment for Denning to catch his breath, they moved at a walking pace along the fence so as not to make noise.

When they approached to within a few feet of the pack, Denning ran up behind a rotter in mechanic's overalls and swung the machete down. The blade fractured the skull and carved into its brain. The rotter convulsed for a few seconds before going limp, still held upright due to the machete imbedded in its head. Denning twisted the blade from side to side, freeing it. The rotter dropped to the dirt with a thud.

Meanwhile, Windows had circled around to the next rotter in line, a female with long blonde hair that had become disgusting with filth and gore. Windows clutched its hair with her left hand and held the head steady, and with the right jabbed the hunting knife under the base of the skull. It snarled. Windows twisted the blade in a circle, scrambling its brains. The rotter slid off the blade and fell forward.

The commotion had attracted the attention of the remaining pack. The closest had been a cop and still wore a riot control helmet.

"Duck," warned Denning. After Windows crouched down, he stepped forward, brandishing the machete like a baseball bat, and swung. The blade sliced through the rotter's neck, partially severing the spine. It toppled over onto the ground, unable to move, the head still attached by a clump of skin and muscle, biting at Denning's feet.

The fourth rotter, dressed in a white lab coat stained dark brown with dried blood, lunged at Windows where she crouched. She held up the knife in front of her and stood. The blade punctured the soft skin underneath the rotter's jaw and continued up, cutting through the roof of its mouth and into the brain. Its mouth gaped open and it spasmed once before going limp. Windows pulled out the knife and jumped back to avoid being hit by the body as it fell to the dirt.

Denning took care of the final one. Moving in a circle around Windows, he got its attention. It maintained eye contact with him. Once the rotter had positioned itself with its back to the fence, Denning rushed forward and shoved it against the wooden slats, momentarily disorienting it. Lifting the machete, he brought it down hard, cleaving its face from the base of its nose to the top of its head. This time he had imbedded the blade so deep he could not remove it.

"Need help?" Windows asked.

"Please."

Windows placed her hand on its shoulders and ducked her head so her face would not be splattered. Denning twisted and yanked for several seconds before the machete finally pulled free with a sickening suction noise. The rotter slid along the side of the fence and onto the ground.

"We should bury the bodies before we let the others out," Windows suggested.

"Good idea. First, I want to check the access road leading in here and make sure there aren't any more of these things roaming around. I don't want us to be surprised while making our rounds."

The two headed for the access road, all the while scanning the area for any living dead that might be lurking in the woods. Windows felt, although she could not put a finger on it. Then it dawned on her. The background noise came not from birds and insects, but from rotters. It was the incessant shuffling and moaning of the living dead, though she had no idea where it came from. Only when they rounded the bend and came within sight of the main road two hundred feet away did she understand.

"Get down." Denning took Windows' arm and pulled her into the trees where they melded into the shadows.

A steady stream of the living dead headed south. Windows counted on average twenty every minute. They did not seem agitated. Occasionally, one would glance down the access road, neither acknowledging it nor moving in its direction. It seemed like they were on a road trip, which might have amused her if this exodus was not taking place less than a mile from their compound.

"What's going on?" she whispered. "Are they running from something?"

"Those things don't run *from* anything. They're chasing after survivors from Montreal."

"Why so many?"

"It's a pack mentality. One sees food and goes after it, and the rest follow. Like lemmings going over a cliff. They could be following someone who passed by here days ago."

The thought dawned on Windows that if these rotters had been around when Miriam and the kids had found the barn, they would have led this horde right to them.

"What do we do now?"

"There's nothing we *can* do. Hopefully, the gate across the road will prevent any of them from wandering down here, though that won't help if any come through the woods. Until these things pass by, we need to be as quiet as possible. We'll keep the kids indoors to be safe. And we'll continue standing guard at night."

"Maybe we can get Miriam to help with that."

"Maybe, though I'm not sure if she's up to it." Denning moved deeper into the woods and headed back to the farm. "Let's get out of here before one of those things sees us."

Windows followed, trying to blot from her mind the images of the rotter-filled road.

CHAPTER THIRTY-FIVE

"**M**IKE, WAKE UP."
Robson heard Roberta's voice, though he pretended to be asleep, hoping she would go away. He did not want to talk to anyone.

"Come on, Mike. I know you can hear me."

Leave me alone, he thought.

"We have to talk about last night."

"What's to talk about?" Robson asked without opening his eyes. "Linda threw us all under the bus. The vampires now have the advantage."

"Only if we let them," James said. "That's why we need to plan how we're going to handle the situation when they come back tonight."

"There's only one way we can handle the situation." Robson opened his eyes and sat up, resting his back against the barn's center support. "We have to stand together and refuse to join their ranks."

"Do you think that'll keep us alive?" Caslow asked.

Robson shook his head. "Not permanently."

"Then why bother?"

Robson stretched and rubbed the sleep out of his eyes. "If the vampires think we're vulnerable, they'll divide us. They'll pick off the weak, and those of us who are left won't have the numbers to resist. Our only chance of making it out of this situation is to unite against them."

"Maybe we'll have a better chance if we join them," suggested Caslow.

"Do you really want to become one of the undead?"

Caslow hesitated. "It's…it's better than being dead, isn't it?"

"No," said James.

"If we do stick together," Yukiko said, "do you think they'll spare us?"

"No. But it might buy us some time so I can talk to Dravko."

"The bloodsucker who's supposedly your friend?" Cory laughed derisively. "That means we're all screwed."

"Dravko isn't like Vladimir or Tibor. He still has a touch of humanity in him. If anyone helps us escape, it'll be him."

"What if he doesn't?" Magda asked.

"Then we're all going to have some tough choices to make.

CHAPTER THIRTY-SIX

CASSANDRA STOOD AT the glass door leading to the balcony, holding the blackout curtain aside with one hand so she could look out over Montreal.

"They should be here soon."

Derrick stepped from the bedroom with the backpack he had finished preparing.

"Cassi, get away from the window before you draw attention to us."

"It doesn't matter anymore. The military is almost here."

That's the problem, Derrick thought. He placed the backpack on the couch and crossed the living room to the balcony. They had a good view of the city from their tenth-floor residence in one of the three apartment buildings along the west bank of the Ile de Soeurs. From this vantage point, they had tracked the fires that raged through the LaSalle District before ending at the Saint Laurent River. They had also marked the path of the Canadian military as it advanced through the city. He estimated them to be around Mont Royal Park, three kilometers distant. Cassi saw that as a good thing, hoping they would be rescued soon. Derrick viewed the approaching military as being only slightly more welcome than the hordes of rotters roaming the city.

Though others disagreed, Derrick had always thought of himself as practical. He had been arrested twice for shoplifting, although he never did time for it. Once, a storekeeper went after him with a baseball bat, giving Derrick a nasty welt on the arm before he made it out of the store. Purse snatching did not fare much better. He had made a few thousand dollars over the years, giving up that venture after he had grabbed a pocket-book from some bitch waiting to meet her boyfriend, who happened to be approaching from the direction Derrick used to escape. The ass-kicking he got that afternoon put him in the hospital for two days. He was not using the money to buy drugs or liquor or whores. He needed the cash to live. As a high school dropout, he could not get or keep a job, and resorted to petty theft to make ends meet. Besides, he only stole from those who had more than him, so he was merely redistributing the wealth. Christ knew those people could afford to spare some.

Derrick saw himself as reasonable. The authorities viewed him as nothing more than a thug.

That was why he and Cassi had to get out of Montreal.

Everything Derrick had acquired during the past year had been commandeered. He had taken over the apartment during the first few weeks after the outbreak when all the residents had abandoned the building, and then spent a week fortifying every window and entrance on the ground floor so nothing could get in. The Harley he kept garaged in a first-floor apartment had been taken from a dead biker he had found while scouting out the northern part of the island. He scrounged for supplies in other apartments or local shops. Derrick figured that in this new world disorder everybody did what they had to in order to survive, despite the fact that argument had never worked for him before the outbreak.

Derrick took the curtain from Cassi's hand and let it fall back over the balcony door, then moved her away from the window to distract her from what was going on outside. She was still pretty after a year of isolation. Her blonde hair hung down past her shoulders. Sure, she looked older than twenty-three and had lost some weight. Everyone had these days. She smiled, which he had rarely seen her do when they moved in. Cassi would be what got him into trouble. He had come across her cowering in a public loo in one of the nearby parks and offered to give her a place to stay in exchange for sex. After all, fair was fair. If he shared his limited supplies of food and water, she should give up something in return. Besides, she had agreed to go with him and to put out, and he never hit her, although several times she could have used a crack off the side of the head. They had a mutually agreeable relationship and had gotten along well, so there should not be any problems. Yet every experience he had with the authorities told him otherwise, and he did not want to have survived the apocalypse only to be put up against a wall and shot for rape or slavery or some other feminist bullshit charge.

Derrick took Cassi's hands in his. "We have to get out of here."

The smile drained from her face. "The military will be here in a day or two at most."

"That's the problem. I... we can't be here when they show up."

"Why?"

For a moment, Derrick contemplated leaving her behind to be rescued. He ruled that out. Once she told them about their arrangement, they might come after him. It would be difficult enough avoiding rotters without having to worry about the authorities trying to track him down. So, he thought up a plausible lie.

"We don't know how they're going to treat us. Remember when the outbreak started, and the police rounded up anyone who broke curfew and tossed them into detention centers?"

"Yeah."

"Everyone in those centers died when some of them became rotters. We've made it too far to die now because of some government fuck up."

Dejection crushed what optimism Cassi had only moments before. "I guess you're right."

He needed to offer Cassi something to keep her spirits up.

"I don't plan to stay on the run forever. We need time to figure out how the military is treating survivors. If they're cool, we'll sit tight and wait for them to catch up. Deal?"

"Deal." Cassi faked a grin, the same grin she wore every time they fucked.

Derrick headed for the front door, grabbing the backpack off the couch. "Let's do this."

"Right now?"

"We need to go while we still can."

"I need time to pack."

Derrick held up the backpack. "I got everything we need. Get your jacket and haul ass."

As the two exited the apartment, Derrick grabbed the Glock 23 and extra magazines from the end table, sliding the firearm between his back and belt, and the magazines into his leather jacket pocket. Cassi took the baseball bat. They followed the stairwell to the first-floor apartment where he kept the Harley. Derrick handed Cassi the backpack. She slid it on and took her place on the rear of the motorcycle, with the bat across her lap. Derrick went down to the main entrance. It was secured by three 2x4 boards stretching from jamb to jamb and held into place by L-shaped hooks bolted into the wall. He removed the boards, opened the door a few inches, and peered out. Nothing moved. Opening the door all the way, he raced back to the Harley and hopped on.

"Ready?"

"Do you think we should wait and take our chances with the military?"

Derrick ignored her. He started the engine, maneuvered the motorcycle into the hallway, and drove outside. Normally, Cassi would close and secure the door behind them. However, since they would never be coming back, he took off across the front concourse and left the building wide open. Derrick made his way through the side streets to Boul de l'Ile des Soeurs and headed north toward Highway 20. At the first roundabout, he veered right onto Boul Rene Levesque.

"Why aren't we taking the highway?" Cassi asked.

"Too many abandoned cars and rotters. I know another way to get to the mainland."

Upon reaching the car dealership at the end of the road, Derrick steered onto the lot and gunned the engine, darting between the rows of dust-covered vehicles, and bumped over a grassy curb onto a back street. A few seconds later, the street merged with a narrow, two-lane bridge spanning the river. Only a few of the living dead sauntered along the span. He accelerated, maneuvering around them. After two kilometers, the bridge connected with a causeway that paralleled the east bank of the river. A bicycle trail ran the length of the causeway. Derrick maneuvered onto the trail.

They traveled another few kilometers before spotting a rotter. Derrick rushed past. It spun around and lunged at the noise, its outstretched arms barely missing Cassi. Ahead of them, two more of the living dead shambled abreast along the path. He drifted to the right side of the trail. The rotters moved toward him. At the last second, Derrick swerved left and went around them. Thirty meters ahead, three more lumbered along the path, with another half dozen fifteen meters beyond that.

"We should go back," Cassi whined.

"We've got a few more kilometers to go, so hang on."

Though he did not admit to Cassi, Derrick wondered if they would make it. The farther they drove, the more rotters they encountered. Right now, there were not enough living dead to swarm them, but he had no idea what lay ahead. Those they passed closed in behind them and followed. Soon there would be too many to their rear for him to return. Derrick considered going back now while they still had a chance.

Up ahead on the left Derrick saw Saint Catharine Island and, beyond that, Island of the Maritime Lane where a series of bridges reconnected the causeway to the mainland.

"We're going to make it," he said to Cassi, although he still had doubts.

Derrick sped up, wanting to get off the restricted causeway and back onto land where he could maneuver.

The rotter presence grew denser. With some adept maneuvering he avoided being overwhelmed. A few hundred meters up ahead he could see the cement counterweights of the drawbridge leading from the causeway to the mainland, which meant the bridge was lowered and they would be able to get across. If they made it that far. Before the bridge, chain link fences lined either side of the trail for twenty-five meters, channeling the living dead into a more confined space. Derrick accelerated, taking the Harley up to eighty kilometers per hour, and leaned over the handlebars to present a smaller target. Cassi held on tight and cowered against his back.

The Harley barreled through the pack, racing past most of them and shoving several aside. Decayed hands reached out and slapped against them, but they moved too fast for any of the living dead to get a grip. One was able to clutch Cassi's backpack. The motorcycle's momentum knocked it over and dragged it several meters before the rotter released its grip. If Cassi had not been holding on to Derrick so tight, she would have been ripped off the back.

Only a few rotters blocked the entrance to the bridge. Slowing enough not to tip over, Derrick wound his way between the living dead and throttled the engine. The Harley raced across the drawbridge onto Island of the Maritime Lane, and then across another two-lane bridge into the residential neighborhood of Saint Catherine where a handful of the living dead milled around the streets, the closest over three hundred meters away. Derrick pulled over and idled.

"Why are we stopping?" Cassi asked.

"I'm trying to figure out the best way out of here."

"Take a left."

"Why?"

"My grandmother used to live in this area." Cassi pointed east. "Boul des Ecluses is a kilometer that way. It runs through the city and will take us into the countryside."

Derrick steered left and headed in that direction. They drove for a minute, passing residential homes on the right, the Saint Laurent River on the left, and an occasional rotter. It appeared as if this part of the city had escaped the outbreak unscathed. Derrick assumed everyone here had evacuated during the first few days and died somewhere else.

They approached a street on the right blocked by police barricades and an abandoned squad car. Cassi tapped him on the shoulder and pointed. "Turn here."

Derrick drove around the barricades and halted. Boul des Ecluses was a two-lane residential street divided down the middle by a grass median with trees planted every ten meters and lined on both sides by single family homes. He scanned ahead of him for any signs of rotters and, seeing nothing, continued.

Approaching the first intersection, he understood the reason for the police roadblock. Between the connecting streets, the one off to his right and the second one fifteen meters ahead on the left, stood a two-vehicle accident. A transit bus had been making a U-turn around the break in the median when an SUV coming out of the street on the left collided with it head on, blocking both lanes. There was more than enough room for them to get by. Using someone's driveway, Derrick maneuvered onto the sidewalk and raced behind the bus.

Right into a horde of the living dead.

Derrick braked the Harley so hard the rear tire skidded. The motorcycle tipped over, spilling them both onto someone's front lawn. He felt a jolt of pain shoot up his right leg. Fortunately, it had not been broken, and the Harley's still ran. He counted his blessings until he glanced up. Nearly a hundred of the living dead wandered around behind the bus, stretching from one side of the street to the other, including sidewalks and lawns, the closest only ten meters away. As one, the horde twisted toward the sound of the Harley. In a matter of seconds, they would close in around him and Cassi.

Derrick used his leg to push the Harley upright. His knee throbbed and his vision blurred. Shifting his weight onto his left leg, he rebalanced himself.

"Help me!"

Derrick glanced over his shoulder. Cassi stumbled to her feet, her left hand cradling her right arm. A shattered piece of her radius bone had torn through the skin. Derrick knew if he tried to save Cassi. They would both be overrun, so he accelerated and raced along the side of the bus.

A girl rotter no more than twelve moved into his path. He lifted his right arm and elbowed it across the face as he passed, knocking it out of the way before swerving around the front end of the bus.

"Fuck you, you fucking asshole!" Cassi screamed behind him.

Backtracking to the first intersection, Derrick steered left onto it, and then left again onto the first street that paralleled Boul des Ecluses. There were only a few rotters here. Racing down it, off to his left he saw Cassi running between the houses, clutching her bleeding arm, with the horde chasing her. She spotted him and frantically waved her one good arm, hoping to catch his attention and have him come to her rescue. He focused his attention back to the road. At the end of the street, he steered left and then swung right back onto Boul des Ecluses.

After traveling for two kilometers, signs advised that Route 302 was ahead. As Derrick drew closer, the number of abandoned vehicles lining both sides of the road increased, so he rode up onto the sidewalk and slowed, keeping an eye open for rotter activity. He cruised past a Burger King on his right and approached a Shell station when he saw movement down by the intersection fifty meters ahead of him. Pulling into the gas station, Derrick rolled over to the side of the building, parked by the men's room, and shut down the engine. He reached for his Glock. It was not there. Damn thing must have fallen out when the Harley overturned. Nothing he could do about that now. Moving along the side wall, he checked behind the building to make certain nothing lurked there, then retraced his steps back to the front. He could not see inside the station because of the darkened windows. Crouching low, Derrick rushed across the parking lot to the outermost bank of fuel pumps and hid behind them to get a better view of the intersection.

From this distance, he was unable to make out much. Abandoned vehicles blocked the intersection in all four directions, and he could discern movement between them. He estimated a couple of hundred of those things roaming around, most moving along Route 302. He could never cross from here and, judging by the number of living dead, he figured he would run into the same problem anywhere along this route. Fucking Cassi. She made him come this way, and now he was trapped. If the living dead had not gotten her, he had half a mind to go back and—

A sound off to the right caught Derrick's attention. A figure stood in the open doorway leading into the gas station's concession area. Derrick froze, hoping it would not see him.

"What are you waiting for?" the figure said in a low voice and waved him forward. "Get your fool ass in here before one of those things sees you."

Ducking down, Derrick ran over to the gas station. The figure stood aside and, once Derrick entered, closed and locked the door behind him. The darkened interior resulted from boards having been secured over the glass from the inside. A series of battery-operated lamps lit up the interior. The figure moved away from the door and walked over to Derrick. He appeared to be about fifty, with graying dark hair and mustache, and a gaunt physique. He extended a hand.

"My name's Andre."

"Derrick," he replied, taking the hand and giving it a half-hearted shake.

"It's good to meet you." Andre stepped close and gave him a hug. "Damn, it's been a while since I've seen another human."

"How long has it been?"

"Several months, maybe more. I've lost track of time."

"How long have you been here?" Derrick asked.

"Since the third day of the outbreak."

CHAPTER THIRTY-SEVEN

LINDA STIRRED. GRADUALLY she regained consciousness, as if coming out of a deep slumber, only this time she rose from the dead as a vampire. The grogginess associated with sleep had been replaced with a heightened sense of awareness. She could hear a spider spinning its web and a mouse scurrying across the floor in the other room. She could smell things around her she never knew emitted an odor, like the age of the wooden beams behind the walls, the accumulated dust and sweat in the mattress she lay on, and even the staleness of the air. That all paled in comparison to the powerful aura inundating her senses, pushing its way to the forefront of everything else.

"Good evening, my child."

Linda opened her eyes and rolled over. Vladimir sat in the corner on the floor. Although the room was pitch black, she could make out every detail as if she wore night vision goggles with a red hue.

"Good morning… what do I call you?"

"Vladimir. I don't like formalities." He stood and crossed over to the mattress. "How do you feel?"

"More alive than I've ever felt."

Vladimir laughed. "So many people say that after waking up from death. I find it ironic."

"I never knew it could be this way. The sights and smells and sounds I've never experienced before. And I feel so strong, so confident, so… so…."

"Hungry?"

Linda met his gaze, her eyes filled with lust. "Horny."

Vladimir laughed again. "That's natural. Right now, it's intoxicating. Some people find these sensations overwhelming. In time you'll learn how to deal with them. The sights and sounds will fade into the background, like they did when you were human. You'll always be able to tap into them. It's what makes us superior to the humans. I'll be here to mentor you."

Vladimir held out his hand. Linda took it, lifted herself off the mattress, and moved up against her master. She wrapped one arm around his waist and ran her hand up and down his chest. Her voice grew lustful. "Will you also be there to take care of my desires?"

"Of course." Vladimir took her hand, raised it to his lips, and kissed the knuckles. "Right now, you must feed. The euphoria you're experiencing is temporary. Like your other feelings, once the hunger strikes, it'll be overwhelming."

"Okay." Linda clutched his hand.

"Let's get the others, and then we'll all get something to eat."

WHEN ROBSON HEARD the chains on the barn door rattle, he braced himself and hoped tonight's outcome would be different. This time he knew what to expect and had prepared the others to stand up to Vladimir. He had no delusions about his position and knew full well being forewarned did not give him an advantage over the vampires. It only made them less vulnerable than they had been yesterday.

The door opened and the coven entered the barn. Everyone except Vladimir and Linda carried a lamp. They stopped by the entrance and formed a line. Vladimir continued inside with his latest sire holding his arm.

Robson had not expected the extent of Linda's transformation. Yesterday, she had been a frightened, broken, abused woman. Now she strode into the barn with a confidence rivaled only by Vladimir. Rather than lower her head to avoid contact, like she had done at their first encounter, she kept it held high and met the gaze of everyone held captive. He also detected a sensuality about her he had not seen before. Robson cursed himself for miscalculating so badly. He had hoped when the others saw what Linda had become, it would strengthen their resolve not to join the coven. Instead, Vladimir paraded Linda before the others like a fucking poster girl for vampirism.

Vladimir stopped in the center of the group. Linda let go of his arm and walked in front of the others as if she were a model on a catwalk. Vladimir extended his hands toward her.

"What do you think of your friend?"

"She's not our friend anymore," said James. "She's one of you now."

Linda stepped over and crouched in front of him. "That's not true. Nothing has changed."

"It hasn't?" Ed asked. "What if we refuse to become like you? Are you going to drink our blood?"

"Yes." Linda's tone bore no guilt or remorse.

"Then you're not our friend," said James.

"I am, and I want what's best for you. If you continue following Robson, you'll wind up being eaten by the living dead."

"How do you...?" Yukiko glanced over at Robson. He glared at her, his eyes warning her to stop. Yukiko went silent and bowed her head.

Linda moved over to the young woman and knelt in front of her. "How do I what?"

"Nothing."

Placing her hand under Yukiko's chin, Linda gently lifted her head until their eyes met. She spoke in a soft, comforting tone. "What is it you wanted to ask?"

Yukiko hesitated. "How do you feel?"

"I feel stronger, more confident, and more alive than ever."

Robson laughed at that one, intentionally trying to goad Linda.

She ignored him. "No one is ever going to push me around again. Or take advantage of me. Or force me to do things against my will. I'll never fear someone like Price again. The Prices of the world will fear me."

"Everyone will fear you," said Robson.

"Mike, I don't have a grudge against you," said Linda. "I wouldn't be here now if it wasn't for you. I had hoped you'd see how much better off we would be as part of the coven and would encourage the others to join us. If you don't want to, that's fine. Don't stop the rest of them. You have no idea what we endured under Price, the threats, the humiliation, the physical abuse. I do. I spent months living among monsters."

"And now you've chosen to live among monsters again," said Robson.

Tibor leaned closer to Dravko. "I told you he never liked us."

"You know that's not true." Robson appealed to Dravko. "We worked well together."

"And where did it get us?" asked Tibor. "Most of the coven was wiped out. We won't let that happen again."

Robson sought support from Dravko. The former master averted his gaze.

"That's the difference between humans and vampires," said Robson. "Paul offered you hope. You offer only death."

"That's not true," Vladimir said, maintaining his pleasant demeanor. "We offer you a choice."

"Some choice. Become one of you or become your food. It's no better than what the rotters offer."

Linda placed her hand on Yukiko's shoulder. "Do you want to join us?"

The young woman shook her head and sobbed. Linda stood up and glared at her, doing nothing to hide her disgust.

"Wait." Caslow stood. "I want to become one of you."

Vladimir nodded to Linda. She stepped over to Caslow, unshackled the chain around his ankle, and escorted him toward the master.

"Who are you?"

"That's Caslow," Tibor snarled.

Vladimir's expression grew stern. "You're the one who abandoned his wife and daughter, and then hid during the raid on the compound?"

"Y-yes."

Vladimir moved closer to Caslow, who lowered his head.

"Look at me."

Caslow swallowed hard but obeyed.

"Now tell me," said Vladimir. "Why do you want to become one of us?"

"B-because I don't want to die."

"Interesting." Vladimir walked away a few feet. "You're saying you don't really want to join the coven, it's simply preferable to dying."

"No…. I mean…. it's…."

Vladimir spun around and held up a hand to silence Caslow. "Let me tell you something, human. You are the only person in this group I would not allow to become a vampire. You're a coward. If you can't find the balls to stand up for your own family, how do you expect to stand up for the coven?"

"No!" Caslow said, starting to panic. "I could if I was as strong as one of you."

"The only reason you want to join us is to save your worthless life."

Caslow lowered his head again, his bottom lip quivering.

"I would walk out into the sunlight before I allowed someone as pathetic as you into the coven." Vladimir stepped back over to him. "However, you can be of use to us."

"How?" Caslow asked hopefully.

"As food."

Clutching Caslow by the shirt, Vladimir spun around and

flung him across the barn. Caslow slammed into the dirt in front of the others, the wind knocked out of him. The vampires looked to Vladimir for guidance.

"Eat. And don't leave a drop behind."

The coven morphed into their vampiric forms, dropped to their knees around Caslow, and plunged their fangs into his body. Except Dravko, who stepped back and tried to hide in the shadows. Linda's eyes pleaded with Vladimir. When he approved, she rushed forward to the others. The sound of fangs piercing skin and of sucking was drowned out by the howls of fear and pain from Caslow. Yukiko refused to watch, closing her eyes and shaking her head back and forth in a futile attempt to block out the noise. Ed and James stared on impassively, while Corey's face contorted in horror. Magda kept her head lowered. Roberta stared at Robson, her eyes pleading for solace he could not provide.

After a minute, the screaming and thrashing tapered off. One by one, the vampires stood and wiped the blood from their mouths. Linda kept on sucking even after Caslow's body gave its final twitch. Tibor stopped her and helped her to her feet. She gazed at him, a euphoric expression on her face. Vladimir came forward, cupped Linda's face between his hands, and licked her skin clean. He turned to the humans.

"Caslow made his decision. We'll be back tomorrow for the next human."

Vladimir ushered his coven outside. Tibor stepped up and gestured toward Caslow's body. "What should we do with him?"

"Leave it. It'll serve as a reminder of what happens to those who refuse to become one of us. Leave one of the lamps in front of the body so they can see it all night."

Tibor obeyed and then joined the others, closing the barn door and chaining it shut behind him.

A deathly silence fell over the barn. Everyone avoided each other's gaze and dealt with the event in their own manner.

Robson had to contend with the horror of the spectacle that had happened as well as the burden of knowing he had failed. He had hoped to keep his people united, to present a strong front to Vladimir and hopefully work out a compromise. Any such hopes died along with Caslow. He knew he could count on Ed, James, and Roberta. The others were in doubt. If even one of them broke ranks, it would be impossible for him to maintain discipline.

Even worse, he now knew he could no longer rely on Dravko to intercede on their behalf. Based on Dravko's behavior, Robson assumed the coven's former master had given up hope. Robson had to face the realization he had no one way of stopping them from turning the rest of his people or draining them of their blood.

Robson did take comfort from the fact that he still had an ace in the deck. It would not stop the vampires from doing what they wanted to his people, although it would prevent them from harming anyone else.

BEFORE THE VAMPIRES reached the farmhouse, Vladimir stopped and motioned for Dravko and Tibor to stay back. He waited for the rest of the coven to go inside then spun around to confront Dravko.

"What the fuck was that back in the barn?"

Caught off guard, Dravko took a step back. "What do you mean?"

"You know damn well what I mean." Vladimir moved forward, shoving his face into Dravko's. "When the rest of the coven drained Caslow, you stood back and did nothing."

"I wasn't hungry," he lied.

"Fuck you, you weren't." Vladimir shoved Dravko with his chest, forcing him to retreat. "Why didn't you join in?"

Dravko could not admit he found it impossible to terrorize

Robson, or that he felt he owed a greater loyalty to the humans than to the coven. He bowed his head.

"Answer me!"

Tibor inserted himself between the two vampires. "Dravko was holding back because Robson has been good to us."

"Have you forgotten that he banished me from your camp?"

"I haven't. But Robson changed after that. He learned to trust and respect us."

Vladimir glared at Tibor. "Don't tell me you've gone soft on the humans, too."

"I agreed to work with them because Elena ordered it, and the arrangement worked. Elena's dead, and you're the master. My allegiance is to you." He stepped aside and motioned to his friend. "Dravko has an emotional attachment to the humans, much like humans have to their dogs. He needs to realize that, like dogs, humans have to be put down when they are no longer of any use."

Vladimir grinned. "You're full of shit, though I respect your loyalty to Dravko."

"My loyalty is to him. My allegiance is to you."

"I appreciate that." Vladimir said to Dravko, "Keep this up, and you're banished from the compound."

Vladimir stormed back into the farmhouse, leaving the two outside. When he was gone, Dravko confronted Tibor.

"So, you recognize Vladimir as the new master of the coven, not me?"

"You're welcome for me coming to your defense."

"I didn't need your help."

"You fucking well did. You're just too stupid to realize it."

Dravko felt the anger well up inside him. "How dare you talk to me that way?"

"I can talk to you any way I want. You're no longer the master. Vladimir is. And it's because he's rebuilding the coven, like the humans are trying to rebuild their society. What have you done? We've spent the past two weeks putting our lives on the line saving humans who we don't even know, and who turned their backs on Robson after we saved them. Robson has done nothing for us. He keeps us around because we're strong, and we bolster his numbers for whatever asinine adventure he decides to go on. All that's over."

Tibor took a deep breath. When he spoke again, the anger had left his voice. "I don't like terrorizing Robson, but I won't let sentimentality get in the way. My loyalty is to our own kind. We need to rebuild our coven if we're ever going to survive. Sadly, you're not up to the task. Vladimir is. You're my friend and always will be, and I want you to be a part of this. If you refuse…."

Dravko did not need his friend to finish the sentence.

Tibor placed a hand on Dravko's shoulder. "What I said about the dogs is true. They're the inferior species, and your sentimentality for them can't stand in the way of the greater good. The sooner you accept that, the better off we'll all be."

Tibor entered the house, leaving Dravko alone. A sense of emasculation filled him, both by the dressing down from Vladimir and Tibor's betrayal, and by his own inability to fight back. The reason he did not was because everything they had said was correct. As the master following Elena's death, he should have put the needs of the coven above his misguided loyalty. Tibor had been telling him that for weeks, and he had refused to listen. Not only had he lost the leadership to a vampire who Elena had banned from the coven, as well as the respect of Tibor, he had also lost his dignity. Despite all that, Dravko still felt Robson deserved better than whatever Vladimir had planned for him. He was unable to save the others. He might be able do something for Robson. Dravko felt he owed him that much.

All he needed to do was find a way to help Robson without getting himself killed or banished in the process.

CHAPTER THIRTY-EIGHT

D ENNING FELT A little more relaxed as he and Windows walked back to the house. Fewer rotters had appeared around the farm in the past twenty-four hours. Three had shambled out of the woods during the course of the previous day, and this morning only two roamed near the perimeter fence. That was the good news. The bad news was that when he and Windows checked the main road a few hours ago, it still flowed with a stream of the living dead. As long as the horde stayed to the main road, his farm and everyone in it should be safe.

Denning and Windows entered the kitchen through the back door. He inhaled deeply, savoring the aroma of eggs and coffee. Miriam stood by the stove scrambling up breakfast while the three children sat around the table eating.

"Good morning," she said.

"Morning," said Windows, stepping over to the table to hug Cindy.

"You're up early," Denning remarked.

"The kids wanted breakfast, so I thought I'd feed them. I'm cooking your plates now."

"Great. I'm starving." Denning stepped over to the coffee-maker and poured a mug.

"Making breakfast is the least I can do, especially since you're the ones out there…." Miriam let her sentence trail off so as not to upset the children.

"Mom," asked Cindy. "Can Rebecca and Philip help me

feed the chickens and Walther?"

"I don't know," Windows said, glancing at Denning for guidance.

"I think it'll be okay, as long as you stay quiet and keep close to Windows."

A chorus of cheers rose from the table. Cindy jumped up. "Let's go now. You will love Walther. He's so cool."

"Hang on," laughed Denning. "Your mother hasn't even had breakfast yet."

"It's okay," said Windows. "I'm not hungry yet. Save me a plate and put it in the oven. And don't drink all the coffee."

"No promises there."

Windows ushered the children outside. Once the chaos had settled, Denning took his mug of coffee and sat down at the table. A minute later, Miriam finished cooking the eggs, dished out the contents onto two plates, and brought one over to Denning, taking the chair opposite him.

"Thanks." He scooped the first forkful into his mouth.

"I'm the one who should be thanking you. You saved my life. More importantly, you saved the lives of my children." Tears welled up in her eyes and streamed down her cheeks.

Denning did not know what else to do, so he kept on eating.

"I want to pull my own weight around here. And the same goes for Rebecca."

"Cindy has that taken care of." He pointed out the window to where the two girls raced across the backyard holding a container of food for the chickens, with Philip struggling to keep up.

"I'm glad they have someone to play with. You have no idea how lonely it was in that apartment." Miriam became embarrassed. "Sorry. I forgot you were by yourself since the outbreak began. I didn't mean to be rude."

"You weren't being rude. I wanted it that way."

"Can I sit some of the midnight watches and do the perimeter sweeps with you and Windows?"

"Are you up to it?"

"I'll learn. It's not right for me to let you two do all the dangerous stuff. I need to take on some of those chores as well."

Denning thought about it as he finished his eggs. He was not sure Miriam could handle cleaning out rotters along the fence, although he admired her willingness to learn rather than take the easy way out. It was a skill he could teach her easily enough. It would be useful to have someone else who could handle themselves in a crisis in case they did have a run in with a large number of the living dead.

"It's a deal." Denning placed his fork onto the empty plate and wiped his mouth with a napkin. "You can sit the midnight to six shift tonight, and tomorrow morning we'll do the perimeter check together."

"Thank you."

"Don't thank me yet. Wait until you have to put a machete through a rotter's head." Denning stood up and brought his empty plate over to the sink. "If you want, once we've cleaned up, I'll give you a tour of the farm."

CHAPTER THIRTY-NINE

I F NATALIE HAD her choice, she would rather be standing in the cupola of an Abrams than the open hatch of the Stryker because the former made her feel more secure. Since the tradeoff was dealing with only a few hundred rotters rather than a few hundred thousand, she could live with it.

The military had spent the last thirty-six hours conducting air sweeps of San Jose, using Apaches or napalm to eliminate major concentrations of rotters. A final air recon of the city at sunrise detected no large bodies of living dead, so they did not expect to encounter any surprises like Tango Alpha had two days ago. To be on the safe side, the three-pronged attack would proceed at the same pace. The main body would advance in a line abreast stretching from the southernmost tip of San Francisco Bay to the foothills of the Santa Cruz Mountains to the south, a front of almost ten miles. The mobile recce units would remain behind and support them in their drive across the city rather than dash ahead like they had attempted the other day. With luck, they would reach their goal by sundown—the foothills of the Diablo Mountains ten miles to the east. On the opposite side of the range sat the less-populated suburban areas of the Joaquin Valley and the Sierra Nevada Mountains and, beyond that range, the open desert of Nevada.

Reserve troops moved up to the Jersey barriers and began shooting the mass of rotters that had collected on the opposite side. Natalie glanced at her watch. 7:53. The unit would be moving out in less than ten minutes.

Ari and Doreen banged on the side of the recon vehicle.

"Are you ready?" asked Doreen.

"I guess." Natalie remembered the unpleasantness of her last mobile experience.

"You guess?" Ari chuckled. "You should be enjoying this."

"'Enjoying'?" Doreen stared at her friend, incredulous. "Were you in the same recon vehicle as me two days ago?"

"Think of it this way. Right now, we're being chauffeured around the city like VIPs. Once we get to the Diablo Mountains, we'll have to walk like everyone else. And that's all uphill."

Doreen held up her hand in mock exasperation. "Okay, okay. You win."

Natalie had not seen her girls act like this since before Site R. At least now her Angels, or what was left of them, showed the same bravado they had in the past. It felt good to have them back.

Napier made his way down the line of troops, with Mesle in tow. "All right, people. Uncle Sam has arranged a nice little ride for you this morning. Thanks to our friends in the Air Force, this should be as easy as a stroll along the beach. Mount up and get ready to roll."

Ari tapped the side of the Stryker and pointed to Natalie. "Good luck, boss."

Natalie wished she had not called her that. It reminded her of Robson.

Mesle led his squad inside the Stryker. Along the line, other squads loaded up into their recon vehicles. The troops who had been gunning down the rotters pulled the corpses out of the way while others used forklifts to move the Jersey barriers. Once the highway had been cleared, the ground troops moved forward and the line made its way through the surrounding neighborhoods. To the south, it detoured around Mineta San Jose International Airport where clean-up crews cleared out the mound of charred corpses along the scorched remains of the airport's perimeter fence. An Apache flew by overhead and took up position a few miles ahead of the front, serving as their forward scout.

Once the line had reached a point five hundred feet ahead of them, Tango Alpha moved forward, keeping pace with the ground troops. They passed through the previous day's battleground, with the piles of slaughtered rotters along the route and the pools of crushed bodies and gore.

The line maintained its precision as it advanced. Occasionally, a lone rotter would emerge from a side street and would be put down with a well-placed shot to the head. The surge reached the intersection with Interstate 880 when a voice came across their CVC. Natalie recognized the call sign as belonging to their Apache escort.

"Tango Alpha Leader, Sierra Echo Three. I have engine failure and am going down. I can't make it back to our own lines."

"Sierra Echo Three, Tango Alpha Leader copies. Set her down in an open area and I'll send someone to pick you up."

The blare of the collision alarm came across the radio, drowning out the pilot's voice. A metallic crash came through the headphones, and the radio went dead.

"Sierra Echo Three, Tango Alpha Leader. Are you all right?"

Silence.

"Tango Alpha Leader, Sierra Echo Four. Sierra Echo Three went down on the baseball field of a school near the foothills."

"Is the crew alive?"

"Let me check." A minute passed that seemed interminable before the pilot responded. "Tango Alpha Leader, Sierra Echo Four. Sierra Echo Three's crew is alive, but the chopper went down hard. The pilot has a broken leg. The school is Piedmont Hills High, about six klicks northwest of your position. There are half a dozen revenants surrounding the chopper, with another twenty or so nearby. They're too close for me to fire on. Can you send assistance?"

"Sierra Echo Four, copy that. Tango Delta Leader, dispatch two Bradleys and an AMEV to Sierra Echo Three's location."

"Tango Alpha Leader, Tango Delta Leader. Copy that."

"Tango Alpha One, Tango Alpha Leader. Send a Stryker ahead to assist Sierra Echo Three."

"Tango Alpha One copies."

The Stryker picked up speed and the line separated to let it through. Once safely beyond the troops, the driver accelerated. The recon vehicle raced pass Interstate 880. Natalie pulled out a street map of the area and compared it to their surroundings, trying to find the best path to the crash site.

Half a mile out from Interstate 860, the Stryker stopped.

"What's going on?" Natalie asked without taking her eyes from the map.

"Up ahead of us. We can't get through there," said the driver.

Natalie glanced up. Abandoned vehicles blocked all lanes of traffic, including the breakdown lanes, part of the gridlock caused by congestion on Interstate 860. On the other side of Route 101, a single lane road merged on to and off the main freeway.

"What about off to our left? There's a path that's open."

The driver turned and rolled over a broken section of freeway divider, bouncing over the crushed cement. Entering the exit lane, he maneuvered the Stryker around a burnt-out ambulance and steered right onto Old Bayshore Highway. There were few vehicles or rotters on this road. The Stryker rushed through the commercial district, slowing down at the intersection with Oakland Road where a twelve-car accident narrowed the path. When Old Bayshore Highway ended at Berryessa Road, the driver steered left and floored the Stryker.

Natalie studied the map, checking it with the street signs that raced by to get her bearings. After several minutes, she said, "Turn left here. We'll be there in a minute."

From inside the Stryker, Mesle ordered, "Be ready to roll."

Sierra Echo Four hovered above the rooftops on their left. The pilot had positioned his Apache over the school parking lot to draw the rotters away from the crash site. The stunt worked, because over a dozen of the living dead stood beneath the helicopter, frantically clutching skyward. Swinging left, the Stryker rolled over the chain link fence surrounding the compound, raced across the parking lot, and plowed through the pack.

The downed Apache sat at the far end of the school grounds in the middle of the track field. Other than some bent rotor blades, it looked to be in good condition. A dozen rotters swarmed the cockpit, scratching at the glass to get to the pilot and gunner.

The Stryker raced across the football and baseball fields, Sierra Echo Four falling in behind to provide fire support. As they passed beyond the school building complex, Natalie spotted fifty rotters crossing the playing fields behind the facility, spread out so far none of them posed an immediate threat.

"Tango Alpha One, Sierra Echo Four. I'll take care of the revenants around the school. You retrieve Sierra Echo Three."

"Tango Alpha One copies."

The Stryker stopped one hundred feet from the downed Apache. Natalie and the others disembarked and rushed to the crash site. Intent on the food inside, none of the rotters around the helicopter heard them approach.

The squad could not shoot without risking a stray round accidentally hitting the pilot, so Natalie removed her hunting knife from its sheath and approached a rotter in a crossing guard vest. When she got to within ten feet, one of the soldiers from the Stryker, Stephenson, raised his M-16A2 and fired off five rounds. The bullets whizzed inches by her head. Four of them slammed into the side of the Apache, three ricocheting off the metal and one fracturing the cockpit glass. The fifth thumped into the shoulder of the rotter in the crossing guard vest. Upon seeing them approach, it moaned and shambled toward them. The others around the Apache did the same.

Natalie had no time to switch weapons or fall back. Reaching out with her left hand, she clutched the rotter by its vest to keep it at a distance, plunged the hunting knife into its right eye, and twisted the blade. It convulsed once, went limp, and slumped to the ground. Another in Piedmont Hills High gym shorts and shirt came snarling at Natalie from the left, lunging for her outstretched arm. Before it could get to her, Ari ran up and struck it in the head with the stock of her M-16A2. The rotter swayed off balance for a moment and lunged again. Ari pummeled its head with the butt of her automatic weapon, churning its face into pulp until it eventually fell over backward. Even went it hit the ground, Ari kept up the assault until the rotter's head erupted. Ari was so intent on the rotter that Natalie and Doreen had to take down three others which went after her.

Mesle had withdrawn his Glock 23 and shot through the forehead the remaining rotters on this side of the Apache. By now, the eight from the other side were coming around the helicopter. Stephenson fired off another four rounds that missed.

Natalie and her Angels had done this numerous times and fell into their familiar pattern. They stood abreast, lined up their shots, and fired. Three rotters went down. They lined up and fired again, and three more went down. Natalie stood back and let Ari and Doreen take out the last two. With the threat gone, they rushed forward and opened up the cockpit to the Apache.

"About time you guys showed up," the pilot said, forcing a grin through his pain.

Mesle remained all business. "Where are you hurt?"

"My left ankle's broken."

"An AMEV is the way." Mesle tapped the gunner on the shoulder. "How are you doing?"

The gunner gestured toward the pile of corpses. "Fine now that those things are gone."

"You ladies stay here and keep an eye on him," Mesle said. "We made enough noise to attract every revenant in San Jose."

"Copy that. What are you going to do?"

Mesle glared at Stephenson, who stood fifty feet away from the others and avoided eye contact. "I need to kick someone into shape."

He strode off purposefully.

Ari stepped up between Natalie and Doreen. "We made it."

"Made what?" Doreen asked.

Ari pointed ahead of her. "We made it to the edge of the city."

Natalie followed her gaze. During all the excitement, she had not focused on her surroundings. A few hundred feet to the east stood the green foothills of the Diablo Mountains.

CHAPTER FORTY

AFTER PARTAKING OF their first good meal in weeks, the coven had slept soundly all day. Everyone except Vladimir and Gabrielle, who had taken Linda into a spare bedroom and introduced her to the heightened carnal pleasures that came with being a vampire before falling to sleep around dawn. As was his usual custom, Vladimir had woken up an hour before sunset to use the time to plan out the night's hunt. Gabrielle slept naked beside him, her head resting in his lap. Linda, also naked, had woken up half an hour ago. She nestled against his shoulder, running her fingers up and down Vladimir's bare chest.

"You're very pensive," he said. "What's on your mind?"

"Nothing."

"You're my progeny. I know you better than you think."

Linda hesitated. "Is there any way we can use Robson as the coven's familiar?"

"Do you have a sentimental attachment to him, too?"

"I wouldn't call it a sentimental attachment, but he did save me and the others from Price. I owe him my life."

"As a human, you did." Vladimir's tone was soft yet firm. "You're a vampire now, and your allegiance is to us. Robson doesn't like us."

"He seems to like Dravko and Tibor."

"He tolerates Dravko and Tibor." Vladimir cupped Linda's cheek and raised her head so their eyes met. "Let me ask you this. After he rescued you from that camp, did he show the

247

same level of concern with meeting Dravko's and Tibor's needs as he did those of the humans?"

Linda frowned. "No."

"You see? He was friendly with them because he had to be, and because he wanted their strength to fight rotters. He never considered them as equals. It's like the mobsters who hire thugs to do their dirty work, but never allow them to be made." Having made his point, Vladimir let go of Linda's chin. "If I made Robson our familiar, he'd stake us in our sleep."

"She does have a point," said Gabrielle, whose head still lay in his lap. "We're vulnerable here. Maybe it would be a good idea to have a familiar who can protect us during the day."

Vladimir tried to hide his frustration. "The covens have had bad luck with familiars betraying us to hunters to save their own skin."

"There are no hunters to worry about now. Only rotters."

As much as he hated to admit it, Gabrielle had a point. They were exposed living in this farmhouse in the middle of nowhere. So far, the coven had been lucky. It would be irresponsible for him to assume that their luck would hold indefinitely.

"We do need a familiar, at least until we find a better place to live. It won't be Robson, though." Vladimir squeezed Linda's shoulder. "What about the members of your group?"

Linda thought for a moment. "Yukiko and Magda might do it out of fear."

"They're weak and useless. I wouldn't want to rely on them during a crisis."

"Corey's a possibility," Linda continued. "He's an opportunist. Promise him immortality and he'll go along. You'll never get any of them to join with us as long as James and Ed are around. They're too hardheaded, and I'm sure they've teamed up with Robson to keep the others in line."

While Vladimir would have loved to add James or Ed to the coven, he knew neither of them would agree to be a vampire. The smartest thing would be to get them out of the way first, and then maybe he could convince the others to join. If not, they would make a pleasant meal.

CHAPTER FORTY-ONE

D ERRICK LAY PRONE on the roof of the gas station. He took a bite out of a 3 Musketeers bar and lifted the binoculars Andre had loaned him, scanning the intersection of Boul des Ecluses and Route 132. Hundreds of rotters meandered along the main road. Derrick wondered how Andre had survived so long in this gas station so close to so many of the living dead.

Actually, Andre had told him last night. Derrick had only been half listening, even though Andre had talked for almost two hours. Sure, the poor guy had not seen another human in almost ten months and was lonely as hell, if not a little bit nuts from being isolated, but that was not Derrick's concern. Still, Andre had been nice enough to offer him a place to hang out for the night, as well as some of his dwindling supply of junk food, so it would have been rude not to let the guy ramble on while Derrick pretended to be interested.

Andre had talked about escaping the outbreak and winding up here at the Shell station. Rotters had already attacked the rows of vehicles stuck in traffic, eating those passengers not lucky enough to escape in time and chasing after those that did. Andre had decided to hole up in the station, figuring he would be rescued in a few days once the military sorted out the crisis and, in the meantime, he would have plenty of access to food and water. He had boarded up the place with lumber he had found in a contractor's pick-up truck parked out back and hunkered down for what he thought would be a week or two at most. At that point, Derrick had stopped paying attention because Andre had gone into agonizingly boring details about how he had run out of nutritious food and water within the first two months and, after that, had been surviving on bags of potato chips, candy bars, soda, and beer. When Derrick had asked Andre why he did not abandon this place and try to find something better, Andre had answered it would have been pointless. He refused to head back north into the city, and would never be able to continue south as long as rotters lined the road.

At first that answer had sounded like a copout until Derrick climbed up on the roof this morning to check out the situation. Now he understood what Andre had meant. From this vantage point, he had a view of a kilometer stretch of Route 132. Rotters shuffled between the abandoned vehicles. Several dozen stood and stared off into space. Only a few of the living dead had left the main road, and even they had not wandered far. The nearest one to the gas station was a good one hundred meters away. The good news for him was t none of the living dead were bunched together. By being spread out, it gave him a chance to get away without being swarmed if he moved quickly and got across the road before they realized what was going on. However, the mass of vehicles made that impossible.

Dereck took another bite of his candy bar and went back to studying the road, this time concentrating on the jammed traffic. The way the vehicles had been left, the only way across would be to zigzag between them. With four lanes of traffic as well as those vehicles abandoned on the shoulders, he would never make it. The rotters would be all over him before he got to the other side. He considered driving east or west until he found a break, ruling that out because it would attract attention. If he could not find a place to cross within a few minutes, he would have to head back into the city and find a place to hide out with a few hundred rotters on his ass. No way was that worth the risk.

He saw only one possibility, slim as it might be. In the middle of the intersection was a thin break in the traffic, a gap about a meter wide that ran straight across Route 132 except for a dogleg at the rear bed of a pickup truck. He had not noticed it at first because it was so small. If he could get to that gap before the rotters, he had a better than even chance of making it across and out of Montreal. If not, then he would spend the rest of his existence wandering along the road with the rest of the living dead, assuming they left behind enough of him to reanimate.

Derrick checked his watch. 9:12. He considered going now, which would give him plenty of time to clear Montreal and find a place in the countryside to hide out, but changed his mind at the last second. His leg still ached from the fall he took yesterday, and he wanted to give it another day to heal in case his plan went south and he needed to escape on foot. Plus, if he left before sunrise, he might be able to sneak up on them without being seen, getting him closer to the gap and giving them less time to react. And, honestly, he needed an extra day to convince himself this was not the most fucked up thing he had ever done.

Derrick took the last bite of his 3 Musketeers and tossed the wrapper over the side of the roof. Crawling backwards, he went to the far end where he had set up a ladder out of the rotters' line of sight. Once back inside the station, he would fill Andre in on what he planned to do and then get a good day's rest.

CHAPTER FORTY-TWO

ROBSON HAD SPENT the last twenty hours going over in his mind how tonight would play out. In every scenario, he won the moral high ground over Vladimir. In reality, he knew he had no chance of coming through this that did not end disastrously for both sides. So, when an hour after nightfall the coven approached the barn, Robson braced himself for the unexpected.

As the vampires unhooked the chain holding the barn door shut, he propped himself up against the support beam, running his fingers through his hair in an attempt to look presentable. The others did the same, except for Corey, who still sat hunched over. The doors swung open and the coven entered, stepping over Caslow's body. The kerosene lamps they carried cast a soft light inside the structure and threw long, eerie shadows across the floor and walls. Vladimir stopped in the middle of the barn, his coven spreading out in a circle around him.

"Here to offer us salvation?" taunted Robson.

Vladimir was unfazed. "Salvation is a religious word which implies holy deliverance from harm. I think we both agree that does not apply here. I'm here to correct a miscalculation I made."

"Vladimir the Great made a mistake."

"I miscalculated. I assumed you'd be the only one in your group to reject joining the coven." Vladimir addressed the others. "It appears there are others equally as stubborn."

"You mean me," said James.

"You and Ed." Vladimir walked over to James and knelt. His gaze went back and forth between the two men. "That's why I'm giving you both one final chance. You would make excellent vampires and be valuable in reestablishing our dominion on Earth. How about it?"

"Go fuck yourself," Edward answered.

"I'd rather die," said James.

"So be it." Vladimir stood and backed away from James. He raised his hands like a messiah calling his flock to the fold. "Feast, my children."

Morphing into their vampiric forms, the coven split into two groups and converged on James and Edward, except for Dravko who stood by the barn door.

James rose to his knees, closed his eyes, and prayed. "Yea, though I walk through the valley of the shadow of death I shall fear no evil for thou art with me, thy rod and thy—"

The Psalm was cut off when Tibor plunged his fangs into James' throat. Gabrielle and Sean each grabbed an arm and stretched it out, drinking from the arteries in his wrist, while Mia and Tamara fell to their knees and fed off the arteries in his inner thighs. James' grunts devolved into pathetic whimpers as the undead drained him of his blood and his life.

Edward opted to fight back. When the vampires approached, he climbed to his feet, propped himself against the wooden rails of the horse stall, and coiled the loose chain around his right fist.

Linda glided up to him, her movements enticing, her voice seductive yet threatening. "You wouldn't hit me, would you?"

Edward slammed the bunched-up chain into her face with all the strength he had left, spinning her around. The crack echoed through the barn. Linda's left cheek had been gashed open, revealing the shattered hinge to the jawbone. Her mouth fell open at an obscene angle. Linda covered the wound with her hand and backed away.

As she retreated, the other four vampires attacked. Edward uncoiled the chain and, holding it in both hands, strung it across Lewis' throat to strangle him. Stamos swung around to Edward's flank and side kicked his right leg on the torn Achilles' heel. Edward cried out and fell to his knees, releasing his grip on the chain. In one rapid move, Lewis pulled the chain from across his throat, wrapped it around Edward's neck, and looped it around the top slat of the horse stall, choking Edward and holding him in place. Edward kicked out with his right leg despite the agony of his wound, catching Lewis in the groin. Lewis snarled and butted the human's forehead with such force Edward's skull fractured. His body slid down the stall until the chain grew taught, snapping his neck. Lewis used the chain to lift Edward's lifeless body off the ground and bit into his neck. Stamos, Jonathon, and Miles each took a limb, the four drinking quickly while his blood was still warm.

"Stop it!" screamed Yukiko, pounding her fists into the dirt. "Stop it! Stop it! Stop it!"

Magda closed her eyes and mumbled a silent prayer. Corey could not avert his terrified eyes from the horror taking place before him. Roberta looked to Robson for solace. All Robson could do was yell at Dravko.

"Aren't you going to do anything?"

Dravko lowered his head and exited the barn.

Vladimir chuckled, his back still toward Robson while he enjoyed the feeding frenzy playing itself out. "I hope you realize how futile it was to count on Dravko to intercede for you."

"I thought he was our friend," Robson confessed.

"You mistook his weakness for friendship," Vladimir said. "Humans and vampires can't be friends. You knew that when you banished me from your camp. Tibor always knew it. I'm sure Sultanic and Tatyana did, too. What you had was a marriage of convenience. That's over, and things are going back to the way they should be."

"You mean where humans hunt you down."

Vladimir laughed.

"What's so funny?" Robson said, trying to control his anger.

"I don't see you humans doing any hunting." Vladimir crouched in front of Robson. "When I say going back to the way things should be, I'm referring to vampires having dominion over humans."

"You mean vampires keeping us as cattle."

"Yes." As if to emphasize the point, the rest of the coven joined Vladimir after having finished feeding off James and Edward, their hands and mouths covered in blood. Vladimir snapped his fingers and motioned to the barn door. The coven exited, leaving behind the drained bodies to rot alongside Caslow's and one lamp so the surviving humans could dwell on the fate awaiting them if they refused to join the coven.

Once the chain had been secured around the barn door handle and the vampires had left, Yukiko curled up in the fetal position and sobbed. Magda shifted so she did not have to face the corpses of her friends. Roberta moved as close as the chains would allow to Robson.

"What are we going to do now?" she asked.

"I don't know. Things didn't go as expected tonight."

"Seriously?" Corey asked. "Do you fucking think? I hope you have a better plan for tomorrow night before—"

Magda backhanded Corey across the face. "Knock off your shit. Give him time to think of something."

"He should already have a plan." Corey ran his tongue around the inside of his mouth and spit a wad of blood at Magda's feet. "Well? *Do* you have a plan, or are you winging this?"

Robson said nothing.

"That's what I thought." Corey lay dawn and snuggled against the wooden wall of the stall.

Roberta mouthed, "Do you have a plan?"

Robson closed his eyes and leaned his head back against the main support. He did have one, although he could not let the others know it.

CHAPTER FORTY-THREE

THE THREE ANGELS sat in the top row of bleachers facing Piedmont Hills High's baseball diamond, munching on their MREs. Natalie would have preferred to be alone, but Ari and Doreen wanted to join her, so she accepted. The other two chatted amicably, Natalie occasionally adding something to the conversation so as not to appear rude. In truth, all she wanted to do was get some sleep. After the day they had gone through, she needed it.

Following the race across San Jose to rescue the downed Apache crew, headquarters had ordered Tango Alpha One to set up a Forward Area Refuel Point and be ready to provide support for the ground troops, if necessary, which never happened. The drive through San Jose encountered no concentrations of rotters the regular forces could not handle. Natalie and the others saw no activity until half an hour before dusk when the advancing line swept past the school and continued on to the foothills of the Diablo Mountains half a mile to the east. The rest of Tango Alpha joined them and, after setting up a makeshift perimeter, settled down for the evening.

Doreen finished her MRE and packed the remnants into the main pouch. "If you'll excuse me, I have the nine to midnight watch."

"Better you than me," Ari joked.

"Good luck," Natalie said.

"Thanks." Doreen stood up and made her way down the

bleacher, pausing long enough to place her hand on Natalie's shoulder. "I'm glad we're back together again."

Natalie patted her wrist. "Me too."

Ari waited until Doreen had reached the bottom of the bleachers before saying, "She's right."

"About what?"

"About us being back together."

For the first time in days, Natalie thought about the Angels no longer with them. Leila had died at Site R after being bitten by a baby rotter. Bethany had succumbed at the beginning of the trip west from an infection caused by a bite. Rotters had killed Tiara on a sandbar north of St. Louis and Katie during the evacuation from Omaha. Sarah and Emily were lost in the explosion on the Golden Gate Bridge. The losses that hurt the most, however, were Josephine, Stephanie, Amy, and Sandy. Deaths were understandable, and she could deal with that. Those four joined other parts of the government-in-exile. Having them walk away from what they had built, what they had gone through for so long, felt like betrayal.

Natalie also thought about Robson, which weighed even heavier on her heart. She had not wanted to leave him behind in Portland. They had only recently fallen in love. Going ahead without him shattered what little hope she had left for the future. Deep down, she knew she had no choice. Every life lost over the past month would have been wasted if the Angels had not at least tried. She had no illusions about ever seeing him again, or even about his still being alive. Natalie only wished she knew what had happened to him. The closure would have been nice.

"You okay?" Ari asked.

Natalie suddenly realized tears were streaking down her cheek. She nodded and wiped the back of her hand across her eyes.

"You're thinking about Robson, aren't you?"

"I know he's probably dead. Even if he isn't, the chances of us ever seeing each other again are...." Natalie choked back a sob.

Ari slid across the bleacher and wrapped an arm around Natalie's shoulder.

"I'm fine," Natalie lied.

"No, you're not."

"I am. Believe—" Natalie never completed her sentence before the tears flowed again. She cried for five minutes. Ari cradled Natalie's head against her shoulder, stroking her hair. She said nothing, letting her friend purge. When there were no more tears left, Natalie lifted her head.

Ari rubbed her shoulder. "Do you feel better?"

"I do. It's...."

"What?"

"I hate for anyone to see me weak like this."

"Look at me," said Ari.

"No."

"Why?"

"I'm a mess."

"No. You're as beautiful as ever." Ari placed her hands under Natalie's chin and raised her head. She used her thumbs to wipe away the tears. "As for being weak, no one could have done what you did over the past year without crying at least once."

Natalie chuckled. "You're biased."

"I admit it. You're the most amazing woman I've ever known."

Natalie smiled. "Thanks."

Ari leaned forward and closed her eyes. Before Natalie could respond, their lips touched. The kiss was gentle. Ari's tongue glided along Natalie's lips. Natalie did not know what to do. When she pulled back a little, Ari released her.

"I'm sorry," Ari said quickly. "I shouldn't have done that. It was—"

Natalie placed her hands on Ari's cheeks and pulled her

close. Their lips met again, only now the kiss was more passionate. Their tongues explored each other's mouths. Ari slid her hands around Natalie's waist and leaned onto the bleacher seat, pulling Natalie on top of her. She ground herself against Natalie, who moaned deep into Ari's throat.

Ari broke the embrace. "Are you sure you want to do this here?"

"Are you changing your mind?"

"No," Ari said. "I mean out here in the open."

"Who cares? I need you now."

For the next hour, Natalie and Ari lost themselves in each other's love.

CHAPTER FORTY-FOUR

"WILL I BE okay?" Linda said, her voice cracking from the pain.

"You'll be fine." Vladimir stroked the back of her head. "Your body will regenerate quickly. By tomorrow night, you'll be healed."

"It's agonizing," Linda moaned.

"You get used to it after a while and learn to control it. Remember, we have a much higher tolerance than humans. Levels of pain that would shock their bodies into closing down have little effect on us."

A quiet knock sounded on the door. Tibor stuck his head inside the bedroom and mouthed the words, "We found him."

Vladimir nodded, and Tibor discreetly exited.

"I have to go," he said.

"Please don't leave me."

"I have things to attend to." Vladimir raised his right arm and placed his wrist in front of Linda's mouth. "Take some of my blood."

"I'm not hungry."

"It's not for food. A vampire's blood is curative to other vampires. It'll help you regenerate."

Linda placed her mouth over the veins in Vladimir's wrist. She extended her fangs, bit through the skin, and drank. After a few seconds, she let out a sigh that sounded part relief and part sexual. Vladimir let her continue for a minute before pulling his arm away. When Linda leaned forward for more, he placed a hand on her shoulder and gently pushed her back onto the bed.

"When you wake up tomorrow night, you'll be back to normal."

Linda fell asleep before her head hit the mattress.

Vladimir exited the bedroom and closed the door behind him. Tibor stood further down the hall at the top of the stairs.

"Where did you find him?"

"Miles and Tamara found him wandering the woods," Tibor replied.

Vladimir descended the stairs. "What was he doing out there?"

"Brooding." Tibor fell in behind the master.

"About what?"

"What else? Having to turn Robson and the others."

Vladimir reached the bottom of the stairs and entered the room the coven used as their living area. Dravko stood by the fireplace, his back to the door. Vladimir crossed the room.

"Do you mind telling me what your fucking problem is?"

Dravko turned to face him. "I don't know what you mean."

"Bullshit." Vladimir moved up close and got into Dravko's face. To his credit, the vampire did not back down. "Why did you leave the barn during the feeding?"

"You know I have a problem with us going after Robson."

"I know. You're protecting your pet human." Vladimir nearly spat the words. "But tonight, we fed on the other two."

"They're friends of Robson's."

Vladimir took several steps back to lessen the temptation to rip out the insolent bastard's throat. "You betrayed the coven back in Maine when you went along with banishing me from the humans' camp. Even after I offered to give you another chance to redeem yourself, you betrayed the coven again."

"I didn't be—"

"Shut up!" screamed Vladimir. Even Tibor jumped at the virulence seething from him. "I've fucking had it with you. You need to get something straight. You are no longer the master of this coven. You never should have been. I'm in charge now. The only way to keep our species alive and rebuild our numbers is to create a coven of vampires who are strong and loyal. You're undermining that effort. I'm sick of coddling you. Tomorrow night, one way or another, I'm making you an example for the rest of them."

"An example?" asked Tibor from the open doorway.

"Yes." Vladimir glanced over his shoulder at Tibor, his icy glare warning the vampire not to question him, and then back to Dravko. "Tomorrow night you are going to turn or feed on one of the humans and show the rest of the coven you're a loyal member of our group. If not, then Tibor and I are going to cut you down where you stand. Is that understood?"

Dravko hesitated.

"Do you understand me?" Vladimir hissed.

"Yes."

"Good. Now get the fuck out of my sight."

Dravko stalked across the room and exited the house, refusing to make eye contact with Tibor. Once he had left, Vladimir stepped up to Tibor.

"Don't you dare tell me you think I'm out of line."

"On the contrary. I think what you're doing is long overdue." Tibor pushed himself off the door jamb. "He's grown weak after spending so much time with the humans. And you need to exert dominance over every vampire in your coven."

"Even you?"

"I didn't think my loyalty was in question."

"It's not," Vladimir said. "It's good to know I can count on—"

The opening of the front door interrupted Vladimir. Jonathon and Stamos entered. They were agitated.

"What's wrong?" Vladimir asked.

"We're in no immediate danger," said Stamos. "We were hunting north of here when we heard something that sounded like gunfire, and plenty of it. We investigated."

"What did you find?"

"The noise was too far away, thirty or thirty-five miles from where we are. It sounded like the humans are battling rotters and trying to push their way south."

Vladimir stepped away from the group as he thought this over. He had always expected eventually the humans would try and take the world back from the rotters, he just never thought it would happen this soon. Based on what Jonathon and Stamos told him, he would have to change his plans and move the coven before it reached the size he had hoped for. Even with eleven vampires, they would prove no match for a heavily armed group of humans on the hunt. It sucked because this was the ideal location to rebuild the coven. At least he had a contingency plan.

He stepped back over to Jonathon and Stamos. "You said this gunfire was about thirty-five miles away?"

"Yes."

"Then we have time."

"Time for what?" Tibor asked.

"To move the coven to a safer location."

"If we have to move, shouldn't we do it tomorrow night before the humans get too close?"

Vladimir shook his head. "Tomorrow night we'll turn or feed on the rest of the humans. The night after that, we'll take care of Robson once and for all."

CHAPTER FORTY-FIVE

DERRICK FILLED THE spare backpack Andre had lent him with five cans of Red Bull, two dozen stale candy bars, and some rudimentary medical supplies such as rubbing alcohol, bandages, and Motrin. The food and drinks were the healthiest items left in the store. He did not intend to live off them for long, merely for a few days until he found someplace else to ride out the apocalypse and get a better feel for whether the approaching forces were going to rescue him or throw him in a prison camp. He would deal with that later. Right now, his goal was to get across Route 302 without getting killed.

Stepping over to the boarded-up window behind the cash register, Derrick peered through a gap between two boards. It grew brighter outside, although the sun had not yet crested the horizon. He still had enough light to see by and, with luck, could sneak by the rotters before they spotted him. He had to move now if he wanted to take advantage of the pre-dawn.

"It's time for me to go."

"All right." Andre stood ten feet away, another backpack hanging off his shoulder.

"Thanks. I don't need a second backpack."

"It's not for you. It's for me." Andre stepped closer. "I want you to take me with you."

"I can't do that."

"Hear me out," Andre pleaded. "I'm not asking to go on a road trip with you. If I stay here much longer, I'm going to kill myself, and if I try to make it out of the city on foot, I'm as good as dead. Take me as far as the countryside and we'll go our separate ways. I promise."

Derrick hated the idea of trying to cross the road with a passenger. He still remembered what a pain in the ass Cassi had been. On the other hand, Andre had given him a place to hide out and shared what little food he had left, so it would have been douchey of him to leave the guy behind. Besides, he did not have time to argue.

"Okay, you can go. But only to the city limits."

Andre rushed forward and hugged him. "Thank you."

"Have you ever ridden a motorcycle before?"

"No."

"Then do exactly as I tell you."

Opening the front door, the two silently crept to the back of the Shell station where Derrick's Harley stood. He would have loved to top off the gas tank, but that would have made too much noise. Raising the kickstand with his foot, Derrick wheeled the Harley around the corner and toward Route 302, keeping the gas pumps between them and the rotters' line of sight. It seemed like there were fewer rotters in the intersection than yesterday. Derrick climbed on first and motioned for Andre to get on behind him.

"Wrap your arms around my waist," Derrick whispered.

"It's hard because of your backpack."

"It'll only be until we clear the rotters, then you can sit upright. When we get to the intersection, hold on tight and don't move. Let me worry about keeping us upright. If you squirm around, you'll throw us off balance and then we're dead. Got it?"

"Yes."

"Okay." Derrick placed his foot of the starter pedal. "Wish us luck."

He pushed down on the starter. The engine roared to life. The living dead heard the noise, and glanced around in various directions, having no idea where the sound came from.

Now or never, thought Derrick, throttling the engine. He drove out of the parking lot and raced for the intersection.

Several of the rotters on their side of the road saw the Harley approaching and moved toward it. Derrick ignored them, keeping his attention focused on the gap in the traffic he needed to traverse. As he approached the intersection, he cut his speed in half to maneuver through the thin line between the vehicles. A few rotters headed toward them. Derrick steered left, swung around the rear end of the pick-up truck in his path, and steered back right.

Only then did he notice a rotter with two broken legs spread out across his path. It raised its arm, clutching at him. Derrick throttled the Harley. The motorcycle drove over its head and outstretched arm, the weight crushing the skull beneath it. When its head exploded, Derrick lost balance, tipping the motorcycle to the left. He reached out and prevented himself from falling by placing his left hand on the hood of a nearby car, then righted the Harley.

Loud moaning caught his attention. A rotter two meters away approached on his right and two more ahead of him threatened to close off the gap at the other end of the intersection. He throttled the engine again. The Harley shot forward as the rotter to the right lunged, falling into the space he had been a second ago. Breaking through the other side of the intersection, Derrick felt two pairs of dead hands clutching at him, fortunately not grabbing hold of anything. The road ahead was wide open.

"How are you doing back there?" he asked Andre.

"Okay," the other man croaked.

Derrick felt something warm and wet collect around his ass. *Jesus fucking Christ*, he thought. *The wanker pissed himself.*

The next thirty minutes passed without incident. Derrick drove down Rue Saint Pierre. The residential neighborhoods gave way to suburbia, which then became the countryside. The farther they got from the city, the fewer rotters they encountered, which was fine with him. Once he came to the next intersection, he would drop off Andre to go his separate way.

Derrick raced around a bend in the road into a mass of living dead moving south. The Harley was traveling so fast they were twelve meters amongst them before Derrick could react. The horde had already started to close in around them. Going back was not an option and continuing ahead would be suicide.

He headed for the side of the road through a tight opening between the rotters on his left, weaving between them. The road became a rocky shoulder merging into a slight incline leading up into the woods. They made it halfway to the top when Andre glanced over his shoulder to see how close the rotters were, knocking Derrick off balance. The Harley flipped over backward, throwing off the two men. Andre tumbled down onto the shoulder. Derrick fell to the side, cursing under his breath when he felt a sharp pain across his left hip. He rolled onto his back to assess the situation.

Five rotters had dropped to their knees around Andre, dead hands clawing at his face and digging into his chest. Andre screamed and flailed. Even if Derrick wanted to help him, there was nothing he could do. A dozen more of the living dead surrounded Andre, fighting the others for space to join the feeding frenzy. Another two dozen shambled up the incline toward Derrick. He went to stand and screamed when his left leg collapsed under him. The pain was unbearable. His vision blurred and his senses dulled, and for a moment he thought he might pass out. That would have been a death sentence. Derrick forced himself to get back on his feet, this time favoring his right leg, his left still throbbing. So long as he did not put pressure on it, he could manage the pain.

Hopping on his one good leg to the nearest tree, he pushed off it with his left hand and hobbled along to the next, his left foot dragging beside him. Every time it bumped into a rock or tree branch, his vision blurred and his stomach heaved. It took him several minutes to scale an incline no higher than four meters. When Derrick reached the top, he glanced over his shoulder to check on the living dead. Except for those that had stopped to strip Andre clean, every rotter along that stretch of road followed him up the incline, a line of decaying bodies stretching for over thirty meters. Derrick assumed there were at least one hundred converging on him. The closest were within ten meters.

Derrick ran. Being on level ground, he hoped to be able to outrun them, an idea that proved futile after he had limped about ten meters. The faster he moved, the greater the pain became until he could barely suck in air. He paused for several seconds at a time to catch his breath. Each time, the mass of living dead got closer. He spotted a large stream flowing thirty meters away to the southeast. If he could get across that, then maybe the water would slow down the rotters enough for him to escape. Granted, it did not offer much of a chance, but right now it was the only one he had. Pushing off the tree he leaned against, Dereck headed for the stream.

He mustered his energy and kept going, refusing to stop. Any more rests would be fatal. However, with every step the throbbing grew more intense. He focused on the opposite bank, pushing out all thoughts of the pain and the moans of the rotters chasing him. Step by step, he got closer to the stream. After a few minutes that seemed like hours, he approached the bank. The closest rotter was still five meters behind him.

Wading into the water, Derrick took only two steps before his right leg sunk into a muddy patch of the bed. His ankle twisted and snapped. Crying out, Derrick collapsed into the stream. He attempted to crawl across, or at least he thought he did. He could not tell for sure, the pain in his leg and hip overwhelming his senses. Derrick did not even feel it when the first rotter splashed into the stream, dropped to its knees, and sank its teeth into his neck. Another dozen joined in, shredding the skin and organs from his body and feeding off the meat.

Unable to join in the feast, the other hundred living dead

crossed the stream. Once on the opposite bank, they stumbled into the woods and continued their slow march south. They had no idea where they were going, and merely shuffled along in the same direction they had been heading after chasing the two humans, like thousands of rotters that roamed aimlessly throughout the area.

Except that this horde was on a path that would take them directly to the Denning farm.

CHAPTER FORTY-SIX

WINDOWS CAME DOWNSTAIRS to find Miriam standing in front of the stove cooking scrambled eggs and the kids gathered around the table eating. She inhaled. Why was it that food always smelled better when someone else cooked it?

Miriam peeked over her shoulder. "Good morning."

"Morning." Windows stepped over to the stove. "I'm surprised you're still up after pulling the midnight shift."

"I won't be for long. I walked the perimeter with Denning, and when I got back to the house the kids were up wanting breakfast." Miriam lifted the skillet off the burner. "I made some for you, too,"

"Thanks."

"Don't mention it."

"How many rotters were on the perimeter?" Windows whispered.

"Only three. Each day there's less."

"Thank God."

"I know." Miriam tilted the skillet over a plate and emptied out the eggs. "*Bon appetit.*"

"*Merci.*" Windows took the plate and sat down at the table with the children. "Good morning, guys."

"Good morning, Aunt Windows," said Rebecca.

Philip waved.

"Can we go out and play today?" asked Cindy.

"We'll see."

"Please. We've been stuck in the house for two days."

"I said, we'll see."

"Pleeeaase."

"They're going stir crazy," said Miriam as she cleaned the skillet in the sink.

"Is it okay with you?"

"I trust you."

The two little girls bounced in their chairs.

"Calm down," Windows chuckled. "Let me finish breakfast first."

"Okay," Cindy said with dramatic exasperation.

When Miriam bent over the table and gathered the kids' dirty dishes, Windows asked, "Where's Denning?"

"Not sure. He had some chores to do. He said he wanted to check on the combine, whatever that means."

"I know where he is."

Miriam washed the dirty dishes while Windows finished her breakfast. Five minutes later, after Miriam had gone upstairs to bed, Windows grabbed her automatic weapon and hunting knife. She herded the children outside with an admonition to be quiet and stay close, knowing that would do as much as good as telling Walther not to shit in the pasture. Only when she promised them they could feed the chickens if they listened to her did the kids settle down.

After leaving the chicken coop, Windows led the kids to the pasture. As expected, she found Denning working on the engine to the combine. Walther stood nearby, curious about what his owner was doing, his tail swishing every few seconds. Upon seeing the children approach, the bull wandered over to the fence in expectation of being fawned over. Cindy led the way, rushing to the fence and making sure she got to him first. As the children jostled each other to pet Walther, who basked in the attention, Windows hopped the fence and walked over to Denning.

"How's it going?" she asked.

Denning put down his wrench and sat facing her. "Quiet

morning. We found only three of those things along the fence."

"Miriam told me. Hopefully, the horde has passed us by."

"Let's hope so. We'll check later this afternoon." Denning glanced over at the children. "I see you're playing day care today."

"Only so Miriam can get some rest." She gestured toward the combine. "I thought you fixed that thing a few days ago."

"I did."

"What's wrong with it?"

"Nothing. Tinkering with it gives me something to do. I have a lot of free time on my hands now that you're here."

Cindy ran over and hopped up onto the fence. "Good morning, Mr. Denning."

"Morning, Cindy. Why aren't you petting Walther?"

"I want to give Rebecca and Philip a chance."

Windows crossed over to the fence and rubbed Cindy's head. The girl ducked out of the way and rolled her eyes. "Mom, stop that."

"Get Rebecca and Philip," said Windows. "We're heading back to the house."

"Can't we stay outside a little longer?"

"Yes, but in the backyard close to the house."

Cindy moaned in disapproval.

"Do as your mother says," said Denning. "I'll let you guys feed the chickens later and say good night to Walther."

"Okay." Cindy ran off to get the others.

"Are you heading back?" Windows asked Denning.

"Give me a minute."

Denning packed up his tools and headed for the fence. Windows saw him wince when climbing over the top with his toolbox and become winded when he got on the other side. However, since it did not seem to slow him down, she expressed no concern in front of the children, although she made a mental note to ask him about it later.

Gathering up the kids, Windows led the way back to the house.

CHAPTER FORTY-SEVEN

ROBSON WAITED FOR the sun to be at its highest before talking to his group. Although he knew none of the vampires would be out during the day, he allowed his paranoia to get the best of him. If Vladimir and the others suspected what he planned, he would fail, and all their deaths would be in vain.

"What's this about?" Corey asked snidely. "We gonna get a pep talk about not joining the bloodsuckers?"

"Shut up!" Roberta snapped. She focused her attention on Robson. "What do we want to talk about?"

Robson took a deep breath. He knew how this would go. "Corey's being an asshole, but he's right. I want to make a final plea to all of you not to join the coven tonight."

"Screw you, man." Corey threw his hands in the air and rolled his eyes. "I'm not getting involved in this game of yours with the vamps."

"It's not a game."

"Yes, it is. And we're the fucking pawns. You two are whacking your dicks at each other because you threw him out of your little group back in Maine, and now he wants to take your people from you. When the two of you get together, you can choke on the testosterone. Vladimir doesn't care if we join him or feed him, which I can live with. He's a vampire. We put our trust in you, and you don't care about us either."

Out of the corner of his eye, Robson saw Magda and Yuki-ko nodding in agreement. "That's not true."

275

"Really? What have you done to get us out of here? When there were nine of us, enough to put up a fight against these things, did you come up with a plan of action? Or an escape plan? Jesus Christ, man. You haven't even asked them to give us food and water. We've been living on that one bucket of water the vamps brought us the first night."

Robson took a deep breath. "What good would any of that have done? We're too weak to fight them, and with our cut Achilles' tendons we'd never get away."

"So, you decided to give up and sacrifice all of us to the vampires?" Corey huffed.

Robson hesitated, trying to convince himself to tell the others what he intended, to give them a reason why he was asking them to make this sacrifice. He could not bring himself to do it.

"I know it seems that way, but it's not."

"Bullshit," said Corey.

"Mike," said Yukiko, "you must understand. We're scared, and we're looking to you to tell us what to do. And all you've been telling us is that we should allow ourselves to be drained like James and Edward. How do you expect us to go along with that?"

"Because becoming part of the coven is worse," said Robson.

"Why?" asked Magda. "It sure is less scary than being fed on, and in return we're immortal. How can that be worse?"

"It is. Trust me."

"We want to," said Roberta. "I've known you for almost a year, and you've always been straight with me and everyone else in camp. This is different. You're asking us to trust you, to accept a horrible death, without telling us why it's important. You have to be up front with us."

Robson met Roberta's gaze, his eyes expressing his determination. "I can't."

"Fuck this shit," Corey mumbled.

Yukiko and Magda were crestfallen.

Roberta shook her head. "I expected better from you."

The others avoided making eye contact, not that Robson could blame them. He was asking them to accept a painful, terrifying death based only on his good faith, which he knowingly violated. He felt confident Roberta would stand by him, although he doubted any of the others would. He could not do anything about it now, other than hope that when this was over anyone who survived might understand why he took this course of action and forgive him. However, he doubted that.

Robson could not even forgive himself.

CHAPTER FORTY-EIGHT

NATALIE STOOD ON the ridge of the Diablo Range overlooking the east slope, using her hand to shade her eyes from the noon sun. Down below sat farms and towns stretching along the San Joaquin Valley and, beyond that, the Sierra Nevada Mountains. From up here, the view looked less so apocalyptic.

According to military intelligence, when the outbreak spread through the Bay area, traffic jammed up around the passes before evacuees could make it across the Diablo Range. A few of the larger cities to the north, such as Sacramento, suffered the same fate as San Francisco. However, for the most part, those living in the valley had a chance to flee. A few buildings or city blocks had been burned out, but there were no signs of the societal collapse she had witnessed traveling across the country. Not even highways and roads packed with abandoned vehicles. If there were hordes of rotters in the valley, she could not see them from up here, which was a good thing. Natalie wondered if the evacuation from the valley meant it had been spared from the worst of the apocalypse. She would find out tomorrow. The top of the range was the farthest line of advance for today.

Taking back San Jose from the living dead had changed the dynamics of the drive across the country. Additional troops were being deployed daily, with the new recruits clearing out major pockets of rotter activity while those who had already seen combat were diverted to less-stressful mop-up operations.

The main campaign now broke into two drives. One would push north between the east bank of San Francisco Bay and the Diablo Range, with Berkeley as the first objective. Once Berkeley had been recovered, the drive north would split into two, with the primary push being toward Sacramento and then due north up the valley until it reached the national forests around Redding.

The secondary push would move along the West Coast to Eureka. At this point, the northern advance would establish a defensive position until it linked up with the troops heading south from the Pacific Northwest. The second drive would move south along the coast toward Santa Barbara where the Sierra Nevadas swung west and connected with the coast. Here they would contact units pushing south through the San Joaquin Valley and join with the forces fighting to regain control of Los Angeles and the territory south to the Mexican border. Once these three major drives had linked up, the campaign would push east and head across country.

Those units that had been involved in the cleaning out of San Francisco and San Jose had been ordered to the top of the Diablo Range. Tomorrow morning, they would sweep through the valley to the foothills of the Sierra Nevadas, establish a northern perimeter running along Route 132 through Modesto, and begin their push south toward Santa Barbara. Mesle had told them that being assigned this area of operation was their reward for what they had gone through in San Francisco and San Jose. Natalie stared down into the valley below, thinking this time they had gotten a break.

The rest of the squad joined her, with Ari and Doreen on Natalie's right and Mesle and Stephenson beyond them.

Mesle ran his hand across his scalp to wipe off the sweat. "There's our target for tomorrow."

"Which one?" Doreen asked.

He pointed to a small town a few miles south of Modesto sitting directly across from them in the center of the valley. "That's Delhi. Air recon reports no signs of revenant activity there, so it should be an easy day."

"Good," Stephenson said.

"It looks so peaceful down there," Ari said.

"Don't get overconfident. Looks can be deceiving." Mesle took a step forward and raised his voice so the rest of the squad could hear him. "Okay, people. This is as far as we're going today, so find a good place to set up camp. I doubt we'll have to worry about revenants up here but, to be on the safe side, I want guard shifts throughout the night. Any questions?"

There were none.

"Outstanding. Now get moving."

As the others sauntered off, the three Angels still studied the valley.

Ari moved close to Natalie until their shoulders touched. "It'd be a peaceful place to settle down once this is over."

"Hell, no." Natalie shook her head. "I want a place out in the middle of nowhere, preferably in the mountains, where there's no one around for miles. If things go to shit again, I don't want to be surrounded by tons of people."

"I'll go anywhere you want to." Ari slid her hand into Natalie's. Their fingers interlocked, and Ari squeezed affectionately. Natalie wanted to kiss Ari, although not out here where everyone could see.

"Sorry." Doreen started to walk away. "I don't mean to intrude."

"You're not intruding," Natalie said.

"I didn't know you two were…."

"Since last night," said Ari.

"Good for you. I'm glad you two found some happiness in the middle of all this. God knows how long it'll be before anyone else will be happy again."

Natalie squeezed Ari's hand before breaking the grip, and then maneuvered so she could put her arms around both women's shoulders.

"Let's set up camp and enjoy the rest of the day. We've got a lot of walking ahead of us tomorrow."

CHAPTER FORTY-NINE

THE NOISE OF the children playing in the living room tapered off and a suspicious quiet settled over the house. One thing Windows had learned years ago as a babysitter was t if pets or kids were quiet, that usually meant they were up to no good. She stopped cleaning the dinner dishes, dried her hands on a towel, and snuck into the living room to see what trouble the kids had gotten in to.

The three of them were asleep. Philip lay face down on the sofa, his left arm hanging off the side onto the floor. Cindy and Rebecca had been playing a card game when they crashed, Rebecca leaning back against an easy chair, her head at an awkward angle and her mouth open, and Cindy curled up on the rug. Windows cherished peaceful moments such as these.

Stepping into the living room, Windows gently shook the children awake.

"We're playing a game," Rebecca mumbled, half asleep.

"You can finish tomorrow. I promise." After finally rousing them, Windows herded the girls upstairs and carried Philip in her arms. Cindy woke up enough to help pull back the covers so Windows could place the boy into bed.

As she tucked in Rebecca, the girl asked, "Where's Mommy?"

"She's asleep. She's standing guard tonight. Remember?"

Rebecca rolled over and hugged her pillow. "What if I have a bad dream in the middle of the night?"

"Come into my room and get me," Windows answered. "Is

that okay?"

Rebecca nodded and immediately fell to sleep. Windows motioned for Cindy to be quiet, and then led her out of the room and closed the door. Windows brought Cindy to their room, helped her into bed, and pulled the covers over her. Bending over, she kissed Cindy on the forehead.

"Mom?"

"What is it?"

"I like it here. I feel safe, not like at...." Cindy could not bring herself to mention the place.

"I feel safe, too. Mr. Denning has been nice to us."

"Can we stay here forever?"

"I don't think that'll be a problem. Mr. Denning enjoys having us around. I don't see any reason we need to leave."

"Good." Cindy drifted off to sleep. Windows kissed her again on the forehead and then quietly slipped out of the room to go back and finish the dishes.

THREE MILES TO the north, the horde of rotters that had killed Derrick and Andre continued moving south through the woods on a path that would take them to the Denning farm.

CHAPTER FIFTY

ROBSON BRACED HIMSELF at the sound of the approaching vampires. He glanced at the others to gauge how they would respond and feared the worst. Magda kept her eyes closed and prayed. Yukiko lowered her head and cried. Corey was determined to go through with this. Roberta would not make eye contact. Robson resolved himself that tonight would not go well.

The coven entered the barn, spread out in a circle around the humans, and placed their kerosene lamps on the ground. Vladimir entered with more fanfare than usual, reminding Robson of a country preacher sermonizing to his flock, which, in a sense, he was.

He stood in front of the prisoners. "Did you all have a chance to think over what I said last night?"

No one answered.

Vladimir addressed Robson, his tone dripping with sarcasm. "Are they going to let you speak for them?"

"No." Corey struggled to his feet, showing as much defiance as he could, the torn Achilles' tendon making it difficult. "Robson doesn't speak for any of us, especially me. I want to join the coven."

Vladimir stepped over to Corey. "Are you sure?"

"Yes."

"Why?"

Corey hesitated, remembering what had happened to Caslow when he gave his answer. "The last thing I want is to become one of those decayed corpses eating people. I want to survive, and I have a better chance of that as one of you."

Linda moved up beside Corey. "Are you sure about this?"

"Yes."

Linda crouched down and unlocked the shackle from around his leg. When she stood again, she rubbed a tender hand through his hair, kissed his forehead, and rejoined the circle.

Vladimir moved up to Corey. "You know how this is done."

Corey nodded and tilted his head to one side, exposing his carotid artery.

"Not me." Vladimir stepped aside. "Dravko."

Robson's eyes snapped open. He had not anticipated this.

Dravko hesitated. The other vampires glared at him, a few growling threateningly. Tibor and Gabrielle positioned themselves to Dravko's rear, ready to take him down if he refused.

Finally, Dravko's shoulders drooped in defeat, and he stepped over to Corey. Corey backed away, unsure what to do. Vladimir nodded his approval and the teenager moved forward and exposed his neck. Dravko hovered over the teenager. He looked around, hoping for a reprieve. When his gaze met Tibor, the latter snarled a warning to proceed. Dravko morphed into his vampiric form and leaned forward, his fangs slicing into Corey's neck. The teenager winced and his body tensed. As Dravko sucked, Corey's body relaxed. He moaned, not from pain but pleasure. Corey's complexion paled and his legs grew unsteady. Dravko stopped drinking.

Propping up Corey with his right arm, Dravko used his left hand to unbutton his shirt and drag a taloned finger across his chest, drawing blood. He bent Corey's head forward, placing the teenager's mouth over the wound.

"Drink," Dravko said.

Corey did not respond.

Vladimir came forward and leaned into Corey. "You must drink his blood if you want to become one of us."

Corey began sucking Dravko's chest, doing so for a few seconds until the teenager collapsed. Dravko and Vladimir lowered him to the ground. The teenager's life drained from him.

"Did he take enough?" Vladimir asked.

"I think so," Dravko answered.

"Good." Vladimir tapped Dravko on the shoulder and stood. He glanced over at Robson and smirked, arrogant satisfaction on his face. Then he crossed over and stood between Yukiko and Magda.

"Are you ladies also ready to join the coven?"

Yukiko raised her head. Her eyes glared with defiance. "Fuck off."

The smugness drained from his features. "What did you say?"

"You heard me, bloodsucker. I told you to fuck off. We're not going to cower before you."

Vladimir glowered at Magda. "Do you agree with this one?"

Magda refused to make eye contact with the master. Her body shuddered as she sobbed. Finally, she managed to nod. Vladimir turned back at Yukiko.

She remained defiant despite the terror in her eyes. "I'd rather die horribly as a human than be one of you."

"So be it." Vladimir stood and walked away from the two women. "Drain them."

The coven swarmed, half descending on Yukiko and half on Magda. Only Vladimir and Dravko refrained from feeding. Magda stayed hunched over and cried as five of the undead grabbed her, one feeding off each wrist and upper arm, and one off the back of her neck.

Yukiko halfheartedly fought back against the four vampires that attacked her. When Linda approached, Yukiko lashed out and ripped her fingernails across Linda's face, tearing three gashes across her cheek. Linda snarled, clutched Yukiko by the collar, and knocked her back onto the ground. She ravaged Yukiko's neck, gnawing off chunks of flesh as she drank. The other four vampires each took a limb and fed.

Vladimir crouched beside Robson. "I hope you're enjoying this. This is your fault."

Robson said nothing.

"If you hadn't talked them out of joining the coven to spite me, we'd be siring them rather than tearing them apart." He pointed to the corpses of Jim, Ed, and Caslow. "Everyone who has died is your fault. You tried to lead them to safety and wound up getting them killed. I hope you can live with yourself."

Robson refused to be goaded. "I doubt you plan on letting me live much longer."

Vladimir grinned and stood.

Finished, the vampires took their places back in the circle, wiping their mouths and licking their hands clean. What little blood remained in the two women flowed out of their wounds and puddled in the dirt. Yukiko's limbs convulsed a few times before the shriveled corpse stopped moving. When the entire coven had resumed its position, Vladimir went over to Roberta and crouched beside her.

Roberta swallowed hard. "I assume your pack of blood-suckers is going to kill me next."

"We're not going to touch you." Vladimir motioned toward Robson. "He might."

The comment caught Robson off guard. "What do you mean?"

"The coven is abandoning the farm tomorrow night. Humans are moving in from the north, and we don't want to be here when they show up. However, we are leaving them a little gift. Before we head out, we're going to turn you. When you wake up the next night, you'll be what you despise most. You'll be one of us, and you'll have the hunger of a newborn vampire." Vladimir reached out and stroked Roberta's hair. "And this pretty young thing will be chained up waiting for you."

Roberta shoved his hand away and tried to slap his face. Vladimir caught her wrist and squeezed. "You might be lucky, little one. Maybe the humans will show up before Robson turns. Then you can watch the humans kill him like they've always killed our kind."

Vladimir released his grip on her wrist and turned his attention back to Robson. "And if they don't show up in time, then her fate is up to you. You've always viewed us as savage and bloodthirsty. Well, let's see if you can control your hunger and refrain from feeding. Let's see if your human *moral superiority* is more powerful than instinct. I wish I could be here to see it."

Robson had no idea how to respond. Though he had always known he would never get out of this alive, he never suspected Vladimir would turn him and force him to feed off his own people, and not in a manner as insane as this. He stared at Vladimir in hatred.

Vladimir took great pleasure in his reaction. "Not so fucking high and mighty now, are you, human? Good. The two of you enjoy your last night together. We'll see you at sundown."

The coven left the barn, with Dravko and Tibor carrying out Corey's body. This time they took all the lamps with them. There was no need to leave one behind. No one was left other than Robson and Roberta, and Vladimir had made his point.

Once the barn doors had been closed and sealed and the vampires had gone back to the farmhouse, Robson and Roberta were left alone in the dark to ponder their imminent fate.

CHAPTER FIFTY-ONE

THE RATTLING OF the chain securing the barn door jarred Robson out of his sleep. For a moment, he thought he had slept through the entire day until he realized whoever removed the chain did so cautiously so as not to make noise. Nor did he see the glow of kerosene lamps.

The door opened a few feet and a lone figure slid inside, shutting it behind him. Because of the dark, Robson could not see who it was. The figure approached before lighting the kerosene lamp he carried.

"I bet you're surprised to see me," said Dravko.

"That's an understatement. What are you doing here?"

Dravko knelt down by Robson's legs and placed the lamp beside him. "I'm letting you and Roberta go."

"Why?"

Dravko removed the lock key from his pocket. "Do you really need to ask?"

"Yes."

Dravko stopped and stared at the ground. "Vladimir is determined to create a new coven, and he has the full support of the others."

"Including you?"

"No. And that's the problem." Dravko raised his head. "Following Elena's death, I should have concentrated on rebuilding the coven. Tibor kept on urging me to leave your group, to go our separate way and start over. He was right. I kept on stalling, placing my loyalty to you over the coven."

"You felt more akin to humans than your own kind?"

"Not to humans. To you." Dravko inserted the key and opened the lock. He scooted over to Roberta. "During the trip to Site R, you had plenty of opportunities to leave us in the middle of a rotter-infested city during the day and let us fend for ourselves, yet you didn't. You took our side when Compton wanted to inject us with the vaccine and kill us when we became infected. But then things changed, and you didn't treat us as one of your own."

"I never stopped treating you as part of our group."

"You did." Dravko unshackled Roberta and stood. "Once you got it into your head to go after Price and help the survivors, you assumed Tibor and I would go along."

"You could have asked to leave at any time. I would have allowed it."

"*Allowed* it?" Dravko's temper flared briefly but he brought his emotions under control. "It wasn't your decision to make. It was mine, and I made the wrong one."

"No, you didn't." Robson tried to reason with him. "Remember all the lives we saved."

"You really don't get it, do you?" Dravko pointed to the decaying, dehydrated corpses of Caslow, James, Ed, Yukiko, and Magda. "These people were not our responsibility. Simmons and Wayans knew that. That's why they refused to allow them to stay in Gilmanton. For some reason, you felt you had to save everyone in that camp. Where has it gotten you? You and Roberta are the only two left from your group and I've been ostracized by the last coven of vampires."

Robson realized Dravko was right. He never asked Dravko for his advice and expected that everyone would follow his lead. "I don't know what to say."

"There's nothing to say. We're in this situation because of the bad choices we both made." Dravko picked up the kerosene lamp. "This is my final act of friendship. It'll be dawn soon. Once the sun rises, you and Roberta get as far away from here as possible. Vladimir had all your vehicles pushed into the lake, so head north. There are humans coming from that direction. If you're lucky, you can reach them before the coven hunts you down."

"What about you?"

"I'm hoping Vladimir will let me live and give me a chance to redeem myself. If not... things have changed so much this past year I'm not sure I want to live in this world any longer."

Dravko extinguished the kerosene lamp. He pushed the barn door open enough to stick his head out and checked to make certain no one saw him. He paused long enough to say, "Goodbye, and good luck."

Roberta gave Dravko time to get out of earshot before asking Robson, "Do you think we have a chance of making it to safety by nightfall?"

"We're not going anywhere."

"Are you nuts? We have a chance of getting—"

"We stand little chance of getting away. We can't travel far with our Achilles' tendons cut and, if we try, they're going to bleed, creating a scent that will lead the coven right to us."

"You heard what Dravko said. The coven may try to escape rather than hunt us down."

"Vladimir will never let me go."

"So, we're going to sit here and wait to die?"

"No." Robson paused. "We're going to take down the last coven of vampires."

"You *are* crazy."

Robson hesitated, wondering if he should reveal his plan to Roberta. He knew he could trust her because she had always been a loyal member of the team. And now, thanks to Dravko's last act of friendship, she would play an integral part in his scheme. He spent fifteen minutes going over what he had in mind and answering her questions. At first, she was incredulous. The more he explained it, the more convinced she became. When finished, he sat against the support and waited for her response.

Roberta thought for a moment. "You realize what you're proposing is suicidal?"

"For me it is. You might still have a chance. Besides, this is the only way we can stop Vladimir."

Roberta's gaze fell on the bodies of the five survivors who had been ravaged at the hands of the coven. "Count me in."

"Thanks." Robson closed his eyes. "Now let's get some sleep. We'll need it."

BOOK THREE

CHAPTER FIFTY-TWO

THE LEAD ROTTER stumbled through the woods. It was once female. It wore the tattered blue uniform of an EMT technician, its right shoulder and breast shredded and encrusted in dried blood from a bite in its neck. It remembered nothing of its past life or the wound that killed it. All it knew was hunger, the voracious need to feast on human flesh. Something had sent it off in this direction, although the decayed brain could not recall what had prompted this exodus of the living dead. Instinct drove it now, pushing it forward in a quest for food.

The rest of the horde followed. Chance had placed the rotters on this path. A few hundred yards to the east or west, and they would have continued through the woods unnoticed. As fate would have it, the EMT rotter emerged from the trees and ambled into the wooden fence forming the northern perimeter of Denning's farm.

Normally it would have continued walking along the fence line and wandered off in another direction, leading the rest of the living dead behind it. However, a noise on the opposite side attracted its attention. It detected movement. The EMT rotter had no idea what it was, only recognizing that noise and movement meant food. Stretching its arms across the fence, it grasped at its prey and moaned in anticipation of satisfying the insatiable hunger consuming it. The moan served as a signal, attracting the rest of the horde.

Grazing on the opposite side of the fence, Walther heard

the commotion and went over to investigate. As he drew closer, his presence agitated the horde. The rotters spread out thirty wide, with the remainder swarming behind them, pushing to get to the food. Walther retreated a few paces. Although not afraid of anything, a sixth sense warned him this opponent was more fierce and powerful than anything he had faced before. He bucked from side to side and stamped his hoofs to warn off the intruders and bellowed a battle call. Rather than scare off the horde, it excited them even more. The living dead let out a collective moan and pushed forward, desperate to get to the prey.

Along a forty-foot section of fence, the support beams bent and cracks formed in the horizontal slats.

MIRIAM SAT ON the front porch. She was not asleep, though after close to six hours on watch her attention had lost its focus. She had worn the night vision goggles throughout her shift, keeping an eye on the access road leading to the farm, and at four o'clock had even walked the perimeter. The only thing out of the ordinary had been a family of deer grazing near the fence and a few raccoons scavenging for food. Her eyes had grown tired from staring into the device all night, so she had taken them off half an hour ago.

The first hint of sunrise colored the eastern horizon a soft azure. She doubted anything would happen in the last half an hour of her watch.

Leaning back in her chair and resting her head against the wall, Miriam thought about how lucky she and her kids had been in finding the farm. If not, they would either be dead right now or… she pushed those thoughts out of her mind. After listening to Windows' story, it made her nauseous to think about the other possibilities that could have befallen them. Not only had Denning and Windows saved their lives, but they also offered a safe environment to ride out the apocalypse. And

God knew her kids enjoyed having someone their own age to play with. She could see her family staying—

A commotion from Walther's pen cut through the silence and ripped Miriam back to reality. It sounded like a stamping of hoofs and bellowing. Maybe he was trying to scare off a wolf or some other predator. Then she heard the moaning. A cold chill passed through her body, extinguishing the flame of hope she had felt moments ago.

Miriam slid on the night vision goggles. From this distance, she could not see anything. She grabbed the Bushmaster, chambered a round, and headed toward the field where Walther grazed.

Fear gripped her stomach and spread through her body. Through the goggles, she saw the mass of living dead pressing against the fence. At this distance and in the poor light she could not determine exactly how many. She knew there were far more than the three of them could handle. Even worse, she could see the fence bulging and fracturing, and heard the crack of wood snapping. They had minutes, at best, before the farm was overrun.

Spinning around, Miriam raced back to the house to warn the others.

WINDOWS HAD ROLLED out of bed when she heard Miriam burst through the front door and bound up the stairs.

"We've got trouble!"

Windows ran out of the bedroom half-dressed and nearly collided with Miriam in the hall. The woman bordered on full-blown panic.

"What's going on?" Windows asked.

"We have to get out of here!"

"You have to tell me what's going on." Windows grabbed Miriam's upper arms and squeezed, hoping the pain would bring her back down.

"There's a horde of rotters along the northern perimeter of the farm trying to break in!" Miriam gasped, regaining her focus. "It won't take them long. The fence is about to collapse under their weight."

The door to Denning's room swung open and he stepped out. He wore a pair of jeans not yet zipped up and pulled a shirt onto his arms. "Did you see them?"

Miriam nodded. "I heard a commotion in Walther's pen and went to investigate. They're all along the northern fence."

"How many?"

"There were too many to count. I figure at least fifty or sixty, probably more."

"Shit," mumbled Denning, buttoning his shirt.

"What are we going to do?" Windows asked.

"We need to get out of here now before they reach the house," Miriam suggested.

"That's not going to happen," said Denning.

"Why?"

"I don't have a car or truck. The only way we're getting out of here is by walking."

Miriam blanched with the memory of the last time she had tried to escape from the living dead by foot.

Windows felt a hand press against hers. Cindy stood by her, fear in her eyes.

"Are we going to be okay?"

"Yes," Windows lied. She knelt down in front of Cindy. "Mr. Denning and I will take care of it. I need you to go sit with Rebecca and Philip. I'm sure they're scared and need someone who's older than them to calm them down. Can you do that?"

"Sure."

"Good girl. Now off you go."

Before Cindy left, she threw her arms around Windows' neck and gave her a long hug, the type of hug you give to someone when you are saying goodbye. Windows felt a tear run down Cindy's cheek and onto her own. The young girl broke the embrace and rushed off into the bedroom where Rebecca and Philip slept.

When the bedroom door closed, Windows asked, "What do we do?"

"We find a way to stop them from getting in here."

"What about me?" Miriam asked.

Denning took the rifle from her. "Stay here with the kids and keep a close watch on what goes down. If we don't stop them, you're on your own."

"What do you mean?"

"I mean, don't worry about us. Grab the kids and head south. If you don't think you can outrun them, lock yourselves in here and hope for the best." Denning reached under his shirt, removed a .38 revolver, and handed it to Miriam. "You'll need this."

Miriam took it and stared at the weapon in her hand. "I'll never stop all of them with this."

"That's not what it's intended for."

Both women stared at him, fully aware of the reality of what they faced.

Denning clapped his hands. "Let's haul ass before those things break through."

Miriam slid the revolver between her back and pants and lowered her shirt over it so the children would not see it, then ran off to be with them. Windows raced back into her bedroom to put on pants and shoes.

WALTHER POSITIONED HIMSELF in front of the fence. He stomped and bellowed, unable to comprehend why the intruders were not scared off.

The EMT rotter could only move its arms, the mass behind it pinning it against the support. It leaned forward and flailed at the food. The additional weight on the fence proved too much.

The support beam ripped free from the ground. The horizontal boards either snapped in half or were torn from their mountings. A fifteen-foot section of fence collapsed. The rotters toppled forward, sprawling into the pasture. Those to the rear surged forward, tripping over the fallen. A pile of living dead formed in front of the collapsed fence.

A male rotter in blue mechanic's overalls climbed to its feet and moved toward Walther. Walther stamped his hoof and snorted. When the attacker did not back down, Walther lowered his head and charged. His left horn sliced through the rotter's abdomen and out the back, the tip grazing off its spine. Raising his head, Walther lifted the thing off the ground and shook it violently, shredding decayed skin and rupturing partially liquefied organs. The rotter tore in half, its legs and abdomen being flung in one direction and the upper torso in another. Coagulated blood and bits of intestines and skin splattered Walther's face. The stench repulsed him. He ran back a few feet and shook off the human debris.

Another rotter lunged, this one a female wearing gym shorts. Walther charged, butting it with his head and throwing it into the air. It came apart like a broken piñata, raining internal organs on the pasture.

By now, several of the living dead had risen to their feet. Five of them circled Walther, led by the EMT rotter. The bull stood his ground. When the first one approached, Walther charged, driving his horn through its lower gut. This one did not fall apart. It leaned to the side, grabbed Walther by the head, and sunk its teeth into the skin above his left eye. Walther lashed around, attempting to throw it off. Being impaled on the horn, the rotter held on and continued chewing. Walther lowered his head and dragged the rotter backward along the ground to dislodge it. After a few feet, it slid off and dropped to the grass. Walther faced down the other four, ready to attack.

He had not realized that, while thrashing about, he had spun around and backed up against the fence. Eight rotters grabbed him from behind and the sides, dead hands and teeth ripping into his flesh. The four in front surged forward, pushing Walther even further back into the horde where more of the living dead latched on to him and fed. The bull might have been able to break free if pain and fear had not overwhelmed him. Instead of fighting back, he allowed himself to be dragged to the ground, bellowing his last cries of defiance.

Those rotters that could not get close enough to feed continued on toward the farmhouse.

THE SUN HAD crested the tree line by the time Windows and Denning arrived at the southern fence to Walther's pen, giving them a clear view of his death throes. Denning started to climb over the fence, tears streaming down his face.

Windows placed her hand on his shoulder. "It's no use," she said softly. "You can't help him now."

"There is one thing I can do."

Denning raised the rifle, aimed, and fired a single round. Walther's head jerked back as the round slammed into his temple, putting the animal out of his suffering. His body slumped. The horde did not care and continued to tear off chunks of flesh and organs.

"Goodbye, old friend," Denning said under his breath.

When Windows looked out over the pasture, her heart sank. Close to a hundred living dead were heading toward the house. A pack knelt beside Walther, stripping the carcass clean, while others flowed through the break in the northern fence. Another thirty or so shambled across the pasture, heading for them. She knew the children could never outrun a swarm this large, and they had no way of putting down so many rotters with a pair of rifles. A part of her wanted to race back to the house and be with Cindy for their final minutes together. Instead, she unslung her AK-47 and fired at one of the approaching rotters. The shot was low and to the left, punching into its shoulder. She took aim again when Denning placed his hand on the barrel and pushed it down.

"We're never going to stop them this way. There's too many. They'll be at the fence before we can take out even a fraction of them."

"Do you think the fence will hold long enough for us to kill them?"

"Doubtful. And once they break through, there's no stopping them." Denning glanced back at the house.

"What about gasoline?" she asked excitedly. "We could burn that at the fence line."

"I don't have any gasoline since I don't own a vehicle. The only gas I have...." Denning's eyes lit up. "I have an idea. Follow me."

Windows fell in behind Denning as he ran along the fence toward the eastern perimeter.

MIRIAM STOOD BY the window to the bedroom, watching the nightmare unfold. From her room, she could see the pasture. In the sunlight, she realized how badly she had underestimated the number of rotters converging on the farm. The .38 pressing against her back felt more ominous than ever.

Rebecca came up to the window, rubbing the sleep out of her eyes. "What's going on?"

"Nothing much," Miriam lied, lowering the shade so none of the children could see. "A few rotters showed up along the fence last night. Windows and Mr. Denning are taking care of them, and we have to wait here until everything is cleaned up."

"Okay."

"Tell you what," Miriam said, forcing herself to sound happy. "Why don't you kids get dressed and, when the others get back, I'll make breakfast for all of us."

Rebecca's face lit up. "Can we have some of that bacon Mr. Denning keeps stored away for a special occasion?"

Miriam fought back her tears. "Of course."

"Yay!" Rebecca ran over to Philip. "Come on. I'll help you get ready."

While the children were preoccupied, Miriam pushed aside the shade again to see what was taking place in the pasture. The rotters stumbled to the southern fence.

Windows and Denning were going somewhere in a hurry.

DENNING LED WINDOWS down to the southeast corner of the pasture where he kept the combine. He hopped the fence and ran over to the ladder leading up to the cab. Windows stayed close.

"Are you planning on escaping with this?" Windows asked. "We all won't be able to fit on it."

"I know." Denning opened the cab door and pointed to the rotters crossing the pasture. "I plan on using it against them."

"What can I do to help?"

"Stay on the other side of the fence and take down any of those things that get by me."

"You got it. Good luck."

While Windows climbed back over the fence, Denning crawled into the cab, closed the door, and propped his rifle in the corner behind him. He switched on the ignition. The engine roared to life. When he shifted into gear, the combine lurched forward and made its way along the fence line.

Thirty feet ahead of him and ten feet to the right, a rotter in military cammies lumbered toward the fence. When it saw the combine, it changed direction and headed toward it. Denning steered right and plowed into the rotter. It became trapped in the maize header. The oscillating blades sawed through decayed skin and bones, severing its legs below the knee cap. The rotter fell forward onto the guides and began crawling, grasping for Denning. When it reached the end of the header, t clutched the horizontal spiral blade. The rotating blade tore apart the rotter piece by piece, severing its hand, lower arm, and upper arm. The rotter did not notice. It kept its face arched upward in Denning's direction, snarling and snapping its jaws, until its shoulder and head were pulled into the blades. The skull burst, exploding blood and gore across the maize header. The rest of its body went limp.

Denning swerved back toward the fence. The head of a rotter in front of him exploded from a round fired by Windows and it went down. Denning drove the combine over the body, the vehicle rocking as if crossing a speed bump. He maneuvered around two more nearing the fence, figuring Windows would take care of them, and steered toward a cluster of four a few yards distant. The combine knocked one of them over, its left front wheel crushing it under the vehicle's massive weight. The other three were scooped up in the maize header and shredded.

By now, four corpses jammed the header. Denning stopped and shifted into reverse, hoping to dislodge the bodies. The one closest to the edge slid off into the pasture. The other three remained lodged in the blades. Even reversing and swerving back and forth could not clear them. He slammed his left hand against the steering wheel, ignoring the bolt of pain that shot up his arm. There were still over ninety of those things out there and, without the combine, they would never be able to clear them out. They had lost. Unless....

Denning knew of a way around this. It sucked, but they had no alternative.

WINDOWS PAID NO attention to Denning, concentrating instead on shooting those rotters that got near the fence. She had taken down three when Denning backed up the combine opposite her and opened the cab door. He leaned out and yelled to be heard over the engines.

"I need you to clean out the header!"

"What?"

He pointed to the front of the combine. "The blades are clogged. I need you to stay by me and clean them out, otherwise this plan's not going to work."

Windows climbed over the fence. Her eyes darted back and forth to both ends of the machine, waiting for rotters to swarm around it. "You realize I'll be exposed?"

"I know. There's no other way."

Windows moved toward the front of the combine. Every one of the living dead converged on them.

"This is insane!" she yelled up to Denning.

Denning grabbed his rifle. "I'll cover you."

Slinging her AK-47 over her shoulder, Windows raced over to the header. The blades were jammed by three decapitated bodies. She grabbed the first by its shirt and pulled. It came loose with little difficulty, spilling muscles and skin across the header. Windows dragged it onto the grass and went back for the second. This one also came free with no trouble except for its trachea and lungs that had wrapped around the spiral blade. Swallowing back the vomit in her throat, she ripped the organs free and rolled the body off the header.

She did not have the same luck with the third body. Its upper torso was wedged between the spiral blade and back shield and would not dislodge. She climbed onto the header, her feet slipping on the blood-coated metal. Grabbing it by the waist, she pulled. The body would still not budge.

A shot rang out over her head and Windows ducked. A rotter in a blood-darkened yellow sweat suit near the front of the combine fell over backward, a bullet wound in its forehead. A second rotter, this one without a right arm, closed in. A second shot exploded its head, and it collapsed onto the grass. She glanced up to see Denning in the cab, his rifle pointed out the side window.

Moving to the end of the header, Windows dropped to her knees and reached her hands in between the blades and back shield. She felt the cold, dead flesh and rotting muscles, and nearly threw up. She yanked at the body again, but it was stuck fast. Windows felt around inside the torso until her hands touched the ribcage. She grasped the bones and pulled, and the body moved a few inches. Windows paused, took a deep breath, and pulled again. This time it slipped free. Dragging it along the header, she dumped the body on the grass and retreated to the left side of the combine. When Denning saw she was clear, he sat back down and shifted into gear. The combine lurched forward again.

Windows wiped her hands on her jeans. That only cleaned off the surface gore. Unslinging her AK-47, she followed the combine, staying at a distance of twenty feet and keeping the machine between her and the approaching horde.

When Denning approached the west end of the fence, he turned the combine to the right and headed in the opposite direction. He missed a rotter in the tattered remnants of a hospital gown that stayed close to the fence. Windows stepped up to it, fired a single round through its brain, and then fell in beside the combine.

DENNING ATTEMPTED TO sideswipe the rotters, hoping to knock them over and crush them beneath the wheels rather than scoop them, thus cutting back the number of times Windows had to clear the blades. He was able to do that with most, although two staggered into his path at the last moment and were shredded.

Denning attempted to swerve around a naked, bloated rotter that wandered in front of the combine. Before he could steer away, the header caught it up and dropped it onto the guides. The spiral blades caught the rotter's right arm and pulled it into the machine, shredding its arm, shoulder, and head. When the blades reached the torso, rather than becoming jammed in the system, the body erupted. A mix of putrefying liquid and blood splashed across the windows. The stench of decay filled the cab. Unable to control himself, Denning vomited across the steering wheel and dashboard. He pushed open the door to let out the reek, which did little good.

Wiping the vomitus from his lips with the back of his hand, Denning took the steering wheel and aimed at the next rotter in line.

ONCE MIRIAM HAD gotten the kids preoccupied with a card game, she sat down on the edge of the bed, reached behind her, and removed the revolver from her pants. It felt cold and ominous. Bringing it around front, she covered it with her left and placed it between her knees so none of the children would see it. She heard the battle raging and cringed with every rifle shot or ghastly moan. It would only be a matter of time before those things overran Windows and Denning, then burst their way into the house. She thought back a few days ago to when the rotters killed Paul, and the agony he went through in those final minutes. She refused to let that happen to Rebecca and Philip, or to Cindy. Placing her thumb on the revolver's hammer, she cocked it back.

God forgive me.

WINDOWS CRAWLED UP onto the header for the sixth time. It resembled a slaughterhouse floor, completely covered in blood and shreds of tissues and organs. Windows pushed the image out of her mind and concentrated on the job at hand. By now the procedure had become routine, and she could clear bodies in a matter of seconds. She had to work faster because of the increasing number of the living dead converging on them. Several times, she had to pause to help Denning gun down rotters before they got too close.

Following along beside the combine had also become more

difficult. Seven passes along the pasture had covered the grass in a slick coating of human debris. She had already slipped half a dozen times, twice landing on her ass, which would have been fatal if the rotters had been too close. After doing this for ten minutes, Windows was soaked in blood, emotionally drained, and physically exhausted.

While Denning prepared to make his eighth sweep across the pasture, three more rotters moved into his path. Each was scooped up and shuffled into the blades. A loud grinding came from the header, followed by a loud snap. The combine jerked to a stop. Windows ran over to check. The spiral blade sat an angle. Its left mounting had shattered, and the blade had dropped down, the jagged end digging into the ground. The three mangled rotters were still moving. Windows raised her rifle and fired one round into each head.

Denning opened the cab door and stuck out his head. "What's wrong?"

"The header is broken. The blade is stuck in the ground."

"Shit!"

A moaning came from behind the combine. Six rotters approached from the rear. Denning warned Windows to stand clear and sat back in the cab. Windows moved away, and Denning shifted into reverse. The spiral blade in the header strained and scraped, eventually breaking loose from the ground. Swerving from right to left, Denning backed over the living dead, knocking them down with the rear chassis and crushing them beneath the wheels. Each one exploded under the weight, sending a spray of blood and organs across the pasture. When the last one had been crushed, Denning stopped, waved Windows over, and opened the cab door.

"Climb on," he ordered.

"Why?"

"You're going to direct me."

Moving around front, Windows climbed up on the header and used it as a ladder to mount the combine. When she had taken up position on the thresher machinery casing by the cab's window, Denning shifted into reverse.

THE ROTTER IN the EMT uniform lifted its head from Walther's body, attracted by the noise. Something large moved across the field, and something smaller moved around it. The rotter was unable to comprehend what it saw or distinguish the noises. Its primitive mind knew only one thing—noise and movement meant food. Climbing to its feet, it circled around Walther's stripped corpse and set off for the commotion in front of it.

The other eleven rotters got to their feet and followed.

DENNING WAS HALFWAY through the ninth sweep of the pasture when the combine bucked several times. The engine stuttered and died. The combine ground to a halt.

"What's wrong?" Windows asked.

"We're out of petrol."

"Now what?"

Denning scanned the pasture. They had taken down every rotter except for a pack of a dozen approaching from the north thirty meters away, the same ones that had been feeding on Walther. He wanted to kill these things more than any of the others. Reaching into his jacket pocket, he pulled out the AK-47's magazine and counted the remaining rounds. Only six left.

"How many bullets do you have?" he asked.

"Five."

"Make them count."

Windows crouched on top of the combine and took up a firing position while Denning crawled down from the cab and circled around the machine. The pack focused on Windows, which gave him a clear shot. He aimed, lined up on a rotter in a soiled bathrobe, and fired. The back of its head exploded. It dropped face first into the grass.

Denning felt a sense of satisfaction that suddenly turned to rage, rage that these damned creatures had consumed everything. They had not been content destroying civilization. They had to ruin his farm, threaten the lives of him and his friends, and murder Walther. Denning fired off the last five rounds without even focusing on his targets, venting his fury. All he saw was the rotter in the EMT uniform, now covered in Walther's blood. It tottered toward him, its arms outstretched, wanting to rip the life out of him.

Raising the rifle above his head, Denning approached it. When he got close enough, he slammed the butt into the EMT rotter's face with such force its skull cracked. The thing's head shot back, and then it surged forward. Denning crashed the rifle into the rotter again, this time knocking it off balance. Another blow and it fell over backward. Standing over the EMT rotter, Denning repeatedly slammed the rifle butt into its head, knocking out its eyes, breaking most if its teeth, and dislocating its jaw. He kept up the assault until the skull ruptured, spilling its brains onto the grass. Only then did Denning stop, his anger having dissipated along with the threat.

He hovered over the body, breathing heavily from the exertion. He suddenly felt drained. His arms ached. His vision blurred. He had overworked himself. Once he had rested for a bit he and Windows could—

WINDOWS WATCHED IN horror as Denning collapsed onto the grass. She ran up to him, fell to her knees, and rolled him over. His eyes had rolled up into his head and his breathing had stopped. Placing an ear to his chest, she could not hear a heartbeat. Tearing open his shirt, Windows placed her hands over his sternum and pressed hard three times. Listening again, she still heard nothing. She repeated the process another five times. Denning's heart never responded.

Sitting down cross legged on the blood-soaked grass, Windows cradled Denning in her arms and sobbed.

CHAPTER FIFTY-THREE

THE HARDEST PART of the morning so far had been descending the eastern slope of the Diablo Range. Once on the valley floor, the line proceeded toward their objective: the Sierra Nevadas on the eastern side of the valley. Headquarters had cautioned them to move slowly since the armored and recon units as well as air support were dedicated to the drive on Berkeley. That suited Natalie fine. For over an hour, her section of the line had leisurely advanced through farmland and open fields toward their destination, the town of Delhi. Those abandoned farm animals that had escaped from their enclosures had done well, for she saw clusters of cows, chickens, and pigs roaming across the valley as well as an abundance of rabbits and deer. After walking for over an hour, they had not encountered any rotter activity.

As they closed to within a mile of Delhi, gunfire sounded to the north, a few rounds at first that increased in intensity within a minute.

Ari moved closer and nudged Natalie's arm. "You hear that?"

"Yeah."

"Makes me nervous," said Ari.

Natalie saw Mesle a few paces to her left talking into his microphone. When he finished, she sidestepped over to him. "What's going on?"

"I'm not sure, so don't let your guard down. Get back in line and stay alert."

"Copy that." Natalie rejoined her unit.

The line continued its advance to the town outskirts. A few hundred yards ahead of them stood a fairground. A large, windowless building dominated the center. This was surrounded by five roofed-off open-walled areas, one of which contained animal stalls. At one point during the outbreak, the grounds had served either as a Combat Surgical Hospital or containment center. A military-style ambulance with its back door open sat parked to the right of the windowless building. Beside it stood a white tent with a large Red Cross emblazoned on the side. A two-and-half-ton ruck stood in front of the building at an angle, partially blocking the view of the area. One hundred feet behind that sat a Humvee with its hood raised. There were no signs of combat or that the camp had been overrun. There were no bodies, blood, or debris. The military had packed up, pulled out, and left these vehicles behind.

Napier held up his hand, signaling for the line to stop. Natalie placed her forefinger on the trigger guard of her M-16A2 in case she needed to fire quickly.

"Some of the squads outside of Modesto are reporting revenant activity," said Napier. "Nothing compared to San Jose, though. We've been ordered to stop so the line doesn't overextend. Take five."

Napier walked up to Mesle and pointed at the fairground. "Take your squad and check out what's inside those vehicles. They've already been cleaned out, but I'd hate to leave something useful behind."

"Copy that." Mesle stepped away from the line and faced his squad. "You heard the man. Move."

Stephenson sighed. "So much for taking five."

As they approached the abandoned vehicles, Mesle pointed to the ambulance and tent. "Branson, see if there's anything of use in them. And see if that ambulance still runs."

Branson nodded and led half the squad to the tent.

"Natalie, Ari. Check out the Hummer," Mesle ordered.

"We'll take the deuce-and-a-half."

BRANSON'S UNIT APPROACHED the tent. When they were fifty feet away, he ordered them to stop. "Akers, you're with me. The rest of you provide cover."

He raised his M-16A2 into the high-ready position, moved up to the tent, and motioned for Akers to open the flap. Akers pulled it aside and Branson stepped inside. Nothing looked out of place. Five cots lined each wall, with a desk and medicine cabinet located at the far end. Walking between the cots, Branson crossed the tent to check out the medicine cabinet even though the drawers and doors had been left open. As expected, everything had been cleaned out. They only items left behind were sheets and pillows. Moving over to the desk, he opened each drawer, finding only office supplies. Branson exited the tent.

"Whoever was here last took everything of use when they left."

"Should we check out the ambulance?" Akers asked.

"It couldn't hurt."

The rear doors to the ambulance had been left open. All the drawers were open and empty, just like inside the tent. Moving along the left side of the vehicle, he stood on the runner and peered into the cab. Nothing. Opening the door, he slid into the driver's seat and pressed the ignition button. The engine sputtered. Branson pumped the gas pedal twice and tried again. This time the ambulance's engine roared to life.

"That's weird," said Akers. "I wonder why they left it."

Branson pointed to the fuel gauge. "Probably because it's on empty. We can siphon some gas from those vehicles to use in this one."

Akers ran off. Branson shut down the engine to conserve what little fuel he had left.

MESLE AND DOREEN approached the truck while Stephenson wandered off to check out the rest of the fairground. The back deck had been left down. Even at this distance, Mesle could see nothing in the bed. The two right rear tires had gone flat, and the gas cap lay on the ground, indicating the military had siphoned off the fuel. What a shame. They could have used it to help clean out the valley.

Motioning for Doreen to follow, he went around to the driver's side door. Doreen raised her M-16A2 into the high-ready position. Mesle opened the door and jumped back, a comical gesture since there was nothing inside the cab. Crawling up, he rummaged around for anything that might be of value.

"Find anything?" Doreen asked.

"A few empty MRE packages and a map of the San Francisco Bay area." Reaching down to the floorboard, Mesle picked up a pack of crackers and offered them to Doreen. "Are you hungry?"

"I'll pass."

Mesle dropped the crackers. "Let me check under the seats."

NATALIE AND ARI approached the Humvee on each side, their weapons in the high-ready position. Natalie stopped by the engine and checked under the open hood.

"Do you know what's wrong with it?" Ari asked.

"Not a clue. It must be something serious otherwise they wouldn't have left it."

Moving over to the driver's door, Natalie opened it. "Holy shit."

"What?" Ari sounded concerned.

"Somebody fucked up big time. They left an M240 machinegun sitting in back with several belts of ammunition."

"Dibs."

"No way," said Natalie. "Finders keepers."

Ari flashed Natalie a seductive smile. "How about I trade you for it?"

"Now that's a possibility." She handed Ari her M-16A2. "Hold this while I get this thing from the back."

STEPHENSON STEPPED UP to a door along the rear wall of the windowless building. If the military had used the fairground as a camp, then they must have set up some type of headquarters or supply room inside. If he could get in, maybe he could find something they could use. He tried the knob. It was locked. Moving along the rear wall, he made his way down the left side of the building, trying the next door he came to. It was also locked. There must be something valuable inside if the military had secured it this good. Stepping down to the double doors in the center of the building, he grabbed the knob.

At that moment, Branson started the ambulance at the other end of the building. Stephenson looked toward the sound as he opened the door and did not see the hundreds of rotters trapped inside until the horde pushed its way through the exit. Caught off guard, he had no time to react. Seven of the living dead swarmed him, grabbing hold of his arms and chest and knocking him down. They had already begun to gnaw on his flesh and rip open his abdomen before Stephenson's body hit the dirt.

The rest of the rotters fanned out and stumbled toward the humans gathered around the truck and the Humvee.

DOREEN HAD SECONDS to respond. She raised her M-16A2, switched to fully automatic mode, and fired into the horde until the magazine was empty. Only two rotters went down with head shots. The remaining bullets either slammed into dead flesh or missed. The horde still surged toward her, now only a few feet away. Doreen dropped to the ground and crawled under the truck.

Bent over checking underneath the front seats, Mesle was vulnerable when the living dead attacked. He climbed into the cab. Because of the awkward position, his foot slipped on the landing and he fell onto the floorboards, his legs dangling out. Dead hands clutched him. Mesle kicked, preventing any of the living dead from getting a hold and pushing several away. That gave him the seconds he needed.

Crawling into the cab, he grabbed the door and pulled. Several pairs of hands wrapped around the edges, preventing him from closing it. He slammed it several times. Each time he did, more rotters clasped the door. When they yanked it open, it knocked Mesle off balance. Several rotters grabbed him by the legs and dragged him out. He thrashed around, but there were too many to escape. Dozens of dead hands clawed at him, stripping off his uniform and tearing away chunks of flesh. Others ripped open his chest, plunging their hands inside and tearing out his internal organs. A rotter in a tattered and discolored lab coat clutched Mesle's intestines and unwound them. A dozen of the living dead fought over the length like dogs over a link of sausages. Mesle remained unaware of any of this, His mind already had shut down from pain and fear.

Doreen had made it halfway under the truck when several pairs of hands grabbed her ankles. Rolling onto her back, she wrapped her hands around the axle and held on, kicking furiously and breaking free of their grip. More hands clutched at her. One rotter in a Navy ACU and missing its right arm crawled under the truck. Doreen struck at it with her left foot, ripping off its nose. She slammed her foot into its face three more times. The first two kicks shattered several of its teeth and tore open its gums. The third caught it under the chin and bent its head at an awkward angle, snapping its neck. It went limp, blocking others from getting under the truck.

In her struggle, Doreen had not noticed the five rotters that circled around the front of the truck and doubled back along the other side. They dropped to the ground and crept under the vehicle. One bit into her left shoulder, the other into her right hand. The pain caused her to loosen her grip. When she did, the pack on the other side of the truck pulled her out. More than a dozen rotters tore into Doreen's body and fed off her.

Those that did not get close enough to feed swarmed around the truck and headed for Natalie and Ari.

WHEN THE HORDE burst out of the building, Napier had seconds to assess the situation. Stephenson was down, and Mesle and the women were about to be overwhelmed. So far, none of the horde seemed aware of Branson and his people. Under normal circumstances, he would dispatch troops to assist them. Doing that, however, would endanger the entire line. He needed at least a hundred and fifty men to engage the revenants in hand-to-hand, which meant pulling off a quarter-mile section of line and exposing the northern and southern sectors to a flank attack. He could not sanction that for the lives of four people. When he saw the horde drag Mesle from the truck, he knew he had made the right decision.

Napier called out to those troops closest to him. "Hold the line and don't let any of these motherfuckers past! Fire at will!"

BRANSON HEARD A commotion on the opposite side of the building. He motioned for his men to be quiet and shut off the ambulance's engine. It sounded like a horde of revenants. His fears were confirmed when gunfire broke out along the line.

"Follow me. Stay close to the building and be ready for anything."

"FUCK," SAID ARI. "We've got company."

Natalie pulled her head out of the back of the Humvee in time to see the rotters from the building converge on Doreen and Mesle. Unslinging her M-16A2, she and Ari were about to rush over and help t when a pack tore Mesle out of the cab and another crawled under the truck and set upon Doreen. The rest of the horde approached their Humvee.

Natalie reached out and stopped Ari as a hail of gunfire shot across the fairground, most of it aimed at the rotters grouped around the deuce-and-a-half. Because of the angle at which the truck was parked, it stood between the line and the horde, making the soldiers' aim inaccurate. The few rotters that had circled around the vehicle to get at Doreen and some of those still emerging from the windowless building went down. Most of the rounds slammed harmlessly into the side of the vehicle. Several went wild, shooting past Natalie's head or ricocheting off the Humvee.

One struck Ari in the right leg above the pelvis. She cried out and collapsed, dropping her M-16A2 into the grass. The rotters were only twenty feet distant. Natalie bent over, wrapped an arm around Ari's back, and lifted her to her feet. The two women limped as fast as they could to the Humvee. Ari nearly tripped, but Natalie held her up and dragged her along. When they reached the vehicle, Natalie shoved Ari inside and slammed shut the door. Before she could make it around the front of the Humvee, a female rotter in an Air Force ACU reached the fender, and a second in a California Highway Patrol uniform grabbed her by the shoulder. Natalie body checked the latter, knocking it into the approaching horde.

Climbing onto the Humvee's hood, she ran across, jumped down on the other side, and raced for the driver's door. A stray round impacted against the back plate of the Humvee, sending a tiny fragment of metal ricocheting across the roof and into Natalie's left eye. Involuntarily closing both eyes, she felt around for the opening and slid into the driver's seat, closing the door seconds before the horde swarmed the Humvee, closing around it in all sides four or five deep. Those closest to the vehicle clawed to get in, leaving streaks of gore across the glass.

Ari had removed her belt and used it as a tourniquet to stop the flow of blood in her leg.

"How bad is it?" Natalie asked.

"It didn't hit an artery, but the bone might be fractured. It hurts like a... Oh, my God." Ari moved closer to Natalie. "Are you okay?"

"I got something in my eye, that's all."

"It's worse than that. You're bleeding."

Natalie studied her reflection in the rearview mirror. When she opened the lid, pain stabbed through her face and her eyes shut. Opening the left lid with her fingers, she examined the pupil. She could see a tiny fragment of metal lodged in the eyeball. Natalie carefully closed the lid. "Do you have anything I can put over this?"

"Hang on." Ari unbuttoned her ACU and pulled out her t-shirt. Removing her hunting knife from its scabbard, she cut off the bottom two inches and passed it to Natalie. "Here."

Natalie wrapped the makeshift bandage around her face, covering the left eye.

"What do we do now? Sit here and wait for them to come and save us?"

"Screw that." Natalie tied the bandage tight in the back so the pressure would keep her lid closed. "I still have a lot of fight left in me."

She crawled between the seats and into the back where the machinegun was.

BRANSON AND HIS men reached the end of the building where Akers waited for them. When Akers heard them approach, he spun around and aimed, stopping when he realized it was his own team.

"What's going on?" Branson asked.

"We have three men down. Two women are stuck in the Humvee. I think they're both wounded."

"Bites?"

Akers shook his head. "Friendly fire."

"Shit." Having them trapped inside the Humvee limited his options. He could not risk firing at the horde without the possibility of a stray round punching its way into the vehicle and wounding or killing one of them. With that many revenants swarming the Humvee, it would only be a matter of time before they smashed their way in.

"What are we going to do?" Akers asked.

"Go down to the other corner of the building by the med tent and keep watch. Don't let anything sneak up behind us."

"Copy that." Akers rushed off.

"The rest of you, switch to single shot. Concentrate your fire at the revenants at the front and rear of the Hummer."

"We'll never take them down doing it like that," said a private.

"I'm not trying to take them down. I want to draw them to us so the women have a chance to escape."

NAPIER SAW THE ineffectiveness of the line's fire against the horde and ordered his men to stand down. He was recalculating his options when he spotted Branson's team moving along the edge of the building. That gave him an idea.

"McDaniel, Jonesy, take your squads and reinforce Branson. The rest of you, tighten up the line and make sure nothing gets past us."

NATALIE PICKED UP the M240 and the belts of ammunition

and dragged them up front.

"How many rounds do you have?" Ari asked.

"I don't know. Hopefully more than enough." Natalie draped one belt around her neck and handed the extras to Ari. "Start linking them together so I have one continuous belt."

"Be careful."

Natalie crawled over the SINCGARS radio in the central console and onto the transmission tunnel. She popped open the hatch, hefted the M240 through the opening onto the roof, and stood up through the hatch. The rotters worked themselves into a frenzy upon seeing her. Mounting the machinegun onto its pivot base, Natalie fed in the belt of ammunition, chambered the first round, and fired a one-second burst into the horde.

At this range, the 7.62mm rounds ripped the rotters apart. Heads exploded and torsos ruptured, spewing blood and chunks of flesh across the side of the Humvee. Natalie swung the machinegun back and forth, firing a few bursts every few seconds so as not to burn out the barrel. Except for those next to the vehicle and out of the machinegun's lowest declination, every burst took down the living dead.

Every time one rotter went down, another climbed over the body to take its place.

WHEN BRANSON SAW Natalie emerge from the top hatch of the Humvee with the M240, he ordered his unit to shift their fire from the horde around the Humvee to the deuce-and-a-half. As McDaniel's and Jonesy's squads arrived, they joined in. It took only a few minutes to clear the area around the truck. Those around the Humvee were too intent on getting at the women inside to care about his squads.

"What now?" Akers asked.

"We move up to the other side of the truck and get ready to get the women out." Branson waved his hand over his head. "All of you, on me."

The three squads moved toward the truck.

ARI FINISHED LINKING the last belt of ammunition to the main line when the driver's door flung open. A rotter in a Scoutmaster's uniform centered itself in the doorway and climbed into the cab. Ari had dropped her gun outside when she got shot. Thankfully, Natalie left hers resting against the center console. Ari leaned over and clutched the barrel as the rotter lunged for her. It missed, and Ari yanked the M-16A2 toward her. The barrel faced away from the rotter, and she had no room to maneuver it around, so she used the stock to hammer the Scoutmaster rotter in the face. Each blow disfigured its features, fracturing the skull or knocking out teeth. With each strike, the rotter drew a little closer. The fifth blow dislocated its lower jaw. The sixth broke open its skull along the top of the forehead, exposing the brain. With the seventh hit, the stock smashed into its brain. The rotter shuddered once and fell onto Ari, spilling blood and gore into her lap.

Another rotter attempted to crawl over the Scoutmaster to get to her.

Ari grabbed Natalie's pants leg and pulled. Natalie stopped firing and yelled down the hatch. "What's up?"

Ari pointed to the driver's side of the Humvee. "I could use a little help."

When Natalie saw the rotters climbing in through the driver's door, she swung the M240 around and fired on the living dead along that side of the vehicle. Each one fell under the fusillade of fire, except for the one half inside the Humvee and the five gathered by the door.

BRANSON SAW NATALIE rotate in the open hatch to shoot on the opposite side of the Humvee. By now, only eighteen of the living dead remained on the passenger side, so he took advantage of the situation and moved forward. When within ten feet, he signaled for his men to stop and fire. Each of the revenants went down with shots to the head. Those last five on the driver's side went after the new source of food, making it only a few steps before they were also taken out. With the last shot fired, an eerie silence fell across the fairgrounds.

"McDaniel, Jonesy, stay here." Branson pointed to the mound of bodies piled up along the passenger side of the Humvee. "If anything so much as twitches, put a round in its head."

"Copy that."

"The rest of you, let's get the ladies out of here."

NATALIE DROPPED DOWN inside the Humvee and gasped when she saw the Scoutmaster and the pile of gore in Ari's lap. She crawled over the transmission tunnel and placed her hands on Ari's shoulders. "Are you okay?"

"I look like shit, but I'll live."

Branson stuck his head inside the Humvee. "Jesus H. Christ. Are you two all right?"

"We're banged up pretty bad," said Natalie.

"Give me a few minutes to clear out some of these bodies and call up a medic, then we'll get you out of here." Branson stood up and shouted orders to his squad. He bent over and leaned back into the Humvee. "Congratulations, by the way."

Natalie was confused. "What for?"

"Wounds like you two ladies have will get you yanked from the line and placed in a cozy desk job somewhere. For you, the war is over."

Ari reached up and squeezed Natalie's hand. "We made it."

"Thank God." Natalie leaned forward and wrapped her arms around Ari from behind, embracing her tightly.

CHAPTER FIFTY-FOUR

ROBSON HEARD THE vampires approaching, only this time he anticipated the encounter. He had mentally prepared himself all day for this. Even Roberta had bolstered her courage, although he could tell by the tremble in her hands that she was still terrified about what would happen. As well she should be. The next ten minutes would be the most dangerous either of them had faced since the vampires had released the Revenant Virus against mankind. Yet they both agreed it had to be done. As the sound of the chains being removed from the handles echoed through the barn, Robson mouthed, "Are you ready?"

Roberta swallowed hard and nodded.

A moment later, the doors swung open. Light from the kerosene lamps bathed the interior of the barn, sending shadows dancing along the walls as the coven entered. Dravko was prepared for the verbal and most likely physical abuse he would suffer once Vladimir realized his captors were gone. The vampire's eyes went wide with surprise when he saw the two humans sitting in the same spot he had left them the night before. Robson ignored him and focused his gaze on Vladimir.

The coven spread out in a semi-circle around Robson, with their backs to Roberta, and placed their kerosene lamps on the ground. They each stared at Robson, hatred for humans and a lust for violence in their eyes, especially from Corey, who sneered. Vladimir positioned himself in front of Robson, a sardonic grin on his face.

"I hope you enjoyed your last day as a human."

"I slept most of it." It took every ounce of courage Robson could muster to sound nonchalant.

"What a shame. You should have taken advantage of it. You'll never see sunlight again."

Robson shrugged. "I thought a condemned man would get a last meal."

"I have given you a last meal." Vladimir glanced over at Roberta and leered. He then crouched in front of Robson. "And don't think of it as being condemned. You're being given an opportunity few humans have ever been offered, though that will change in the future."

"The difference is that once you turn me, you're going to leave me out here on my own to fend for myself or die."

"Just as you did to me. It's fitting, don't you think?" Vladimir patted Robson on the leg and stood. "Enough talk."

"So, this is it?" Robson asked.

"I'm afraid so." Vladimir faced his coven. "Are you ready?"

The other vampires nodded or stretched their jaws, including Tibor, who had fought beside Robson for close to a year.

Dravko stepped back, moving away from the coven. "I won't do it."

"I didn't think you would," snorted Tibor.

Vladimir brushed off Dravko with a wave of his hand. "We'll deal with you later."

Dravko stepped forward to confront Vladimir. Tibor and Corey morphed into their vampiric forms and blocked his path. When Tibor and Corey moved toward him, Dravko backed off into the shadows. He looked over at Robson, his expression questioning why he and Roberta had not escaped when they had the chance.

Vladimir grabbed Robson by his collar, yanked him to his feet, and dragged him to the center of the barn. The coven closed in around him, all except Dravko. Rather than resist, Robson stood his ground. The master morphed into his vampiric form, bent his head at an angle, and plunged his fangs into Robson's neck. Robson winced as the tips penetrated his skin but refused to cry out or show pain. That became more difficult when the other vampires moved in to feed. Corey and Tibor held out his arms, each biting into a wrist. Vampires fed from each of his forearms, inner elbows, and upper arms. Linda and Gabrielle stepped up behind him and leaned forward, plunging their fangs into his shoulders. Robson felt his lifeblood being drained. He felt his pulse growing weaker and his respiratory rate increase.

He cast a glance over at Roberta.

MORE THAN ANYTHING, Roberta wanted to avert her gaze. However, she could not allow herself that luxury. She crawled into a crouching position, doing so slowly so as not to draw attention to herself or the fact her ankle had been freed from its shackle. When Robson glanced at her, she focused on his eyes. Once he had lost enough blood to slip into unconsciousness, she would act. Until then, she fought back the tears.

DRAVKO LOWERED HIS head to avoid witnessing Robson's death. He had failed his coven, both as a vampire and as their leader. He had failed his human friends. Worst of all, he had failed himself. Dravko contemplated sneaking off while the rest of the coven were busy and heading north until the morning sun would end his existence. Maybe then—

An agonized scream came from the center of the barn.

VLADIMIR STEPPED BACK from Robson and clutched his chest. Over the centuries he had been shot, set on fire, and doused with holy water. Never had he experienced an agony as intense and crippling as this. The burning began in his stomach, ate its way through his veins, and spread through his body. The muscles in his chest and arms contracted violently, causing his upper body to twist and spasm. The skin on his hands darkened and shriveled, and the fingers bent in until his talons dug into his palms. As the pain raced up his neck, Vladimir's throat constricted. His vision blurred. When the scorching sensation reached his head, the torment became unbearable. It felt as though his brain was melting. Memories and motor functions seared away, leaving behind an overpowering hunger.

Falling to his knees, Vladimir howled in agony. He stared over in Robson's general direction, unable to see him clearly through the murky gray cloud in his eyes. He tried to speak, his voice croaking out unintelligible sounds. Vladimir focused the remnants of his mental skills to ask one final question.

"Wha' did 'ou do to me?"

WHEN VLADIMIR DROPPED to his knees and howled, the rest of the coven jumped away from Robson. He saw the uncertainty and fear in their eyes as they shifted their attention between him and the master. Then Stamos clutched his abdomen and doubled over in pain. It struck Tamara a moment later. She tore through the skin on her chest trying to rid herself of the searing agony.

Dizzy from the loss of blood, Robson stepped back and propped himself against the central support.

"Wha' did 'ou do to me?" screamed Vladimir.

"I infected you with the Revenant Virus."

"How?" Vladimir asked, the word so twisted and distorted it was barely recognizable.

"The vaccine Compton developed was derived from samples of the virus. When I was inoculated, my blood was infected. And now, so are all of you." Robson chuckled. "Kind of ironic, isn't it? You nearly wiped out the human race with the Revenant Virus, and I wiped out the vampire race with the vaccine."

Vladimir struggled to stand, and instead fell over onto his back. In his mind, he ordered the coven to tear Robson apart. The command left his mouth as a gurgle. Not that it would have mattered. One by one, the other vampires succumbed, each too busy being consumed by the infection to have obeyed.

Only Tibor and Corey had not yet begun the transformation. The two vampires lunged at Robson.

For a brief moment, Dravko thought things would be all right. With the rest of the coven dying off, he could sneak out and start over, and rebuild the vampire nation in the manner he and Elena had envisioned. That thought was short lived. Even though staying meant his own death, he could not allow a pack of rotter vampires to roam the countryside.

And he refused to betray his friend again.

Dravko saw that Tibor and Corey were about to attack Robson. He launched himself across the barn and slammed into Tibor. Both men crashed against the opposite wall. Tibor came off the wood and swiped at Dravko with his right hand, the talons tearing across the Dravko's face. Dravko fell back, stunned by the pain. Tibor lunged again, slashing half a dozen more times. Dravko felt the lacerations on his face open wider with each blow and the skull around his eye socket fracture. Tibor grabbed Dravko by the collar, spun him around, and slammed him face-first against the wall. He leaned in close and snarled in Dravko's face.

"I'll be damned if I allow you to be the last vampire on Earth."

Tibor bent his neck to bite Dravko and gasped. He fell back several paces and collapsed, clutching his gut. His body convulsed and twisted in a violent angle as the virus took hold, coursing through his veins and changing him from the undead into the living dead. Tibor's skin discolored as decay set in. He turned his head in the direction he assumed Dravko stood, unable to see through the gray film covering his eyes. Tibor issued a final plea to his friend, the rotting brain making it slurred and disjointed.

"No let me be one of them."

Dravko circled around behind Tibor. He would eventually kill Tibor, but not before offering his friend the same mercy Tibor would have showed him and Robson. Raising his foot, he slammed it down on each of Tibor's ankles, shattering the bones so he could not walk. If Tibor felt any pain, it did not show. He lay amongst the hay and thrashed around.

Dravko checked on Robson.

LINDA HAD NEVER felt anything as painful as this, including the other night when James had broken her jaw. She knew she would be dead in a few minutes. No, worse than dead. She would be one of the living dead. Linda tried to summon up the courage to stick her talons through her eyes and scramble her own brains.

She heard a commotion and lifted her head in time to see Dravko tackle Tibor to the other side of the barn, leaving Corey to face off against Robson by himself. Hatred seethed in her as painful as the infection. Robson had taken immortality from her before she could enjoy it and condemned her to an eternity of walking the Earth and feeding on human flesh. Now he stood with his back to her, only ten feet away. Her last conscious thought was she could not let him live.

Pushing herself to her feet, Linda lumbered toward Robson.

ROBERTA STRUGGLED TO stand, using the wall of the horse stall as support. Limping over to the nearest kerosene lamp, she picked it up and lifted it above her head to see. Most of the vampires were still turning, except for Dravko and Tibor, who battled in one corner of the barn. She found Robson against the center support, with Linda sneaking up behind him. She did not have time to go to his aid or warn him, which left only one option.

Roberta threw the lamp at Linda.

It crashed against the vampire's back and shattered, dousing her in kerosene. The fire from the wick ignited the fuel, engulfing her in flames. Linda howled. Throwing herself against the animal stalls on the opposite side of the barn, she slid to the ground and slumped forward. She tried to extinguish the flames until her muscles burned away. Linda's body teetered for a moment before rolling to the side into a pile of dried hay.

The hay ignited.

WHEN DRAVKO TACKLED Tibor out of the way, Robson focused his attention on Corey. The teenager paused, confused by both the transformation of those vampires around him and the sudden disappearance of Tibor. That second bought Robson the time he needed. Reaching down, he picked up the chain that had shackled him to the central post and twirled a length of it around both hands. The noise snapped Corey out of his daze. He snarled at Robson and lunged.

The vampire had taken only a few steps when he stopped, clasping his arms tight against his chest to lessen the pain of the infection gnawing through his abdomen. Limping behind Corey on his one good foot, Robson looped the section of chain between his hands around the vampire's neck and yanked his arms to the side, tightening it. Corey gagged and choked, too consumed by his transformation to fight back. Balancing himself on his good foot, Robson placed the knee of his bad leg between the vampire's shoulder blades. Pushing down with his knee, he pulled back on the chains. Corey flailed his arms and reached back, clawing at Robson's face. A cracking sound emanated from Corey's neck and his head tilted to one side. Robson loosened his grip on the chain. Corey collapsed face-first onto the barn floor, his head at an obscene angle. Although Corey's body remained motionless, his mouth still snapped at Robson.

The sound of shattering glass behind Robson caught his attention. He glanced over his shoulder to see Linda burst into flames. That gave him an idea.

"Get Roberta out of here," he yelled to Dravko. "Then use the lamps to set the others on fire."

DRAVKO RAN OVER to Roberta and scooped her up in his arms. Making his way through the coven, he carried the woman to the double barn doors and placed her outside. As she fought to steady her balance, Dravko closed one of the doors. He had closed the second one halfway when Roberta grabbed the edge and stopped him.

"I want to help," she pleaded.

"You can." Dravko bent over, picked up the chain that lay on the ground that Vladimir had used to secure the handles, and handed it to her. "Once I close these, lock us in."

"No!"

"It's the only way."

Roberta nodded. "Then what should I do?"

"Get out of here as fast as you can."

Dravko slammed the doors shut.

THE VAMPIRES THAT still survived had only a few seconds left before they were completely transformed into rotters. Hobbling over to the lamps, Robson grabbed one in each hand and moved over to the closest vampire. Stamos raised his head and glared, any semblance of humanity having been replaced by the soulless mind of the living dead. Robson swung one of the lamps and smashed it across Stamos' face, then hobbled back as flames engulfed the vampire's head. It snarled even as its tongue shriveled. Its eyes exploded within their sockets. Dropping to the ground, it thrashed around until the heat cooked its brain.

Mia was next. She knelt, her body doubled over in agony. Robson smashed the lamp on the back of her neck. She never even attempted to stand as the burning kerosene poured down her back and over her head and shoulders, preferring the ultimate death to becoming one of the living dead. Robson limped away from the charred corpse to get two more lamps.

When Robson reached the closest, something jumped him from behind, knocking him onto a pile of hay and pinning him. He fell on top of a pitchfork but could not get to it because of the weight holding him down. He felt a pair of cold hands on his shoulders and decayed breath against his neck. Robson braced himself. Then the weight was suddenly lifted. Rolling over, he saw Dravko standing beside him, holding Tamara's head between his hands. She struggled to break free, but his grip was stronger. Dravko squeezed as tight as he could, his arms straining from the pressure. Tamara cried out as her skull caved in. Her body slipped through his fingers and onto the dirt, covered in a rain of skull chunks, brain, and skin. Dravko wiped his hands on his pants, then reached out his right to help up Robson.

"Thanks," said Robson, struggling to regain his balance, favoring his good leg.

Dravko patted his friend on the shoulder. "Let's end this now."

Robson picked up the pitchfork, using it as a makeshift crutch. Taking one of the nearby lamps, he lobbed it at the barn doors. The glass shattered, splattering kerosene across the wood and bursting into flames. Robson tossed three more against the other walls, creating a conflagration that would consume everything inside the barn. Dravko had culled out the coven, having snapped the necks of Jonathon, Sean, Lewis, and Miles.

Clutching the pitchfork, Robson limped over to Dravko. "You should get out of here while you still have a chance."

"I'm the last of my kind, so I'll die here with the rest of my coven." Dravko took a step back to stand beside his friend. "I could say the same about you."

"I've lost too much blood. I'd never make it to morning. Besides…." Robson pointed ahead of him. "You're going to need help."

Vladimir and Gabrielle had completed their transformation into the living dead. Both rotter vampires had risen to their feet and stared at the two men with dead gray eyes. Vladimir tilted his head, sizing up his prey. His lips curled at the corners and he growled. Vladimir and Gabrielle lunged.

ROBERTA HAD FINISHED wrapping the chain around the barn door handles and securing the lock when something smashed against the other side. A moment later, a searing heat shot through the cracks, followed by a whoosh as flames engulfed the interior. Roberta limped backwards, forgetting about her wounded ankle, and fell onto the dirt. She crab-walked twenty feet away before stopping to rest. By then, the flames had moved to the exterior walls and lapped at the roof. More fires sprang up along the other three walls.

Robson and Dravko were burning down the barn, and she had trapped them inside. Roberta crawled to her feet and hobbled forward to unchain the handles to give them a way to escape. By now, flames had engulfed the twin doors, making it impossible for her to reach the chains. She stepped back, searching for a way to get inside.

That was when a howl emanated from inside the barn, a sound so ungodly it made her blood run cold.

ROBSON RAISED HIS pitchfork and jammed it into Gabrielle's face when she came within range. One prong punctured her left eye, one lodged in her throat, and the other pierced her neck. She lurched from side to side, trying to break free. Clawing at them had no effect and biting on the center prong succeeded only in shattering her teeth. Gabrielle grew frustrated at not being able to get to the food. Grasping the handle and balancing himself on his good leg, Robson shoved the pitchfork in deeper. Because of his weakened condition, he was unable to puncture the skull.

Gabrielle snarled and lunged, her outstretched arms grasping for his throat. Robson fell over backward. Still holding the pitchfork, he lodged the end in the dirt, locking it in place so Gabrielle impaled herself. The prong in her eye smashed through the skull and scrambled her brain, while the one in her mouth severed the spinal column. Her weight broke the handle below the metal connection. Her body dropped to one side, the pitchfork still imbedded in her skull. Gabrielle convulsed a few times, then her body went limp.

Robson tried to climb to his feet but did not have the energy. His heart pounded in his chest. His breathing was shallow from the exertion. He wanted to do nothing more than lie down and go to sleep. He knew he had to push on, although he could not remember why. Rolling over, he sat up on his knees.

A roar to his left caught Robson's attention. Dravko and Vladimir were engaged in a death struggle. The confusion cleared. Mustering the last remaining reserves of strength, Robson stood. Grabbing the wooden handle from the ground, he brandished the broken end like a stake and went to help his friend.

VLADIMIR SPRANG AT Dravko. Dravko had anticipated the attack and moved aside at the last second, allowing Vladimir to rush past. As he did, Dravko spun around and grabbed

Vladimir, one hand wrapped around his neck and the other around his forehead, hoping to snap his spine and immobilize him long enough to destroy him. It did not work out quite as planned.

Vladimir bucked. Dravko knew if he lost his grip, Vladimir would be on him in a second, and he could not win a one-on-one with something that had the determination of a rotter and the strength of a vampire. Dravko dug in his talons and wrapped his legs around Vladimir's waist. The rotter vampire thrashed about more violently, and Dravko had all he could do to hold on. Vladimir spun around so he his back faced the central support beam and rammed against it, driving Dravko into the wood. He kept up the pounding until Dravko was not sure what would break first, the beam or his spine. Yet he held on tight, knowing if he let go Vladimir would tear him apart.

"Hey, asshole!"

Vladimir looked up. Robson stood in front of him. The rotter vampire did not register who the person was or what he wanted. It only saw food and lunged, then felt a sudden pain in its chest. A broken handle stuck out from below its sternum. In its last shred of conscious thought, the rotter vampire knew the piece of wood posed a danger and reached up to pull it free. Dravko reached around and dug his talons into Vladimir's neck, hoping to tear it out. The rotter vampire forgot about the stake in its chest and slammed back into the support again. Dravko felt his right shoulder blade shatter and his arm go limp. He clasped Vladimir even tighter with his left. Vladimir grabbed Dravko's left arm, raised it to its mouth, and bit, ripping a chunk of flesh out of his arm that he chewed. Dravko cried out, knowing he had only minutes left to live.

Robson stood hunched over, all of his energy spent. He had failed because he no longer had the strength to push the makeshift stake through the vampire rotter's heart, and now they would all die. Raising his head, he prepared to meet death straight in the eye, and instead witnessed the struggle between

Vladimir and Dravko that ended in Dravko being bit. Robson had one chance left. He placed both hands on the end of the wooden handle. Then he paused, realizing that if he staked Vladimir, he ran the risk of killing Dravko directly behind him.

Dravko caught Robson's attention and nodded.

Vladimir growled.

Robson leaned all his weight against the handle. The broken piece of wood slid through the rotter vampire's chest, pierced its heart, and continued out through the back until it lodged into Dravko less than an inch from his own heart. Vladimir tensed. The skin around the stake began to fall apart, the decayed skin breaking down into ash. The cavity spread quickly, across its chest and deep into its abdomen, and then fanning out down its legs and arms. The Vladimir rotter cocked its head to one side, contemplating Robson. Its eyes registered hatred. It snarled as the disintegration engulfed its head. By now, Vladimir's entire body was an outline in ash. Its form remained intact for a moment before crumbling apart.

With the rotter vampire gone, Dravko fell back against the support beam and slid into a seated position, the broken handle still in his chest.

Fire engulfed the barn, burning along all four walls and the wooden outlines of the stalls, and lapping at the rafters. Smoke filled the area, making it difficult to see or breathe.

Robson knelt beside Dravko. "Come on. We can still get out of here."

Dravko shook his head and lifted his arm to show the bite wound. "It's over for me."

"Is there anything I can do?"

"Yes." Dravko motioned at the stake protruding from his chest.

"I can't kill you."

"You'd be doing me a favor. I'd rather die as a vampire than burn to death as one of those things."

Robson shifted his position to get better leverage and

placed his hands on the end of the broken handle. "Are you sure?"

Dravko nodded.

Robson leaned forward, driving the stake into Dravko's heart.

Dravko winced. The disintegration took place immediately, spreading out across his chest and along his entire body. Laying his head back against the support, a sense of contentment washed across his face. He closed his eyes as his head disintegrated. A second later, Dravko crumbled into a pile of ash.

Robson fell onto his back, not caring anymore. He had no energy left and only wanted to sleep. He no longer realized fire consumed the barn. For the first time in months, his mind was at peace, even if it was a peace induced by confusion from lack of blood to the brain. He could not remember much other than his life had been difficult the past year. Something told him that was over now.

As Robson slipped away, the final thought that crossed his mind was of Natalie.

ROBERTA HAD CRAWLED to the end of the driveway when she heard the groaning of wood over the furnace-like roar of the fire. She stopped and rolled over in time to see the barn collapse, sending a shower of sparks billowing into the night sky. Bracing herself, she half expected a swarm of flaming rotter vampires to emerge from the rubble and bear down on her. Thank God, nothing walked away from the inferno.

The sound of engines caught her attention. A military-style Humvee pulled onto the farm followed by a pair of Bradleys. They stopped in a line abreast thirty feet from her. A dozen soldiers exited the vehicles, some taking watch on all four quadrants while the rest approached her. They stopped ten feet away, their guns in the high-ready position and aimed at her. A young lieutenant in a Canadian army uniform continued toward Roberta.

"Ma'am, stay still and don't move."

"There's no chance of that." Roberta lifted her left leg to show the gouged Achilles' tendon.

The lieutenant knelt in front of her and shined a flashlight in her face and over her body. "Have you been bitten?"

"No."

The lieutenant turned to one of the soldiers behind him. "Woods, get the medic over here."

"Yes, sir."

The lieutenant's eyes fell upon the remains of the burning barn. "What happened here?"

"It's a long story."

"Are you all right, ma'am?"

Roberta sighed. "I am now."

CHAPTER FIFTY-FIVE

WINDOWS STOOD BY the two freshly-dug graves. Both sat to the right of Anna's marker under the oak tree. A pair of makeshift crosses composed of sections of fence marked the final resting place of Denning and Walther. She knew that was how Denning would have wanted it. He and his wife were at peace and would not have to endure the hardships of building a new world from the horrid remains of this one. Most importantly, Denning had joined his wife, which was where he always wanted to be.

That still did not stop the heartache.

For the survivors, the worst was over. Five hours after the rotter attack on Denning's farm, a Canadian military unit pushing south from Montreal came upon them. Based on previous experiences, she had feared the worst. In reality, the soldiers were entirely professional. As the line pushed father south toward the U.S. border, their commanding officer agreed to leave five of his men behind for a day to help dispose of the bodies. They had dug the two graves for the deceased and oversaw the laying-to-rest ceremony, and then cleared the pasture of the living dead, placing the corpses in a pile. Two of the soldiers even volunteered to repair the fence. Windows thanked them by preparing scrambled eggs, the last of their bacon, and chicken.

Before the five men left the next morning, they set fire to the pile of bodies. The stench had been sickening. Windows did not mind. With the soldiers' departure, she realized that the farm was now in human territory, and the rotters to the south were being destroyed. For the first time in almost a year, she was safe. No rotters. No rape gangs. No constantly looking over her shoulder to see what danger was closing in on her. Life had returned to a semblance of its former normalcy, and Windows had been one of the few lucky enough to make it through Hell and come out on the other side.

Too bad she could not say the same for those she loved.

A tiny hand slid into hers and squeezed. Windows glanced over at Cindy, who was also sad.

Cindy sniffed back a tear. "I miss them."

"I know you do." Windows wrapped her arm around Cindy's shoulder and hugged her. "We both do."

The two stared at the graves for Denning and Walther, remembering them in their own way.

After a few seconds, Cindy asked, "Will Walther go to heaven?"

"Of course, honey."

"Good. I want to see him again someday. And Mr. Denning, too."

"You will, but not for a long time."

Miriam and her children stood thirty feet away, also paying their respects while not wanting to intrude. They would be leaving tomorrow morning. Windows had offered to let them stay for a while, but Miriam declined. She wanted to go back to Montreal and try to rebuild her life. Hopefully, they could settle back into their old house and see if any of their neighbors who survived would return. If not, Miriam was certain new people would move in. She figured if she could rebuild the life they once had, that would be her memorial to Paul. Windows envied her. Miriam had a former life worth trying to regain.

Cindy tugged on her hand. Windows crouched down. "What's up?"

"What's going to happen to us?"

"We'll stay here and take care of the farm for Mr. Denning.

Maybe we'll even take in a few people who have nowhere to go so they can help us out."

"Like Mr. Denning took us in?"

Windows nodded. "Would you like that?"

"As long as I can stay with you."

"Always, honey." Windows put her arms around Cindy and hugged her tight. "Always."

EPILOGUE

Sixteen months later

"LADIES AND GENTLEMEN, we're beginning our descent into Portsmouth International Airport at Pease. Military personnel, please check in at Hanger 3 for your assignments. All civilian passengers can proceed directly to the terminal. Thank you."

Natalie stirred from her nap and stretched. It seemed unusual flying into Portsmouth rather than Logan. That was one of the changes following the war. Most of the major airports were either still inside exclusion zones or were so severely damaged during the outbreak it would take years to clean them up and make them operational. Not that it mattered, because there was still little in the way of air travel in the country. Until recently, all flights had been military. Three weeks ago, President Fogel had allowed civilians with a justifiable reason to book transport aboard military aircraft. He considered it one of the many first steps in restoring a sense of normalcy to the country, although it would be quite a while before people could hop a flight to visit relatives in another state.

She still found it hard to believe the war was over. It had taken fourteen months to clear the United States of rotters. After securing the West Coast, the drive continued east from the Sierra Nevadas. The United States linked up with the Canadian campaign near the Idaho-Montana border, and from there the two armies combined forces into a juggernaut that maintained its advance until it reached the East Coast,

343

sweeping up every one of the living dead. A long defensive line had been established along the border with Mexico to keep out rotters until the Central American campaign met up with the Americans. Major cities were bypassed for later clean up. Some areas were so heavily infested, or were so difficult to get to, they were sealed off into exclusion zones—the Hawaiian Islands, Chicago, Boston, New York City, and Long Island. Once the rest of the nation could get back on its feet and more troops could be trained, then the exclusion zones would be taken back, although that could take years.

The rest of the world fared about the same. The Russians had been able to stop the rotter advance at the Ural Mountains and had built up camps of European survivors in safe areas stretching into Siberia. They had launched their own reclamation campaign a few months after the Americans and in a year had cleaned out most of Europe except for the Italian and Iberian Peninsulas. The campaign to take back the United Kingdom was scheduled to begin in six months.

The Chinese spearheaded the campaign to reclaim Asia, launching their efforts from eastern Siberia. The massive population centers of China and India slowed their progress considerably and, as of a few weeks ago, the advance had made it only as far as the 23rd Parallel, leaving the southern part of India and all of Southeast Asia still occupied by rotters, as well as the Korean Peninsula and Japan. Australia would begin its rescue operation next year. For now, almost five hundred thousand survivors had set up a self-sustained fortified region in the Outback and had been able to keep out the living dead but did not have enough resources to take back the continent. The rest of the region—Indonesia, the Philippines, New Guinea, New Zealand, and the thousands of islands strewn across the Pacific—would more than likely be left to the living dead for the foreseeable future.

As for the Middle East, they had made out better than anticipated. Comprised mostly of desert, the surviving military forces had taken back the majority of the region earlier than anticipated. The major cities took longer, especially along the Levant. The safe zone began at the Red Sea in the west, stretched to the Dardanelles and the Caucasus where it met up with the Russians, and extended north where it met up with the Chinese in Turkmenistan. The push east was only a hundred miles away from linking up with Indian troops pushing west from Pakistan and Afghanistan. The only area not accounted for was Africa. No word had come from that region in over a year, and everyone assumed the continent was completely dead. As of now, no efforts would be made to reclaim that part of the world.

The C-5 banked left. Natalie glanced out the window at the airfield below, having to turn her head to compensate for the patch over her left eye.

Ari reached out and held her hand. "We'll be there soon."

"I know."

"Are you sure you're up for this?"

Natalie nodded, although in fact she did not know if she was.

Despite what Branson had predicted, Natalie and Ari did not spend the rest of the war behind a desk. They could have if Natalie had not refused to take the easy way out while so much work still needed to be done and requested a return to duty. Of course, Ari volunteered to go with her. Headquarters had assigned her to take over command of a company on the Utah front. They would see service throughout the Midwest, including heavy action around St. Louis and Cincinnati, before ending the war with the reclaiming of Washington, D.C.

Elections were held a month after that, and Secretary Fogel was elected president by a landslide. Natalie and Ari were released from military service and talked about moving back to Colorado to begin their new life together.

She found it funny how fate always intervened. Most of the states had not yet re-established their governments, so as a temporary measure Fogel had divided the country into districts that would remain under federal control until such time as the states could rebuild their infrastructures. Fogel had requested Natalie take over as security commander for the Northeast District that comprised the New England states. Of course, she accepted, and now she and Ari were flying into Portsmouth to begin that assignment.

First, however, she had one stop to make.

The C-5 touched down. Five minutes later, it pulled up to the terminal and everyone disembarked. A corporal stood by a Humvee holding a sign that read BAZARGAN. As they approached, the corporal straightened to attention. "Miss Bazargan. Miss Fleitman. How was your flight?"

"Not bad. I miss business class."

"Ma'am, for the military, that *was* business class."

Natalie chuckled. "Is that my Hummer?"

"Yes, ma'am. If you want, I can drive you to Portland. Security Command is waiting for you."

"No, thanks. I need to make a detour first. Were my earlier instructions followed?"

"Yes, ma'am. I carried them out myself." The corporal paused. "If you don't mind my asking, what is so special about that place? It's a burnt-out wreck."

Natalie did not respond, so Ari answered for her. "It holds a personal meaning to us."

"Copy that. Sorry to pry."

"No need to apologize." Ari tapped his shoulder, reassuring the corporal that no offense was taken. "That'll be all."

The corporal headed back to the terminal. Ari opened the trunk of the Humvee and tossed their duffel bags inside. She closed the hatch and said, "I'll drive."

Leaving the airport, Ari headed for downtown Portsmouth. The trip took the women past sights that had become all too familiar to them and harbored as many bad memories as good. Getting onto Route One, she crossed the bridge over the

Piscataqua River into Maine. A few miles up ahead sat the Kittery Trading Post where the Angels had once provided protection from rotters for the numerous raiding parties that had stripped the shops clean.

As they passed, Natalie realized how much things had changed. The last time she was here, the living dead swarmed the area. Now not a single rotter could be seen, and dozens of tractor trailer trucks parked outside the strip malls as crews rummaged through the shops, commandeering anything of value to help rebuild society.

When Ari steered right onto Haley Road, Natalie felt her anxiety grow. Soon they would be back at Fort McClary, where they had started from so long ago. She needed to visit here, not out of a sense of nostalgia, but for closure.

Natalie had spent the last month tracking down information on those Angels who had not joined the campaign against the rotters, and it depressed her. Sandy had joined a Combat Surgical Hospital that had been overrun by a rogue horde of rotters west of Dallas, killing everyone in the hospital. Amy had gone into logistics, driving supply trucks that reinforced the line; a convoy she was part of had been hijacked by looters who killed the drivers, including Amy. Stephanie spent the war training recruits in San Francisco before sending them to the line. Once the fighting ended, she moved back east and disappeared. While recovering from her wound, Fogel had asked Josephine to assist Chief of Staff Thomas in rebuilding San Francisco, which had become the home of the government-in-exile. The two had worked hard to restore the city, doing such a good job that in elections held six weeks ago, Thomas and Josephine had been elected mayor and deputy mayor, respectively.

Yet one person remained unaccounted for.

Ari pulled the Humvee into Fort McClary's parking lot. Nothing had changed since the night her Angels had left Portland to bring the vaccine to Omaha. It was one of the thousands of battlefields across the country that would sit untouched for years before someone had the time and re-sources to clean it up. The only difference was the structure erected near the main entrance to the compound. Ari stopped in front of it and the two women climbed out.

Natalie had ordered a cork board set up on the compound. It stood five feet square, with walls extending out on both sides and a roof overhead to protect the board from the elements. She had hoped Robson or someone from his group would post a message letting her know what had happened to the others after they went their separate ways. Not that she intended to get back together with Robson. She desperately needed to know what had happened to him, and that others beside her and Ari had survived.

Natalie stepped up to the board, then closed her eyes and lowered her head. Nothing was attached.

Ari moved up alongside Natalie. "It's okay. Not much time has passed since the end of the war. We'll have it checked once a week. I'm sure someone will post up here soon."

"Thanks." Natalie paused a moment before asking, "Was it worth it?"

"Was what worth it?"

Natalie pointed to the destroyed fort. "Everyone we lost here. Everyone we lost at Site R and on the trip to San Francisco. For all we know, there are only four of us left. I want to know they didn't die in vain."

"You're missing the most important things."

"What?"

"If it wasn't for you and Robson, we never would have been able to retrieve the vaccine and get it to the government-in-exile. Yes, we lost a lot of good people doing that, but how many lives were saved because the troops were inoculated? None of this could have happened without you two."

Natalie smiled, more to hide the pain of her loss than to celebrate her achievement. "What's the other thing?"

"We have each other." Ari took Natalie's hand and squeezed. "We survived the rotter apocalypse."

Acknowledgments

I want to thank all my readers who have patiently and faithfully followed the *Rotter World* saga. What had originally been a one-off novel about humans and vampires trying to survive a zombie apocalypse turned into an epic trilogy that not only explored the darker aspects of how we would react to a complete collapse of the social order but concluded with humans bringing the war back to the living dead. I loved writing this series, became attached to the characters (which didn't prevent me from killing off most of them), and am sorry to be leaving the rotter-infested world behind.

A major debt of gratitude goes to Felicia A. Sullivan, my editor, who worked closely with me to tighten up the manuscript. Felicia is a consummate professional who did a superior job, and I value her expertise as well as the fact that she is also a fan. I also want to give a special shout out to Judy Knuth who proofread the final product. They both did an excellent job in making this book read and look as professional as possible. However, any errors in the final product are mine to own.

Zach McCain provided the cover art for *Rotter Apocalypse*. We played around with several ideas before finally coming up with the artwork used for this cover, which perfectly captures the essence of the entire novel.

I also want to express my gratitude to James Jackson, the author of the *Up From the Depths* series and a military and technical advisor for The Ward Room: Military and Technical Assistance for Writers. James reviewed all the military-related scenes in *Rotter Apocalypse* and provided pages worth of feedback, correcting the many mistakes I originally made in depicting current U.S. weapon systems and offering some constructive feedback on how the military would wage war against the living dead. If the battle scenes in and around San Francisco seem realistic, it's because James made me look smart.

I am grateful to my readers for reviewing the first draft and providing their honest feedback. I rely on my Beta readers to point out my mistakes and plot flaws, and they did a fantastic job.

As always, a special thank you goes to my family. For the past three years they have tolerated the long hours I spent roaming through my own sick, twisted, and undead world. My wife and fellow writer, Alison Beightol, has been supportive and understanding; I would never be able to do this without her love and support. The pets, however, cannot fathom why that strange glowing device on the desk is more important than them. I cannot remember how many times I sat in front of my computer with Walther's drooling snout resting on my leg and his large brown eyes staring up at me begging for attention. To all of you, thank you for sharing me with my passion. I love you all.

About the Author

Scott M. Baker was born and raised in Everett, Massachusetts, and spent twenty-three years in northern Virginia working for the Central Intelligence Agency. He has traveled extensively throughout Europe, Asia, and the Middle East, incorporating many of the locations and cultures he has visited in his stories. Scott is now retired and lives outside of Concord, New Hampshire, with his wife, his stepdaughter, two cats who treat him as their human servant, his Boxer Roxie, and Fred, a Bassett Hound puppy who is a lovable bundle of energy.

Scott is currently writing the *Nurse Alissa vs. the Zombies* and *The Chronicles of Paul* sagas, his latest zombie apocalypse series, as well as his paranormal series. Previous works include *Operation Majestic*, his first science fiction novel described as *Raiders of the Lost Ark* meets *Back to the Future* – with aliens; *Frozen World*, his first non-zombie post-apocalypse novel; the *Shattered World* series, his five-book young adult post-apocalypse thriller; *The Vampire Hunters* trilogy, about humans fighting the undead in Washington D.C.; *Yeitso*, his homage to the giant monster movies of the 1950s that he loved watching as a kid; as well as several zombie-themed novellas and anthologies.

Blog: scottmbakerauthor.blogspot.com
Facebook: facebook.com/groups/397749347486177
MeWe: mewe.com/i/scottmbaker
Twitter: twitter.com/vampire_hunters
Instagram: instagram.com/scottmbakerwriter

YouTube:
youtube.com/channel/UC5AyCVrEAncr2E0N5XoyUdg/playlists
Wyrd Realities Homepage: www.wyrdrealities.net
TikTok: tiktok.com/@scottmbakerwriter

You can also sign up for Scott's newsletter, which will be released on the 1st and 15th of every month. He promises not to share your email with anyone or spam the recipients. The newsletter contains advance notices of upcoming releases/events and short stories from the Alissa, Paul, and Tatyana universes that will not be available to the public. You can sign up by going to the link below.

Newsletter: mailchi.mp/0b1401f1ddb2/scott-m-baker-writer

www.ingramcontent.com/pod-product-compliance
Lightning Source LLC
Chambersburg PA
CBHW071212250626
47159CB00001B/288